CONTEMPORARY AMERICAN FICTION

EDWIN MULLHOUSE

Steven Millhauser was born in 1943 in New York City and grew up in Connecticut. *Edwin Mullhouse*, his first novel, was published in 1972 and won the Prix Médicis Etranger in France. His second novel, *Portrait of a Romantic*, appeared in 1977. He lives with his wife in New York.

# EDWIN MULLHOUSE

### The Life and Death
### of an American Writer
### 1943–1954

**by JEFFREY CARTWRIGHT**

*A novel by*
**STEVEN MILLHAUSER**

PENGUIN BOOKS

PENGUIN BOOKS

Viking Penguin Inc., 40 West 23rd Street,
New York, New York 10010, U.S.A.
Penguin Books Ltd, Harmondsworth,
Middlesex, England
Penguin Books Australia Ltd, Ringwood,
Victoria, Australia
Penguin Books Canada Limited, 2801 John Street,
Markham, Ontario, Canada L3R 1B4
Penguin Books (N.Z.) Ltd, 182–190 Wairau Road,
Auckland 10, New Zealand

First published in the United States of America
by Alfred A. Knopf, Inc., 1972
Published in Penguin Books 1985

LIBRARY OF CONGRESS CATALOGING IN PUBLICATION DATA
Millhauser, Steven.
Edwin Mullhouse: the life and death of an
American writer, 1943–1954, by Jeffrey Cartwright.
I. Title.
PS3563.I422E3    1985      813'.54      84-26378
ISBN 0 14 00.7782 0

Printed in the United States of America by
R. R. Donnelley & Sons Company, Harrisonburg, Virginia
Set in Janson

*To my mother, my father, and my sister*

# Introductory Note

I FIRST MET JEFFREY CARTWRIGHT in the sixth grade. I can barely remember him. He was the sort of vague industrious boy who gets A in everything and excels in nothing. He was the sort of boy who wears eyeglasses and sits in the front row. He knew all the countries of Central America and their capitals; he liked to draw maps of South America showing the major products of each country. On the playground in the morning before the bell he stayed by himself, staring at his toes or gazing through the diamond-shaped spaces in the tall wire fence; during recess he joined in games only when Miss Thimble required everyone to play; after school he walked home by himself, carrying his books girlishly in the cradle of his arms. I can recall nothing physical about him except his tremendous eyeglasses, which seemed to conceal his eyes; somewhere in the dark attic of memory I have preserved an image of him turning his head and revealing two round lenses aglow with light, the eyes invisible, as if he were some fabulous creature who lived in a cave or well. I never spoke to him. Indeed I rarely thought of him; and after the sixth grade, when I moved from Newfield to another town, I promptly forgot him.

Ten years later while browsing in a gloomy secondhand book-store near Columbia University, on one of those dark and rainy New York afternoons when all the colors of the world seem washed away, I came across a book called *Edwin Mullhouse: The Life and Death of an American Writer (1943–1954)*, by Jeffrey Cartwright. A vague image stirred. Could it possibly be . . . ? The preface left no doubt: "Newfield, 1955." I immediately purchased the book, vowing to live on gingerale and potato chips for the next two days, and hurried back to my snug cell in Livingston Hall, where locking the door and preparing a cup of steaming black coffee with my forbidden aluminum heating coil and my smuggled cup, I settled at once into the comfortable leather chair, clicked on the double-barreled fluorescent light, and accompanied by a soothing sound of rain against glass and a hushed swish of traffic on Amsterdam Avenue six flights below, I read from cover to cover the astonishing book which it is now my privilege and my pleasure to introduce. Only in the final pages did I realize that Jeffrey must have been writing it during the very year I went to school with him (1954–55). I deeply regretted never having struck up an acquaintance. But who could have guessed that the quiet boy who wore eyeglasses and sat in the front row was secretly composing one of the most remarkable documents ever recorded in the annals of biography?

Such was my modest connection with Jeffrey Cartwright, that vague industrious boy with his secret fever; and such was my first acquaintance with a work that I have no hesitation in proclaiming to be a modern classic. Interested readers are referred to my definitive article in the *Journal of American Letters,* XXII (1966), 22–43, which compares Jeffrey's very American life of Edwin with Boswell's very British life of Johnson; and to my recent article in JAL, XXVII (1971), 1–17, which takes issue with a number of lively misreadings of Jeffrey's pellucid work. But this is no place for academic polemics and ivy beleaguering. The proof, after all, is in the pudding—and the pudding is piping hot. This new edition of a major American biography, long overdue, reproduces faithfully and without abridgment the original (1956) edition, long out of print, written by a marvelous boy. It is my fond, my sober hope that this handsome and happily priced volume will win for Jeffrey that wider circle of readers which his masterpiece so richly deserves.

Meanwhile the search for Jeffrey Cartwright continues. I, for one, hope they never find him. Edwin's novel, some will recall, was discovered in 1969 by the daughter of Professor Charles William Thorndike of Harvard: in a children's library, of all places! One fondly imagines Professor Thorndike—who has written so well about Elizabethan children—poring over the text in a room frequented by little girls in pink frocks and yellow pigtails. The fate of *Cartoons* has proved a strange one indeed. Published by some grotesque mistake as a children's book (ages 8 to 12) in 1958, it has remained unreadable by children and unread by adults. Professor Thorndike has called it "a work of undoubted genius," and he is not a man given to hyperbole. I myself have sternly resisted the temptation to read *Cartoons*, knowing full well that the real book, however much a work of genius, can no more match the shape of my expectations than the real Jeffrey could, should he ever materialize. I shall probably succumb, one sad day. Meanwhile Edwin's genius lives undimmed for me in the shining pages that follow. One can only regret that his work has proved less popular than his life.

WALTER LOGAN WHITE

*New York, 1972*

*—Phew! A biographer is a devil.*
                    —E.M., in conversation

## Preface to the First Edition

EDWIN MULLHOUSE IS DEAD. I shall not qualify the noun of his memory with the insolent adjectives of insufficient praise. Edwin Mullhouse is dead. He is as dead as a doornail.

I have studied them carefully, those smug adult prefaces. With fat smiles of gratitude, fit thanks are given for services rendered and kindnesses bestowed. Long lists of names are cleverly paraded in order to assure you that the author has excellent connections and a loving heart. Let me say at once that in this instance there are none to thank besides myself. I am not thankful to Dr. and Mrs. Mullhouse for moving away with the remains. I am not thankful to Aunt Gladys for mislaying eleven chapters. I have always done my own typing myself, using both index fingers, and I have never received any encouragement at all from anyone about anything. And so, in conclusion, I feel that grateful thanks are due to myself, without whose kind encouragement and constant interest I could never have completed my task; to myself, for my valuable assistance in a number of points; to myself, for doing all the dirty work; and above all to myself, whose patience, understanding, and usefulness as a key eye-witness can never be adequately repaid, and who in a typical burst of scrupulousness wish to point out that the "remains" mentioned above are, of course, literary remains.

J.C.

*Newfield, 1955*

# Chronological Table

|  | Year | Age |  |
|---|---|---|---|
|  | Aug. 1 1943 | 0 |  |
|  | Aug. 1 1944 | 1 |  |
| **THE EARLY YEARS** (Aug. 1, 1943– Aug. 1, 1949) | Aug. 1 1945 | 2 |  |
|  | Aug. 1 1946 | 3 |  |
|  | Aug. 1 1947 | 4 | —*Nursery School begins* |
|  | Aug. 1 1948 | 5 | *Oct., lasts 14 days* —*Kindergarten begins Sept.* |
|  | Aug. 1 1949 | 6 |  |
| **THE MIDDLE YEARS** Aug. 2, 1949– Aug. 1, 1952) | Aug. 2 1949 | 6 | —*1st grade begins Sept.* |
|  | Aug. 1 1950 | 7 | —*2nd grade* |
|  | Aug. 1 1951 | 8 | —*3rd grade* |
|  | Aug. 1 1952 | 9 |  |
| **THE LATE YEARS** (Aug. 2, 1952– Aug. 1, 1954) | Aug. 2 1952 | 9 | —*4th grade* |
|  | Aug. 1 1953 | 10 | —*5th grade* |
|  | Aug. 1 1954 | 11 |  |

# Part One

# THE EARLY YEARS

*Aug. 1, 1943–Aug. 1, 1949*

# 1

EDWIN ABRAHAM MULLHOUSE, whose tragic death at 1:06 A.M. on August 1, 1954, deprived America of her most gifted writer, was born at 1:06 A.M. on August 1, 1943, in the shady town of Newfield, Connecticut. His father, Dr. Abraham Mullhouse, after a long instructorship in English at the City College of New York, transferred to Newfield College in September 1942 as an assistant professor, having in July of that year moved into a modest two-story house with his wife Helen, nee Rosoff. In March 1947 their second child, Karen, was born; and so forth. It's about here that Edwin would have flung the book away, or in a milder mood would have looked up from the page with the nuance of a frown and said: "The only thing that doesn't interest me is facts. Jot that down, Jeffrey." My name is Jeffrey Cartwright.

"When I think of my youth," he wrote (in a letter undated by him but dated by me April 26, 1954), "I think of comics and cartoons, crayons and cotton candy, clowns and kaleidoscopes." The clowns are a lie, circuses always bored him. And kaleidoscopes never meant as much to him as picture puzzles or cereal boxes or bubblegum machines. But the spirit of his remark, as distinct from its alliterating letter, may certainly be trusted. Edwin was always playing. No occasion was too slight to serve as the pretext for another gift; his parents seemed to celebrate a perpetual Christmas. Edwin went through games very quickly, throwing himself feverishly into them for days or weeks or months at a time and suddenly abandoning them forever. But he never could bear to throw anything away, so that his beloved room gradually assumed the characteristics of a museum. In a sense, Edwin never stopped playing: he simply passed from Monopoly to fiction.

I see him now, sitting Indian-fashion on the striped bed before the double window, the tip of his tongue escaping from a corner of his mouth as he bends over a piece of tracing paper that he holds in place over a favorite comic book. Ten feet away, on the windowless side of the room, little Karen Mullhouse sits on another bed, in red corduroys and a yellow t-shirt, looking up at the ceiling light with a Viewmaster pressed to her eyes. Between them, seated at a rickety green folding table on which the empty frame of a picture puzzle lies beside a jumble of knobby pieces, is myself. Suddenly there is a blinding flash. Karen screams and drops the Viewmaster. I look up, startled to see Mr. Mullhouse standing in the doorway, blinking and grinning over his twin-lens reflex with its silver flash attachment. Only Edwin remains as before, bent in furious calm concentration over his tracing paper. He knows that as soon as the hot blue bulb cools, his father will bring it to him so that he can press his fingernails into the soft warm bumps of glass.

Now turn to summer, 1953. Edwin, wearing eyeglasses, sits crosslegged on the striped bed before the double window, bent over a blue examination booklet. Across the room, Karen Mullhouse, dressed in bluejeans and one of Edwin's old cowboy shirts full of bucking broncos, sits on the edge of the other bed beside a rickety green folding table and moves a white marble in zigzags across a board full of holes. I am seated as before on an old folding chair, wishing she knew how to play chess instead of Chinese checkers. Again the flash. "Oh, Dad!" cries Karen. I burst out laughing. "Shhhh," says Edwin. Behind me, on the upper shelf of one of the two gray bookcases on both sides of the single window, you can see Monopoly, Clue, Camelot, Sorry, Pollyanna, Parcheesi.

# 2

AND YET, OF COURSE, he had always written. In three black bindings intended for a triplicate of her husband's dissertation, Mrs. Mullhouse preserved every scrap of Edwin's writing she could get her hands on, from his earliest experiments in printing ("A IS FOR APPLF") to the last, hastily scribbled note. She collected it all from the beginning, before she had any idea that Edwin was especially gifted in that way. She also preserved his crayon drawings, his pastel sketches, his report cards, his baby booties, even the old Schaum music books. Those first-grade exercises on blue-lined yellow paper are most interesting. It would be absurd to pretend to see the future author of *Cartoons* in the early word-lists (tip, top, tap, pit, pot, pat, spit, spot, spat), and yet the student of Edwin's work cannot help being struck by this intimation of the later word-play. And it is true that Edwin was always fascinated by his own writing. I suppose it must have given him a sense of his own specialness to see his clumsily pencilled "family newspapers" (containing his earliest stories) and his carefully typed poems bound up in a sizable book at the age of nine. No doubt Mrs. Mullhouse intended precisely that effect. She was raising a little wunderkind, god bless her, and she wasn't about to let him forget it. Long before Edwin began to take pictures of himself with his own camera, he lost himself in the perusal of his early manuscripts. At least as early as the third grade he had a distinct sense of having produced juvenilia. When Edwin entered the fourth grade, a friend of the family tried to interest a publisher in the Rose Dorn poems. The venture fell through. Lucky for Edwin.

# 3

IN THE SUMMER OF 1953 I rode Edwin to White Beach. It was a brilliant day. The tall highway, raised over us on vast concrete pillars that looked slim and fragile at a distance, as if a flung stone could smash them, seemed lifted out of darkness into the light. Way up there, in all that blue, even the black-tipped factory smokestacks towering over us seemed necessary to the sky. The blinking caution light, the shady roof of the highway, the sudden yellow splash of a MERGING TRAFFIC sign, tanned elbows sticking out of windows, a distant helicopter, the near rush and chrome—Edwin was taking it all in, I knew. And yet some stubborn or malicious streak in him, what his father once called the traditional feigned toughness of the American writer, made him say, as I turned to look at him: "Aren't we there yet? I have a splitting headache. Watch the road, Jeffrey."

As we passed under the highway onto the steaming tar I began to feel an uncontrollable excitement. Ever since beginning his immortal novel in the autumn of 1952, Edwin had shut himself away from the world, fearful, I suppose, of distorting his fiction with reality; his sudden reversal seemed to mark an epoch. But I did not wish to spoil the purity of my observations by direct questioning. In the summer of 1953 I had not yet revealed to Edwin my plans for his biography, and so I could not explain to him the importance of his reactions. He was like one of those unsuspecting people whom you see being filmed by a hidden television camera: at the right moment I would reveal everything to him, his eyebrows would rise, his mouth would open, he would flash a nervous smile at the unseen audience and look away in a paroxysm of delighted embarrassment. Meanwhile I snatched eager glances at his face but he hid everything behind an absurd clownish mask.

Upon reaching a familiar billboard I turned right toward the distant wooden bridge that connected the mainland to the island of

White Beach. Soon the old two-story houses with their rickety outdoor staircases gave way to empty lots and long low factories behind wire fences, as if the town had died on its way to the water. As our wheels rolled from tar to rattling wood, the smell of salt-water mingled with the old sound of water slapping against piles. From narrow footpaths on both sides of the bridge, big children and little old men stood and sat with their fishing rods, while on a solitary pile that stood farther out in the water, as if someone had had an idea and changed his mind, a white and gray seagull sat as if posing for a postcard. "Look!" I cried, "the same one you painted in forty-nine!" "Really?" said Edwin, looking with sudden interest. One remarkable fact about my friend was his mystifying inability to appreciate the humor of others; the most obvious kind of buffoonery often left him puzzled and uneasy, and he always dreaded the telling of a formal joke because he never knew when to laugh. Yet he himself loved the crudest kind of practical jokes and was master of a subtle, biting wit. It is as if he assumed an earnestness in everyone in the world except himself—an assumption that revealed at once a deep self-disparagement and a subtle contempt for the imagination of his fellowman. As we left the bridge and entered a sandy weedgrown parking lot: "I was only pulling your leg," I said. "Oh," said Edwin, crestfallen. But a moment later he tapped me on the shoulder and said eagerly: "But how do you know it isn't the same one, Jeffrey? It might be the same one, after all." In the distance, above the line of trees, to my surprise I did not see the glinting arc of a ferris wheel.

I parked the bike between a DeSoto and a Studebaker, and as Edwin and I began to walk straight ahead toward the invisible rides, my mind plunged and burst with memories. To the right of the parking lot, past the shady picnic grounds and across a black road with a double yellow line in the center, lay the curving beach itself. We had never gone swimming there, since a day at White Beach was barely long enough for only the rides, but we had picnicked under those trees, listening to the nearby noises of the invisible amusement park and the less interesting shouts from the beach, mere static to the park's music. Indeed the name "White Beach" summoned up neither whiteness nor sand but bright yellows and reds and the plunge of a roller coaster, the bursting open of spookhouse doors. Edwin and I walked on. That, incidentally, is the kind of unspecific sentence that used to make Edwin gnash his teeth or giggle when he came across one in a book: "Time passed," "she said," "he killed the Indian," "they walked on." But the modest biographer on his humble slope cannot aspire to the heights of fiction; Edwin and I walked on. The parking lot with its gleaming cars passed gradually into a miniature forest, and as we came out of the trees I stopped in confusion.

We were standing at the edge of a wide dusty space, like a vast abandoned parking lot, on which a number of odd-shaped structures were scattered about. On our left stood a long low windowless building painted dull red and attached to a row of black posts by means of a long narrow roof. On our right stood a white many-sided structure that seemed to be composed of garage doors with rows of little high windows and a low, cone-shaped roof. Some half-dozen other buildings, mostly white, spread themselves to the tree-fringed distance. A few people were strolling about in the bright summer light, wives and husbands arm in arm, an occasional little boy, all of them kicking up clouds of dust, peeping in windows, peering under doors, pointing—haunting the place, I couldn't help thinking; and for a second I thought: I have fallen asleep on a bright white beach beside some distant ocean, and this is my sad, sad dream. "Where the devil are we?" I exclaimed roughly. Edwin, sniffing allergically and pointing a languid finger, said: "Isn't that the merry-go-round?" And as he pointed I recognized the small white many-sided structure with its cone-shaped roof. And suddenly I recognized in the dull red building with its row of posts the vast bright arcade that we had always passed through first on our way to the bigger rides, an arcade that once had contained a shooting gallery with its row of chained rifles and its dipping ducks, a dart-and-balloon booth with shelves of shining radios and tall stuffed animals (and the invisible shelf under the counter that contained the only prizes we ever won, the glass ashtrays, the painted fans, the straw tubes that trapped inserted fingers), a stand where pink spun sugar whirled in a circular vat and collected magically on paper cones to form cotton candy, and at the very end, which my memory had imagined to be blocks away, the spookhouse itself with its two sets of swinging doors and its painted ghost. Even at the age of eight I had known that White Beach was a small amusement park, yet in the summer of 1953 I was stunned, stunned I say, to see the long arcade of my childhood shrink to a dwarfish old age. I glanced at Edwin. His eyes were squeezed shut as his mouth opened for a sneeze. Hiding my disappointment, I hurried across the hard ground toward the old merry-go-round; under a blazing sun the points of my polished shoes kicked up little mushroom clouds of dust. I was just tall enough to see through a dusty pane. In semi-darkness, on the motionless round platform, the painted horses stood frozen, their hooves raised, their heads lifted or jerked to one side. I turned back to the blinding light. Edwin, coming up beside me, glanced into a window and quickly glanced away. His eyes tightened to lines; he sneezed. "Let's go," he said. "My handkerchief is soaked. My allergy is killing me. I have a terrible headache." In the bright light his pale face and neck seemed almost white against his dark hair and dark zippered jacket, as if he were a black-and-white photograph, slightly overexposed. In one hand he held a sopping handkerchief; behind his flashing lenses his eyes gleamed with an unpleasant moistness. Altogether he did not resemble one's notion of the youthful American writer. "Yes yes," I said, "in two seconds," and hurried across to the little arcade. Edwin followed. At the end where the spookhouse used to be, two boys were lying on their stomachs and peeping under the wide locked door; an old man wearing a gray uniform chased them away. "Ourselves," I murmured. "What?" said Edwin. "Forget it," I said, remembering how he and I had once dreamed of being inside that black scream-filled chamber and suddenly turning on a powerful overhead light, revealing what we imagined to be a vast clutter of tracks and cars, and astonished people staring open-mouthed at walls filled with cages, niches, statues, skeletons, levers, gearwheels, treasures. As we passed the lowered, locked door—but where were the swinging doors, the outer tracks, the operator's booth?—Edwin said: "Forget what? Say" (turning to the old man in gray) "wasn't there a roller coaster around here somewhere?" The old man eyed Edwin suspiciously, and turning to me said: "Ain't nothin' but a motor there now, son. Back o' them trees there, over thataway." He was what Edwin called a living cartoon. Thanking him in appropriate cartoon fashion ("Thanks, mister"), I hastened around the corner of the building, followed by sniffling Edwin. Here the hard sand began to sprout clumps of grass and occasional clusters of bushes and trees; some hundred feet away a strip of tall grass banked a narrow creek, an inlet of the sound; across the water lay a flat grassy waste containing a row of spherical white oil tanks and two tall radio towers rising crisscross in the rich blue sky; and on the hazy horizon, where the sky looked bleached, the stalks of distant smokestacks blossomed in white. "Edwin!" I cried, "don't you remember!"— for my memory had preserved the little creek as a vast lake, toward which the roller coaster plunged on its most fearsome dip. Behind a cluster of tall bushes stood all that remained of that towering nightmare of tracks and screams: a peeling shed with broken windows, housing four-foot-high black generators with sinister corrugations. A little sign read: DANGER ELEC. "To think," I said, turning to Edwin, "that"—but he was twenty feet away, walking off with his white handkerchief hanging from his fist. Reflecting once again upon the coldness and aloofness of the creative temperament, I resolved to leave my friend to himself and pursue my own investigations. I walked toward the building whose arcade was invisible and whose irregular concrete back was now facing me; a number of high windows, all broken, held fragments of glass shaped like puzzle pieces. The windows were all above my head. Grasping the concrete ledge of one, I pulled myself up and stared. At what? At a wooden partition, against which leaned a bicycle with rusty handlebars. I dropped down and tried a window on another side: only the wooden partition, striped with light and shadow. I dropped down. My palms were stinging; here and there the flesh was torn. Below my hands I saw my broken shadow, stretching along the ground and standing up suddenly against the concrete wall. With a kind of feverish melancholy I abandoned the spookhouse windows, and in the dazzle of a perfect day, as I walked to the front in search of Edwin, it seemed to me that he and I were nothing but a couple of spookhouse skeletons, surprised by light.

Through the perspective of the archway I saw him, framed in a polygon of light, seated with his back to me at the edge of a concrete basin. Again I walked along the shady archway, and as I stepped through the polygon into the sun I saw that the basin was about two feet deep and fifty feet long, shaped like the state of Nevada. Weeds pushed through the cracked concrete floor and in one corner a small tree was growing; crumpled cigarette packs, popsicle wrappers, wooden ice-cream spoons, bottlecaps, smashed soda bottles lay scattered about. Edwin sat with his right leg dangling over the side and his left foot resting on the edge, his left knee raised; his left elbow rested on the knee, and his left fist leaned against the side of his tilted head. I walked up behind him and was about to address him when suddenly, as I watched, bright green water rose from the weedgrown floor and filled the concrete basin, long wooden dividers formed a maze, red motorboats with white steering wheels rode into the shining distance along green avenues that trembled with spots of yellow light, while at the dock under the shadow of a wooden roof Edwin and I watched the waiting boats, vast at our toes, knocking up against the sides in the greenblackness of the shadowed water. With one hand resting on top of his pole, a man in a t-shirt waited for us to get in. It was too late to turn back because of the line behind us and Mr. and Mrs. Mullhouse watching with little Karen from behind the rail. As we stepped down onto a rocking sputtering floor we noticed a thin trembling coat of water, our boat had a leak, we were going to drown in the dirty green water that was fifty feet deep but already the pole had given us a push, already we were set afloat, already we were entering a dark tunnel, we were going higher and higher, pressed back in our seats we gripped the bar with aching fists and climbed steadily up in blackness until at last, at last, a glimmer of gray in the distance, oh hold on tight, a twist to the left and the bright sky blinding us as unbelievably we still climbed up and up, staring fiercely at our red-spotted white knuckles that seemed to be bursting through the skin, pretending we were anywhere else but miles in the sky, knowing it was death to look but looking anyway at the hideous tracks, the little red motorboats, the field at the edge of the crystal water, and as the track leveled out a scream came from the car in front of us, a girl's hair streamed, for an instant we were poised at the top of a tall dream waiting for the fall, then our shirts billowed out behind us and in the clattering rattle we clenched our teeth as through the spaces in the tracks, faster and faster the ground rushed up to meet us until we saw with the distinctness of a photograph three tall blades of grass sticking up through the bottommost tracks, and as we crashed into the ground the doors burst open and we entered a house of screams, jerking along on a crazy track where luminous skeletons rose in their cages till strings brushed our faces and we burst through the doors into the sky, leaning over the side and watching the shadow of our plane flying under us in a long slow circle, floating along smooth grass, rippling over a bench, passing like a black ghost among the bright crowded mall aflower with pink cotton candy and yellow and red balloons, standing suddenly upright against the side of a ticket booth, again floating along smooth grass, rippling over a bench, passing among the crowd as a child begins to scream and faces turn upward to watch a red balloon rise lazily over the spookhouse roof into the bright blue air, growing smaller and smaller above its dangling white string until it becomes a bright red spot in the sky, and as we come to a rocking stop at the top of a towering wheel oh see below the manikin faces, the dollhouse roofs, the diorama trees, the shining mirror of the motorboat pool, the blue line of the creek, the distant fields, the white oil tanks, the crisscross towers, the line of factory smokestacks blooming, and as we float slowly down, an odor of mustard and sauerkraut mingles with the taste of pistachio ice cream in a sugar cone, carousel music rides in bright circles as brass shells pop from cocked rifles, red tickets stream as all the colors of a summer afternoon glow like a glossy postcard, shimmer in memory like a color transparency projected in darkness onto a sparkling white screen. And as the lights went on, there was Edwin, sitting at the edge of a shrunken weedgrown basin, his hair rumpled, his skinny wrist sticking out of his jacket sleeve, and pierced by memory I cursed the blue day, as now again, seated in lamplight, shut in a heated room, I curse the unending night. "Edwin!" I cried, "a penny for your thoughts!" Whirling, as if he had not known I was standing behind him, he looked up through his dusty lenses with a frown, and wiping his nostrils, reddened by allergic discharges, he said testily: "Can't we go now? I have a splitting headache." You were always so cunning, Edwin.

# 4

I FIRST MET EDWIN on August 9, 1943. At the time I was exactly 6 months 3 days old, having been born on February 6, 1943. It is with no desire of thrusting myself forward, but only of presenting the pertinent details of a noteworthy occasion, that I thus intrude my personal history into these pages. With my stated object in mind I may add that we lived next door to the Mullhouses on Benjamin Street (we were 293, they 295), that mama had been waiting all the sunny morning for Mrs. Mullhouse to return from the hospital, and that many people have remarked upon my extraordinary, my truly inspired memory.

As I bumped along the sidewalk under the dark blue shadow of my carriage top, I wiggled my toes delightedly in a warm band of light. The shadows of passing trees rippled over my sunlit legs, and in one corner of the carriage a delicate silky spiderweb sparkled like a jeweled maze. Over the rim of the carriage I saw the dark spars of a telephone pole sailing in the bright blue sky. I also recall a little white cloud, very like a rubber whale I played with in the bathtub. Mama was chattering away in some kind of babytalk that made no sense to me or anyone else and I did my best to drown her out with my pink rattle, on one end of which Tweedledum stood with his arm around Tweedledee. Despite my efforts she managed to communicate to me a sense of intense excitement, as indeed she had been doing all morning long with her fussing and her fidgeting and her endless brushing of my silky locks. Luckily for literary history my senses were immensely alive to the importance of the occasion, that bright August morning.

A sudden stop; a turn to the left; two nasty bumps; and again

I was rolling merrily along a sidewalk, but now the blue shadow
of the carriage top came down to my ankles, the spiderweb hung
limp and gray, smashed by mama's thumb, and over the carriage
rim I saw the familiar top of a bright white door, and over that a
triangle of white shingles roofed in red, and over that an endless
repetition of white shingles and a piece of window. Another turn,
a change from loud concrete to quiet grass, a stop, the gathering
arms, and why not skip all that and get to the good part, as Edwin
used to say.

My half-year-old heart was hammering away as with a sudden
hush and hurried breathing mama tiptoed after Mrs. Mullhouse up
the carpeted stairs. In an anguish of anticipation I sucked my
thumb. He was sleeping—Edwin was always sleeping—and as
mama stepped through the door into the strange dim room I was
later to know so well, the women's hushed excitement and the
sudden darkness frightened me, and I would have burst into tears
had I not been fearful of incurring some strange, dim punishment.
Edwin, for his part, lay sound asleep in the wooden crib by the
double window. The green shades, later replaced by blinds, were
drawn, though not yet luminous, and as mama bent over the crib
uttering sounds of endearment, I had my first glimpse of the
future author of *Cartoons*. He lay under a skyblue blanket with a
repeated pattern of red apples and yellow pears; a fat red book
with gold letters lay by his toes, which rose up under the blanket
like a miniature mountain. Years later when Edwin and I were
looking through the big mahogany bookcase by the stairway I
came across that very book with a shock of remembrance. The gold
letters spelled "David Copperfield." I should like to report that
eight-day-old Edwin was wandering precociously among those
timeless pages, and perhaps he was, but a more reasonable explanation is that Mr. Mullhouse was teaching a course in the Victorians
that fall (the Victorians, Edwin once said, sounded to him like one
of those movies full of swordfights and slashed red curtains) and in
a fit of absentmindedness had left it in the crib, and probably was
searching for it distractedly somewhere downstairs at the very
moment I was being introduced to his son. Edwin lay absolutely
still. He looked as if he had died of old age. His chubby bare arms

lay outside the blanket and were folded across his chest, the elbows by his sides and the fists together at his throat. Beneath a fringe of hair the little old face had a meditative expression. Domed over the sleeping eyes, the unlashed lids resembled the sightless white eyes of marble statues. As I watched, the little fists began to turn over, revealing handfuls of wrinkled fingers; the head rolled toward us slightly; and slowly, dreamily, the eyelids opened over large gray irises (later so deeply brown). Edwin was staring straight into my eyes. Ten years later as we sat talking late into the night, gathering material for his biography, I asked Edwin (half in jest) if he remembered our first meeting, and he replied (half in jest) that he remembered it very well indeed: "a vague sensation of someone bending too close to me." He smiled, and I instantly moved away, and I was never able to ascertain whether or not he did in truth remember; but I record this snippet of midnight conversation in support of the very real possibility that I was Edwin's first memory. Be that as it may, Edwin as I was saying opened his eyes and stared straight into mine. Perhaps it was the suddenness of it all, perhaps it was the strangeness of waking up in his new home, perhaps it was simply the first of his many jokes, at any rate his little wrinkled hands began to roll back and forth at the wrists, his smooth face filled with creases, and fiercely, as if he had just been born, the destined subject of these pages burst into a shriek of tears.

# 5

"Oн," said mama, "poor Edward."

"Ed*win*," said Mrs. Mullhouse.

"Oh yes of course how— Ed*win*, not Ed*ward*."

"It's a perfectly natural mistake, everybody makes it. You see, we wanted to give him a special name, but not a funny one of course. This way the boys can call him Ed but he won't just be any old stupid Edward. Shhhhhh, bubbele, shhhhhh."

"Such a cunnin'," cooed mama. In her own way she was a clever if haphazard punster.

# 6

DESPITE THAT FIRST MEETING, with its unfortunate aura of ill-boding, we were soon inseparable. Edwin was like that: he resisted all change violently, but as soon as the change became part of his normal scheme of things he clung to it violently, resisting all change. We developed an intimate speechless friendship. Through the mist of years I look back upon that time as upon a green island of silence from which I set forth forever onto a tempestuous sea. In green and blue August we stared at one another through the lacquered bars of his crib. In orange and blue October we rode side by side in our carriages along Benjamin Street; a yellow leaf came down out of the sky onto Edwin's blanket. In white and blue December I gave him a snowball, which he tried to eat. He liked his father to hold him upside down and blow on his feet. On my first birthday (February is a gray month) I gave him a piece of cake; he threw it up in the air, where I shall leave it. April showers bring May flowers. Time, as Edwin would never have said, passed.

Not that we were literally silent. Before Speech the Intruder came crashing into our private party he made quite a preliminary ruckus, pounding on the door and rattling the knob and tossing snowballs at the windows. That is to say, in the early months we had an elaborate system of gasps, purrs, chuckles, burbles, sniffs, smacks, snorts, burps, clicks, plops, clucks, yelps, puffs, gulps, slurps, squeals, ho's, hums, buzzes, whines, chirrups, grunts, hisses, hollers, yowls, rasps, gurgles, gargles, glugs, and giggles, not to mention a vast number of hitherto unclassified sounds: gurshes, jurbles, fliffs, cloffs, whizzles, mishes, nists, wints, bibbles, chickles, plips, and chirkles, to name a few, as well as occasional norples, nufts, and snools. Edwin's pre-speech vocabulary was impressive and I bitterly regret that I was unable to record his earliest experiments with language. I do remember a number of them, however, for from the beginning I observed him with the fond solicitude of an elder brother and the scrupulous fascination of a budding biographer. I can confidently state that the following utterances issued from the mouth of Edwin before he had attained the age of three months:

> *aaaaa* (crying)
> *nnnnn* (complaining)
> *kkkkk* (giggling)
> *ggggg* (giggling)
> *cheeeooo* (sneezing)
> *hp hp hp* (hiccuping)
> *haaaooo* (yawning)
> *tatata* (singing)
> *fsssss* (drooling)
> *eeeee* (screaming; singing)
> *b-b-b-b-b* (unknown)

By six months (I was a year old and walking) Edwin had achieved more elaborate combinations:

> *kakooka*
> *pshhh*
> *dam dam dam*
> *chfff* (an early version of Jeffrey?)
> *keeee* (accompanied by a grin and flapping hands)
> *kfffk*
> *dknnnnz*
> *shksp-p-p-p*
> *kaloo*
> *kalay*
> *aaaaaeeeee* (singing)

Some of his bolder adventures in the realm of sound were later suppressed by the polite requirements of civilized noise. I refer not so much to his intricate belches and exquisite winds as to his astonishing salivary achievements. How I long to convey to the adult reader his breathtaking combinations of the buzz and drool, his dribbles and drizzles, his bubbles and burbles—whole salivary sonatas enhanced by gushing crescendos and hissing fortissimi, gurgling glissandi and trickling pianissimi, streaming prestissimos, spouting arpeggios, those slurps and slops, those drips and drops, those spluttering splattering splurts of sputum and drippy splish-splashings of melodious spittle. Adult speech, Edwin used to say, is ridiculously exclusive.

The questing biographer gazes with fondness upon this slightly damp picture of brighteyed baby Edwin sporting among sounds, a happy porpoise, untouched by purpose, diving blissfully in the moneybins of language like a latterday Scrooge McDuck. Surely Edwin's later and highly sophisticated delight in language may be traced back to these early months, when sound was not yet a substitute for things but rather a thing itself, the gayest of his toys: a toy that could be rolled and bounced and licked and swallowed and twisted into a thousand delightful shapes. In general, language for little Edwin combined the virtues of rubber dogs, rattles, and breasts. Later Edwin tried to recapture by a variety of methods this early experience of what I shall call the thingness of speech. Thus, extracting from the mahogany bookcase a fat volume which he said was written in Hebrew, he would open to the first page and begin reading very slowly in a voice as solemn and deep as possible:

> *Tiurf eht dna ecneidebosid tsrif snam fo.*
> *Etsat latrom esohw eert neddibrof taht fo.*
> *Eow—*

losing control at "neddibrof," gaining it at "taht fo," and sputtering into helpless laughter at "eow," which he pronounced in imitation of a rocket in a war movie: eeeeeeowwwww. And he would torment his mother, who was concerned for her daughter's intellectual development, by speaking to eighteen-month-old Karen for hours on end in carefully enunciated nonsense syllables, to which Karen would respond as in a secret code in solemn or laughing nonsense noises of her own.

I should like to end this noisy reminiscence, which began so quietly, with a description of Edwin at his pre-language prime, at the age of six months. Dressed in a red t-shirt and baggy underpants, he is seated in the center of his playpen with his back to the fireplace, facing the inner front door (a glass door covered with venetian blinds and opening into a little front hall full of boots and umbrellas). To his right looms the piano, to his left stands the little oval table before the empty couch, over which one can see the top of the mahogany bookcase and the row of balusters disappearing diagonally into the ceiling. The narrow rugless passage between the couch and staircase leads to the open doorway of the vast invisible kitchen behind Edwin, where Mrs. Mullhouse is making clinking and whooshing noises. I am seated between the playpen and the piano on the dark brown rug with its dark green leaves, facing Edwin's right profile. Through a brilliant sliver of window running along a venetian blind, I can see gleaming snowdrifts and a powder of blown snow under a blue sky. Inside it is summer. Through the upward slanting blinds of the room's four windows, bright light pours. Bright light pours around the edges of the blinds, bright light streams from the kitchen archway, bright light presses against the house and passes through the icecold glass into the sudden warmth of the living room where, unstiffening, it glows and tingles and stretches and expands and fills the whole room until the frail walls are ready to burst with the pressure of the morning. The bright light polishes the corners of the mahogany bookcase, waxes the brass base of the piano lamp, fills a glass picture-frame brimful of shine so that the picture underneath is invisible. On the mantelpiece a large oystershell shows its rainbows. Reflections of bright water in transparent vases lie pale green and blue on the ceiling, and tremble as a car passes with clinking chains. An odor of tobacco lingers in the air and is traceable to a curving pipe lying in a deep ashtray on a lamp-table to the right of the inner front door, beside a brown armchair with white lace doilies over its shiny arms and a sagging cushion whose depression seems to hold an invisible Mr. Mullhouse. To the left of the door stands a tall carved chest whose top can open to receive shiny black discs. As I sit dreaming of the day when I shall be tall enough to look into the top, for even biographers dream, a sound seems to issue from the magic chest. The light buzzing or humming grows louder, as if a flock of locusts were approaching. Edwin grins suddenly, catching my attention; the sound leaps from the box to him, changing with his grin from nnnnnn to eeeeee. The eeeeee grows louder and switches to a giggling kkkkkk; bits of saliva appear at the edges of Edwin's lips; he clenches and unclenches his little fists. He is tuning up for a soundfest. Silence, as Edwin used to say, puh-lee-az! A hum begins again, accompanied now by a plopping or flopping or flapping sound made by his fingers plucking his lower lip (a trick he learned from me). The plopping continues steadily against a changing background of nnnnnn, aaaaaa, eeeeee as he reaches a new theme, a series of sputtering explosions produced by the insertion of his tongue between his lips. The explosions lead to a series of loud clucks, quickly transformed into spluttering p's; streams of saliva pour down, brightening his chin, darkening his t-shirt. The sounds become wetter and drop to a gurgle or gargle, rise suddenly to another grinning eeeeee which changes in pitch: eeeeee-EEEEEEeeeeeeEEEEEE. He drops to a long pshhhhhhhhh, thinking. His little fists clench and unclench, his t-shirt is sopping, he raises his eyes to the ceiling and at last bursts into song:

> *keeeeeeeeeeee aaaaaaaaaa*
> *keeeeeeeeeeee aaaaaaaaaa*
> *keeeeeeeeeeeeeeeeeeeeeeeeeeeeeee*
> *koooooooooooo aaaaaaaaaa*
> *koooooooooooo aaaaaaaaaa*
> *kooooooooooooooooooooooooooooooo*

The astute reader does not need to be told that Edwin has just composed his first poem. (Later he eschewed the blaze of improvisation for the steady warmth of patient toil.) His voice becomes louder, and rounding his lips he passes on to a rapturous French yyyyyyyyyyy. The rich yowl rises to a magnificent piercing EEEEEEEEEEEE as Mrs. Mullhouse appears in the kitchen doorway. She holds a white dishtowel in her dripping hands. Her nostrils are dilated, her lips tense, her eyes filled with terror. Facing the other way, Edwin sings on, blissful, beslobbered, indulgent, exultant, indifferent.

# 7

MY HAND

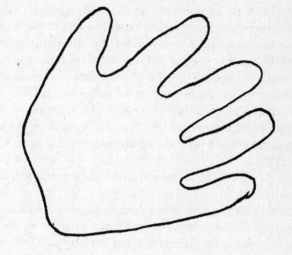

MY FOOT

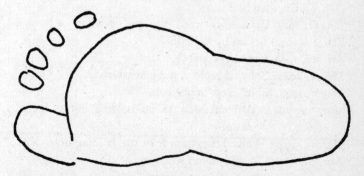

*Traced from Prints, Feb. 18, 1944. Age 6½ months.*

These instructive diagrams were taken from a slim faded volume with a padded cover entitled *My Story: A Baby Record*, wherein Abraham Mullhouse recorded a wealth of doting data concerning the early months of his first child and only son. Edwin was quite fond of this volume, which was divided into numerous sections with titles such as "I Am Born," "Height and Weight," "First Steps," "Travel," "Happy Birthdays," "Some Things I Said and Did," "Days to Remember"; his favorite page was "My Baby Hair," to which an actual lock of his six-month-old hair is carefully taped. As a biographer I must judge the volume more severely. Mr. Mullhouse's loving and indiscriminate fascination with all the details of a developing life, though undoubtedly commendable in a budding father, cannot but be looked at askance by the true biographer, who, an artist in his own right, is interested solely in destiny's secret designs. Indeed I hope that these diagrams will lead the reader to reflect upon the nature and meaning of true biography; for it is the purpose of this history to trace not the mere outlines of a life but the inner plan, not the external markings but the secret soul.

It was about this time that a number of commonplace physical events began to take place, even in Edwin. They are of small interest to this biographer. With the aid of *My Story: A Baby Record*, I here record them in cold mechanical fashion:

Dec. 31. Crawled backward.
Jan. 22, 1944. Crawled forward (not real crawling—a lurch).
Feb. 22, 1944. Sat up by himself.
Feb. 29, 1944. Crawled (really).
Mar. 2, 1944. Crawled rapidly and extensively.
Mar. 3, 1944. Stood erect in playpen.
Mar. 11, 1944. Walked sideways by holding onto edge of
          playpen.
Mar. 31, 1944. Walked two steps forward, holding onto table.
Apr. 13, 1944. Knelt without support.
Apr. 30, 1944. Stood without support.
May 26, 1944. Rose from crawl to standing position without
          use of hands.

June 4, 1944. Took single step.
June 11, 1944. Walked! (8 or 10 steps at a time).
Aug. 1, 1944 (1st birthday). Climbed onto couch, unaided.

I should like to add my own brief note to the entry of April 30: Edwin drew himself to an upright position by means of my pants pocket and then let go (the pocket was torn, though not badly). That spring he began to stand in front of his carriage in the pose of a solemn captain. He enjoyed eating ice-cream cones and chewing buttons, and for a while he enjoyed biting tables. I remember him trying desperately to remove the yellow flowers from a red dress of his mother's, and I remember a way he had of tilting his head to one side with a coy flirtatious smile. He moved his lips ecstatically at the sight of custard, he patted his favorite animals on the head, he pressed his face against the legs of people he liked, he sucked his thumb with his little finger crooked aristocratically. On July 4, to a sound of distant firecrackers, he climbed the back stairs. On his first birthday he did a little dance (on the couch). I gave him a lovely box of eight crayons, which he mistook for candy.

And here, at the completion of Edwin's first year, I should like to pause briefly in order to consider my special relation to Edwin, then and in the months and years to come. From the moment of our first meeting I was the watcher, he the watched. True, I was older by six months, a great stretch of time in the early days, and Edwin looked up to me, learned from me, and sometimes even copied me; and if I add that I was an unusually bright child, always advanced for my age, the reader will not be accused of leaping without looking if he jumps to the conclusion that I in my own small way exerted an influence, however humble, on the development of Edwin's style and soul. But he was the special one, not I—not, at first, because there was anything special about him but simply because his parents breathed into him a glow of specialness. Mrs. Mullhouse added to her instinctive pride of motherhood and the pride of her race in its firstborn sons the certainty that any boy of Abe's was bound to be special. Edwin, always an obedient son, did not disappoint her. Fortunately for the history of Western literature she happened to admire books and famous writers, though she also admired professors, painters, surgeons, lawyers, opera stars, and famous violinists and pianists. If she had happened to loathe literature and love airplanes, there is no question in my mind that Edwin would have become a pilot, yes, and probably crashed into a rainbow; for he was always an obedient son. Oh you were, Edwin, you were. You may have mocked the whole world as a dream or cartoon but you were always an obedient son. He was like one of those people in India who disbelieve in the world of appearances but adhere rigidly to the rules of their caste. As for Mr. Mullhouse (Dr. in 1949), he seemed indifferent to Edwin's future, for the very good reason that he knew Edwin's future could not possibly resemble anything he would not approve. And so from the first unrecorded howl, from the first flap of the wings of the stork, Edwin glowed with his parents' love and expectations. He was one of the watched, and I a watcher. I have never regretted my role; far from it; for there is a joy of watching as well as a joy of being watched; and what of the pain of the watched, what of that? Do you think it was easy for Edwin? Don't you know how he longed for the bliss of not being noticed? Thus the spotlight flies from shadow to shadow, longing to hide itself, but in vain. Edwin looked up to me as a prince looks up to a trusty servant; there was never any question of a clash of privileges. In bitter loneliness the prince asks his man to decide a subtle question of policy, and so the unseen man has a hand in the affairs of state. Then perhaps the prince forgets the existence of his man for a week or weeks or months at a time, until suddenly he needs him again. But the man never forgets his prince, and in the servant's chamber, which the prince never enters, who can tell what strange midnight thoughts flit through a skull?

# 8

IT WAS A PERFECT SUMMER MORNING. The sky had been soaked for hours in blue easter-egg dye and the grass shone like green cellophane. From the kitchen window at the side of our house mama had seen Helen Mullhouse step from her back door with Edwin in her arms, had watched her walk down the four gray steps and make her way along the green back yard in our direction until, turning the corner of her house, she disappeared, cut off from view by the detached Mullhouse garage. Moments later mama stepped onto our own back porch holding me by the hand. Together we walked down the steps, across the ambiguous part of the lawn that was both side and back, down a little slope that marked the border with the Mullhouse lawn; and passing between a small vegetable garden and the rickety chicken coop at the back of the red-roofed white garage, which seemed a miniature version of the red-roofed white house, we turned to the right and entered a little paradise. A white trellis covered with pink roses stretched from the side of the house to the front of the garage. In the center of the lawn stood a round white table semicircled by three brightly painted slope-backed wooden chairs and surmounted by a white-fringed red umbrella, whose shadow spilled over the edge of the table, fell onto the lawn, and rolled toward us. Mrs. Mullhouse, wearing green sunglasses, red shorts, and a white halter, sat reading in the yellow chair on the left, pulled slightly back from the table and turned so that her pale legs could stretch out in the full glare of the sun. A pair of white sandals rested on the grass by her feet, and on the arm of her chair stood a blue eyeglass case. Beside the sandals lay a small cloth zebra with a red ribbon around its neck. Puzzle: Find Edwin.

"Oh," said Mrs. Mullhouse, looking up from her book at mama and me and removing her sunglasses. She frowned at the sunlight and smiled at us.

Behind her, in a narrow strip of soil lying along the side of the house, orange and yellow zinnias blossomed among clusters of purple-and-black pansies. A fat yellow-and-black bumblebee threw a stripeless shadow against a white shingle. At the corner made by the trellis and the row of flowers lay a pale green tasseled cushion, on top of which sat a red-handled tool with three curved silver prongs; beside the cushion lay a pair of stiff gardening gloves, one of which lay on its back with the fingers curled as if to receive an orange. Behind the table was an empty white chair, gleaming in the bright sunlight. To the right of the table was an empty green chair, shining as if wet.

"I can't stay more than a sec," said mama, "but as I was telling Jeffy I just had to come out, it's too nice for dishes. I saw such a lovely dishwasher the other day but actually they say they're more trouble than they're worth. You've done worlds with this place, Hel, I can't get over it. It's really so lovely, all the roses. Oooooooh, look at the big bad bumblebee, look Jeffy, see? Where's Edward?"

"Ed*win*," said Mrs. Mullhouse.

"Did I say Ed*ward?* Isn't that funny!—it just comes out that way every once in a blue moon or so. I think Ed*win* but I say Ed*ward*, there's probably some psychological reason."

"I guess if you just called him plain old Ed. But I don't know, Ed, Ed, somehow it's just not Edwin. Oh please sit down and stay. Hi, Jeff, my you're looking—oh don't!"

Mama had stepped to the shiny green chair and placed her hands on the sloping back in preparation for pulling it out from the table. At Mrs. Mullhouse's cry she yanked her hands away and looked at them. Mrs. Mullhouse burst into laughter. "It's not wet, it's just that— Edwin, come out of there. Edwin." Placing one hand by the side of her mouth she whispered: "It's his choo-choo." We all looked at the choo-choo chair. The space under the side of the seat was covered by a wide strip of wood, raised about two inches from the ground; underneath, toward the back, I thought I saw a little pink fist. From where I was standing I could not see under the front part of the seat, but I saw that Mrs. Mullhouse's chair was unboarded in front. "Edwin," she said, "Jeff's here. Come on out, Edwin. Edwin!" She rose, placing her book on the seat but keeping hold of her sunglasses, and walked around the table past the trellis of roses to the choo-choo. She bent over, resting her hands on her knees, and said through the slatted seat: "Edwin, listen to mommy. Come out, Edwin." She was answered only by a rustling sound, as if she were speaking to a snake. I thought I could make out a little white shoe. Mrs. Mullhouse fell to her haunches, and gripping the chairarm with one hand she tipped her head to the side and peered under the front of the seat. "Edwin, come on out now, honey. Come on, Edwin. Edwin! Bad boy! Bad, bad boy!" She stood up, flushed and frowning. "Can you give me a hand? I'd like to get him out of there." She put on the sunglasses. "Let's lift, okay? But slowly." Mama and Mrs. Mullhouse each gripped the back and an arm; taking deep breaths they began to lift the heavy chair slowly from its cushion of grass. As the legs rose I saw, from left to right, a white shoe, a knee in red corduroy, a bare elbow, a hand, a bit of hair. As the chair rose higher I saw the complete shoe, resting on its toe and sloping upward from toe to heel, I saw the line of the red corduroys change from horizontal to vertical and curve around a little buttock, I saw a stripe of pale belly followed by a t-shirt in blue and red stripes, and a silky gleam of brown hair over a pale face buried in the grass and half hidden by a hand. He seemed to be peering into the earth, shading his eyes. Perhaps he was looking for China. "Higher!" gasped Mrs. Mullhouse. "This way! Oy! Careful!" Taking little abrupt shuffling steps, they moved the chair slowly toward the garage, carrying its angular shadow with them and leaving behind the naked lawn with Edwin crouching there. When Mrs. Mullhouse saw his head she nodded at mama and they lowered the chair. "Edwin!" said Mrs. Mullhouse, but he remained motionless; she walked over and stood looking down at him, hands on hips. Mama stepped over, and I came toddling up. "He's just shy," said mama. Mrs. Mullhouse said: "He's a baaaad boy." Edwin said nothing. I said: "Dad doy, dad doy." Edwin's head turned slightly; an eye flashed over the hand, and was gone. "I don't know what's the matter with him," said Mrs. Mullhouse. "What a cute outfit," said mama. "Dad doy," I said. "Oh well," said Mrs. Mullhouse, "oopsy daisy"; and bending over she reached down to Edwin. He gave a sudden jerk, and snapping up his head he crawled furiously forward and disappeared under the chair. "Oh Edwin!" cried Mrs. Mullhouse, clapping her hands in exasperation. Mama tried to soothe her: "It's all right, Jeffy was like that too." "But he's not like that!" insisted Mrs. Mullhouse. "I don't know what's gotten into him. He's been so withdrawn lately. He was making such progress. You know, he hasn't made one single sound for two whole weeks. I really don't know what to think." Meanwhile I had ambled over to the chair and was peeking under. "Dad doy," I said. "Oh Jeff, stop that," said mama, and in another tone: "He's just learning to make phrases, it's so exciting." "Edwin can say 'too-too,' " said Mrs. Mullhouse, "which means choo-choo; but," she added sadly, "Abe says it's not really talking." "Jeff can sing 'O Susannah.' " "Edwin can hum." As they talked they seemed to forget Edwin, who was in the process of turning around under his too-too. As Mrs. Mullhouse was saying "Abe says it's foolish to worry about talking when he's only just learning to walk, but he was making such progress," Edwin peeped out from under the front seat. I was struck, as always, by his large dark eyes and the extreme pallor of his skin—a pallor that was not unhealthy, as it later became, for the cheeks were rosy. He looked up and said loudly: "Dadoy." Mrs. Mullhouse broke off in the middle of a word. She took off her sunglasses. "Dadoy," said Edwin. "Did you hear that!" cried Mrs. Mullhouse. "He's talking!" "Dadoy," said Edwin. "Oh thank you!" cried Mrs. Mullhouse, addressing either me or God; her eyes were moist. "Dadoy!" cried Edwin. "Dadoy! Dadoy! Dadoy!"

# 9

IN THE BEGINNING WAS SILENCE, womb of all words which all words seek, mother of these: breath of my life. How or when the first word sprang thence hither, I'll never know, nor why. Does it really matter? Perhaps sound is only an insanity of silence, a mad gibber of empty space grown fearful of listening to itself and hearing nothing. Thus are we madmen all. Or perhaps we are silence talking in her sleep, perhaps we are a long nightmare of silence as she thrashes in torment on her downy bed. And when she wakes? Idle speculations of an eleven-year-old soul, brooding on whence and whither. Edwin once agreed with me that the ideal order of words on a page creates in the ideal reader an ideal silence; thus words regain their mother; and all the shrill noises of adulation are nothing to an artist but evidences of his imperfection.

Mrs. Mullhouse's thanks proved premature. Edwin seemed content to play with his noises and showed no interest whatever in attaching meanings to them (quite a different game). As Indian summer passed into the ragged end of autumn Mrs. Mullhouse began to look a bit ragged herself. "Spoon," she would say. "Spoon. Spooooooooon." "Pooooo," Edwin would reply, grinning hugely and flapping his hands; and reaching for the shiny spoon he would put it in his mouth, close his eyes, and pretend he was a silverware drawer. I, to her dismay, was making extraordinary progress. At eighteen months I had a vocabulary of over five hundred words, and by the time of my second birthday (February 1945; Edwin gave me a rubber snowman) I knew over one thousand words and was speaking in ten-word sentences. In February 1945 Edwin was eighteen months old and had an active vocabulary of three words: mama, dada, and dead (a version of his name). He alternated brief bouts of delighted babbling with long fits of absolute silence; both affected Mrs. Mullhouse as if she were witnessing in her eighteen-month-old child the remorseless onset of senility. Babbling summoned up in her mind images of toothless old women in peeling rooms; silence to her was a form of insanity. For the rest of her son's brief life she would be plagued by his love of silence, never understanding that it was intimately related to his love of sound; for silence is to sound as the whiteness of pages is to the blackness of words: tempters both, though whether to hell or heaven no man knows.

And so he played—now with sound, now with silence, now with his other toys. My most vivid memories of that winter, Edwin's second, are evening memories, for from the age of two I was a frequent evening visitor there. Mama, I think, was happy for a few hours' peace, and Mrs. Mullhouse seemed to hope that my articulate presence would inspire Edwin into speech. Bundled up in boots, mittens, snowsuit and hood, I would walk with mama each evening after dinner along the dark sidewalk between heaps of snow, watching on my left the line of the snowy pricker hedge, the open space of the Mullhouse driveway, the snowy pricker hedge again, and the open space of the steps; and holding tight to mama I would make my way down the same two steps I had bumped down in my carriage long ago, and would walk along the wavily shoveled walk toward the lit-up front stoop with the little cone-shaped bushes set back on both sides under the yellow windows. Over a thick brown mat rose the tall white door with its three red numerals screwed into the wood at the top: 295; and as mama rang the two-note bell I wiped my snowless boots carefully on the fuzzy mat and listened to the sound of the inside door opening with a rattle of blinds, heard the click of the inside light, the three steps in the hall, the hand on the knob—I watched the door swing inward at my toes, revealing the feet of Mrs. Mullhouse in vast puffball slippers that looked like white kittens—and looking up I saw breath coming out of her smile. Mama usually went right home, and Mrs. Mullhouse would help me off with my boots and snow-suit in the chilly front hall. Then opening the door, and turning off the light, we would enter the lamp- and firelit living room, which seemed to have contracted from its huge daylight propor-tions to a small warm circle defined by armchair, couch-corner, and fireplace, yet seemed at the same time somehow vaster: for the dark stairway with its diagonal row of balusters was alive with dangerous shadows and the tall chest housed a hundred eyes. Edwin sat on the flickering rug before the fire in a bright circle of toys, solemnly rolling an empty wooden spool back and forth or drop-ping purple wooden hoops onto an orange pole. Mr. Mullhouse was always seated on the brown armchair to the left as I entered, smoking a pipe and reading, one leg hooked over a chairarm and a vast black moccasin, trimmed with white, dangling from his toes. He would look up and say solemnly: "Good evening, Jeffrey," or "How do you do, Jeffrey," for he believed that little children should be addressed as adults, and I would reply: "Good eeving,

Mistuh Muh-how"; and sometimes in his eyeglasses I could see flames from the fireplace. Edwin would watch all this carefully out of the corner of his eye but would show no enthusiasm or even recognition. Mrs. Mullhouse would say: "Say hello to Jeff, Edwin. Say: hewwo, Deffy, hewwo!" "Oh for the love of Christ," Mr. Mullhouse would say, and in a waggish humor I would echo: "Oh for luwa cries." "Oh fine, that's just great, they'll just love that over there," Mrs. Mullhouse would say, but already Mr. Mullhouse was back in his book; and I would join Edwin silently on the floor, and silently we would play. Mrs. Mullhouse sat on the end of the couch near the fireplace, reading or knitting by the light of a small lamp on the wall bookcase, and looked up sadly from time to time at her soundless son. Sometimes she turned out her light, moved to the other end of the couch, and sitting with her legs tucked under her, watched the fire. Sometimes she sang. After a time that always seemed too short she would say: "Well, Jeff, I guess it's time to go bye-bye," and a long time later she would go to the front hall, pull down her big furry coat and pick up her furlined red boots, return to the couch, and begin to pull on her boots with a frown. She would say: "Well, Edwin, mommy's going far away across the snow," but of course he knew perfectly well she'd be back in two minutes. When she had me all bundled up in my snowsuit, and herself bundled up in the big furry coat that made her look like a bear, I would go up to Mr. Mullhouse and say: "Good eeving" or "Fankoo, goonye." He would look back at me and say solemnly: "Good night, Jeffrey." Once, looking up from a fat book, he said: "Marry, God you good den." And Mrs. Mullhouse always said to Edwin: "Say goodnight to Jeff, baby," but Edwin would be knocking wooden pegs into holes with a red wooden hammer or rolling a little wooden horse on silver wheels along the fireplace bricks or just sitting there.

One evening I appeared as usual and joined Edwin on the floor. The room was cozily dark, lit only by the crackling fire behind its screen and the light by Mr. Mullhouse's chair. Edwin was seated on the rug before a large white drawing pad with the broken remains of his eight crayons in a shoebox beside him; he was making wavy lines in an aggressive fashion, delighted at being allowed to scribble all over the nice clean sheets of paper (Mrs. Mullhouse persisted in seeing dogs or houses among those joyful scrawls). The red crayon was only a little stump without its paper sheath, and Edwin had discovered a new stroke, made by pushing the stump across the paper on its side. As I watched him making a winding pale-red river across a world of blue and orange wiggles, Mrs. Mullhouse began to sing:

*"This old man, he played one,*
*He played nick nack on my drum,*
*With a nick nack paddywhack give a dog a bone,*
*This old man came rolling home.*

*This old man, he played two,*
*He played nick nack on my shoe,*
*With a nick nack paddywhack give a dog a bone,*
*This old man came rolling home.*

*This old man, he played three,*
*He played nick nack on my tree, sing along with mommy honey,*
*With a nick nack paddywhack give a dog a bone, come on baby,*
*This old man came rolling home.*

*This old man, he played four,*
*He played nick nack on my door,*
*With a nick nack paddywhack*

Oh Abe he just won't sing."

Mr. Mullhouse looked up from his book and stared at Mrs. Mullhouse solemnly through his flickering lenses. Placing the book over one leg, and removing his pipe, he said:

> *"Columbus said to Isabel*
> *Just give me ships and cargo.*
> *I'll be a lowdown sonofabitch*
> *If I don't bring back Chicago."*

"Oh really, Abe," said Mrs. Mullhouse. Mr. Mullhouse said:

> *"For forty days and forty nights*
> *They sailed in search of booty,*
> *When on the shore they saw a whore—*
> *By god she was a beauty.*
>
> *The sailors all jumped overboard*
> *Without their shirts and collars.*
> *In fifteen minutes by the clock*
> *She made nine thousand dollars."*

"Oh Abe," said Mrs. Mullhouse. "Really."

Mr. Mullhouse put the pipe back in his mouth, picked up his book, and began to read. A few moments later he took his pipe out of his mouth and said: "Snip snap candlewax for the love of Christ."

"Nick nack paddywhack," said Mrs. Mullhouse, "and Abe I wish you'd watch your language in front of the children. And besides," she continued, "oh now I've forgotten what I wanted to say." She returned to her fire-watching. Edwin all this while had been sitting with his back to me, but with great stillness, as if listening intently. After a while Mrs. Mullhouse began to hum, and soon she broke into song:

> *"This old man, he played five,*
> *He played nick nack on my hive,*
> *With a nick nack paddywhack give a dog a bone,*
> *This old man came rolling home.*
>
> *This old man, he played six,*
> *He played nick nack on my sticks,*
> *With a nick nack paddywhack give a dog a bone,*
> *This old man came rolling home.*
>
> *This old man, he played seven,*
> *He played nick nack"*

"THE EYES AGAIN!" cried Mr. Mullhouse in an unearthly screech.

"Oh God, what?" gasped Mrs. Mullhouse, lifting a hand to her cheek.

"Staggering as if struck by lightning," said Mr. Mullhouse, "he lost his balance and tumbled over the parapet. The noose was on his neck. It ran up with his weight, tight as a bowstring and swift as the arrow it speeds. He fell for five-and-thirty feet. There was a sudden jerk, a terrific convulsion of the limbs, and there he hung, with the open knife clenched in his stiffening hand. The old chimney"

"Oh Abe, for heaven sakes. You frightened me."

"Good. Excellent. The old chimney quivered with the shock, but stood it bravely. The murderer swung lifeless against the wall, and the boy, thrusting aside the dangling body which obscured his view, called to the people to come and take him out, for God's sake. A dog, which had lain concealed till now, ran backwards and forwards on the parapet with a dismal howl and, collecting himself for a spring, jumped for the dead man's shoulders. Missing his aim, he fell into the ditch, turning completely over as he went, and, striking his head against a stone, dashed out his brains."

"Oh really," said Mrs. Mullhouse, "where do you dig up that stuff, anyway."

"Dickens, m'dear," said Mr. Mullhouse, and returned to his book.

Edwin, attracted by the unusual sound of his father's voice, had turned during the reading from the pad to his father's face. Afterward he continued to sit motionless and unblinking, seeming to stare at his father but seeing nothing; while in the gleaming obsidian heart of each wide pupil, ringed with its smooth iris of polished mahogany, a small and perfect image of the lamp was clearly visible to the casual observer, complete with its ivory figure on top, its glowing shade, and its swelling porcelain belly on its base of brass.

The next evening I arrived as usual and took my place beside Edwin, who was trying to feed his zebra an empty spool held in an old soupspoon. After a while he put the spool in his crayon box and began hitting the zebra on the head with the back of the spoon. Mr. Mullhouse sat puffing away beside the glowing lampshade, one leg hooked over the chairarm and the vast moccasin dangling; from time to time he raised his eyes from the page to frown at the bowl of his pipe. Mrs. Mullhouse sat in the knitting corner of the couch with her legs thrown under her and a red ball of yarn resting on the groove between the two cushions. The puffball kittens slept on the rug beside a straw bag filled with colored balls of wool and long pink and green knitting needles with silver buttons on the end. As she clicked away at a pair of red mittens for Edwin she began to sing.

> *"Lavender blue, dilly dilly,*
> *Lavender green.*
> *When I am king, dilly dilly,*
> *You shall be queen.*

Actually that doesn't make any sense sung by oh damn I've dropped a stitch."

There was a pause, followed by the sound of clicking, pipe-puffing, and fire-crackling. After a while she sang again:

> *"Baa baa black sheep have you any wool?*
> *Yes sir, yes sir, three bags full.*
> *One for my master, one for my dame,* ·
> *And one for little Edwin who lives in the lane.*
> *Baa baa black sheep have you any wool?*
> *Yes sir, yes sir, three bags full."*

She sighed, and again the living room filled slowly with its sounds. Edwin was crawling about, dragging his zebra by the tail over the fireplace bricks, bumping him down onto the rug and over the mahogany paws of the little table before the couch, dragging him up and down among the dark leaves and swirls of the rug until he came to the puffball slippers. He placed the zebra headfirst into one, with its hind legs and tail sticking out, and lost interest. Reaching up to his mother's knees he pulled on her dress and drew himself up to a standing position before her.

"Why Edwin," said Mrs. Mullhouse, looking up from her needles with a smile. "Did you want to see mommy?"

Edwin toddled around to the side of the couch. Mrs. Mullhouse followed him with her eyes; from my post of observation before the fireplace I followed her eyes, wherein I detected an amused perplexity. For a time Edwin simply stood there with his back against the wall bookcase and both hands resting on the white doily of the couch-arm. He was staring at the needles and Mrs. Mullhouse said: "Do you want to see mommy knit, Edwin?" She began to work the needles loudly, frowning down at her lap and occasionally giving to the strand of red yarn a jerk that caused the yarnball to jump. As she knitted away before the eyes of her son, Edwin leaned closer until his face almost touched her shoulder. Looking up at her ear he shouted: "ICE AGAIN!"

Mrs. Mullhouse jerked her head away and at the same time, as if to ward off a blow, jerked up her hands. The ball of yarn gave a jump. It rolled to the edge of the cushion, tottered over, and dropped softly to the floor. Making its way crookedly among the gleaming table-paws it came tumbling crazily toward me, leaving on the dark rug behind it a sudden bright red slash.

# 10

Mrs. Mullhouse recovered her composure and her yarn; and now every evening Mr. Mullhouse read aloud to Edwin from books without pictures, while Edwin, understanding nothing, listened in fascination to his father's voice. It was the sound alone that held him, undistorted by meaning; and the sense I think of a special occasion, a sacred rite requiring in the profane listener a hush of awe. Mr. Mullhouse's reading voice was not his everyday voice but a formal, artificial, ideal version of it; a voice, you might say, that formed literature out of the dust of speech and breathed into its nostrils the breath of life. For the next few months Edwin experienced the great passages of English literature as a feast of babbling. Besides a few standard courses in English Composition, Mr. Mullhouse was teaching a course called Survey of English Literature from Beowulf to Joyce and another called Victorian Fiction. Edwin's favorite poets at this time were Chaucer, Spenser, Shakespeare, and Milton; he showed a special interest in medieval alliterative verse; and in prose, aside from his beloved Dickens, he listened with pleasure to passages from *Le Morte D'Arthur*, Boswell's *Life of Johnson*, and *Finnegans Wake*. In the months that followed, as sounds increasingly came to be associated with things, Edwin lost his interest in adult literature, which curiously enough ceased to have any meaning whatsoever as the words themselves began to acquire meanings.

For his second birthday I gave Edwin a tall child's dictionary with a glossy cover. "Say thank you," said Mrs. Mullhouse. "You wackum," said Edwin. He was making excellent progress. The nightly readings from Dickens or the Survey anthology stirred Edwin to imitate the fine sounds he heard, so that in a sense his interest in speech was really an interest in reading. By his second birthday he knew numerous passages by heart and loved to recite them with all the gusto of a budding actor:

*A bee a noppity: assa question!*

*It wuzza besta time, it wuzza wussa time, it wuzza age a whiz, it wuzza age a foo!*

*Wanna opril wishes sure as soda!*

At the same time, try as he might, he could no longer avoid the knowledge that sounds had meanings, and so at first reluctantly, then resignedly, at last passionately, he began to acquire a vocabulary. He became obsessed by the notion that there was a name for everything; perhaps he felt that the world contained a finite number of things and that to learn the names of all of them was to define the universe. Or perhaps he felt a sense of discovery and even invention, as if objects he had never noticed before were springing into existence by virtue of being named. Indeed in the Late Years, during the era of long moonlit conversations that followed the completion of *Cartoons*, Edwin once claimed that to name things is to invent the universe; the more names, the larger the universe, or some such nonsense; and when I reminded him drily of his initial resistance to language, he turned to me with a puzzled expression and said: "But I was always advanced for my age. You must be wrong, Jeffrey." For of course he had forgotten everything.

His favorite word between the ages of two and three was "Wussat?" accompanied by a pointing finger; his favorite game was to search for objects without names. "Wussat?" he would cry, pointing to his foot. "Shoe," Mrs. Mullhouse would say. "Unless of course you mean foot. Or did you mean toe, Edwin?" "Wussat?" he would say, bending over and pointing again. "Shoelace," Mrs. Mullhouse would answer. "You know: shoelace. A lace for your shoesy-woozies." "Wussat?" "That's a whatchamacallit, Edwin. You know: a whoosiewhatsits. Oh what is the name of that stupid tongue. Oh: tongue. Only it's not a real tongue, Edwin, it's a shoe tongue." "Wussat?" "Oh dear, Edwin, I really— it doesn't have a name, it's just a sort of hole for the shoelace to go through. You'd better ask daddy." Daddy was the real test. Daddy knew everything, or almost everything, and what he didn't know he knew how to find out. "Wussat?" "Window." "Wussat?" "Windowsill." "Wussat?" "Frame. All of this is called the frame, boys. This piece here is called the sash; it holds the glass. This is a rail. Look: top rail, bottom rail. These things are stiles. And up here too: top rail, bottom rail, stile, stile." "Wussat?" "Damned if I know." There followed a search through the mahogany bookcase, interrupted by cries of "Helen, have you seen my carpentry book, you know, the one with the blue and red cover?" and at last pulling out a book Mr. Mullhouse sat crosslegged on the floor before the bookcase and turned pages wildly until he came to a picture of a window. "Aha!" he cried, looking up and raising a finger. "The correct term, gents, is: sash bar." He sighed and shook his head. "You'd think it would have a more splendid name."

There is a picture of Edwin from this period showing him seated on the armchair, leaning forward with a frown and pointing a finger. Under the picture, in Mr. Mullhouse's small neat print, is the single mysterious word: "Tripod."

I must report that although Edwin proved unready for my child's dictionary, with its small illustrations and its elaborate pronunciation apparatus, he did prove ready for two simple alphabet books that Mrs. Mullhouse had given him during his silent phase, and which he now pondered for hours at a time. The first contained on each left-hand page a vast capital letter, and on each right-hand page a ridiculous jingle. What fascinated the future author was not the jingle but the letter. Each one, drawn in three dimensions and casting a shadow, was inhabited or infested by little two-dimensional manikins with eyes and smiles and shoes. Thus one manikin hung by his arms from A's bar while another slid down a side; one lay on his stomach on top of B while another scaled the straight side like a mountain-climber and yet another peeped up over the bar; and one lay on his back in the curve at the base of C, with his legs crossed and his hands behind his head, looking up at another who was hanging by his knees from C's top. I cannot help thinking that this early experience of letters as *places* lingered on in Edwin's imagination, so that when much later he spoke of building a world of words he was thinking partly of a real place where he could play, climbing among the letters, poking his head out of holes, swinging from bars, and sliding down slopes. The second alphabet book gave each letter a personality. Thus A had two eyes in his triangle and his bar was a handlebar mustache; B was a snowman with a tall black hat; and C wore a cowboy hat and had an eye under the top curve. And here we have the evident origin of Edwin's later theories concerning the personalities of letters and the physical properties of words. He loved to spout all sorts of nonsense about the pointy head of A, the pot belly of B and his son b, the moon C, the ladybug D, and so forth, and he used to claim that all words looked like things: "yellow" was a ship with a rudder and two smokestacks, "bad" was two chairs on opposite sides of a table, "did" was three people standing on line. All of which struck

me then, and strikes me now, as highly ridiculous, except perhaps
as evidence of Edwin's endless fascination with words. And yet
they tease me, these books in which letters are more than letters;
and I cannot help wishing that Edwin had never laid eyes on them
at all.

Edwin's passion for adult literature barely survived his second
birthday. That summer a vast number of children's books appeared
in the house. Some volumes contained on each page a single line
of large print and over it, as if the words were dreaming, a towering illustration. Others contained eight or ten lines of print per
page, arranged variously in relation to the illustration. Still others
contained whole pages of print, inhabited here and there by little
colored pictures, like birds in a tree of words. These books multi-
plied with bewildering rapidity until, by his third birthday, Edwin
was the proud owner of his personal bookcase, made by his father
from two orange crates and painted a dark shiny blue. In the
course of the next year, as the room began to assume its final shape,
acquiring a second bed and the first of its two large gray bookcases
(see Chapter 1), the orange-crate bookcase became a random
repository for picture puzzles, small stuffed animals, cowboy
pistols, and shoeboxes filled with marbles or broken crayons; but
with the acquisition of the second gray bookcase, the little orange-
crate bookcase found its way into Karen's room, where for a while
it housed dolls and coloring books, until one day it found its final
resting place in a corner of the vast damp cellar beside Mr. Mullhouse's mahogany folding desk, gathering to itself old notebooks,
piles of damp white paper, boxes of index cards, manila envelopes,
and a small silver model of the Washington monument with a thin
glass thermometer running up one side. Farewell, bookcase: the
memory of your history has touched me deeply, as if by escaping
the chronology of this chapter you had made some last proud
effort before lapsing into oblivion.

And since I have broached the subject, let me say that memory
and chronology simply do not make good bedfellows. Indeed it
sometimes seems to me that I should abandon the madness of chro-

nology altogether and simply follow my whims, launching immediately, for instance, into Edwin's bloody death and passing from there to a portrait of Edwin's grandmothers, whom I haven't even introduced yet even though they have been hovering about for years, and from there perhaps to the death of Arnold Hasselstrom. And yet, after all, no. My task does not resemble the making of a jigsaw puzzle, here a shoe and part of a baggy cuff, there a piece of cloud shading into blue, but one of those connect-the-dots pictures that lead you in a series of invariable steps from a seeming chaos of numbers to a sudden recognition of the still incompleted pattern to the final closing of the gap, when number 63 is at last joined to number 1 and you see before you a flower, a kitten, a weeping clown. And of course there are Edwin's favorites, the ones with part of the picture filled in beforehand, so that in a swarm of buzzing numbers you see a lone hand holding the top of a watering can. Or to change the image: let chronology be the meter of my biography, memory my rhythm: now matching so closely as to be barely distinguishable, now tugging against one another, now drifting so far apart that the reader begins to frown and tug at his chin, now coming together with a bang. Where was I?

All of Edwin's earliest books contained on the inside front cover a space for his name, usually preceded by the phrase THIS BOOK BELONGS TO. In each of them obedient Edwin entered, in careful wiggles, the illegible scribble of his name. He seems to have abandoned this practice on or before his third birthday, since the book I presented to him on that occasion, *A Child's Golden Treasury of Immortal Poems,* is not signed by him, and a large number of other books, which by their vocabulary and general nature unquestionably belong to the Early Years, are likewise unsigned. When his name again appears it is printed in five large tilted capital letters. Since Edwin did not learn to copy the letters of his name until his fourth birthday, when he received a tall blackboard on an easel with an alphabet running around the sides, the volumes he acquired during his first bookish year may be determined with a satisfying accuracy. Here follows a complete list of all the books Edwin is known to have owned between the impressionable ages of two and three:

Thumbelina, Ali Baba and the Forty Thieves, Rapunzel, The Adventures of Pinocchio, Aladdin and the Wonderful Lamp, Rumpelstiltskin, The Three Billy Goats Gruff, The Immortal Moment: A Survey of English Literature from Beowulf to Joyce, The Valiant Little Tailor, The Little Pretzel Who Had No Salt, The Absent Minded Wizard, Doctor Dumpling, Archibald and the Jumblejacks, The Pinch-me Punch-me Bounce-me Bump-me Toss-me Tumble-me Tickle-me O, Spiderella, Rambambolo, Ha Ha the Hee Haw and the Moo Moo Who Said Meeow, Donald Dandelion and Oopsy Daisy, Snow Red, Periander Pippintop, The Azurl of Climpertoy, Prince Imlo of Nax, The Golden Nose, Solomon Snudge, Bicklebuck and the Binglebat, Billy Bimbo, The Hippopota Mister and the Hippopota Miss, Ho Hum and Heave Ho, The Near-Sighted Ogre, Gerald the Intelligent Grape, The Lonely Island, The Little Shadow Who Had No Boy, The Snow-girl Who Melted Away, The Timid Troll, Coralora, Swanita, The Hunchbacked Imp, King Crunch, Nibble Nibble Nosebeam, The-odore the Moose, The Boy Who Never Grew Up, The Teeny Weeny Genie, Willy of Chile, The Picture Book of Snowflakes, Andy the Amoeba and His Friends, Why Is the Sky Blue?, Jerry the Giraffe Has His Tonsils Out, The Tired Hiccup, The Pipe-Lover's Guide to Real Smoking Enjoyment, The Jewel in the Grass, The Queen in the Lake, The Door in the Tree.

If the emblem of Edwin's first year is a boy with a shiny chin seated in a playpen, and if the emblem of Edwin's second year is a boy seated in front of a fireplace in the bright circle of his toys, the emblem of Edwin's third year is a boy kneeling on a chair with his elbows on the kitchen table and his chin on his hands, his hair touching his father's shoulder as he stares in a stern trance at the open book before them on the table. Mr. Mullhouse was fond of changing his voice whenever someone in the story spoke: he squealed, he growled, he lisped, he stuttered, he wheezed, pounding his chest. Once during the speech of a fire-breathing dragon he moved his lips soundlessly, and when Edwin angrily complained, his father argued that the fire had burned away his vocal cords. Some-times, tired, Mr. Mullhouse would leave out a word or an entire sentence and start to turn the page. But Edwin had many pages and even entire books by heart, and clutching his father's arm he would say with a look of shocked reproach: "Oh *no*, oh *no*, you left it out," whereupon Mr. Mullhouse, looking a trifle guilty, would start at the top of the page and read straight through in his best manner, glancing from time to time at Edwin with secret pride.

From the age of two and a half Edwin began to make up stories. These early tales were remarkably unremarkable except for the energy with which he recited them and the sudden, startling, dreamlike, and ultimately boring shifts that occurred whenever some new idea popped into his head. For the most part his stories were unintelligible and interminable, consisting of bits and pieces of whatever had just been read to him combined with obscure references to some real incident that was weighing on his mind: a broken kangaroo, an angry door, a missing head. How often, in those days, might you have found us in some shady corner of the bright back yard or in a striped rectangle of window on the living room rug, I with downcast eyes and Edwin with a wild look about him as he tried my patience with some tedious story about a glass king who had wandered into the kitchen in search of a golden key and mommy said for god sakes for god sakes and the water was boiling and then we all had coffee and ice cream and cups and spoons and zebras. Stories were all energy in those days; Edwin the dreamer, Edwin the plotter and planner, Edwin the flat-on-his-backer in his room at noon, is a later though no less determined Edwin. In the Late Years, during difficult stretches of writing, Edwin would complain clumsily—his conversational powers were distinctly third-rate—that he had lost his early fluency, and one slowly gathered from his incompetent mutterings his amusing notion that now he had to construct with all the cunning of a jaded intellect and all the cruel pressure of a totalitarian will, self-consciously and painfully, syllable by weary syllable, the faded reproductions of those early fluent masterpieces. The notion of a "fluent masterpiece," had anyone else suggested it, would have made Edwin laugh scornfully through his nose or blink rapidly in a feigned idiocy of incomprehension. He never abandoned the myth of an earlier ease and naturalness of expression; perhaps in some fashion it was necessary for his work, heating him to a yet higher fever of scrupulous artifice. Easy and natural his early stories may have been, but masterpieces they most emphatically were not. It is only my word against Edwin's, I know; but he is dead, and besides, I was the one who had to listen to that drivel.

Each of Edwin's early books was at one time or another his favorite; but his constant favorite, his favorite of favorites, which he knew line by line and page by page despite his illiteracy and which he insisted on having read to him at least twice a day for more than a year, was *The Lonely Island*. Because of its importance in the spiritual history of my immortal friend, I shall here transcribe the simple text of its 44 pages, leaving to the reader's imagination those vast gloomy illustrations hovering over the words in shades of green, blue, and midnight black.

Page 1.   Once upon a time there was an island.
     2.   It lived all alone in a great big ocean.
     3.   In the summer the sun shone brightly.
     4.   In the winter it snowed.
     5.   At night it was very dark on the island.
     6.   No people lived on the island.
     7.   Sometimes rain came to the island . . .
     8.   . . . but then it went away.
     9.   Sometimes the wind came to the island . . .
    10.   . . . but then it blew away.
    11.   Once a bird came to the island.
    12.   It built its nest in the highest tree.
    13.   The island liked the bird in the tree.
    14.   The bird sang to the island.
    15.   One day the bird flew away.
    16.   The island was very sad.
    17.   Its tears fell into the ocean.
    18.   That night the island had a dream.
    19.   It dreamed of an ocean with many islands.
    20.   The islands played leapfrog.
    21.   The islands played ring around the island.
    22.   The islands swam in the water all day long.
    23.   All the islands were very happy.

24. The island woke up. It was all alone.
25. The sky grew dark and snow began to fall.
26. Snow fell for many days and many nights.
27. Great waves fell on the island.
28. One day the sun came out.
29. The ocean lay all about as far as the eye could see.
30. The island was very lonely in the ocean.
31. That night the island had another dream.
32. It dreamed of an ocean with many islands.
33. It dreamed that the islands came out of the dream . . .
34. . . . into the ocean.
35. The island woke up. It saw . . .
36. . . . another island and . . .
37. . . . another island and . . .
38. . . . another island!
39. There were islands as far as the eye could see.
40. The lonely island now had many friends.
41. The islands played leapfrog.
42. The islands played ring around the island.
43. The islands swam in the water all day long.
44. The lonely island was lonely no more.

# 11

EDWIN'S GRANDMOTHERS never appeared together. Before Karen was born, the grandmothers slept in the empty bed in the extra room, but after Karen was born the empty bed was moved into Edwin's room and the grandmothers slept there. The empty bed was never moved back; and after Karen had a bed of her own, the grandmothers slept in Karen's bed and Karen slept in the empty bed in Edwin's room.

Edwin's favorite grandmother was Grandma Mullhouse. She had thick white hair that broke at her neck into a froth of curls;

a single comma-shaped curl came down over one eyebrow. She wore vast-brimmed hats that shook when she walked or brimless hats with short black veils and hatpins tipped with red or blue or yellow knobs. She wore bright silk neckerchiefs, tying them at the side of her neck like a pirate. She liked bright red dresses with wide shoulders and she always carried a huge pocketbook, which Mr. Mullhouse called her briefcase. On her dress, over her heart, she wore a big pin that she called a brooch; Edwin's favorites were the three gold leaves joined on a single curving stem, and the silver galleon sailing on silver waves. On each wrist she wore two heavy round bracelets that banged together whenever she moved. At the ends of her thick fingers, which were bent in different directions at the last joint, her nails were fiery red. She smoked cigarettes, leaving bright red stains on the ends, and she always coughed, saying: "It's not a cough, Abe, believe me." She could put out a cigarette by squeezing it with her fingers, because she had no feelings there any more. She brought Edwin white bags of soft-centered raspberry candy in cellophane wrappers that were twisted at both ends, handfuls of blue and red and white poker chips, and decks of shiny playing cards that she got from someone called Max. Once she gave him a gold compact with a round mirror and an orange powderpuff that looked like a beanbag. After the first day, when she talked to Mr. and Mrs. Mullhouse about arthritis, rheumatism, and rising prices, Grandma Mullhouse spent almost all her time with Edwin and me, playing Go Fish and Old Maid, making vast bowls of custard or huge yellow cakes with orange icing, and telling stories about the man who thought she was thirty-eight or the man who thought she was thirty-five or the time she used to give piano lessons before her fingers got crooked or the time she was thrown from a merry-go-round halfway across the park and landed on her back and stood up without a scratch; it would have killed most people. After a week she went home, spending the last afternoon with Mr. and Mrs. Mullhouse and talking about arthritis, rheumatism, and rising prices.

Nanny had straight gray hair and no lipstick. She had a stern face with wide cheekbones and she talked with an accent. Edwin tried to like her but he was afraid of her; when she bent down to kiss him he thought she was going to scold him. She had pale cool cheeks full of fine wrinkles, and although Edwin was surprised at the smoothness of her skin, he preferred the thick pink powder on Grandma's cheeks. Nanny wore little hats and little pins without pictures. She wore tight black shoes with thick heels, and her thick ankles came over the top. When she wore a kerchief she called it a babushka. She wore dark clothes and looked much older than Grandma Mullhouse; later Edwin was amazed to learn that she was five years younger. Whenever she came, Edwin knew he would have to eat red soup for dinner; and she always told him to rub his nose up, not down. Sometimes she brought him special foot-long pretzels or brown bags of peanuts, but usually she brought gifts for the whole family: chocolate cakes in white boxes tied with white string; and sometimes she brought nothing. She spent most of her time with Edwin's mother, helping with dinner or sitting stiffly with her hands in her lap. There was a faint holiday feeling when she came, but Edwin was relieved when she went away.

The most important thing about the grandmothers was their connection with the railroad station. Twice a visit Edwin and I accompanied Mr. Mullhouse by bus or cab to the vast brown waiting room with its rows of black wooden seats where tired people sat among shopping bags and suitcases while lively people strode up and down or pushed in and out the doors that opened onto the dangerous tracks. There were glass machines full of pistachio nuts, free piles of blue and red and green timetables arranged neatly in wooden compartments (Edwin always took two of each), and round red seats on silver poles, where you could turn round and round and see the shiny counter, the ticket windows, the doors, the shiny counter, the ticket windows, the doors, the shiny counter, the ticket windows, the doors. And of course there was the train itself: the loud voice shouting, the people standing up, the rush outdoors onto the wooden platform with its carts full of mailbags and the safe tracks right in the wood and the nearby deadly tracks with wires overhead and black bridges in the sky, and at last the train in the distance getting closer and closer and louder and louder until the wind of its passing almost knocked you over

and you stared at the vast iron wheels with the white steam shooting
out. But better than the timetables, better than the turning seats,
better than the snorting train itself was a certain corner of the waiting room near the photograph booth. There, standing in two rows,
were the tall brown machines with footstools in front of them and
colored pictures at the top. We were still too short for the stools
to be of any use and so Mr. Mullhouse had to hold each of us up
in turn. Edwin placed a nickel in the silver tongue and I quickly
leaned forward, placing my face carefully against the cold metal
of the viewer and shading the sides with my hands. Edwin pushed
in the tongue and pulled it out, and I knew without looking that the
nickel had disappeared. A buzzing began; and suddenly in the
viewer I saw brightness, and words, and then a gang of cowboys
was galloping silently toward me on white and black horses with
great clouds of dust coming up behind. Whenever the words appeared I quickly drew back to let Mr. Mullhouse look in and read
them aloud; then I rushed back, bitterly disappointed if the picture
had already reappeared. I liked the Hopalong Cassidy pictures, but
Edwin liked the cartoons.

A black cat, wearing goggles, stepped into the cockpit of a small
white airplane. Reaching forward, he spun the propeller with his
paw. White puffs came out the back; the plane shook and at last
began to move forward. But it failed to go up in the air: continuing
along the smooth airstrip it passed onto a bumpy field, where disappearing into a haystack it still moved forward, carrying the hay
along. The moving haystack startled a man with a pitchfork, whose
hat rose in the air. It frightened a cow, who lay down on her
stomach and covered her eyes with her hooves. Another haystack
opened its eyes, lifted its skirts, and ran away. The moving haystack hit a bump and shot into the air, revealing the cat in the
plane; loaves of bread began to fall from the sky. The plane continued along the field, chasing cows and scattering chickens and
coming at last to a big barn; it crashed through and came out the
other side, leaving a plane-shaped hole. As a farmer came running
out of his house the plane rose into the air with a chicken on each
wing. It tipped to the left and one chicken fell off; it tipped to the
right and the other chicken fell off; it turned upside down but the

cat remained seated. The plane bumped into an eagle and with its propeller gave the bird a haircut so that its head resembled an egg with a few hairs sticking up. Still upside down, the plane began a long curving nosedive and turned rightside up as it skimmed the ground, knocking over the farmer and again rising into the air. The farmer ran into his house and came out with a shotgun; he shot twice into the sky, falling over backward each time. Two birds landed at his feet. At last he shot one wing off the plane and the plane began to perform wild looping spins until it plunged straight down, spinning like a top. The cat leaped out, holding his nose, and the plane crashed through the roof of the farmer's house as the cat landed on a large haystack. The farmer shot the haystack; an angry bull emerged; and as the circle closed the farmer ran zigzagging into the distance, becoming smaller and smaller, pursued by the bull.

One machine was different from all the others. It stood by itself, dark and old, and advertised the same picture week after week in the faded announcement at the top. This machine had a crank on one side; when you put a nickel in, the crank could be turned, and you could make the movie go faster or slower. If you turned very fast the motions were speeded up and the brown-and-white lady pushed the brown-and-white man onto the brown-and-white bed and the man bounced up and the lady pushed the man and the man bounced up and the lady pushed the man and the man bounced up and the lady flung up her hands, looked at the ceiling, and then reached for the chair; if you turned at a medium speed the motions were jerky so that the lady seemed to lift the chair over her head in many stages, with pauses between each stage; and if you stopped turning altogether you saw the lady standing motionless with the chair breaking on the man's head over the frozen beginnings of a grimace, and beyond the margin of the picture you saw a whole pile of cards reaching down underneath, and if you turned very carefully you could make a single new card come down, with everything looking exactly like before except that one of the lady's elbows now touched a corner of the photograph hanging on the wall, and the jagged crack in the breaking chairleg was wider.

# 12

TIME PASSED. I suppose it comes to that, in the end. If I were direct-
ing a movie I would now show one of those calendars with the
pages being torn away one by one against a changing background:
September October November December (popped cork, shouts of
Happy New Year!) January 1947 February March April May
June July August (the 1 is circled). At the very end I would introduce a headline effect: superimposed against a background of
clattering printing presses you see a small turning pinwheel which
gets larger and larger as it comes closer and closer and reveals itself
to be a newspaper—and stops (to an orchestral blare), enabling
you to read in big black letters: HAPPY BIRTHDAY EDWIN. If I were
writing a novel . . . but time is passing, the reader is growing older,
we wake from green dreamed islands to drown in the dark. Lights!

On a brilliant afternoon in August, when grass too green and a
roof too red and the precise and luminous white shingles among the
windows seemed not so much to be opaque and shining with a surface brightness as to be transparent, penetrated by color, and illuminated from within or behind, like the glowing objects in one of
Mr. Mullhouse's color slides mounted in glass and held up to a hot
bright lightbulb; on such an afternoon in August, shortly after
Edwin's fourth birthday, a group of four people were to be found
seated on the large white wooden family swing in the center of the
Mullhouse back yard. On the right sat Mrs. Mullhouse and five-
month-old Karen, with their backs to the vegetable garden and
their faces toward Robin Hill Road; on the left sat Mr. Mullhouse
and Edwin, who was slumped in the near corner with his bare legs
extended and his feet resting on the edge of the seat opposite, a few
inches away from Karen. The two bench-like seats of the swing
were fitted into a tall roofed frame in such a way as to move back
and forth upon the application of pressure to the fixed wooden

floor or to the seat opposite. Hidden from the view of all four, a bright cardinal was pecking at the ground beside the little mountain laurel at the side of the house near Robin Hill Road. "And so," Mr. Mullhouse continued, "the king—" "Not so fast, Edwin," said Mrs. Mullhouse, frowning slightly and pulling Karen closer to her, though to all appearances they were swinging lazily back and forth with gentle creaking sounds. "Remember the baby," she said, stroking Karen's hair. Edwin pushed harder. "Stop it, Edwin. Abe, make him stop." "Edwin!" said Mr. Mullhouse sharply; Edwin's feet dropped, dangling just above the wooden floor. "And sit up, for heaven sakes," said Mrs. Mullhouse, "you're ruining your posture." Slowly, with great precision, Edwin moved one inch. "And so," continued Mr. Mullhouse, "the king took the pebble from Chicken Little's head and said: 'Thees ees awnly a leetle pebble, Señorita Cheeken, eet ees nawt thee sky.' Whereupon Turkey Lurkey said: 'Blimey, 'e says it's only a bloomin' pebble.' And Henny Penny said: 'You mean it's jes a lil ol pebble? Ah do dee-klay-uh.' To whom Goosey Poosey said: 'Pebble, schmebble, the sky is falling down and you're talking pebbles.' And Ducky Daddles said: 'Chees, if it ain't one ting it's anudda.' And Gander Pander said: 'Reckon we oughta mosey on back, ah reckon.' And Cocky Locky said: 'Cockadoodle doo! Cockadoodle doo!' And Chicken Little said: Edwin, if you don't want to listen, don't listen, but don't sit there making faces. I don't know what's gotten into that boy."

"I'm sure he didn't mean anything, he's just tired, aren't you, Edwin. Let's see, whose turn is it? Mine?" And putting a fingertip to her cheek, and pursing her lips, Mrs. Mullhouse looked off with a frown of concentration. Edwin, crossing his arms and yawning loudly, swung his chin toward his right shoulder and pretended to fall asleep.

"Once upon a time," said Mrs. Mullhouse, "there was a little boy called Edward. He lived in a great big house with his mommy and daddy and he was such a quiet little boy. Well, one day Edward's mommy said to Edward's daddy, 'You know,' she said, 'I'm worried about Edward. The way he just sits around moping around all day.' 'Hmmmpf,' said Edward's father, 'I wouldn't worry about it if I were you. Just let well enough alone and everything will work out all right in the end.' "

"A very wise, very judicious man," said Mr. Mullhouse.

"Please don't interrupt, dear. You know you always tell *me* not to interrupt. Well, the next day Edward's father bought him a great big fire engine. But it was the wrong color, so Edward refused to play with it and just moped around. The next day Edward's father bought him a toy farm with a silo, and also a great big blackboard on a stand with boxes of chalk and a real eraser, but still Edward just moped around. Soon Edward was known in the neighborhood as The Boy Who Moped Around. Then one day Edward's mother got an idea. She put on her coat and hat and went to the Stork Department at Howland's. 'Hello, Mr. Stork,' she said. 'I'd like one of those pink bundles, please.' 'Well,' said Mr. Stork, 'here you are, sweetheart.' 'Thank you,' said Edward's mother, 'and you can keep your remarks to yourself if you don't mind.' "

Mr. Mullhouse raised his eyebrows.

"As soon as Edward's mother got home, she went up to Edward and gave him the pink bundle. And do you know what was inside?" Suddenly Mrs. Mullhouse turned to her left, picked up Karen, and placed her in Edwin's lap. "Karen!" cried Mrs. Mullhouse. Karen began to giggle and grin. Edwin, scowling, pushed her away. Karen burst into tears. "Oh what a rotten spoilsport," said Mrs. Mullhouse, drawing Karen onto her lap. "Don't cry, baby. Mmmm, thaaat's right, such a schatzkele. You just ignore Mr. Smartypants over there. Edwin, you make me so *damn* angry sometimes."

"I think," said Mr. Mullhouse, "that Edwin is anxious to go to bed."

Mrs. Mullhouse made a secret signal to Mr. Mullhouse with her face. Mr. Mullhouse took out his pipe, and the cardinal hopped about as Karen's sobs became fewer and fainter and stopped. "Well!" said Mrs. Mullhouse, "that's better. Whose turn is it? Edwin's?"

"Once upon a time," said Edwin, "there was a cow. This cow had two heads, three eyes, four mouths, five tails, six hands, seven feet, eight toes, nine shoes, ten shoelaces, eleven"

"Oh Edwin," said Mrs. Mullhouse.

"If you don't want to tell a story," said Mr. Mullhouse, "then don't tell one."

"I *am* telling a story." Edwin frowned and pushed out his lips.

Mrs. Mullhouse looked at Mr. Mullhouse; she held up a finger and shook it back and forth slightly. "Well, Edwin!" she said brightly, "and what was the little cow's name?"

"Jeffrey," said Edwin.

"Oh," said Mrs. Mullhouse, and paused. "What an unusual name for a cow." She paused again. "And what happened to the cow, Edwin?"

"He died," said Edwin.

Silence.

"And is that the end of your story, Edwin?"

"No."

In those days the Mullhouse back yard abutted on a weedgrown vacant lot from which it was separated by a tall thick hedge.

"Oh look!" cried Mrs. Mullhouse, pointing to the clothestree beside the back steps. A bright cardinal had landed on one of the lines, shaking the row of clothespins. Everyone except Karen turned to look. "Oh the lovely thing. Why don't you ever have your camera?"

"I'd need a telephoto," said Mr. Mullhouse. "I ought to get one, anyway."

"What's telephoto?" said Edwin, still watching the cardinal. It stood with its chest thrust out, its small head moving in quick jerks, as if it were surrounded by invisible enemies.

"It's a lens that makes small things appear big. Like putting a magnifying glass in front of the camera. With a telephoto I could sit here and take a picture of that bird as if I were sitting next to it on one of those clothespins. Yes, I certainly ought to get one."

"Telephoto," said Edwin. "Telephoto telephoto pheletoto pheletoto"

"Oh stop it," said Mrs. Mullhouse.

"Cow went to Hell," said Edwin, "and in Hell he met a bird. This bird had three tails, four heads, five nick nacks, six telephotos, seven"

"Oh Edwin, shhh! You've frightened him!" The cardinal rose from the trembling row of clothespins and flew swiftly over the swing and onto the hedge. Three heads followed its flight, turning completely around and changing from hair to pink. As the others stared eagerly at the upper branches, Edwin's gaze fell carelessly to the leafless spaces at the base of the hedge. Suddenly he stiffened. His lips parted, his eyes widened. "There it goes," said Mrs. Mullhouse, pointing skyward. "Edwin, what are you—oh! Well I'll be. Hi, Jeff! Peek-a-boo! I see you!"

# 13

GOD PITY THE POOR NOVELIST. Standing on his omniscient cliff, with painful ingenuity he must contrive to drop bits of important information into the swift current of his allpowerful plot, where they are swept along like so many popsicle sticks, turning and turning. He dare not delay for one second, not even for one-tenth of a second, for then the busy and impatient reader will yawn and lay aside the book and pick up the nearest newspaper, with all those slender columns that remind you of nothing so much as the sides of cereal boxes. The modest biographer, fortunately, is under no such obligation. Calmly and methodically, in one fell swoop, in a way impossible for the harried novelist who is always trying to do a hundred things at once, he can simply say what he has to say, ticking off each item with his right hand on the successively raised fingers of his left.

His earliest definite memory was of playing with an Erector set while she was still at the hospital. He remembered tiptoeing in to stare at her in her cradle; she had practically no hair. He handed back to her the toys she flung through the playpen bars and he played peek-a-boo with her in the crib. He fed her custard in the highchair, eating half of it himself. He stroked her silky hair and played with her little hands. He made her laugh by pushing his nose with a finger and making his tongue come out. He clasped his hands, saying: "This is the church, this is the steeple, open the doors, and look at all the people!" He said: "This little piggy went to market, this little piggy stayed home, this little piggy ate roast-beef, and this little piggy had none. And this little piggy ran alllllllll thewayhome." He said: "One two buckle my shoe, three four shut the door, five six pick up sticks, seven eight lay them straight, nine ten the big fat hen, 'leven twelve dig and delve, thirteen fourteen maids are courting, fifteen sixteen maids in the kitchen, seventeen eighteen lady's waiting, nineteen twenty the platter's empty." He said: "One two three a-lary, I spy mistress Mary, sitting on her bumbalary, out goes why oh you." He said: "Patty-cake patty-cake baker's man. Stick it in the oven as fast as you can." He said: "Fee fie fo fum, I smell the blood of an English mun." He sang The Farmer in the Dell, A Tisket A Tasket, Twinkle Twinkle Little Star, Lazy Mary Will You Get Up, The Caissons Go Rolling Along, De Camptown Races, Jingle Bells, My Bonny Lies Over the Ocean, Mademoiselle from Armentieres, Clementine, and O Susannah. He sang comic variations like Karen in the Dell, Lazy Karen Will You Get Up, My Karen Lies Over the Ocean, O Karenannah. He sang: "Here comes Peter Cottontail, hoppin' down the bunny trail." He sang:

> *Light she was and like a fairy*
> *And her shoooooooes were number nine.*
> *Herring boxes without topses*
> *Sandals were for Clementine.*

He sang:

> *The general got the car de gare*
> *Paaaaaaar layvoo.*
> *The general got the car de gare*
> *Paaaaaaar layvoo.*
> *The general got the car de gare*
> *The sonofabitch wasn't even there.*
> *Hinky dinky par lay voo.*

Taking a tissue and twisting it in the middle, he held it under his nose and said in a deep voice: "Give me the rent the rent the rent."

Then holding the tissue on his hair he said in a high voice: "I don't have the rent the rent the rent." Then holding the tissue under his nose he said in a deep voice: "Give me the rent the rent the rent." Then holding the tissue on his hair he said in a high voice: "I don't have the rent the rent the rent." Then holding the tissue under his neck he said in his own, triumphant voice: "*I'll* pay the rent." Then holding the tissue on his hair he said in a high voice: "My hero." Then holding the tissue under his nose he said in a deep voice: "Curses!" He told her the names of things and tried to make her say "spoon," not "pooo." He taught her how to say "arny goose," his own old way of saying "orange juice." He taught her how to say "oink oink," "meeow," "hee-haw," "er-e-er-e-errrrrrr," and "puck puck puck puck awwwwwk." He wrote her name in big letters and said: "That's you." He drew pictures of cats, dogs, elephants, mommy with a flower, daddy with smoke coming out of his mouth, Jeffrey with donkey's ears, himself with an upside-down smile, Karen with curly hair and a big smile. He held her hand to help her walk, rolled Tinker Toy wheels to her across the kitchen floor, told her to stay at the bottom of the stairs while from the landing he started a Slinky on its slow way down. He opened the cereal boxes and she found the prize. He showed her how to make the world go round by holding out his arms, spinning around, and falling onto the bed with his eyes shut. He showed her how to say a word over and over and over until it meant nothing at all. He showed her how to pick radishes out of the garden, digging away the soil until the red bulb appeared. He showed her how to make snowballs, how to blow away the tops of gray dandelions, how to catch a trembling bubble on the wire loop. He introduced her to icicles, balloons, spiderwebs, lollipops, and pink worms in black rainpuddles. He showed her how to write with her finger on cold foggy windows. He tucked her in at night and on the dark walls of her room showed her the moving rectangles of light from passing cars. On the tall old phonograph that he opened by standing on a footstool, he played Humperdinck's *Hansel and Gretel*, trying to make her share his terror when the witch cackled from the gingerbread house. At night he moaned: "It's oooonly the wind," terrifying himself and her. On the cover of *Peter and the Wolf* he showed her the frightening picture of a little green duck inside a black wolf. He tried to teach her the letters, the numbers, the days of the week, the months, the refrain of "Jingle Bells." He tried to teach her to say: "Now I lay me down to sleep, pray the Lord my soul to keep." Sometimes, when she would not learn, he lost his temper and shook her by the shoulders, saying: "You stupid stupid jerk, you stupid dumbbell," until her large, beautiful, copper-flecked blue eyes filled with terror, and she burst into hysterical tears.

Karen's favorite toy, in the Early Years, was a bright red parasol with a white handle. When she stood in the sunlight, holding her parasol over one shoulder, the sun streaming through the shade flowed over her hair, her cheek, and her little plump arm in a crimson stain, as if you were looking at her through a piece of red cellophane.

Edwin's favorite photograph of himself and Karen was technically one of the poorest. They stood in the center of the picture, walking hand in hand along a bright, tree-lined road with their backs to the camera. Edwin wore long baggy shorts, held up over his thin legs by dark suspenders that made an X on his short-sleeved cowboy shirt; Karen wore long pants with straps and a little t-shirt. Their very short shadows fell behind them; Karen's shadow, half the length of Edwin's, was almost a circle. It was a touching picture, though no more so than a dozen others; what made it heartbreaking was the fact that it was terribly overexposed. Karen's curly blond hair, even then darkening to brown, was here a pale blaze that seemed to be shooting off light, like the rays that Edwin used to draw about his suns. The pale road had the texture of sand, not tar, and the leaves on the pale-trunked maples were the lightest of grays. In front of the two children the flat road stretched away in a shimmering perspective that became brighter and brighter until all detail was bleached away, as if they were being drawn toward some dazzling vision.

# 14

TWO MONTHS AFTER HIS FOURTH BIRTHDAY Edwin entered Miss
Hersey's Nursery School. He endured Miss Hersey's Nursery
School for fourteen days. By Christmas his entire two weeks at
Miss Hersey's Nursery School had contracted to a single memory:
a wooden ladder at the side of a bunkbed where he napped. Miss
Hersey's Nursery School was considered a preparation for Kinder-
garten. I shall have no further occasion to mention Miss Hersey's
Nursery School.

Meanwhile he continued to pursue the study of literature with
all the desperate passion of pre-literacy. He acquired shiny new
volumes of all shapes and sizes, arranging them scrupulously on the
shelves of his new gray bookcase in accordance with some private
system curiously resembling disorder. The books of the Early
Years were much of a muchness and it is unnecessary to name them
all; if the reader studies the list given in Chapter 10 he will have a
fair idea of the range of literature available to the future novelist.
It is not entirely accurate to refer to Edwin as pre-literate, for by
this time he was able to recognize many words ("Edwin," "Karen,"
"Pinocchio," "island," etc.) and to name most of the letters. But
for all practical purposes he was as illiterate as a mouse.

In the lower right-hand corner of the bookcase, beneath a shoebox filled with marbles, lay a new kind of book that made its appearance one darkening afternoon that fall, and was destined to
exercise a considerable pressure of influence on Edwin's imagination. I remember that afternoon quite well. We were sitting on his
front step discussing a surprise attack on a neighboring village—
Edwin was wearing his new Indian headdress with the feathers
down the back and holding in one hand a tomahawk with a black
rubber head and a red wooden handle—when from the direction
of the distant bus stop Mr. Mullhouse came striding down the sidewalk past my house, swinging his briefcase with one hand and

waving over his head with the other. I took aim with my pistol but a sudden blow from the tomahawk knocked it out of my hand. I protested with some heat as I gathered the gun from the dampish grass. "I was only aiming, Edwin." "Ugh," said Edwin. I knew it was hopeless to converse with him in one of his Indian moods and contented myself with wiping the gun on my cowboy pants. As Mr. Mullhouse turned down the steps from the sidewalk and strode briskly toward us along the cement walk, I watched Edwin staring at the deep pockets of his father's trenchcoat. An endless stream of toys came pouring out of those pockets during the Early Years. "Good evening, Jeffrey. How, chief. You'll excuse me, boys, but I'm tired as the deuce." We bent to the left and right respectively, and as Mr. Mullhouse stepped between us onto the front step Edwin frowned bitterly and began to scalp the grass with his tomahawk. "Now where in God's name are my keys," said Mr. Mullhouse, standing behind us on the fuzzy mat. "Not here," he said loudly, reaching into one pocket and extracting a rumpled handkerchief that emitted bits of dust. "And not here," he said more loudly, shifting his briefcase to his right hand and reaching into his left pocket with a jingle. Edwin turned and looked up. Mr. Mullhouse extracted and replaced a handful of change, a pipe, a flat yellow package of pipe cleaners, a pouch of tobacco, and three books of matches. He sighed. "Maybe they're in here," he said, clicking open the briefcase, "though to tell you the truth, hmmm, what's this," and taking out a slim brown paper bag he looked at it with a puzzled frown. "Here, see if you can make head or tail of it." Edwin seized the package joyfully, and placing it on his lap began to slip out a glossy magazine. "But of course!" cried Mr. Mullhouse. "What an absentminded professor!" He opened the unlocked door. "Oh by the way, Jeffrey." I turned around. "Bang," said Mr. Mullhouse, shooting me in the head with his finger and closing the door behind him before I could reach for my gun. Edwin stared in disappointment at his gift. "What is it?" I asked. "Oh, pictures," said Edwin, flipping through the magazine. "Pictures of what?" I asked. But Edwin had already lost interest, and closing his left eye he reached out his left arm, pulled his right fist back to his ear, and released over a distant rooftop an invisible arrow.

It was his first comic book. When Mr. Mullhouse, in a spirit of glowing anticipation, began to read it aloud in the living room after dinner, Edwin listened politely for a page or two but at last could not conceal his impatience. Mr. Mullhouse sighed and returned to *The Littlest Injun,* Edwin's current favorite, about a boy who rode on the back of a buffalo. One rainy spring day six months later, in the bored restless mood that had seized him after his recovery from a nasty cold and fever, without enthusiasm Edwin set up his red British soldiers with their black hats in a line at one end of the room and his blue American soldiers with their white hats in a line at the other end of the room and removed his box of marbles from the bookcase in preparation for war. Under the marbles he discovered the comic book. From the bed where I sat I saw its glossy cover catch the light; under a bright red sky a vast snowball rolling downhill contained a duck and a pair of yellow skis. And I knew by a certain familiar hush of tension that something had happened inside Edwin, and that this sky, this snowball, this tumbling duck, which six months ago had left him so indifferent, were suddenly the most important things in the world to him, and that we would never play soldiers now and perhaps would never play soldiers again. Lying on his bed in warm yellow light while farther and farther away the gray rain rattled his windows, Edwin plunged into a dazzle of many-colored adventures from which in a sense he never emerged. From that moment he began to live in a world of frames and colors. Mr. Mullhouse, who believed that adults should not impose their own tastes on children, encouraged Edwin's interest, which Mrs. Mullhouse viewed with alarm. Not only did he read comic books aloud over and over again as Edwin sat on the couch beside him, leaning against his vast arm, but I have seen him sitting in his armchair in the evening with one leg hooked over the side, reading one of Edwin's comics with a frown of concentration, while beside him, on the polished lamp-table, a fat book sat under a smoking ashtray.

But having leaped ahead to a rainy spring day I must now return to the fall, as if the last paragraph were one of those sudden warm days that come upon you like a promise of spring in a setting of falling yellow leaves. For it was at this time that Edwin began to

show an interest in cameras, an interest that seems to me not unrelated to his interest in the railroad station machines, not unrelated
to his later passion for comic books, not unrelated, in short, to the
history of his imagination, and thus to the history of his life and
fiction. Mr. Mullhouse's old Graflex was a big black box that sprang
clattering open like a jack-in-the-box with no jack in the box.
Kneeling on a chair beside the kitchen table, enraptured Edwin
looked through the top at a colored blur. As his father turned a
knob the picture became clearer and clearer until he saw the
kitchen sink and the yellow dishrack, glowing in full color in the
square frame. "Extraordinary, the things you come across," said
Mr. Mullhouse, slowly turning the camera; and as the dark lens
pointed at me he said "Egad!" while I frowned in annoyance and
imagined myself in the camera looking up at Edwin with a frown
of annoyance. Mr. Mullhouse liked to explain how his camera
worked, and Edwin loved to listen, nodding happily and understanding nothing as he waited patiently for the part where his
father pushed the button and made the loud and unspeakably satisfying thud-crash-thud. He also liked the part where Mr. Mullhouse opened the camera and showed him the hole getting bigger
and bigger.

More fun than the camera itself were the black-and-white
photographs that emerged mysteriously every few weeks from a
brown cardboard cylinder tied with white string. Edwin pulled
the string; the tight cylinder expanded slightly, as if it had been
holding its breath; and slipping off the string his father began to
unwind the blotter roll slowly along the kitchen table, asking
Edwin to hold down the end. "Nnnn!" said expressive Edwin, if
ever I tried to help. The brown cylinder was white inside, and as
his father slowly rolled it back Edwin waited for the bright white
edges of the first pair of photographs to appear. After the pictures
were selected for the album (Edwin was allowed to keep the remaining pictures, which he added to his collection of timetables
and seed packets), Mr. Mullhouse brought out the dark green
papercutter with the silver blade. Placing a photograph carefully
at the edge, and frowning at us, as if he believed that only the
threat of punishment could prevent us from thrusting our hands

beneath the blade, at last he swung down the handle with a magnificent sound that was a mixture of scissors and crunched snow.

Later Edwin helped to paste the pictures in, bringing the brush swiftly down onto the white back of the photograph that lay on an open newspaper, placing the photograph carefully in the center of the black page, pressing down firmly with the side of his fist so that the rubber cement oozed from the sides, and rubbing the sticky wet cement up and down with a finger until little sticky rubbery balls were formed, which could be brushed from the page.

It was about this time that Edwin was given a Viewmaster. I myself, I must confess, never cared for those gaudy and unconvincing views. But Edwin would spend hours staring at shiny three-dimensional scenes from *Cave of the Winds: Colorado*, or *Glacier National Park: Montana*, or *Desert Scenes: Arizona*, or *Woody Woodpecker in The Pony Express Ride*. He rather enjoyed closing first one eye and then the other, in order to see the slight difference between the two nearly identical pictures—the sole result of a patient explanation by Mr. Mullhouse of the principle of three-dimensionality, during which Edwin had nodded in an enthusiastic hypocrisy of comprehension. He also enjoyed holding up the round, notched reels to a light or window, where he studied them without the machine, in two dimensions.

Comic books, cameras, photographs, Viewmaster reels—such were his simple games, but what omens for the omniscient biographer!

That winter Edwin discovered icicles. Mr. Mullhouse was photographing them and they grew everywhere. Dressed in a new blue snowsuit and a new blue hat with furlined earflaps and a chinstrap that clicked shut at the back of his jaw, Edwin tramped about the yard in search of icicles. A thick jagged icicle came out of the drain; medium-sized icicles hung miles overhead, under the roof; miniature icicles grew on the branches of the hedge and the twigs of the peach trees. There were icicles under the kitchen windowledge, icicles on the white swing, icicles under the roof of the chicken coop; and rows of icicles, like transparent clothespins, hung from the clothestree ropes. One bush in front of the house was abloom with icicle-flowers, hanging in bright transparent clusters. Edwin wanted to dig up the icicle-bush and put it in the refrigerator with the ice cubes, where it would never melt away, but Mr. Mullhouse said he was damned if he was going to serve flowers in the gin. Besides, he would take its picture, which amounted to the same thing; and there is in fact a photograph of the icicle bush showing Edwin bent over as if to sniff a flower (the boot-toe in the left-hand corner is mine). But Edwin wanted the icicle itself—a statement that sounds rather like an epitaph.

He was well aware of the mortality of icicles, for when the sun shone like a summer sun out of the rich blue winter sky he could see the icicles dripping down from the kitchen windowledge onto the brilliant white shingles, leaving ragged gleaming lines of wetness, he could see the icicles dripping from the clothestree ropes and the bars of the icy swingframe, he could see the icicles dripping from the gray back steps and the gutters of the garage and the roof of the chicken coop, and if he listened closely he could hear the dripping of a thousand icicles, splashing onto the woodpile under the kitchen window, splashing onto the cement mound that held up the clothestree pole, falling softly onto the snow and making black pitmarks, he could hear the music of a Peter-and-the-Wolf orchestra of icicles, icicle flutes and icicle oboes, icicle violins and icicle bassoons: a fragile glittering transparent world of icicles, melting, falling, dissolving, dripping away. On the shady side of the house the icicles hung hard and frozen, but they were less lovely than the sunny icicles, shining with dissolution.

Pierced by the sadness of icicles, Edwin determined to rescue one and keep it forever. Searching carefully among the icicles of the steps, the swing, the clothestree, the chicken coop, the bushes, the windowledge, and even the shining peach trees, at last he found a perfect icicle, round and clear and tapering to a perfect point; and breaking it carefully at the root he hurried inside and placed it in the freezer between the icecube trays, warning his mother and father never to touch it and receiving their solemn promises. Day after day, twice a day, Edwin opened the freezer door to check his icicle; it lay on its side in bright perfection. One day he noticed with horror that his icicle was sticking to the icy bottom. Very carefully he worked it loose, leaving only a faint flaw, and quickly added a piece of waxpaper for his icicle to rest upon. Thereafter everything was perfect.

But it snowed again. For three days and three nights the sky was a rippling curtain of snow while the wind howled and the attic made creaking sounds; the flames in the fireplace leaped crazily, blown by the wind. On the fourth day the sun came out. Edwin's back yard was smooth and white and shining, though the front yard was pockmarked with dogtracks and spotted here and there with yellow stains. After the snowplows came, the snow was heaped higher than Edwin on both sides of Benjamin Street. The world was full of snow and icicles; there was more snow than earth, more snow than air. Mr. Mullhouse had finished with icicles and had begun to photograph snowy hydrants and snowy cars; he was especially fond of snow heaped over shiny fenders, with one corner of a license plate sticking out. Edwin and I made snowforts and shouted at the yellow snowplow with its tilted sneer. There was snow wherever you looked, day after day; day after day the pale sun shone helplessly on a white world. One day Mrs. Mullhouse said: "Edwin, do you still want that old icicle?" and Edwin said: "No, I'll get a better one later." "Thank God," said Mrs. Mullhouse, turning on the hot water, "I was afraid to breathe in there." That afternoon we climbed snow mountains and looked for buried hydrants in the snow. The days grew cold and gray, and we played inside, making puzzles on the oval table near the couch or playing with the Erector set in Edwin's room. Then it rained, turning the snow to slush, and a false spring followed, melting all the snow. And again it snowed, and again the sun came out.

One day Mr. Mullhouse took Edwin and me on a long bus-ride to a dark stone building. In a vast brown room that reminded me of the waiting room at the railroad station, except that you couldn't make a sound, books in brown bookcases rose to the ceiling, row on row. There was a special room for children, where on long brown tables large white books lay open or stood on end. At first Edwin failed to understand that he could take as many as he liked: he thought he had to buy them, as in a toy store; but when he understood, he began feverishly choosing book after book, placing them in a towering pile at one corner of a table, until Mr. Mullhouse said that he should take only six and come back next week for more. Edwin finally chose seven, and as we rode home in the bus he read aloud eagerly, making up everything.

Spring came after a winter rain. The blue sky looked up out of rainpuddles, and warm air blew in the afternoons, though the nights were cold. Snow stayed for weeks in shady corners of the house where bushes kept off the sun, while in the front yard between the sidewalk and the street the red maples put out their redblack buds. A yellowgreen haze trembled on distant willows and one day Edwin noticed pale green buds on the sideyard forsythia. Mrs. Mullhouse cut off three branches and placed them in a slim vase on the piano; within three days they had burst into yellow flower. The last snow melted in the mild afternoon air, but the temperature dropped sharply when the sun went down.

One bright afternoon when Edwin and I were playing cowboys and Indians I chased him around the front of the house, backed him into the bushes, and was about to blow his brains out when, in the midst of his frantic looking about for help, he began to stare behind him as if he had forgotten my existence. It was an old trick. "Bang bang!" I cried, "you're dead!" but he took no notice of me, and turning his back he stepped into the evergreens right up to the shingles and crouched down suddenly so that only the red, yellow, and blue tips of his feathers were visible. Nervously fingering the white wooden bullets in my holster I approached warily, expecting him to leap out at me with his rubber tomahawk, but as I came up behind him I saw him squatting motionless, staring at the ground. There, streaking the dirt, lay patches of old snow, miraculously unmelted in the shadow of the little fir tree. "Bang bang!" I cried; but suddenly, as if my shots had brought him to life instead of killing him, he leaped up, rushed from the bushes, and ran along the side yard with myself in hot pursuit, and dashing up the steps he flung open the door, rushed to the refrigerator, and opened the freezer. "Edwin," said Mrs. Mullhouse, "I really wish you wouldn't" but "My icicle!" he cried, "where's my icicle?" "What icicle, Edwin? You mean that old icicle? Why, I threw it out long ago, remember? I asked you, and you said," but Edwin had burst into tears.

# 15

THE STRANGE WEATHER CONTINUED. The yellow jonquils began to open, the maples put out their dark red flowers, but as the sun went down the air grew chilly, and one morning there was a film of frost. "Good old New England," said Mr. Mullhouse. "If you're going out, remember to wear mittens and a bathing suit." It was treacherous weather, a mixture of bloom and chill, and one late afternoon in Edwin's back yard a sudden cool breeze blew against our sweat-shining faces, and Edwin sneezed. The next morning when I hurried over to play, Mrs. Mullhouse told me that Edwin was sick in bed.

A cold, for you and me, is a series of unpleasant sensations in the nose and eyes; for Edwin it was a voyage down the Amazon, a flight through the blue on a magic carpet, a journey to the mountain where grave bearded men drink liquor from kegs and make thunder by playing ninepins. Fever for him was the lifting of the stone with the brass ring: a stairway went down into the earth, and at the end was a door, and opening the door he passed into a palace divided into three great halls. On both sides of each hall stood four brass cisterns full of gold and silver. He had to be careful not to touch the walls, not even with his clothes, for if he did he would die instantly. At the end of the third hall he came to a door and entered a garden filled with trees that bore strange fruit of many colors. Passing through the garden he came to a terrace, and in the terrace was a niche, and in the niche was a lighted lamp. And taking the lamp he passed back through the garden of fruit trees, stopping to take fruit from each tree; but he did not know that the white fruit were pearls, the clear fruit were diamonds, the red fruit were rubies, the green fruit were emeralds, the blue fruit were turquoises, the purple fruit were amethysts, and the yellow fruit were opals. Then he passed through the three great halls with their cisterns of gold and silver, and climbing the stairs he cried: "Pray, uncle, help me out." "Give me the lamp first," replied the magician. But he refused, and the magician, flying into a rage, pronounced the magic words. Then the stone closed over him, and all was darkness.

Colds always took him by surprise. A casual sneeze, no different from a hundred such sneezes, would reveal itself to be the first note of a symphony of fever, chapped lips, burning nostrils, soaked handkerchiefs, and aching bones. There was a fairytale abruptness about it all: at one moment he would sneeze in sunlight, at the next he would be lying in bed beside the shut blinds of his double window with a sopping handkerchief squatting beside his pillow like some pale animal that had crawled up out of a hole. For weeks he would not stir from his sheets except to go to the bathroom just outside his room. Lonely and wretched in my glowing health, I stood with my hands in my pockets in the house-shadowed grass of morning, gazing up at the dark windows where I sometimes saw white clouds, or standing in the emerald grass of noon I would shade my eyes as I stared at the remote sunpolished glass behind which Edwin lay like an invisible Snow White in an opaque glass coffin, or a perverse Rapunzel, content in her tower. Only sometimes, in reply to my shouts, would the window stir with a motion of blinds, and then for a moment I would catch a pale glimpse of a piece of Edwin before he suddenly disappeared, as if dragged away by a witch. Then I would hurry up the back steps, and rapping on the wooden frame of the screen door I would be admitted to the kitchen, where I would try to allay my loneliness in the company of Karen and Mrs. Mullhouse. With unusual precision Mrs. Mullhouse recounted to me the progress of Edwin's illness while I watched Karen toddle about in her new white shoes or played pattycake with her as she sat on the floor. "His temperature was a hundred and two and a half but Dr. Blumenthal said don't worry, it's not polio. Poor Edwin, he has to lie on his stomach cause his heinie's so sore." I saw Dr. Blumenthal once: a vast white-haired man with creaking black shoes and a creaking black briefcase, who talked to Mrs. Mullhouse at the top of his voice. "So what are you telling me from starve-a-fever. Food he needs, food. You want he should win first prize in the Skinniest Boy Contest? You!" (whirling toward me). "How much is five and six?" "Eleven," I answered promptly. Turning back to Mrs. Mullhouse and bending forward he said in a hushed conspiratorial whisper: "He's got smart friends."

The day came when at last I was allowed to visit Edwin. The fever and the infection were gone but he was still weak and needed rest, though Mrs. Mullhouse assured me that now he was taking his meals downstairs. Eagerly I climbed the carpeted stairs, passing the glass-framed photograph on the dark landing; and climbing the five stairs above the landing I stepped to Edwin's door. A sudden nervousness overcame me; I paused. After all, I had not seen him for almost three weeks. Could he have changed? And I thought: three weeks ago he did not resemble the Edwin of three years ago; we do not see the hour hand move unless we look away a while; perhaps a new Edwin awaits me, a pale stranger. To my left, the door to Karen's room was open and a band of sunlight, mad with dust, streamed into the hall almost to my toes. Holding my breath, with swift-beating heart I opened Edwin's door.

Hushed in shadow, the room lay silently before me, as if it had not yet recovered from a prolonged illness. I blinked rapidly, scattering darkness. Before the closed blinds of the double window lay Edwin, fast asleep. The upper sheet, turned over the blanket to form a white band, was pulled up to his chin; one arm, draped in a pale blue pajama-sleeve, rested above, and from where I stood the pale hand blended into the bleached sheet. He was almost entirely covered with Golden Books, which rose and fell gently as he breathed. Straight ahead stood the room's third window, through which, had the blinds been open, I might have seen the black roof of my house; in those days I used to enjoy walking slowly toward that window and watching my house rise higher and higher, slat on slat, until the kitchen window appeared, followed by the red roof of the Mullhouse garage. In the Late Years, while Edwin was writing his immortal masterpiece, I would sometimes creep into my kitchen late at night for a graham cracker and a glass of milk, where I would see, over the Mullhouse garage, the bright yellow rectangle of this very window. To the right of the window stood the large gray bookcase, overflowing with toys and books (including a forgotten comic book); its top was several inches higher than the windowsill, and although its right side pressed against the right wall, its left side extended past the window frame and covered a small portion of glass. To the left of the window, in an imbalance so unendurable that I would have invented a second gray bookcase if I had not known one was coming, stood a blackboard on an easel, a tall dog on wheels, a blue orange-crate bookcase full of puzzles and animals (hello, bookcase), and an open wooden chest filled with holsters, boots, chaps, spurs, green plastic arrows with pink rubber tips, a ten-gallon hat, a rubber tomahawk, a red plastic bow, and an eyeless zebra. The matte wallpaper, pebbled to the touch, contained a repeated series of six vertical maroon lines crossed by a repeated series of four horizontal maroon lines on a silver-gray background. On the left wall, over the empty bed with its two oblong pillows forming a back, was a map of the United States in full color, showing fish and steamships in the dark blue oceans, a palm tree in Florida, a skyscraper in New York, an ear of corn in Iowa, an Indian in Arizona, a log in Oregon, and nothing in Connecticut. At the age of five I knew all forty-eight states; a map to Edwin was still a picture puzzle. The reader will forgive this somewhat detailed description of Edwin's room when I explain that many of Edwin's happiest moments, as well as his last, were spent in this setting.

Closing the door softly behind me, I walked on tiptoe over the blue linoleum with its white leaves and stepped onto the bright red rug before Edwin's bed. His dark blue slipper-socks with the soft leather soles lay crumpled at one side, revealing part of a white Indian and part of a white horse. On a brown chair behind his head stood a solitary glass of water, its surface dulled with dust. The pale hand over his chest, like his armor of books, rose and fell softly as he breathed. As I stood looking down on him, the very picture of tranquillity, the memory of our first meeting stirred in me, and I could not help thinking that his appearance had improved. The early plumpness had stretched into thinness, as if he consisted of a single lump of modeling clay that had been pulled slowly by invisible fingers; but his features still retained the roundness, almost the chubbiness of his babyhood. Indeed that little round nose and little full-lipped mouth would remain with him to the end, clashing with his slender neck and tapered fingers, as if Nature had not been able to make up her mind. As I gazed on him thus, remembering old times and scenes, a sudden fancy took me. Bending quietly over him, I stretched my mouth into a monster's mouth, I screwed up my nose into a monster's nose, I stared ferociously and held up my hands like claws, waiting patiently for the pale eyelids, already trembling, to open slowly over the dark shining eyes.

# 16

THAT SPRING EDWIN INVENTED A GAME. I shall record it here, not for its own sake but because of its connection, as it seems to me, with his later delight in the art of artifice, and more immediately with a small, inconspicuous, but tremendously important event that took place in my presence on the occasion of Edwin's fifth birthday.

Until the black Studebaker appeared, in the Middle Years, Mrs. Mullhouse shopped at the red grocery at the top of Robin Hill Road; but once a week she rode with mama to the big glass supermarket in the center of town, accompanied by myself and Edwin. He looked forward to these weekly shopping trips with an eagerness bordering on frenzy, and not simply for the sake of the peanut machines, not simply for the sake of the silver carriages, not simply for the sake of the rows of cold cereal stretching into the distance and towering overhead in a blaze of color and a promise of masks or prizes: he looked forward to the trips also for the sake of the numbers.

He had noticed them on his first visit, sitting under the boxes in a long metal band, but it was not until his second visit that he discovered they could be moved with a finger. Mrs. Mullhouse had forbidden him to remove anything from the shelves, but the numbers were not on the shelves and he did not remove them. The shiny white squares, each with its shiny red numeral, slid smoothly along the metal band, bumping into the next numbers and carrying them neatly along. Sometimes he could push as many as six together before hitting a snag. His goal was to push all the numbers down to the end, where they formed a long beautiful number. One day as he was working his way past the cookies into the canned fruit, a man in a white apron seized his arm. After that, Mrs. Mullhouse forbade him to slide the numbers. But she did not forbid him to move the numbers in such a way that they seemed never to have been moved at all; and so, carefully and secretly, in dread of the men in white aprons and with a dizzy sense of excitement, Edwin pushed the 7 of 27 against the 3 of 31 to form 731 and the 1 of 731 against the 2 of 29 to form 129, leaving 73 in place of the original 31, and then he pushed the 9 of 129 against the 2 of 23 to form 923, leaving 12 in place of the original 29, and so on, now working among the sad cans of asparagus and yellow beans, now among the gay boxes of detergent, looking carefully both ways before each change and sometimes requesting me to guard one end of the aisle. At first he delighted in the most radical changes, and although at this time he was able to count with certainty only to 29 and could add and subtract only to sums of 10 and 12, nevertheless he knew that 73 was a long way from 31 and that 93 was even further away. He enjoyed watching people say "My God, seventy-three cents for a lousy box of graham crackers," or "Hey, what's going on here, hey, that can't be right." But soon he tired of such crudities, and began to concentrate on changes of two or three cents, which almost no one noticed. He was never caught, but one day he lost interest and never gave the numbers another thought.

Edwin never learned what happened to Abdul the Bulbul Amir, because Mr. Mullhouse could not remember the end of the poem. He always stopped at the same place, smiling happily over the last line, and apparently quite indifferent to the fate of the hero. He called it the most magnificent piece of poetry ever to issue from the mind of man. Often that spring, on rainy afternoons, Edwin would look up from his book in the corner of the couch while I sat at the other end of the couch and Karen played with her dolls in front of the fireplace, and barely able to suppress the excitement in his voice he would ask: "Daddy, could you say Abdul the Bulbul Ah Me?" Sometimes Mr. Mullhouse would refuse, shaking his head impatiently or pleading weariness, whereupon Edwin would plunge into abysses of silent grief; but usually his father would take the pipe from his mouth, place his book over his thigh, and shift his position so that he was facing Edwin, and raising a forefinger for attention he would recite:

> "*The sons of the prophet are hardy and bold*
> *And quite unaccustomed to fear.*
> *But the bravest of all is a man, I am told,*
> *Named Abdul the Bulbul Amir.*
>
> *If you needed a man to encourage the van*
> *Or harass the foe from the rear,*
> *Or storm a redoubt you had only to shout*
> *For Abdul the Bulbul Amir.*
>
> *There are heroes aplenty and well known to fame*
> *In the army that's led by the Czar,*
> *But the bravest of all is a man by the name*
> *Of Ivan Skivitsky Skivar.*
>
> *He could sing like Caruso both tenor and bass*
> *And perform on the Spanish guitar.*
> *In fact quite the cream of the Muscovite team*
> *Was Ivan Skivitsky Skivar.*
>
> *One day this bold Russian he shouldered his gun*
> *And with his most truculent sneer*
> *Was looking for fun when he happened to run*
> *Into Abdul the Bulbul Amir.*
>
> *Quoth the Bulbul, 'Young man, is your life then so dull*
> *That you wish now to end your career?*
> *Vile infidel know, you have trod on the toe*
> *Of Abdul the Bulbul Amir.'*

*Then this bold Mameluke drew his trusty chibouk*
*And shouting, 'Allah Akbar!'*
*With murderous intent he feloniously went*
*For Ivan Skivitsky Skivar.*

*They fought all that night 'neath the pale yellow moon,*
*The din it was heard from afar.*
*Vast multitudes came, so great was the fame*
*Of Abdul and Ivan Skivar."*

And stopping there, he would say, beaming: "The poet was very proud of that line. He got 'em both in." Edwin had at first begged his father to continue, but Mr. Mullhouse had raised his eyebrows and turned up his palms, saying: "I wish I could remember." Soon Edwin stopped asking, and after the recital Mr. Mullhouse would put his pipe back in his mouth, lighting it with a new silver lighter that shot out a flame, and return to his book.

Edwin's fifth birthday was memorable in a number of ways, not the least for its avalanche of gifts. Edwin received among other things an easel and watercolors, a palisaded fort with little rubber cowboys and Indians dressed in colorful costumes who could be mounted on shiny plastic horses, a year's subscription to *Walt Disney's Comics & Stories*, and a wind-up shooting gallery with a row of moving tin ducks and a black plastic pistol that shot rubber-tipped darts. I gave him a magnificent two-volume *Child's History of the World*, which he opened upside down and pretended to read eagerly for two seconds. Grandma Mullhouse baked a tall sagging cake with orange icing; when she cut into it there was a clinking sound, and several cuts later she removed from the cake a doughy teaspoon. Edwin was delighted. After the party Mrs. Mullhouse and Grandma worked in the kitchen while the rest of us retired to the living room. Mr. Mullhouse sat in his chair with his leg hooked over the side and became immersed in Edwin's comic book while Edwin wound up the shooting gallery and watched the yellow tin ducks sailing along and dipping out of sight. After a while Edwin asked his father to say Abdul the Bulbul Ah Me, and Mr. Mullhouse gave a spirited recital, sneering truculently in the proper place and shouting "Allah Akbar!" so ferociously that Mrs. Mullhouse called from the kitchen to see if anything was the matter. After the poem Mr. Mullhouse returned to the comic book but Edwin sat very quietly on the floor, staring at the dark leaf-swirls. Karen was clapping her hands nearby in a pile of ribbons and wrapping paper and I was examining the maps in volume 2 of *A Child's History of the World*. I was less distracted by Karen's mild racket than by Edwin's turbulent silence. Beneath that cool exterior I thought I detected a madness of excitement. I tried to catch his eye but either he cunningly avoided me or else he was wrapped in a thick fog. It was with relief and a certain thrill of presentiment that I saw Edwin rise at last to his feet, walk over to Mr. Mullhouse, and tug his father's sleeve. "Mmmm?" said Mr. Mullhouse, not looking up. Then looking up when Edwin again tugged his sleeve he said: "Mmmm?" Edwin said:

> *"Ivan fell down and broke his crown*
> *And Abdul cut off his head.*
> *And that's the end of the famous story*
> *Of Abdul and Ivan and Ed."*

"Ed!" exclaimed Mr. Mullhouse. "Who's Ed?"
"Ed*win*," said Edwin. "I got all three of 'em in."

# 17

I WONDER if I have sufficiently emphasized a major theme of this biography. I refer to Edwin's naturalness, his distinct lack of what is usually called genius. He did not begin to speak at two months, or read at two years, or write brilliant stories at the age of three— or four, or five, or six, for the very good reason that he could not write anything but his name until the first grade. Nor was he lovably slow or backward in any way, with his talent standing out against his stupidity like an emblematic lightning flash against a black thunderhead. No, he was only a normal healthy intelligent American child of the middle of the twentieth century, fascinated by toys and snow. Oh, he had what may have been an unusually strong attraction for books and words—an attraction amplified, perhaps, by the literary bias of this biography—but my own attraction was equally strong, and both of us were also fascinated by other things: hollow pink rubber balls, for instance, tapered pieces of white chalk, a red record of cowboy songs; and I remember a favorite toy of this time, a magic drawing pad with a thin red pointed stick for a pencil and a transparent sheath: when you pressed the stick against the surface a lead-colored line appeared, and when you lifted the transparent plastic surface and the gray page underneath, with a sound of torn paper the lead-colored line disappeared. The important thing to remember is that everyone resembles Edwin; his gift was simply the stubbornnness of his fancy, his unwillingness to give anything up. In the Late Years, when most of his contemporaries were already being watered down by a dreary round of dull responsibilities and duller pleasures, he alone refused to be diluted, he alone continued to play. Of course there was the little matter of genius. But that is the point precisely. For what is genius, I ask you, but the capacity to be obsessed? Every normal child has that capacity; we have all been geniuses, you and I; but sooner or later it is beaten out of us, the glory fades, and by the age of seven most of us are nothing but wretched little adults. So that genius, more accurately, is the retention of the capacity to be obsessed. Somewhere along the way, probably no later than the second grade, Edwin realized that all around him children were shedding that capacity. And so he clung to it, nursed it, kept an active watch over it, as some people encourage the development of their muscles. For Edwin felt instinctively, I think, that the conditions of life tended to work for the loss of that capacity. Indeed I have sometimes wondered whether the loss may not be inevitable, and obsession, like strength itself, subject to time. Something of the sort was in my mind not too long ago when in the restless workless impatient mood of Edwin's last months we were discussing the advantages of suicide; and I remember the bitterness of his smile as I spoke with unusual magnificence of what I called, in a memorable phrase, the obscenity of maturity.

# 18

ONE SUN-DRENCHED MORNING shortly after Edwin's fifth birthday I came strolling as usual across the Mullhouse back yard, darkened up to the swing by the vast shadow of the house, and quietly climbing the back steps I stood for a few moments meditating on the coolness and darkness of the shadowed porch below and the hotness and brightness of the clear blue sky above. The inner door was open and through the screen I saw Mrs. Mullhouse standing with her back to me over the kitchen table, tying or untying her apron-strings in back as she bent over an open book. I rapped sharply on the wooden strip between the upper and lower screens. She turned with a flutter of dropped apron-strings and a swirl of her apron, which hung from a strap around her neck; and with one hand raised to her cheek she said: "Oh, come in Jeff. Karen, stop that." Karen, seated on the pale linoleum, was banging a cover against a pot like a pair of cymbals. "But Jeff, where's Edwin?"

"Isn't he here?" I shouted.

"Why no. He went over to your house about fifteen minutes ago. That is, he didn't say he was going to your house but I assumed. Oh Jeff, don't tell me. Karen, please!"

Karen, terrified, burst into wails. Immediately the telephone joined in. Edwin had a special fondness for cartoon telephones, which shake angrily or jump up and down impatiently as they ring (while in the next room the wig of the startled gentleman leaps up in surprise).

". . . you for calling. Yes. Oh no, no. Yes. Goodbye. That was Mrs. Whatchamacallum on Beech Street, she was just cleaning her windows and who do you think she saw?" Already she was slipping the apron over her neck, and five minutes later Karen was bumping up and down in Edwin's old stroller and I was skipping to keep up with her as the three of us hurried along sunny Beech Street in pursuit of Edwin.

On the other side of Robin Hill Road, Benjamin Street is no longer called Benjamin Street but Beech Street—an oddity that made perfect sense to Edwin and me, since the street on the other side of Robin Hill Road was a strange new world that had nothing to do with the familiar universe of Benjamin Street, by whose hourly changing shadow-patterns of leaves and telephone wires we told the time. The shadows on Beech Street were always alien to us, even in the Middle Years when we walked freely there, for we never played on Beech Street and never learned it by heart. Half-way down, in those early days, the sidewalks on both sides stopped and the vacant lots began, some with tilted FOR SALE signs half-buried among weeds; and at the very end the road still stops at two brown posts, each with a round red reflector. Beyond the posts the weedridden ground rises gently to a scattering of bushes and trees, beyond which, from the road, only the sky is visible. So often did Edwin and I climb that little slope that years of repeated motions have blended in memory into a single pattern, and I can no longer recall the first climb of all. So much is certain: that having one day reached those two brown posts we could no more resist climbing to the sky than someone contemplating suicide can resist imagining his mourners. It took only a few seconds to scramble to the top. Had we expected some storybook illustration of wind-mills and canals stretching endlessly into a watercolor haze? or a maze of miniature houses charmed into neatness by the spell of distance? Alas. A field of high yellow grass, like a huge empty lot, stretched for a mere block or so to a fringe of trees that was clearly on higher ground than our little slope. To the left, parallel to Beech Street and a block away, a road with its houses was all too visible; to the right the land rose and the field changed abruptly into trees, between which the backs of houses peeped, announcing another street. And so our mountain was merely a low point on land rising on two sides of us, and our view a mere block or so of common fieldgrass. And yet the keen disappointment of our expectations was mingled with the joy of an unanticipated discovery. "Such is life," puts in Edwin with a solemn deadpan from the grave.

But such it was, and please stop haunting me, Edwin. For the little slope, having reached its peak of trees and bushes, dropped down to a shallow brown stream alive with white places where the water bubbled over stones. In the Middle Years Edwin and I sailed many a wooden boat over those brown rapids, following the stream to the left along the length of the yellow field and through a short cement tunnel under a road, after which the stream sank lower and the banks rose higher to form cliffs with green back yards on top until, just before the bakery, the high dirt walls turned to cement and passed into the black vastness of another tunnel under Robin Hill Road itself, emerging in a swampy field on the other side where tall sharp grass came down to the water and the invisible spongy ground was a nest of spotted water-snakes; while above the motionless grass-spears, on hot summer days, transparent-winged insects shaped like sewing needles hovered like a nightmare of the grass. But Edwin was no Huck Finn. He never ventured beyond the bakery, always stopping his boat before the long tunnel; though I have seen him standing on the other side of Robin Hill Road across from the bakery, leaning his forearms on top of the cement wall and resting his chin on his crossed hands as he stared out at the brown stream winding its way on and on among the yellow grass until it turned out of sight at the edge of a distant baseball diamond. But again my memory refuses to behave, again my biography escapes its frame, and I am reminded of certain pictures in Edwin's beloved comic books in which a horse's nose protrudes over the edge into the margin of the page or the hero's toes come over the bottom of the frame as if he were about to step into your lap, brandishing his sword. A curse on chronology! And again: a curse on chronology! I do not refer to the hypocrisy of it all, the stupid wretched pretense that one thing follows from another thing, as if on Saturday a man should hang himself because on Friday he was melancholy, whereas perhaps his melancholy had nothing to do with his suicide, perhaps he hanged himself out of sheer exuberance. Nor do I refer to the vulgar itch to get to the good part, the desire to leave out everything and plunge at once into the bloody horrors of Edwin's end. No, I refer simply to the difficulty of the thing, the impossibility of fitting everything into its proper niche. And if I were to let myself go! If I were to let the horse step completely out of its frame! If for no reason at all except that I have suddenly remembered it, I were to describe the trembling elastic top of an overfull glass of water standing on a yellow rubber mat before the kitchen window. Carefully Edwin holds an eyedropper above it, carefully he squeezes out a single swelling drop. It trembles, stretches, falls. The surface shatters, water sheets the sides of the glass, the little horse steps out of the picture and dissolves instantly in the solvent of a three-dimensional world; and behind him, in the shady greenwood, the hero stares in terror at that horse-shaped white hole in his universe.

As we passed the abruptly ending sidewalks and entered the land of vacant lots, Mrs. Mullhouse began to shout Edwin's name. It was a serious matter, this Beech Street escapade, for Edwin was strictly forbidden to cross Robin Hill Road by himself. But he knew of the slope and stream, for we had walked there a number of times in the company of Mr. Mullhouse and his camera, and in fact a photograph already existed that showed Edwin standing by the stream in his blue workman's overalls with the high front and the shoulder straps. Mrs. Mullhouse must have known as well as I that Edwin was beyond the slope, for even as she called his name and looked anxiously about she pushed Karen swiftly forward over the bumpy tar. Just beyond the posts she was forced to stop with the stroller, and I hurried up alone. I must have been infected by Mrs. Mullhouse's vague fear, for a picture flashed in my mind of Edwin lying on his back under the clear brown water, his eyes staring sightlessly, his hair streaming silkily, his hands bobbing limply on the troubled surface of the water. Within seconds I had scrambled to the top. Standing in the shade of a spreading oak I saw an invisible breeze making a dark line in the tall yellow grass. Directly below, some ten feet away, Edwin stood with his back to me on the near bank of the stream, staring out across the field. He stood with his hands in the pockets of his wide brown shorts, held up by crossed suspenders; his shoulders seemed very narrow in a tight t-shirt I had never seen before, striped yellow and white. Under those billowing shorts his legs looked pale and thin; his knees touched, and between his narrow thighs was a space shaped like the dictionary illustration of a double-convex lens, through which the bubbling brown water was visible. For a few seconds I stood silently watching him as he stood motionless against a background of field and sky. Behind me Mrs. Mullhouse was unaccountably still; and suddenly as I watched I was filled with the sense of his remoteness, it was as if I did not know him at all and had never known him, it was as if he were as impenetrable to my knowledge as the hard tree shading me and pressing into me with its ridges of bark, it was as if, standing there with his back to me, he were as forever unseeable as a transparent negative, which when turned around does not show the other side but the same side reversed; and I wanted to run down to him and spin him around and make sure he was there; a passing fancy; and the sun burning in the field and the empty blue sky burning over me seemed evil puzzles I would never solve; and who knows what would have happened if a pebble dislodged by my foot had not begun to roll bumpily down toward him, jumping like a crazed insect, until it hit him in the heel, and without turning his body, but only his head, he looked slowly over his shoulder with a pale frown. It was not Edwin.

# 19

HIS NAME WAS EDWARD PENN. He was seven years old. He lived in a world of make-believe so intricate and absolute that his occasional eruptions into the world of grass and sky had for him all the elements of a fantastic voyage, as if he were the March Hare or Mad Hatter emerging from the rabbit hole and coming upon a little girl fast asleep on the bank with her head in her sister's lap. He dwelt in a heated cellar beyond the bakery. He suffered from an obscure nervous ailment that was just serious enough to prevent him from attending school but not quite serious enough to prevent him from doing precisely as he pleased. Edwin believed that Penn had invented his disease in order to achieve complete spiritual freedom but I believe that his disease was the real physical expression of an implacable spiritual need. I believe that Penn did not survive the decade but Edwin believed that Penn would continue to exist indefinitely at the unchanging age of seven. Edwin, I should add, had not crossed Robin Hill Road at all that day—for he was always an obedient son—but had simply strayed into the vacant lot on the other side of his backyard hedge, and in fact had seen us crossing Robin Hill Road and had actually called out to us, if you can believe him. His resemblance to Penn was striking only from behind. For if Edwin's thinness was a matter of legs and arms and neck, while his features retained the signs of an early plumpness, Penn's features followed his body in its effort to achieve two dimensions. Penn's nose in profile came to such a sharp point that it seemed capable of puncturing a balloon; his nostrils were so narrow that he seemed barely able to breathe. Each of his eyebrows resembled the mark over the o given in the dictionary for the pronunciation of *horn* or *north*. His little sharp ears, his thin sharp fingers, and his thin sharp mouth with its little sharp teeth, combined to give him a distinct creaturely air, though he lacked the squirrel's sharp quick movements and indeed assumed an air of languor and aloofness, standing with his hands in his pockets and his head tilted to one side as he looked out at you from behind half-closed eyes. Was he really a friend? I think he appreciated Edwin's eager and delicate sympathy for his world, but I suspect that he was incapable of true friendship, for I suspect that he was incapable of sustaining a belief in the reality of Edwins and Jeffreys and other such creatures. As for Edwin, he remarked once that among the three contemporaries who had exercised an influence on his life, only Edward Penn had left a lasting mark, though he couldn't say what that mark was and in fact barely remembered Penn. "And the other two?" I asked with a smile. He replied instantly: "Rose Dorn and Arnold Hasselstrom." There was a brief embarrassed silence. "Oh," he said with a sudden blush, "and you too, Jeffrey." And raising a hand he laid it gently on my shoulder. "Mathematics," I answered harshly, "was never your strong point, Edwin." But he looked at me in bewilderment, for as I have had occasion to remark, Edwin was never one to understand other people's jokes.

How well I remember our first visit to that heated cellar. Mrs. Mullhouse had to accompany us, for Penn lived too far away for us to visit him by ourselves, and during our stay she remained upstairs in the living room with Mr. and Mrs. Penn, a frail couple with four sad eyes. "This way," said Mr. Penn with a sigh and a shake of his head, opening a door in the kitchen and reaching inside to click on a dim yellow light. "Watch your step," said Mrs. Penn with a doleful look. Carefully we began our slow way down the dimly illuminated wooden steps, holding onto a loose and splintery rail as the steps creaked under us. As we descended there rose to our nostrils a damp, sour odor that I was destined to come upon three years later on the day I entered the third grade. It was the first time I had sat at a desk; and when I opened the carved and ink-stained top I was greeted by a damp, sour odor that suddenly cast me back to the cellar of Edward Penn, which now as I write seems mixed with my old desk and its nightmare freight of pencil shavings, a black penpoint, a chewed lollipop stick, a scrap of sticky cellophane. At the dark bottom of the stairs we turned to the right and walked along a narrow passageway past looming barrels ringed with rusty hoops. Turning once more to the right we entered a wider and brighter space, and by the late afternoon light of two high oblong windows we made our way toward the far wall past piles of damp newspapers tied with string, olive-green trunks with rusty clasps, empty paint-cans stained with red drippings, a pair of dusty maroon boxing gloves beside a bright yellow Joe Palooka punching dummy, pencil shavings, a black penpoint, a chewed lollipop stick, a scrap of sticky cellophane. Turning to the right a third time we saw before us a vast faded-blue curtain rising from the dusty floor to a rod a few feet below the high ceiling. The curtain extended from the cement wall on the left to a wooden partition on the right, over which a network of nickel-colored pipes protruded. We stopped, uncertain how to proceed. "Perhaps we should go the other way," I suggested, but at that moment we heard bedspring sounds behind the curtain, and then a small portion of the cloth began to squirm, and finally a small pale hand appeared at the invisible division of the curtains;

and sweeping aside the cloth with a princely gesture, Edward Penn stepped out and said: "Hello. Mother never listens to me. I told her to stamp when you came." And stepping aside he motioned us into his den.

Twenty feet away hung another, less impressive curtain, composed of three different materials; later we learned that all the curtains were old living-room castaways that Penn had collected from the attics of sympathetic neighbors. There were no windows in the den; in addition to a single bulb hanging from the ceiling on a long chain, light came from three old standing lamps with frayed cords. To the right, against the wooden partition, lay a small sagging bed with a mustard-colored bedspread. Beyond it stood a white metal kitchen table with a single white wooden chair. A red-shaded standing lamp, glaring down at the table, was reflected dimly in its bright surface; the table was littered with comic books and tracing paper. Past the table stood an old chipped chest of drawers with brass loops instead of knobs, and past that, with its back to the far curtain, was a brown bookcase entirely filled with comic books. But it was the left wall that transformed Penn's den into a kingdom. For there, illuminated by two tall bright lamps, blazed his masterpiece. The long cement wall had been whitewashed from floor to ceiling and on it, in brilliant glossy colors outlined in black, lay hundreds upon hundreds of cartoon characters of all sizes, tilted at crazy angles, overlapping one another, inhabiting one another's eyes and noses— all jumbled together as if poured out of an enormous box, yet forming at a distance a vast abstract design. It was a fiery cartoon vision, an intricate map of Penn's feverish and patient brain. There was a huge head of Pluto with his orange snout and round black nose and tall eyes, with one ear up and one ear half bent over; when you stood close you saw a miniature Bugs Bunny in his nose, complete with orange-and-green carrot. Woody Woodpecker and Mighty Mouse danced in a circle with Huey and Louie and Heckle and Jeckle and Popeye and Wimpy and Dopey and Sneezy as Dumbo flew over with Scrooge on his back and Dewey floated down at the end of an umbrella. There were hundreds and hundreds of them, I tell you, nay, thousands and thousands: here piled up on one another at the center of a bright red circus ring, there tumbling from trapezes whose ropes went up to nowhere; riding on one another's backs and hats, spilling out of one another's pockets; rowing boats, climbing ladders, leaping from flaming windows; some so small that you could recognize them only when Penn lent you his magnifying glass, one so large that it was a single eye stretching from floor to ceiling, and recognizable only by a rigid attention to certain of its monstrous curves; and mixed in with the real cartoons were Penn's own creations, little Plutos with Krazy Kat heads, an elephant whose raised trunk became the neck of a giraffe, a smiling clock that had swallowed an ostrich, an aristocratic fly with a cane and a monocle. As we surveyed his masterpiece, the result of two years' labor (and still incomplete), Penn watched us in languorous silence, breaking his pose of disdain only to indicate, in a quiet monotone, some marvel we had overlooked, such as a tiny row of twenty Donalds, one of which was different from all the others (it was Penn who introduced Edwin to the puzzle page of the Sunday paper). But he could not suppress a mild flutter of excitement as he pointed out to us a small whale floating in the pupil of a vast eye, and seated on top of its spout, distinctly lifelike through the magnifying glass, Penn himself in his striped t-shirt and brown shorts.

Oh it was a regular treasure-house, that den, and not the least of its attractions was the chipped bureau, each of whose twelve brass loops was attached to the nose of a small brass lion, and five of whose six drawers were filled with the fascinating implements of Penn's many-sided art: bright tins of watercolors, slim paintbrushes whose tips were sometimes no thicker than a single hair, clean tubes of oilpaint squeezed carefully from the bottom, boxes of pastels and crayons, large pads of tracing paper, small pink pads, pieces of charcoal, looseleaf notebooks in black bindings, heaps of scattered pages, brown clipboards with silver clips, boxes of colored pencils, dozens of little plastic pencil sharpeners, thick packages of typewriter paper, red and green plastic rulers, wooden rulers with metal edges, bottles of colored ink, silver compasses holding yellow pencils, metal protractors, black wooden penholders, boxes of penpoints, and even a curious brush that Edwin laughed to see, for his father used exactly the same kind for shaving. Edwin was particularly fascinated by a crazily shaped sheet of transparent plastic approximately the size of a piece of typewriter paper: it was full of oddly shaped holes, like a piece of Swiss cheese, and the outside swooped and rippled in dozens of strange curves. Penn explained that it was from a beginner's Cartoon Kit that had been given to him at the age of four; it was used for drawing difficult lines, one curve being useful for fat behinds and the cheeks of whistle-blowing policemen, another for fingers and long noses, another for birdcages and distant haystacks. Placing it over a clean corner of white paper cluttered with cats and policemen, and turning it about rapidly as he drew, Penn quickly sketched for us a complete cartoon farmer with a tall hat bent over in the middle, a nose shaped like a lightbulb, a fringe of whiskers, droopy pants held up by a single strap, and a pitchfork in one hand. Edwin begged Penn to let him have the picture; in reply Penn tore the page carefully into sixteen pieces and dropped them into the red wastebasket under the white metal table.

The heavy bottom drawer was completely filled with two layers of thick black books; Edwin was disappointed until Penn carefully removed one book, carried it to the table, and lovingly opened it to reveal a familiar burst of color. They were his oldest and most treasured comic books, bound twenty-four in a volume. Penn showed Edwin one so old that it contained many different strips; for it he had traded a precious magic trick consisting of a red cup and a disappearing black ball. Other volumes contained black-and-white comic strips from newspapers, cut out and pasted in to form a continuous series. The bulk of Penn's less valuable comic books were housed in the wooden bookcase that stood with its back against the curtain and one end against the wooden partition. They were arranged by year, beginning with 1941, the year of Penn's birth, and divided into sections by means of green metal dividers on rubber-covered bases. The years 1941 through 1944 filled the top shelf; thereafter each of the remaining four shelves was devoted to a single year. Other comics lay in neat piles in odd corners of the den, and duplicates were stored under the sagging bed. Penn had begun subscribing to several comic books at the age of four; from the age of five he had made it his business to purchase every single copy of every single series put out by Walt Disney: the monthlies, the bi-monthlies, the quarterlies, and the annuals. He was always filling in gaps in the early years, as some people fill in the gaps in stamp collections, and he kept up with several other publications as well as he was able. He eagerly questioned Edwin about his collection and snorted faintly through his sharp nose when Edwin, looking away, confessed to owning "not too many" (actually no more than a dozen at this time). Penn's passion for comic books, incidentally, was not all-embracing; like Edwin after him, he had no interest whatsoever in what he called adult comics: detective stories, adventure stories, horror stories. For Penn, Superman and Dick Tracy and hairy monsters were real inhabitants of the real world, of no more interest to him than the radio news reports which he had stopped listening to at the age of three (World War II, for Penn, was a long adventure serial that his father listened to all night long, and Penn loathed radio serials). Only in the world of cartoon animals was Penn able to breathe with some measure of freedom. But even his beloved animals, he felt, were infected by a taint of caricature that rendered them almost real; he longed for creatures of absolute fantasy, bearing no relation to anything in this world. He showed us sketchbooks containing rough drafts of nameless cartoon creatures who lived under the sea or at the end of the rainbow; he showed us elaborate maps of entire countries in the insides of trees, filled with wavy lines representing rivers and rows of small triangles representing mountain ranges. He spoke of worlds inside a stone, a flame, a snowflake, a flash of lightning, a mushroom. He spoke of creatures made of ice, of glue, of sun, of green. He told us his idea for invisible cartoons, represented only by word-filled bubbles pointing at blank spaces; the cartoonist would represent their habits and adventures both by the words and by the act of pointing the bubbles at different places in a continually changing landscape; each reader would imagine a different creature. And with a mixture of aching fondness and lucid contempt, he showed us a comic book he had made long ago, full of green skies and black moons, red oceans and yellow islands, bound in bright covers and containing a page that advertised dozens of toys and gifts above a scrupulously drawn coupon with a dotted line.

Recently he had begun to experiment with animation. Reaching into one of the bureau drawers he removed a small thick pad with blue, white, green, and pink pages. On the top page was a circle consisting of words, inside of which was a small car driven by a mouse. Penn read the circle to us, turning the pad as he pointed to each word: EDWARD PENN'S COMICS AND STORIES. Then grasping the pad in one hand he began to flip the pages with the thumb of his other hand. Facing left, a mouse wearing a scarf was driving along in a little car past trees and houses and telephone poles; spurts of smoke came out the back, and the scarf streamed out behind him. After a while a string of E's appeared in the air, followed quickly by a motorcycle emerging on the right, on which sat a cat with a policeman's hat. The motorcycle gained on the car; they rode side by side; as they slowed to a stop, the puffs of smoke disappeared and the scarf hung down. The cat stepped off his motorcycle and wrote in a pad. Then the cat got back on his motorcycle, facing the other way, and drove off toward the right until he disappeared, while the mouse drove off toward the left, his scarf streaming, until he too disappeared. The cartoon ended.

Edwin was fascinated. He begged to know how it was done. To my surprise Penn proved quite willing to explain the secret. He opened up to the first page, in the center of which the mouse sat motionless in his car with his scarf standing out stiffly behind him; in the background stood a house and a tree. On the next page the mouse looked exactly as he had before, but the house and tree had moved to the right. Ten pages later the mouse was still in the center of the page but the tree had disappeared, only half the house was visible, and a telephone pole had come into view on the left. Until the very end, when the mouse drove out of sight, he and his car stayed unchanging in the center of the

page as the background moved or stayed still. The motorcycle
appeared first as an arc of wheel on the right-hand side of the
page, then as a half wheel, then as a complete wheel with the
toe of a cat. It was all astoundingly simple, drawn with little
attention to detail; the important thing, said Penn, was to keep
the background moving at a constant rate and to make sure that
each object looked the same on successive pages. He showed us
an early experiment in which he had been careless: the car seemed
to puff along at wildly different rates of speed, and also to shrink
and expand. But his very clumsiness had inspired new ideas; and
he showed us his most recent pad, called PENN IN WONDERLAND,
in which the little mouse drank from a bottle and grew taller and
taller, hitting his head on the ceiling.

Edwin returned from the first visit in a fever of excitement.
Within three days he had hung old sheets all over his room and
had acquired great supplies of tracing paper and pads. Without
success he tried to persuade Mrs. Mullhouse to permit him to
paint pictures on the cellar walls, on the walls of his room, on
the ceiling of his room, on the walls of his closet, on the ceiling
of his closet, on the inside of his closet door; he had to settle for
reluctant permission to tack up tracings on the closet door. Daily
he begged Mrs. Mullhouse to take him back to Penn's but she
said she couldn't just drop in on people she didn't know and besides they were such a funny old couple, talking your ear off
about their son's diseases, and anyway it was their turn to call.
I think Edwin would actually have disobeyed the stern injunction
never to cross Robin Hill Road if he had known where to find
Penn; but in those days the world ended a block away, and houses
"beyond the bakery" might as well have been in China or a comic
book. When at last Mrs. Mullhouse called, a week later, it was
to invite Penn to Edwin's house for dinner. But Mrs. Penn said
that her son never ate out because he was on a special, difficult
diet and required a private bathroom because of various internal
troubles that apparently she discussed in some detail, since Mrs.
Mullhouse kept on making faces at the phone and opening and
closing a hand like a mouth. "That woman," said Mrs. Mullhouse,
when at last she had hung up, "simply doesn't know when to

stop. And that son of hers: really, Edwin, don't you have enough friends already?" Penn, it seemed, had to be consulted about visitors; Mrs. Penn would call back in a little while. "Here we go again," said Mrs. Mullhouse, rolling her eyes toward the ceiling as she lifted the phone; and as she listened she arched an eyebrow, tapped her long fingernails loudly against the receiver, and with a ballpoint pen drew box after box on a white pad, filling them in with parallel diagonal lines and darkening carefully every other stripe. When she hung up she announced that the King of Siam would be receiving visitors the following afternoon at one.

And so at one the following afternoon we found ourselves again in Penn's subterranean den. Edwin sat sideways on the white wooden chair before the white metal table and I sat on one end of the mustard-colored bedspread, listening to the sound of sharp footsteps overhead and an occasional scrape of chairs. "I can't stand that noise," said Penn, and it was almost the only thing he did say; for the most part he sat stiffly on the other end of the bed, plunged in gloomy silence and evidently controlling a desire to ask us to leave. The den itself had changed: though direct sunlight from the cellar windows was shut out by the curtains, at this hour the sun made its presence more strongly felt than on our late-afternoon visit. The blazing cartoon wall was paler, the burning lightbulb at the end of its chain seemed to illuminate only itself, and the air was hot and close, as if we were shut up in a large trunk in a hot attic. Penn himself seemed considerably wilted; only during our third visit, in the evening, did I realize that he became more and more lively as the night approached, like the moonflower, which opens at night and closes before noon. I suspected then, and I suspect still, that Penn had invited us to come in the early afternoon because he was unable to work well at that time and had hoped to create a diversion. After a painfully long silence, punctuated by ineffectual attempts on the part of myself and Edwin to lure Penn into conversation and equally ineffectual attempts to talk naturally between ourselves, as if we were alone in Edwin's room, Penn suddenly stood up and walked away, just like that, sweeping aside a curtain that fell heavily into place behind him and fading away in a series of diminishing footsteps that quickly disappeared, only to become audible again as they creaked upstairs. Edwin and I sat speechless, staring at our toes; when I tried to catch his eye he looked angrily away. After a while Edwin stood up and went over to the cartoon wall, which he pretended to examine with great interest. I coughed into my fist, cleared my throat, sniffed and swallowed and licked my teeth in sheer boredom, and was about to lean back and close my eyes when Edwin whirled around and shouted: "Stop making those water-noises!" I smiled helplessly, raising my eyebrows and turning up my palms in imitation of Mr. Mullhouse; Edwin turned back to the wall. The tense attitude of his neck revealed that he was listening hard for water-noises. I felt saliva rising in a pool under my tongue, I yearned for one of those gurgling sucking things that dentists put in your mouth, I clenched my teeth and pressed my lips together in a fierce determination not to exasperate Edwin with a sound of swallowing, and I think I would have burst like a hydrant if a loud flushing noise overhead hadn't come to my rescue. I swallowed in ecstasy, and soon Penn's footsteps were audible on the stairs, and both of us watched the curtain for that squirming motion. Penn found the opening with difficulty this time; I was reminded of a kitten trapped under a towel. Stepping at last into the den he avoided our eyes, walked to the bed, and sat down uncomfortably on the very edge, clasping his hands stiffly over his knees and staring gloomily at the middle of the floor. I said: "Was that you flushing?" but my attempt at a humorous sally proved a dismal failure: Edwin thrust his hands into his pockets and slumped his shoulders forward, as if he were trying to fold himself in half like a letter, while Penn continued to look wan. We were saved at last by Mrs. Penn, who stamped three times. At once Penn stood up and explained that it was time for us to go; he left it at that, as if the reason were transparent. The profound feeling of relief that overcame all of us put all of us into an excellent humor, especially Penn, who said without a trace of irony that he was sorry we had to go since there were so many things he had wanted to show us, and who cordially invited us back for the following week. The prospect of our leaving had clearly animated him; he talked rapidly and breathlessly, as if he were trying to hold us there—and I have no doubt that he sincerely wanted us to stay, if only for the pleasure of prolonging the sense of our imminent departure. But another three stamps sent us scurrying through the curtains. Penn, of course, did not accompany us out of the den; and as we turned the corner I saw him watching us from between the curtains, with an expression of distinct sadness on his face.

Our third visit to Penn was more successful by far; little did we realize that it would be our last. The next week Mrs. Penn called to say that Penn was "indisposed," which I took to mean "indisposed to see anyone." The very next day, however, she called again, inviting us for the evening. Mrs. Mullhouse fretted and made faces but at Edwin's earnest entreaty finally agreed to go; it was the end of August, Kindergarten was only ten days away, and perhaps she thought that school would put an end to the Penn foolishness. In a way she proved right. But that evening Penn was in wonderful form. Edwin and I used to have a joke about Penn: we imagined him improving steadily as the night wore on, until at about 3 A.M. he became the most civilized person on the face of the earth. At 7 P.M. that evening he was well on his way. The cartoon wall, undiluted by sunlight, glowed in the full splendor of its lamps, and Penn himself, wearing a bright red shirt with white buttons, seemed positively to glow. For the first time since we had known him he asked us about ourselves. Edwin declared that he was going to write a book. It was the first I had heard of it, and I think I would have been a trifle hurt if I hadn't suspected him of inventing his future on the spot. What else could you do, faced with that blazing wall? I myself announced with a chuckle that in that case I was going to write a book about Edwin. The ways of fate, Edwin once said, leaving the sentence unfinished; and I can see why. The ways of fate . . . At any rate, Penn then asked us if there was anything we should like to see; and Edwin expressing an ardent interest in EDWARD PENN'S COMICS AND STORIES, Penn brought out a whole drawerful of pads and proceeded to flip and explain, accompanying several with an elaborate series of sound effects, including a whale's hearty laugh and the delicate sneeze of an eel. Later he told us about his early life: the endless series of white hospital beds, the long hours with nothing to do, the early passion for sketching, and the blossoming of his special talent under the skilled eye of a neurosurgeon whose brilliant cartoons of hospital life had appeared in nationwide magazines. The three stamps, when they came, produced this time a singular effect. Reaching behind the chest of drawers, Penn brought forth a red broom-handle with a brass ring at one end, and climbing up on the metal table he bumped the ceiling three times. Then leaping nimbly down—yes, actually leaping down—he proceeded to march high-steppingly up and down in front of the cartoon wall, holding the broom handle like a flute and emitting distinctly flutelike sounds. This sudden display of boyish humor endeared Penn to Edwin and me forever, allowing us to forgive, finally, his cruel turn-about. For if we never saw him again after that night, it was because Penn never was in the mood for another visit. Evidently he was a boy of sudden passions and sudden coldnesses, and perhaps he simply closed to us, forever, after that night; but sometimes I wonder whether he feared the tremendous flow of energy that is generated by a vital friendship, and hoped by a violent act of severance to save himself for his art. So that perhaps he was capable of true friendship after all, but sacrificed it on the altar of a higher purpose. Edwin called daily for nearly a month, and each time Mrs. Penn said the same thing: he was indisposed. Finally Edwin became caught up in preparations for Halloween and simply stopped trying. He never asked Mrs. Mullhouse to call again, nor did Mrs. Penn call herself. As for me, I felt from the beginning that the vital exchange should be between Edwin and Penn; I simply came along for the ride, a smiling intermediary, watching like a hawk. By Christmas Penn was little more than a summer dream. One day in the Middle Years Edwin and I took a long walk and found his house, but the Penns were no longer living there. Through a dusty cellar window we saw that the curtains had been taken down and the walls painted brick red. A shiny green pingpong table stood in the center of the old den, and in place of the chest of drawers there now stood a little blue step-ladder, three steps high, with an orange paddle lying on top, leaning on a bright white pingpong ball.

When we left Penn that evening he accompanied us to the foot of the stairs. The visit had clearly tired him; tiny drops traced an outline over each sharp eyebrow, and at the side of his neck a pulse beat visibly. Under both eyes lay shadows like faint bruises. He was not reluctant, this time, to see us go. Indeed he did not repeat his former invitation to come again. Did he know already that he would never see us again? Possibly. More likely he was simply thinking of his work: of the night, already deprived of two fine hours, racing toward conclusion; of his exhaustion and agitation, which would prevent both his working well and his sleeping at all; of the empty pages yearning to be filled; of new maps, new universes; of the real world waiting to reclaim him after his restless dream of Edwin and me. As we reached the top of the stairs, Mrs. Penn opened the door; the sudden brightness of the kitchen hurt my eyes. That, no doubt, explains my curious sensation as I looked back down into the darkness for a last goodbye. For Penn, like the Cheshire Cat, seemed to have faded almost completely away; and I saw in that darkness only the vertical row of white buttons on his shirtfront, glowing like miniature moons, and the lone button of a single cuff, raised under an invisible wave.

Ah, Edward Penn, where are you now?

# 20

EVERYONE SEES THE WORLD DIFFERENTLY, said Edwin, but nightmares are pretty much the same. It is to a recent nightmare that I owe the following description of Franklin Pierce Elementary School. A long brown high-ceilinged corridor stretched endlessly into the distance. The floor was covered with several inches of water that soaked into my socks and pantscuffs. Children were standing in rows on both sides of me with their faces pressed against the walls. I advanced eagerly but with great difficulty, as if against a tide, and at last the row of children on my right was broken by a door. I looked in and saw a vast room filled above the level of the distant windowsills with abandoned brown desks. The desks lay twisted among one another in a dark jumble, and as I crawled painfully over them on my way to the far windows my hands and knees became covered with a sticky black substance. Several desks lay upside down on the top of the pile with their black metal bases thrust up and sharp silver screws sticking out. I was trying to get to the windows but a hill of desks rose in front of me and as I tried to crawl over it they kept on falling and tumbling toward me like the boulders in a movie landslide, clattering down at me and bouncing over me as I pushed my head and arms into dark crevices for protection. Somewhere at the side of the room was a space I had not noticed, and there a tall lady with white hair walked along a blackboard, drawing wavy musical staves with a wire chalk-holder that held five pieces of shrieking chalk whose ends kept shattering in white chalk-clouds. I was trying to seat myself at a tilted desk at the top of the pile but my leg was caught and I had to twist it back and forth very carefully as if I were removing a Tinker Toy stick from a Tinker Toy wheel. At last I worked it loose and squeezed myself into the desk, which was tilted forward and to one side so that I had to grip the top tightly to keep from falling. The dark surface was pockmarked with little grooves that were filled with ink or grime, and at one end of the empty pencil trough sat a round black inkwell whose top was flush with the surface. I was trying to get the desk open but it seemed to be stuck, and as I tugged and pulled, always in danger of tipping over and falling onto the sharp screws and edges below, the tall lady with white hair stood with her arms folded across her chest, tapping her foot and watching me. And as I tugged and pulled I knew that the last thing I wanted to do was to open that desk and see what was inside, and yet I had to because the tall lady was watching me, and as I tugged and pulled I saw oozing from under the top a gray rubbery substance like rubber cement. The lady with white hair was watching me, she was tapping her foot faster and faster and at last began to come toward me, I was sitting in a vast windowless room filled with neat rows of empty desks, outside wailed a distant train, and as a white-haired man bent over me the top of the desk came suddenly open though still joined to the bottom by long sticky strands of rubber cement, and inside I saw, lying among yellow-edged pencil shavings and pieces of crumpled tissue paper clotted with mucus, a little baby lying with a blanket up to its chin, its face sheeted with gleaming blood or slime.

# 21

DID HE LEARN ANYTHING in Kindergarten? Oh, everything. He learned Singing, Clapping, and Keeping Quiet. He learned Standing on Line and the Pledge Allegiance. He learned Giggling in the Coatroom, Opening Milk, and Raising Your Hand to Go to the Lavatory. Miss Tipp insisted on the word "lavatory," no doubt on the principle that you couldn't come right out and say you wanted to go to the bathroom, but for Edwin the new word marked a difference. The tall white machines with their shiny silver handles fascinated him; he kept flushing and flushing, watching the jets of water shoot along the back from invisible holes in the top. He was puzzled and upset when he learned what the machines were used for; he had thought them a kind of upright bathtub. Thereafter he transferred his affection to the wax half-pints of milk that were distributed daily at 10 A.M. during Snack Period, and with tireless amusement fitted pennies into the wax flap on top and peeled the wax sides with his wax-filled fingernails. After splashing milk on himself several times, he devised a slow safe method of opening the dangerous top: carefully turning back the edges he tugged gently in different places until the top came up without an explosion. The milk itself was of little interest to him. He enjoyed dipping the straw in it, putting a finger on top, raising the straw, releasing his finger, and watching the white stream come out. Afterward, when the milk was gone, he liked to flatten the straw between his fingers, roll it into a little cylinder, and drop it inside the empty container; and stuffing through the hole his white napkin, the waxpaper from his peanut butter and jelly sandwich, and his brown paper bag, he would close the top carefully, smoothing down the edges and trying to make the bulging carton look like new.

But most of all Edwin learned about Holidays. Before entering Kindergarten he knew that the year contained two special days— his birthday and Christmas—and he realized dimly, but without anticipation, that there were a number of half-special days, like the day the nuts came out in a big brown bowl with two silver nutcrackers or the day he and Karen received chocolate rabbits. And there were special days that might come at any time: a visit from Grandma Mullhouse, for instance, or a trip to the library, or a picnic expedition. But in Kindergarten he learned that the year was a continual round of celebrations and holidays, all of which had to be elaborately prepared for. Hardly two weeks had passed before Miss Tipp began telling us about the Nina, the Pinta, and the Santa Maria. She read us a poem about the Nina, the Pinta, and the Santa Maria, and we sang a song about the Nina, the Pinta, and the Santa Maria. Each of us received his own box of eight enormous crayons, flat on one side, and we all drew pictures of the Nina, the Pinta, and the Santa Maria. Miss Tipp showed us how to draw the sun, and most of us drew fiery yellow suns with long rays streaming down onto the Nina, the Pinta, and the Santa Maria; but Edwin drew at the top of his page a flat black border representing the night, and under that a small round moon, barely visible on the pale paper. But the Nina, the Pinta, and the Santa Maria soon sailed away, and Miss Tipp began telling us about pumpkins and witches, black cats and Halloween moons. She passed out black and orange sheets of construction paper and small round-tipped scissors, and we all cut out big orange moons and big black cats with pointed ears. Vast jars filled with white paste appeared, and when Edwin pasted two orange eyes onto his cat he was rewarded by having it tacked up on the bulletin board. One day Miss Tipp brought in a grinning pumpkin; Edwin took off the top of its head, looked inside, and quickly replaced the top, turning it carefully until it fit precisely. Pumpkins always baffled him. We sang a song about a witch on a broomstick and Miss Tipp read us a tedious story about Halloween in Denmark. For the first time in his life Edwin looked forward in fearful excitement to the night of funny, frightening masks; and no sooner had Halloween passed than he found himself looking forward even more eagerly to Thanksgiving. Miss Tipp brought in three ears of colored corn, a collection of miniature Pilgrims, and a sad headdress without a tail. We all cut out Pilgrim buckles for our shoes and we all told what we were thankful for; Edwin said he was thankful for Thanksgiving. We sang a sad song about God and a happy song about Indians and Miss Tipp read us a tedious story about a little boy called Miles Standish. She turned a page: and suddenly snow began to fall on Miles Standish, and we were making Santa Claus faces with red hats and curly cotton beards. Miss Tipp's Christmas equipment put the rest of her holiday supplies to shame: during the first week alone she brought in a manger, a little team of reindeer pulling a sleigh, a wax Santa with a wick coming out of his head, a prickly wreath with red berries, a white plastic snowman with a black plastic hat, and a long red stocking decorated with white reindeer. She set us to work decorating the windows with green paper trees and red paper Santas, making illustrated Christmas cards for our families, and cutting out decorations for our Christmas trees: little green trees, little white angels, big red bells, and above all candy canes: white paper that we striped with red crayon and rolled from one corner, taping the cylinder, flattening one end, and curving the flat end into a hook; and all the activity and the tense sense of holiday worked us up to a higher and higher pitch of anticipation until we became grateful to the very tasks that fevered us for also distracting us from an unbearable pressure of waiting. It was as if we were tied to the track on which Christmas was a distant howling train. There was a real tree with lights, and a Christmas party with the two other Kindergarten classes; we ate Christmas cookies shaped like trees and stars, sprinkled with red and green sugar and sometimes with little silver balls. And everyone knew that it was all simply a matter of marking time. Then followed the

tense tempestuous week before Christmas, a week that affected
Edwin like an illness, like a fever, like a dream of falling, so that
a sharp word from his father was capable of hurting him like a
thumb: he would burst into a desolation of tears, sobbing hyster-
ically with shaking shoulders while Karen watched in terror,
squeezing her fingers into a soft doll. Mrs. Mullhouse would com-
fort him, stroking his hair as he cried into her shoulder, and soon
the violence would spend itself and he would lift his head, rubbing
his eyes and blowing his nose into a tissue his mother held for
him while Mr. Mullhouse, sitting all alone as if he had banished
himself into exile, would look over uneasily and try to make up
for everything: tenderly, cunningly, he would begin to say something quite harmless and friendly about the prospect of snow for
Christmas, he would put into his voice rich promises of stories of
Indians on intimate lamplit evenings, but the sheer sound of the
voice that had wounded him shattered Edwin, and he would burst
into wails of such pain and bitterness that it was as if Mr. Mullhouse had announced there was to be no Christmas at all that
year. Only after the second fit would he begin to recover, looking
up with big red eyes, rubbing his temples to soothe his headache,
and keeping his mouth open because his nose was stuffed. Within
ten minutes we were all joking and laughing, and it was as if
nothing had happened, except that the air was a web of intricate
tenderness, spun by secret spiders. The glittering day itself, after
such waiting, was flawed for Edwin by a delicate imperfection,
for with each bright wrapping he ripped ecstatically from its toy
he seemed to be falling one step further from a consummation
he had somehow never quite reached.

After Christmas there was a pause, as if someone were thinking
up a new holiday, but soon we were busy cutting vast hearts out
of red construction paper and pasting white paper lace around
the edges, each of us with his own sticky bottle of honey-colored
glue capped by a slit rubber tip. One girl brought in a bag of
little candy hearts with sayings printed on them, which Miss Tipp
dutifully distributed and then read aloud, moving from table to
table amid tempests of merriment. Rather suddenly a huge log
cabin appeared, big enough for two of us to stand in, and in an

atmosphere of hearts and lace we sang a song called "Honest Abe" and Miss Tipp told us that Abraham Lincoln was so honest that he once walked six miles to return a book he had borrowed. Each of us had to bring in a stamp with a picture of Abraham Lincoln on it, and when one girl brought in George Washington by mistake, Miss Tipp was delighted, because he was next. We sang a song about a cherry tree and Miss Tipp told us that George Washington could not tell a lie. Edwin wanted to know who was more honest, Abe Lincoln or George Washington; Miss Tipp said she thought they were about the same. A week later she brought in a cage with a real rabbit inside. Easter was the last big holiday, and Miss Tipp did all in her power to generate enthusiasm. She exceeded herself in the matter of eggs. She brought in a wicker basket full of soft green paper grass on which sat a large chocolate egg, three real eggs dyed red and yellow and blue, and dozens of little eggs wrapped in gold and silver foil. She brought in real eggs that sat on paper collars and had faces on them: one had a black mustache over his mouth and a little black mustache on his head, another was a rabbit with tall ears pasted on. She brought in a delicate necklace of blown eggs, painted in bright stripes. She brought in a large toy egg with a little window in one end: when you looked inside you saw a green field with miniature white sheep against a background of miniature red houses and distant blue hills. We cut out vast construction-paper eggs and pasted gold and silver stars on them or sprinkled silver dust on wavy lines of glue. Edwin insisted on cutting out a black egg, smiling mysteriously to himself and refusing to explain the joke. During one of our recent interviews I asked him about that black egg, but he had forgotten it completely, and could only suggest with another mysterious smile that perhaps it was a rotten egg. After Easter there were no real holidays, but Miss Tipp did her best, distracting us for a while with rehearsals for a Revolutionary War play (Edwin was Paul Revere) and luring us on with visions of the Memorial Day parade. After Memorial Day it was all the Fourth of July: Miss Tipp brought in a huge drum, a toy flute, and a red-and-white striped hat with a blue band filled with spangles, and we sang a song called "The British Are

Coming," during which we all stamped our feet. So the year passed in a trail of white paste and a shower of colored paper and suddenly we were out and the Fourth of July was only five days away; and even as Edwin set off red ladyfingers with his first glowing punk and with his first box of sparklers made sizzling circles in the black night sky, he was calculating the time left until his sixth birthday, which was less than a month away, and less than five months from Christmas. Let no one tell me that childhood is lived in a timeless present. Rather it is a fever of futures, an ardor of perpetual anticipations. Edwin stretched his arms greedily toward the future, bright with unopened presents. As his sixth birthday approached, he was quite unaware that more than half his life was over.

# 22

THE FATAL FLAW OF ALL BIOGRAPHY, according to its enemies, is its helpless conformity to the laws of fiction. Each date, each incident, each casual remark contributes to an elaborate plot that slowly and cunningly builds to a foreknown climax: the hero's celebrated deed. All the details of the hero's life are necessarily related to this central image, which suffuses them with a glow of interest they lack by themselves, as firelight enchants the familiar items of a living room; an interest, moreover, that was probably quite different for the hero himself, sporting in his meadow outside the future cage of his biography. And having borrowed a spurious significance from the central image, the details of a biography move toward it as surely as if each word were a pointing finger. "Biography is so simple," said Edwin one sweltering night not too long ago. "All you do is put in everything." The reader need not be reminded of the traditional unfairness of the creative temperament, an unfairness here carried to the point of fatuity. Nor did he stop at this point, but went on to claim (if I correctly interpret his half-articulate remarks) that the very notion of biography was hopelessly fictional, since unlike real life, which presents us with question marks, censored passages, blank spaces, rows of asterisks, omitted paragraphs, and numberless sequences of three dots trailing into whiteness, biography provides an illusion of completeness, a vast pattern of details organized by an omniscient biographer whose occasional assertions of ignorance or uncertainty deceive us no more than the polite protestations of a hostess who, during the sixth course of an elaborate feast, assures us that really, it was no trouble at all. And since Edwin claimed that good stories always struck him as true, he found himself in the curious position of believing absolutely in the Mock Turtle and the Mad Hatter but experiencing Lewis Carroll, about whom his father used to tell affectionate anecdotes, as an implausible invention.

So much for Edwin's opinions, here recorded in the strict interests of biographical accuracy. They are a typical mixture of subtlety and inanity. Like so many creative people, Edwin was not impressive as a thinker; his brain resembled a murky aquarium, occasionally illuminated by the flickers of a faulty electrical system. Often, in the middle of an argument, he took refuge in contemplations of the vanity of Reason before the awesome mysteries of the universe, or some such tommyrot. At other times, caught in a glaring inconsistency, he would assert the artist's right to inconsistency. At still other times, pressed to develop an idea thrown out carelessly in the heat of argument, he would shrug and say: "It's just a hunch," or "It's not worth talking about," or "How many anagrams can you make out of 'Edwin'?" And he suffered all his brief, too brief life from a weakness for deliberately saying things that he knew would drive people to teeth-gnashing frenzies of annoyance. It is not worthwhile, therefore, to break our heads over his useless opinions concerning the fictionality of biography. But I take this opportunity to ask Edwin, wherever he is: isn't it true that the biographer performs a function nearly as great as, or precisely as great as, or actually greater by far than the function performed by the artist himself? For the artist creates the work of art, but the biographer, so to speak, creates the artist. Which is to say: without me, would you exist at all, Edwin?

But enough of speculation. For one thing is certain: once I had revealed to Edwin that I was going to be his biographer, once he had allowed the idea to take hold and sink in, he became fascinated by my project, indeed obsessed by it, and proved at times almost aggressively helpful in providing me with information— information which, I am grieved to say, was often at variance with my own precise and infallible memories. The point is that for all his mockery of the biographer's art, when it came to the real thing Edwin took it very seriously indeed. No doubt it was a relief to turn from the terrible freedom of the kingdom of Beauty to the quiet strictness of the kingdom of Truth. In one of our late conversations Edwin said that I had saved his soul—he was always saying things like that—by making him think of his life as a biography, that is, a design with a beginning, middle, and end. Smiling, and pushing away the hot lamp where a trapped moth was stupidly beating its wings, I replied that strictly speaking his life could not be considered a design with a beginning, middle, and end until it had ended. Edwin did not answer, but looked away, frowning slightly over lenses that reflected the glowing lampshade; and by one of those curious tricks played on us by our senses, I seemed to hear, faintly in that prophetic silence, the sound of wings beating madly in his eyes.

# Part Two

# THE MIDDLE YEARS
*(Aug. 2, 1949–Aug. 1, 1952)*

# 1

BEHIND THE RICH BLUE LUMINOUS CURTAIN, rippling, the pale blue
luminous letters ripple, mingling with bright blue luminous
melodies jingling in an odor of salt and cardboard, mingling with
jujyfruits, jingling with jujubes, in the black-crow licorice dark.
In light, caught, the letters, transfixed, stiffen. Brighter than licked
lollipops, livelier than soda in sunlight, lovelier than sunshine on
cellophane the colors shine: popsicle orange and lemon-ice white,
cotton-candy pink and mint-jelly green, cherry-soda red and
raspberry-jello red. Cellophane crackles in the green-and-red-
tinted dark. Thick with purple shadows, a dim room appears. In
the center stands a vertical ladder, from the top of which a narrow
shaft of yellow light falls diagonally down, cutting across one end
of a bed and illuminating two round white feet sticking up at the
bottom of a blue blanket. A white rabbit, wearing one red nightcap on each tall ear, lies on his back, asleep. As he exhales, with a
whistling sound, the blanket under his chin rolls down to his feet.
As he inhales, with a snoring sound, the blanket over his feet rolls
up to his chin. Over his head a dream appears: he is sawing a log
in half. As the saw cuts through the log a piece falls out of the
dream and hits him on the head. He sits up, rubbing his head. A red
throbbing bump grows higher and higher, pushing up his hand, and
then grows lower and disappears. The rabbit yawns and stretches
and removes both nightcaps. Putting on a pair of large round black
eyeglasses he walks over to a little stove and begins to fry an egg,
flipping it up in the air and catching it in his pan. He changes hands,
flips it up in the air, and holds out the pan, waiting. The egg does
not return. Sighing, the rabbit walks over to the ladder and begins

to climb. He pokes his head out of his hole into a bright green clearing. In the near distance stand several thin black trees, each with three or four leaves. Beside the hole lies the fried egg. The rabbit picks it up and disappears into his hole. From behind one tree an orange snout with a black nose pops out, followed by a V-shaped frown. In long white eyes, little black pupils move to the left and right. The fox tiptoes quickly to another tree, no thicker than one of his eyebrows, and disappears entirely behind it. His foot peeps out and tiptoes across the grass, followed by his leg, which stretches to twice its length and stops behind another tree; the rest of the fox shoots across to the new tree in an orange blur and disappears behind it. His frowning head peeps out. He looks to the left and right. With hunched shoulders he tiptoes over to the hole. He is orange except for his white toes, his white fingers, and the broad white patch that stretches from the top of his chest to the bottom of his belly. Reaching behind his back, he brings forward a huge red firecracker. He lights the firecracker, pushes it upside down into the hole, and tiptoes a few paces away. With his back to the hole he squeezes his eyes shut and blocks his ears with his fingers. The rabbit flips his egg and holds out the pan. The egg does not return. Frowning, he looks up and sees the firecracker. The egg is speared on the sizzling wick. He climbs the ladder, removes the egg, and pushes the firecracker up out of the hole. The firecracker rolls along the grass and stops behind the fox, who stands with his fingers in his ears. After a while he opens his eyes, removes his fingers from his ears, and turns around. When he sees the sizzling firecracker at his feet his eyes spring out of his head at the ends of springs. He dives headfirst onto the grass, landing with a crash and covering his head with his arms. The sizzling wick goes out. The fox looks up. He rises to his feet, walks to the firecracker, picks it up, and smiles. The firecracker explodes. When the smoke clears, the fox is still standing. He is entirely black, except for his white eyes and his white smile. The rabbit sits in a rocking chair by the stove, reading a newspaper. The frying pan is attached to one foot. As he rocks back the egg flips into the air. As he rocks forward the egg falls into the pan. The fox approaches the rabbit hole, pulling a rope attached to a shiny black cannon. He places a shiny black cannonball in the shiny black cannon, tips the front of the cannon into the hole, and lights a wick at the cannon's back. He turns around, shuts his eyes, and blocks his ears. The front of the cannon swings up, followed by a fried egg, and turns all the way around until it is pointing at the fox. The fried egg goes back into the hole. The fox turns around, sees the cannon, and looks at the audience. The cannon goes off. When the smoke clears, the fox is standing with a hole in his stomach, through which a tree is visible. He reaches down and zips up the hole. Then he collapses onto the grass. A new scene begins on the left, traveling to the right and erasing the old scene. The fox enters pulling a rope tied to the top of a bending tree. He hammers a peg into the ground, ties the rope to a trigger attached to the peg, lays the rope in a circle near the hole, and places inside the circle a bright orange carrot that rests at the end of the trigger. The fox sits down against a nearby tree, crosses his legs, crosses his hands behind his head, closes his eyes, and begins to snore. Above his head a dream appears: he is seated at a table with a napkin tied under his chin and the rabbit bound hand and foot on a plate before him. The rabbit's head pops out of the hole. He sniffs, adjusts his eyeglasses, and sees the carrot. He climbs out of the hole, steps into the rope-circle, and removes the carrot. Reaching into a pocket in his skin, he removes a leg of roast chicken and places it on the trigger. Crunching on the carrot he steps out of the circle and sees the fox asleep against a tree with a dream over his head. He walks over to the fox, unties the dream-rabbit, who runs away, and puts in its place a huge red firecracker. Then he goes back into his hole. The dream-fox bites into the firecracker, which explodes. The real fox wakes up. He spits out a mouthful of teeth. In the circle of rope he sees the chickenleg. He walks over to the rim of the circle and frowns down, tapping his foot. As he stares, lines of odor twist from the chickenleg to his twitching black nose. He bends over, reaches toward the chickenleg, and suddenly straightens up. He looks at the audience and shakes his head slyly. Reaching into a pocket he removes a cane. Gently he prods the chickenleg until it rolls from the trigger. He flinches, but nothing happens. Shrugging, he picks up the chickenleg, thrusts it deep into his mouth, and removes a clean white bone. He licks his chops, rubs his belly, and tosses the bone away. It lands on the trigger. The fox's hair stands on end but nothing happens. Frowning, he pokes the trigger with his cane. Nothing happens. He takes out a sledge hammer and slams the trigger. Nothing happens. He steps inside the rope and kicks the trigger. Nothing happens. He jumps up and down on the trigger. Nothing happens. As he wipes his forehead with a red handkerchief, a small blue bird flies overhead. A tiny blue feather flutters down. The fox watches the feather as it slowly falls, rocking back and forth, descending past his eyes, his neck, his stomach, his knees. It lands gently on the trigger. The rope yanks the fox into the air and out of sight, accompanied by the sound of a whistling rocket. A distant explosion rocks the forest. The fox enters on the left, leaning on a crutch. One leg is bound in a cast and white bandages cover his head. He sits down beside the rabbit hole and thinks. A lightbulb appears above his head. He reaches up and turns it off. Tearing off his bandages and throwing away the crutch, he removes from his pocket a hammer, nails, and pieces of wood. He begins building furiously, working up a cloud of dust that conceals him completely. When the dust clears a vast blue chute is visible. Beginning in front of the rabbit hole, it rises slowly toward the right on taller and taller posts, passing through the forest where small deer gaze up in wonder, passing over the treetops as an old owl frowns and scratches his head, passing beneath a rainbow into the sky, passing clouds and jagged mountaintops until at last it reaches a tall brown cliff on which a vast boulder rests atop a tiny pebble. Beside the boulder, reclining in a yellow and red lawn chair, wearing green sunglasses and sipping lemonade, is the fox. He picks up a straw, tears one end, and blows the paper wrapper at the boulder. The boulder tips onto the blue chute and starts to roll down. It rolls past clouds and jagged peaks, it frightens a buzzard, it flattens a passing airplane, it snaps apart the rainbow, it roars over treetops past the startled owl, and terrified deer take cover as it thunders past. The rabbit's head pops out of the hole. Grasping the end of the chute, with a quick motion he bends it upward slightly. Then he ducks out of sight. The boulder follows the curve of the chute and sails into the air, hitting a distant treetop that catches it, bends backward, and springs forward, flinging the boulder back. The fox is standing on the cliff with his head to one side and one hand cupped over an ear. He removes a watch from his pocket and frowns. As he turns his head to look down, the boulder slams into him, rolling over him and flattening him like dough. For a few moments the fox lies like a colorful shadow. Then one end peels up and he rolls into a tube. His eyes move back and forth in the tube. One leg emerges, one arm, a bushy tail. The fox stands up. Cracks appear in his body and he falls apart with a tinkling sound. The rabbit is lying on his back on the floor, doing sit-ups. He stands up and begins to do quick knee-bends. He lifts a dumbbell over his head. As he begins to skip rope, a sudden crash shakes his house. Frowning, he looks up. The fox, eyes bulging and teeth gnashing, is trapped in the hole at his waist. His arms are pinned to his sides. The rabbit breaks into a smile. Pushing over a small yellow stool, he puts on a pair of boxing gloves and begins to punch the fox's head as the circle slowly closes.

# 2

IF THE EARLY YEARS are the pre-literate years, and the Late Years are the literary years, then the Middle Years may neatly be named the literate years. It was in the first grade that Edwin at last learned to read and print. Edwin was never again so dedicated a student, and we soon distinguished ourselves as the aptest of Mrs. Brockaway's pupils. Very early in the year she divided the class into three reading groups, which met separately twice a day at the front of the room, and of course Edwin and I were in the top group. Otherwise I sat diagonally across from him at one of the room's six tables. Mrs. Brockaway did not seat us alphabetically (a lucky stroke for this observer) but according to unnamed principles so various and elusive as to be comprehended only in the terms homogeneity and diversity. At opposite ends of our table sat quiet Susan

Thompson and that loudmouth Billy Duda, while beside me sat Trudy Cassidy, already a babbler, and across from me, beside Edwin, none other than Donna Riccio, the most popular girl in the class, who in February received thirty-nine valentines, three from Edwin. In the third grade she began to lurk in obscure corners of the playground with Mario Antonio and that crowd, and soon she drifted into the middle reading group and at last into the lowest reading group, from which she never emerged. I suppose Edwin was infatuated with that black hair of hers, and there can be no question that he showed off in front of her in an unspeakable way, yet when all is said and done the whole thing must be dismissed as a light flirtation, not at all comparable to the raging fever later inspired in him by Rose Dorn, of all people. No, Edwin's true passion in the first grade was for reading, and I suspect that he was more in love with the alphabet than with Donna Riccio's red lips and raven locks.

Often I would see him snatching secret glances at Donna Riccio, lifting his gaze from her elbow to her blue short-sleeve, from her blue short-sleeve to her long black eyelashes, from her long black eyelashes to the blue bow in her shiny black hair, from her shiny black hair to the top of the blackboard where, stretching across the room like a vast title, the large green alphabet cards displayed their white letters, alternately capital and small.

In my opinion the instruction in reading progressed with excruciating slowness. For Edwin, who had no opinion, it was all a fascinating game. It was not the first time I had been led to reflect upon the transforming powers of the creative imagination. Our first book, to call it that, was a green soft-covered affair longer than it was tall, whose pages were divided into horizontal rows of little colored pictures. Each row began with a letter. As Mrs. Brockaway named the pictures, we had to put an X through each one that began with the letter on the left. It was the sort of exercise suitable for a three-year-old, or a two-year-old, or a clever cat, and I could not understand why my time was being wasted in this manner. But Edwin crossed out his pictures with tireless rapture. Moreover, he was always contriving difficulties. One row, beginning with *b*, showed a bear, a door, a book, a baseball bat, and a moon. Hurrying ahead of Mrs. Brockaway, who was still on the previous page, Edwin crossed out the bear, the door, and the baseball bat, leaving the book and the moon. When Mrs. Brockaway read the pictures, Edwin was stunned; he insisted that the door was a bathroom door and the book a dictionary. Mrs. Brockaway said he should wait for her to read the pictures. Edwin asked how she knew the book wasn't a dictionary. Mrs. Brockaway said that a dictionary was also a book and that he would never learn anything if he didn't stop asking questions and start paying attention. Edwin stopped asking questions, but he continued to rush ahead. He felt a strong affection for the little pictures, which kept on reappearing, so that soon the goat, the mitten, the bear, the book, the fox, the mailman, the goose, the gate were as familiar to him as Careless Carrie and Hayseed Hank in his deck of Old Maid cards.

He was also fond of the long pale word-cards with thick black letters that Mrs. Brockaway held up from time to time in order to teach us something or other: *bit, fit, sit, pit, hit,* or *dot, not, hot, lot, pot,* or *bat, cat, rat, mat, fat.* Later we went on to *flat, brat, chat, that, spat,* but not *gnat,* not to mention *cravat,* which Edwin and I discovered a year later under the Vocabulary of Rhymes section in the back of a dictionary.

After the book with the rows of little pictures came a slim paper-covered book that Mrs. Brockaway referred to as the first pre-primer, presumably because it was so elementary that it did not exist. On the first page was a black cat on a round red rug, and under him was the word "Fluffy." On the next page Fluffy was lying on his back in the grass with a red ball of yarn in his paws; on one side of him stood a little blond girl with a red bow in her hair who was pointing at him, and on the other side stood a boy with brown shorts and a skyblue shirt. Underneath were the words:

> Look, Bobby.
> Look at Fluffy.
> Look at Fluffy play.

The inanity of it all was positively painful to me; but Edwin was enchanted by every page. I cannot believe that he cared two cents for the ridiculous stories, which for that matter were not even stories; what fascinated him must have been the sense of being initiated into a secret, of turning on a light in the spookhouse, of entering a garden that for years he had looked at through a little door—what fascinated him in short must have been the act of reading itself, as if that act were somehow independent of the particular words that called it into being. And strange to say, he was deeply moved by the insipid illustrations, which were changed by the pressure of his imagination as completely as a ring of green water is changed by the pressure of the breath into a stream of many-colored bubbles. The pictures presented a world of white picket fences and green lawns and tall old trees with rope-swings and such stuff, a world of blue milk trucks on winding country lanes, a world in which it was not at all surprising to come across a white goat or to pay a visit to grandfather's farm. It was a world, you might say, dimly reminiscent of his own but older and more intensely green. And perhaps the secret is this, that he was moved by the sense of having lost something that he could not name. Yes, and I think he also loved the sheer look of the page, whose few words and towering illustrations stirred up memories of earlier pages, so that through each one, as through a sheet of translucent glass, he saw vague shapes of islands and dragons, he saw from some half-remembered library book a dim fox carrying over his shoulder a gray bag that contained a hen, he saw Tootle wearing a daisy chain in a field filled with butterflies, he saw, kneeling at the kitchen table and frowning in stern concentration while his father read to him, himself.

After the first pre-primer came the second pre-primer, as if there were degrees of nonexistence, and after that the third pre-primer, and at last, long after I had given up all hope, the primer itself, memorable for its hard covers, and finally the first reader, more of the same unfortunately. All of these books produced in me the feeling that I was climbing steadily higher and higher on a staircase winding toward a remote room in which I had long since ceased to believe. They were all accompanied by workbooks, which fascinated Edwin with their simple games; he was never happier than when coloring in the pictures beginning with a certain letter, or putting the correct word in the blank, or drawing a

line under the word in the right column that was the same as the
single word on the left. I recall one exercise that required you to
draw a line from a word to the picture it represented: Edwin drew
a line from the word "bell" to a large striped ball, and hastily erased
it as he glanced into my workbook. And I recall another exercise
that reminded me of the rows of Donalds on Edward Penn's wall:

*Find the word that is different in each row.*

| | | | |
|------|------|------|------|
| look | look | book | look |
| run  | can  | run  | run  |
| ball | ball | baby | ball |
| go   | go   | go   | do   |

Along with the reading exercises came the printing exercises.
Edwin, who had learned to copy the capital letters of his name
shortly after the age of four, was nevertheless entranced. He liked
to connect the dotted outlines of the letters, as earlier he had connected the dots in innumerable coloring books, and he liked to
practice printing his name in a dotted version:

Edwin

Later he was fascinated by the yellow paper with its alternately
dark blue and light blue lines. He practiced his letters with passion
and soon had a distinct feeling for each one. He had a special fondness for letters like b and h that rose over letters like e and o to
touch the dark blue line above, and letters like g and y that
plunged below the dark blue base-line to touch the pale blue line
below. He was puzzled by t, which rose above the light blue line
but was not permitted to reach the dark blue line, and fascinated
by i and j, with their dreamlike dots. He liked to form categories
on the basis of similarity of shape: thus b and d were related to
one another in much the same way as q and g, except that the
tails of the latter both began on the same side of the o; m was two
n's and w was two v's; capital G was capital C with something
added. The relation of capital to small letters intrigued Edwin: C
was a bigger c, S was a bigger s, Z was a bigger z, but what

was the relation of D to d? of G to g? of Q to q? of E to e? F and E were clearly related to one another but f and e were clearly not: f was related to t, the only other small letter with a cross-stroke, and e to c. Edwin was always asking Mrs. Brockaway to explain these things, as if she had invented the alphabet, and Mrs. Brockaway was always telling Edwin not to ask so many questions, as if indeed she had invented the alphabet but refused to divulge its secrets. The early printing exercises impressed upon everyone, but especially upon Edwin, a sense of the physicality of letters—a sense that, the reader will recall, he first experienced in the alphabet books of his third year.

The first grade was so much a matter of reading and printing that it would be misleading to do more than mention our other activities. Science meant bringing in leaves and stones; Art meant decorating our pencil-cans and learning how to mix powder-paints; Music meant shouting some preposterous song. Arithmetic was at first almost as interesting to Edwin as reading, for the numerals too had personalities, but the numbers formed from numerals were disappointing compared to the words formed from letters, and the games played with numbers, though they amused him, failed to arouse in him a lasting excitement. Only once did numbers truly move him: one day he learned the secret of rounding 100 and beginning all over again, a secret that seemed to open up vast spaces in his mind. But soon it seemed merely a clever trick, like the story Billy Duda later told in the fourth grade: "Ten boy scouts were sitting around a fire and each boy scout had to tell a story. The first boy scout said: 'Ten boy scouts were sitting around a fire and each boy scout had to tell a story. The first boy scout said: "Ten boy scouts were sitting around a fire . . ." ' "—at which point Mrs. Czernik told him to sit down.

One first-grade subject unconnected with words does call for special mention, for it was the cause of Edwin's first punishment at school. Most of the time Health was a half hour of ingenious tedium, but one day toward Christmas Mrs. Brockaway announced that Mrs. Hotchkiss, the school nurse, was going to pay us a visit. We were to keep our mouths shut and she meant shut. The door opened, and Mrs. Hotchkiss came striding in, wearing a white cap, a white dress with white buttons, white stockings, and white shoes. Under one arm she carried a large white piece of cardboard and in one hand she carried a long thin black cloth case approximately the size of a cheerleader's baton. At Mrs. Brockaway's desk she put down the long black case and proceeded to unfold two wings from the back of the cardboard, as if she were creating an angel. She then stood the piece of cardboard on the desk, facing us. The cardboard showed the vast black outline of a tooth. Edwin and Donna Riccio, who usually sat with their backs to the desk, but had turned their chairs around for this special occasion, both stared up at the huge tooth. It was Donna Riccio who gave the first quiet giggle; I could tell by the tenseness of Edwin's neck that he was desperately restraining a convulsion. And I think he would have been successful had not Mrs. Hotchkiss picked up the long black case and proceeded to remove from it, slowly and carefully, the largest toothbrush I have ever seen. The bristles were nearly two inches high; on the other end was a red rubber point the size of a Hershey's Kiss. It was too much for Edwin; he exploded helplessly, setting off Donna Riccio and Trudy Cassidy and the rest of the class; yet even then it was not too late, for although Mrs. Brockaway resembled a dragon, Mrs. Hotchkiss sweetly smiled. But as the laughter died down she became quite serious; and frowning over her pink-rimmed eyeglasses she began to explain the correct method of brushing one's teeth. Edwin was in agony, he was a rigid knotted muscle of attention, he reminded me of the tightly knotted rubber band on the bottom of a tightly wound balsawood airplane; but again I think he would have been successful had not Mrs. Hotchkiss raised the monstrous toothbrush to the monstrous tooth and quite solemnly, without a smile, begun to brush. It was not the sight so much as the sound that finished him: at the first gentle brshhhhhh he let out a helpless howl. Things happened very quickly then: Mrs. Brockaway stormed over, grabbed his collar, and yanked him out of his seat; Edwin's face filled with horror; and in a state of pallid shock he was half-dragged to the coatroom, where he remained for the rest of Mrs. Hotchkiss's lecture, which proceeded without incident. Afterward, when he was let out, Edwin kept his eyes lowered and buried himself in his work; his eyes were red. Poor Edwin. He could no more understand other people's solemnities than he could their jokes.


Edwin's reading at school was supplemented by his reading at home. He went through all his books, searching for familiar words and trying to solve new ones. The word "bone," which we learned in October, immediately gave him the key to "lonely" in *The Lonely Island*, though "is" threw him into confusion, for he could not understand why "island" was not "is-land." Indeed the relation between spelling and sound perplexed him endlessly; he never forgave the Inventor of Words for "do" and "go." He began to read aloud to Karen from his books, omitting and inventing as the need arose. Strange words that he could not pronounce tormented him; sometimes he would throw the book down and sulk sourly, as if waiting for the offending page to apologize.

Every Saturday Dr. Mullhouse drove Edwin, Karen, and me to the library, where for an hour we pored over tall thin books filled with bright colors and large letters, many of which formed words and even sentences that Edwin could read. Nearby, in low brown bookcases, smaller and fatter books stood in tight rows that reminded me of the crayons in Edwin's stand-up box: blue violet, blue green, green yellow, yellow green, raw umber, burnt sienna, Indian red, maroon. The older you got, Edwin knew, the smaller the letters and the fewer the pictures: the books in the low brown bookcases had only an occasional black-and-white picture at the top of a page, and his father's books had no pictures at all. By the end of the first grade, when Edwin began to read books that contained whole pages without pictures, he was careful to choose for Karen books with very few words and many large pictures, as suited her age. But sometimes he read his own books to her as well, and sometimes he read her books secretly to himself.

As the schoolyear advanced, Edwin noticed that words were springing up all around him. Words grew all over the breakfast table—on cereal boxes, on jars of vitamins, on bottles of Saccharine. He found dozens of words on the way to school: BENJAMIN ST., JORDAN AVE., FOR SALE, STOP, VINCENT CAPOBIANCO, BUZZY LOVES

SUE, OUR HOLY MOTHER OF CHRIST, OLDSMOBILE, MOBILOIL, and of course Edwin's favorite, which made him think of nincompoops and polio: SLOW CHILDREN. There were words on his puzzle boxes, words on his Viewmaster slides, words on his cap pistols, words on his paintboxes, words on his coloring books, words on his pink rubber ball, words on his tennis ball, words on his box of checkers, words on his lightbulb, words on his light switch, words on his pillowcase. On a single penny, read by Dr. Mullhouse, were the words LIBERTY, IN GOD WE TRUST, ONE CENT, UNITED STATES OF AMERICA, and E PLURIBUS UNUM, which even Mrs. Mullhouse didn't understand. On the paper sheath of a single crayon were the words COPPER, BINNEY & SMITH INC., NEW YORK, MADE IN U.S.A. There were words in the kitchen cabinets, words in the medicine chest, words in the closets, words in all the drawers. They grew on pencils, on lamps, on clocks, on paper bags, on cardboard boxes, on carpet sweepers, on the brass prongs of wall plugs, on the bottoms of plates, on the backs of spoons. They grew on his sneakers, in his underpants, on the inside of his shirt behind his neck. They grew even in the yard: on the white swing, on the garbage-can covers, on the oil inlet sticking up out of the frontyard grass; and one spring day he looked up to see an airplane writing words in the sky. And because, as the world passed from winter to spring, Edwin passed from the primer to the first reader, it was as if the very season were a budding and blossoming of words.

# 3

SUMMERS, Edwin and I played in lawn water and real water. Lawn water was the tall fan of the sprinkler, sweeping in a vast lazy semicircle over sparkling grass in the Mullhouse back yard. Edwin liked to wait for the water to reach the lowest point of its arc. Then taking up a position on the other side of the yellow sprinkler he would watch the water, like the dripping wing of some enormous bird, rise slowly from the polished grass, weaving rainbows where the hard jets broke into drops and spray; and as the slowly turning pipe showed its holes near the top and a few drops from the hissing wing above touched Edwin, he would run away over the slippery lawn, shouting as a chill shower shocked him, helped by a wind. But at best the sprinkler was something we had to put up with on days when we were denied the real thing. School lasted until the end of June, but on weekend afternoons Mrs. Mullhouse would take Edwin, Karen, and me on the long drive to Soundview Beach. Wearing bathing suits and t-shirts we entered the steaming Studebaker and felt the hot leather against our thighs. Edwin always sat in front, on a white towel. Crossing his thin legs, barred by light, he would lean back with a book, perhaps a comic or some blue-covered biography from The Childhood of Famous Americans Series (*Oliver Hazard Perry: Boy of the Sea, Andy Jackson: Boy Soldier, Buffalo Bill: Boy of the Plains, Peter Stuyvesant: Boy with Wooden Shoes*). It is here that the humble biographer in his rude cave longs for the golden wings of imagination. For while Karen and I watched the landscape pass through its familiar changes, the houses melting into open fields and long factories, a marsh, an airport, a roadside stand heaped with fruit and corn, Edwin was on a whaling expedition on the high seas or searching for gold with a pack of huskies in the Klondike; and when from time to time he lowered his book to gaze out the side window, for the first hazy seconds he must have experienced the moving landscape as a memory or a dream; while at other times, when he closed his book and fixed his attention on the familiar scene, the eyelashes I was watching would cease to blink, and in the rearview mirror I could see those eyes staring at nothing I could see, two polished lenses, focused on infinity. Edwin never lost what I shall call his capacity for revery, but which he once called, with typical melodramatic verve, the ability to die.

Stepping from the car was an adventure. The sandstrewn pavement of the parking lot gave way to a fringe of tickly grass, where we cooled our feet in preparation for the tar of the seaside road. Once across we stood in grassy sand and steeled ourselves for the long trek across the burning desert, where the danger was less to the soles than to the tender skin on the crest of the foot, over which the bright sand tumbled in scalding waves. Mrs. Mullhouse, dressed in her beach uniform of wide-brimmed straw hat, green sunglasses, black bathing suit, straw sandals, and straw pocketbook slung over a shoulder, carried a blanket over one arm and walked behind with little Karen as Edwin and I, carrying our towels around our necks, hurried ahead over the crest of sand down to the cool brown rim at the water's edge. But before we could enter the water we had to return to the hot part of the sand and help Mrs. Mullhouse lay the blanket. The spot she chose was always far from the water ("You don't expect me to sit right in the water, like a fish") and always as far as possible from the crowded section where colored blankets formed a vast broken quilt ("You don't expect me to sit in everybody's lap"); and it was always with an air of solemnity that she officiated at the laying-out ceremony, during which each of us had to take an end. There were three rules: the blanket had to be free of wrinkles, the sand underneath had to be free of ripples, and the blanket had to be free of sand. Then with warnings not to kick sand on the blanket, not to go over our heads, and not to stay in too long, since Mrs. Mullhouse believed that terrible sunburns occurred in the water, at last she released us, and we rushed down to the water as with great care she began to fold all the towels and lay them in a neat pile at one corner of the blanket. At high tide I liked to plunge right in; but not Edwin. Oh no. For now his own elaborate ceremony began. Walking alone along the shore to a distant and unpopulated section of ocean, he advanced inch by cautious inch into the chill water, dividing his body mentally into sections and preparing each higher stage by preliminary wettings. You stayed out of his way while all this was taking place. From far away we watched him—we, for Mrs. Mullhouse and Karen had by now come down to my part of the water. Poor Edwin. The area of the bathing suit was crucial and often caused him to retreat; he would stand with his hands on his hips and stare down frowning at the dark wet edges of his bathing shorts, as if he had gotten them wet by mistake and had ruined a good piece of clothing. But always a wave would take him by surprise, wetting him a few inches higher than the waterline he had established, so that making a virtue of necessity he would advance boldly up to the new line, waiting for the inevitable cold shock that would propel him forward to his waist. But at waist level he would clench his teeth with the sudden discovery of a more chilling wetness, for he had been concentrating so intensely on the sensations of his wet bathing suit that he had forgotten the pure contact of water on naked unprotected flesh, and the first wave to ripple against his thin stomach would cause a rash of goosebumps all over his arms, accompanied by a shocked stiffening of muscles, as if he had seen a shark. And now the thought of advancing any farther was as fantastic as the thought of inhaling underwater; and his mind's argument that parts of his body were now actually immersed and comfortable in the freezing waves seemed to his body devious, implausible, and theoretical. And so he decided to return to the blanket and lie down in the sun. But as soon as he began to turn back he discovered a new shock of cold, for the submerged parts of his body had been protected by the water from a breeze he had somehow failed to notice, a breeze that combined with his wetness to form an icy wind. And so he quickly returned to waist level, determined to stand motionless indefinitely until some elegant solution to his perplexity should be found. Meanwhile he rose on his toes or jumped with the advancing waves in order to preserve his waterline. He looked about continually, moving to the left or right whenever someone in the water threatened to shorten the distance between them; and far down the shore, at the water's edge, he could see his mother standing ankle-deep, holding Karen's hand, and myself splashing around nearby, watching him. Alone in his private tract of water, he seemed a nervous seabird, frail, alert, unknowable. In fantasy I see him rising from the water with a slow motion of dripping wings. But at last, and suddenly; with pride in his boldness, with terror of pain, with joy at the solution of a difficult problem, and with a look of surprise, Edwin crouched in the water up to his neck.

# 4

IN THE SUMMER OF 1953 I rode Edwin to Soundview Beach. It was a brilliant day. The fields of tall grass stretching into the distance seemed done in green watercolor that melted into a watercolor sky. Two bags of lunch bounced on top of a maroon blanket in the wire basket in front, while Edwin bounced on top of two white towels on the red metal seat in back. From time to time he produced an allergic snuffle. "Let's turn around," he said, and nearly threw me off balance with a sneeze. He was still in a difficult mood. Nearly a month had passed since our visit to the White Beach amusement park, and I still had not revealed to him my important secret. Despite my relentless questioning I had been able to elicit from him nothing about his book except that he had reached some mysterious "point." I had vowed silently, not for the first time, to reveal my plan to him as soon as he should show me his masterpiece. Meanwhile it was all I could do not to jot down my observations in full view of their unknowing subject.

I parked at a gray wooden stand for bicycles and walked with Edwin across the street onto the bright crest of sand. His feet were protected by a pair of high black-and-white sneakers that came almost to the tops of his red-and-blue-striped socks. Over his old bathing suit he wore dark blue dungarees with light blue rolled-up cuffs, and over his shirt he wore a dark brown summer jacket, zipped up to his chin. On his nose sat a pair of dusty eyeglasses with colorless frames. In one hand he held a sopping handkerchief. "Sun," he muttered, squinting and scowling and sweating and suffering but stubbornly, stubbornly refusing to wear clip-on sunglasses, which he said made his eyeglasses press into his nose, or to remove his hot jacket, which he insisted was necessary for the prevention of colds, since one could never distinguish allergic sneezes from cold-sneezes. "Oh, think of the water," I suggested, sweeping out an arm as the first wave rose to greet us. Edwin blew his nose. The sloping beach was aglow with gay blankets, bright sand, and polished people. Here and there a tilted beach umbrella cast a gibbous shadow, while the aluminum legs of partly shaded lawn-chairs flashed in the sun; and quite by chance, at the crowded heart of the beach, a number of blankets formed three neat rows, reminding me of Edwin's old paintbox with its rectangles of color set among white tin. At Edwin's insistence we walked to a high spot far from the crowded section, away from the water. He held his handkerchief firmly in one hand and one corner of the blanket weakly in the other while I did most of the work. After placing the lunchbags and towels on the corners of the blanket I kicked off my sneakers, pulled off my shirt and shorts, and stood in my bathing suit waiting for Edwin, who was still taking off his socks. "You go," he said. "I'll wait here." He placed his socks neatly beside a towel. Barefooted, but still wearing his dark brown jacket and his dungarees, he lay down on his stomach in the blazing sun, and reaching into one of the lunchbags, extracting a book in a violet-red binding, and opening up to a flat Hershey bar wrapper that served as a bookmark, stubbornly, stubbornly, stubbornly he began to read, while lines of sweat formed at the edges of his hair and allergic tears welled in his itching eyes.

# 5

TOWARD THE END OF SEPTEMBER, in the second grade, a strange change came over Edwin. Day after day from the cruel distance of Table 1 (Antonio, Bopko, Cartwright, Cassidy, DeAngelo, Dorn) I watched Edwin idling at the remote island of Table 5 (Litwinski, Mullhouse, Pluvcik, Riccio, Robbins, Robins). Day after day I watched his gaze rise from the placid pages of *Bobby and Betsy* to the clock or the flag or the picture of George Washington or the dark green plants in their red plastic flowerpots on the row of windowsills over the radiators; and leaning his chin on his palm he would stare unseeing, minutes at a time. He stumbled over sentences in the advanced reading group; his lists of spelling-words on blue-lined yellow paper floated dreamily above the lines; and twice during snack period he wound his wet straw absently round and round his finger and had to drink the rest of the milk out of the wax carton, making a white spot on his nose from the milky flap. Once when he was playing shortstop during a game of kickball, bases loaded and two out, a tall easy fly came to him; he moved under it, looking up in the blue sky at the big black spinning rubber ball with its red rubber patch; the outfield was already trotting in, the kicker was rounding first half-heartedly, a few members of the other side had already stepped out of line and begun to head for the outfield; but as the ball plunged toward Edwin it was suddenly clear that something had gone wrong, he was standing there with his hands at his sides, gazing up at the sky and ball as if he wondered what they were doing up there, until suddenly the ball smacked at his toes, startling him into pained alertness, bouncing high; and filled with shame and anguish he had to stand with his arms held out to catch it on the bounce as the second girl touched home and a loud cheer went up from the other side.

Even his manner of walking home betrayed the great change working in him. No longer did he leap up to snatch leaves from low-hanging branches or walk carefully to avoid the cracks in the sidewalk. Instead he walked along listlessly, holding loosely in one hand his spelling book stuffed with pieces of blue-lined yellow paper and drawing the fingers of the other hand bumpily along the pickets of a fence. "Anything wrong?" I would say, as casually as possible. "What?" he would answer. "Oh no, nothing"; and sometimes he would sigh. I tried to fascinate his attention with roadside treasures (the tiny white plastic wheels and axle of a miniature car or truck, a praying mantis sitting on the curb, an old soggy firecracker whose faded colored stripes were run together, half a pingpong ball containing rainwater) but he took no notice of anything, and even more lofty sights, like a red kite tangled in telephone wires with its white tail flapping, or a man standing at the top of a telephone pole, left him unmoved.

Home from school, I would change into my playclothes and hurry over to Edwin's as usual, but when I entered his room I would find him still unchanged, lying on his stomach on the bed beside the double window with his chin on the spread and one hand dangling over the side, or lying on his side with his back to the windows, his head supported on one hand and his other hand tucked between his knees. "Edwin," I would say, "aren't you feeling well?"—and forcing his eyes to focus on me he would say sadly: "I'm okay." Then his eyes would go out of focus and he stared through me as if I were a piece of cellophane. He refused to go outside and play, as if the effort of lugging the burden of his body downstairs were more than his frail spirit could bear, though when I say "refused" I mean only that his lids closed slowly and with terrible finality at my suggestion. He seemed vaguely willing, however, to play inside. With melancholy immobility he listened unhearing as I slid out the green folding table from behind the chest of drawers. With infinite sadness he watched unseeing as I stood on the table's stomach and proceeded to pull up its four white legs. With rigorous remoteness he brooded unthinking as I set up the marbles in two opposite triangles of the Chinese-checkers board and pushed the table against his bed. With weary resignation, with bleary inattention, with a kind of passion of lassitude and a fierce energy of indifference he proceeded to beat me soundly, zigzagging slowly and ever more slowly in one grand weary melancholy move all the way across the board to the very bottom of my triangle with one pale marble.

Mrs. Mullhouse was quick to notice the change, for upon arriving home Edwin would not dash upstairs to change into his play-clothes but would drag himself over to the staircase and pull himself slowly, slowly, slowly up by the banister. When I entered she would be waiting for me in the living room, and would subject me to anxious interrogation. Later she would come upstairs and rap with her knuckles gently twice. "Is anything wrong, Edwin?" she would say, standing in the doorway and looking almost angry with concern. "Aren't you feeling well? Do you have a fever?" And at last going over to him she would lay the back of a hand on his forehead, and then she would touch his forehead with first one cheek and then the other, and then she would stand with the backs of her hands against her hips and frown down at him as if he had broken a window. Finally she would leave, and some time later I would hear Dr. Mullhouse enter below with a rattle of blinds. A muffled conversation would be followed by the sound of his heavy step on the stairs; with a single knuckle he rapped gently three times. "Cm in," Edwin muttered from his bed, and Dr. Mullhouse would respond in one of two ways: he might open up briskly and stride in with an air of joking geniality, or he might turn the knob slowly and peek in as if he were entering a sickroom. Edwin ignored him in either case, and replied to his questions with grim reluctance, in a weary monotone, after an insufferable pause.

At dinner, according to Mrs. Mullhouse, he only pecked at his food. After dinner he said good night and dragged himself slowly, slowly, slowly up to his room. In the morning, when I arrived, he looked pale and worn, as if sleep had been a crushing labor. And at last, one morning, he did not rise at all. Mrs. Mullhouse shook him three times before his eyes opened, and when she returned a fourth time he was sitting up in bed, leaning against the venetian blinds, fast asleep. When I arrived she reported to me in detail and informed me that she had called Dr. Blumenthal. "Oh Jeff," she said, "do you think it's polio?" I assured her that it was not, but as I hurried off to school my mind teemed with images of stunted and twisted legs. The day passed with intolerable slowness. The red second-hand of the big round clock moved in its track with elaborate and unnatural slowness, as if it were moving through honey, while the tormented minute-hand, like a wounded bird, dragged its broken wing painfully forward in tiny dying jerks. That morning, for the first time, I understood the expression on George Washington's face. At the 11:30 lunch bell I hurried away from school as quickly as I could, despite a vast policeman who held out his arms as if to press me to his chest, and without stopping at my house I ran to Edwin's. But Dr. Blumenthal had not yet arrived. The afternoon passed like a long insomnia. Images of wheel chairs and white hospital beds mingled with the green adventures of Bobby and Betsy and their dog Scot. At the 3:15 bell I hurried straight to Edwin's, without even changing my clothes. Mrs. Mullhouse looked grave, and my mind toppled down a flight of stairs as I awaited her news. But Dr. Blumenthal had found nothing wrong with Edwin, nothing, that is, except fatigue and weakness. He had recommended sunshine and orange juice. "Sunshine and orange juice," said Mrs. Mullhouse, "my God, what kind of a prescription is that?" but as we spoke she drifted into the kitchen and began to fill a tall glass with orange juice. "He said there was no infection," she continued, "but he did say to call again in a few days. Now why would he want me to call again in a few days unless it was serious. Be a good boy and bring up this orange juice, won't you, Jeff, and try to get him to take a swallow, and Jeff: see if there's anything bothering him, something one of us said or did, I'm sure there's something bothering him, will you do that, Jeff?" The tall glass was so full of orange juice that she had to sip some of it herself. Holding the dangerous thing carefully in two hands I carried it upstairs. Edwin's door was closed, but not all the way, and pushing it wide open with my foot I entered the familiar dimness. Edwin lay on his back, with one arm thrown over his eyes, fast asleep. I uttered his name, but he did not stir. I closed the door quietly with my foot and proceeded to walk across the room and place the glass on the second gray bookcase. Then I sat down on the bed under the colored map of the United States. "Edwin," I called softly. "Edwin, Edwin, Edwin, Edwin, Ed . . ." A knee moved; slowly his whole body gathered itself together and began to turn toward the wall. "Edwin," I said, "it's Jeffrey"; and I heard him murmur "door." "Door?" I said, glancing at the door I had just closed; and my heart began to hammer. Rising I said softly: "What door, Edwin?" "Doze," he murmured. As I crossed the room on tiptoe the mysterious syllables, so full of possible secrets, echoed in my brain. Door . . . doze . . . doze . . . door . . . what was he trying to say? Standing over him I whispered: "What door, Edwin? What door?"—and with sudden inspiration I added: "Close what door?" His murmuring became confused, stopped altogether, and began again. I was about to give up and shake him awake when suddenly, with no more consciousness than before, but with extraordinary precision, Edwin uttered slowly the words, the burning words, the unbelievable words, that I had so grotesquely misunderstood. It was fortunate indeed that I was not holding the glass of orange juice, for at that moment it would have dropped from my astounded fingers, leaving dangerous slivers of glass in the little red rug while at my toes a dark stain soaked and spread.

# 6

HER NAME WAS ROSE DORN, she rhymed with forlorn, and Edwin was deathly in love. I had always detested her myself. She was a little blond girl with a little black kitten; she had no friends. Her mother was a witch. She alternated between fits of dreamy brooding, when chin on hand she stared with angel eyes out of windows or through walls, and fits of wild violence, destructive cold and cruel. Oh, she was always clamoring for attention. She was a small solid girl with a turned-up nose and large pale eyes. She had thick tight golden hair that she wore in two pigtails, tied with red bows; from neck to forehead her hair was combed in tight lines radiating outward from a central part. Carefully and elaborately bound, her hair was at the same time wilful and wild: pale strands uncaught by the comb lay loosely on her neck and sprang from the part in the middle of her head; often by the end of the day the tight hair in back had become unbound and hung down in long straggling waves. Her favorite dress was a short bright red one with puffed short sleeves, from which her short solid arms hung down alertly, as if she were perpetually prepared to snatch your crayons. Her posture was terrible: sliding lower and lower on her spine, she looked up innocently, raising her blond eyebrows and pointing to herself, when Mrs. Cadwallader scolded her. She was quite a little faker. During the Lord's Prayer she muttered nonsense; during the Pledge Allegiance she moved her lips silently, standing with her left hand over her chest. One day she would pretend to be utterly stupid, stumbling over the easiest words and answering no questions; the next day she would read with fluid mocking ease. Nor was her fakery always so elementary. A terrible speller, always missing early in spelling bees, she would often pretend to be feigning stupidity in order to create the impression that she was only feigning stupidity. If, for instance, she was asked to spell a difficult word like "caterpillar," she might begin easily enough with her c, a, t, and you could see that she was uncertain about the next letter; but instead of making a reasonable guess she would say, very slowly and thoughtfully: x, q, z, h, w—blinking in wide-eyed surprise when Mrs. Cadwallader told her to sit down. Hating to do seatwork, she quickly sank to the lowest reading group; spitefully she stayed where she was, at once contemptuous of the other members of her group and contemptuous of herself for not being in the top reading group. There was something wrong with her, we all knew that; she was like a page on which a waterdrop has dried, leaving a faint ripple. The Carol Stempel episode had frightened all of us, of course. But aside from that there was an unpleasant aura about Rose Dorn, a sense that warned you away unless you happened to be Edwin: a sense of remoteness and difference, as if she were an elf or bat. Those large pale eyes, that too-yellow hair, that sleek black kitten: Billy Duda said she roamed about at night, followed by her cat. They said her mother, the witch, stayed shut up all day in her house in the woods; they said she cut you up in little pieces if she caught you. They said a great many things, and I never paid attention to half of them; my point is simply that Rose Dorn inspired talk like that. Perhaps it was her wildness that attracted poor Edwin so powerfully; perhaps it was her stillness; perhaps it was only her hair. Whatever it was, she held him in her spell for six months, teasing and tormenting him without mercy. Of course she lost him in the end. God knows I hated her; God knows I once pitied her; may she rest in peace. She died horribly but dramatically, clamoring for attention even in her end; and her death spread through Edwin like an infection.

I found her the next morning standing by herself on the playground under a high window, slapping a little red ball attached by a gray rubber string to a wooden paddle. Beside her lay that shiny black kitten, licking its paws in the warm October light. It was a nasty little creature, always sneaking up on you and suddenly leaping at your leg; its ridiculous name was Gray. So absorbed was Rose Dorn in her little game that she did not notice me as in grave meditation I stood there watching her, wondering precisely how to begin. For I had been entrusted with an extremely delicate mission. Upon learning Edwin's secret I had wakened him and told him what I knew; he had grown pink, denied everything hotly, and at last poured forth his passion in a flood of incoherence. I shall spare the reader those tedious details. Suffice it to say that he had not shown so much animation in almost a month; indeed I date his recovery from the moment of his confession. As our colloquy drew to a close with the sound of Dr. Mullhouse entering down-stairs, I remembered the orange juice. Gingerly I suggested that he take a sip. To my astonishment he gulped the whole glass down. It was with an air of triumph that I descended the stairs, bearing the empty glass past Dr. Mullhouse, who was coming up with an-other glass of orange juice; and as Mrs. Mullhouse took it from me at the bottom of the stairs, she told me that she wouldn't be surprised if I grew up to be a famous doctor.

But as I stood watching Rose Dorn paddling her ball, smacking away with a thp-thp-thp, I did not feel at all like a famous doctor. I felt uneasy; I felt afraid; I felt, how shall I say, a fool. For suddenly, standing there in the bright morning light, I felt that I should never be able to carry out my task, and I cursed myself for having agreed to Edwin's plan. Indeed I was tempted to wash my hands of the whole affair, and I bitterly regret that I did not then and there turn away. In a sense it was really all my fault: without me, would Edwin ever have dared to face his blond enchantress? But the kitten was staring at me with its pale green eyes; I had given my word; the bell might ring at any moment. Taking a deep breath I stepped up to her and said: "Edwin is sick." She looked up. The red ball shot past the paddle, stopped at the end of the rubber string, shot down past the paddle on the other side, shot up in the air, and in this fashion gradually wound the string around the handle of the paddle, binding Rose Dorn's extended index finger. She continued to look at me without speaking; I felt she was mocking me in some remote outrageous way. She did not attempt to remove her finger from its rubber trap. I said: "Look at your finger." She frowned in faint incomprehension; then she looked down. Under the paddle the red ball swung back and forth beneath its few inches of rubber string. She looked up, unfrowning, and waited for me to speak. Twenty feet away a line of girls, among whom I noticed Trudy Cassidy and Donna Riccio, were chanting like savages as they waited to jump into the chaos of two swirling ropes. Stepping closer to Rose Dorn I said: "Edwin. Edwin is sick. Edwin . . ." At that moment I felt a hideous sensation on my leg. There, like a big black burr, hung Gray. I shook my leg frantically; finally I tore him off with my hands. He trotted away and began playing with a yellow chewing-gum wrapper, knocking it to one side with a paw and springing after it. Rose Dorn said nothing, but continued to stare with her pale piercing eyes: strange, those eyes, as if the irises had died one day, leaving only the bright black pupils. I was about to address her again when the bell rang. From distant corners of the playground people began running in; nearby, a noisy double line was forming at the flight of concrete steps leading up to two green doors; at the other end of the playground another line was forming at a door above a single step. I continued to stand there, transfixed with confusion; angrily I kicked at pebbles while Gray sharpened his claws on my shoes and socks. The nearby line began to climb the stairs; the far line was being gobbled up by the door; farther away, a few latecomers ran along the sidewalk and down a little slope past the willow onto the playground. I wanted them all to disappear so that I might perform my mission in peace. Were her eyes grayblue? greengray? tawny? I never knew. Behind me, the nearly empty playground was strangely quiet, and suddenly I thought of a bright crowded beach under a blue sky: a ripple of thunder, the upward-gazing faces, the folding umbrellas, the darkening air; and when, hurrying away, you look back for a moment from the crest of sand before scurrying down to the parking lot, you see, under a dark sky from which drops are already falling, the empty brown sand stretching endlessly away before the gray, dangerous, alien water. I turned abruptly. "Here," I said, sticking out a hand that held a small brown paper bag. In a low, significant tone I added: "From Edwin." She continued to stare. "Take it!" I almost shouted; with her free hand she took it, and holding one side of the bag with the four free fingers of her trapped hand, slowly she reached inside. "Hurry," I whispered, looking about; grayly the playground stretched away.

When she removed her hand she stared at her small open palm. In it lay a large pink plastic ring crowned with a transparent plastic dome in which a black needle, pointing North, trembled over a silver disk with black markings. It was a treasure from Edwin's collection of cereal-box prizes. "It's a compass-ring," I said, feeling preposterous. She slipped it onto a finger—it was much too big—and making a fist she stared at it, tilting her head to one side. "We'll be late," I said, looking about again; and suddenly she was running away toward the far door, her pigtails bumping on her back, and Gray bounding after her. On the playground, beside the wall, I noticed her bright red pencil-case. I picked it up and hurried after her, wondering if I had performed my task successfully; wondering what I would tell Edwin. Far away I saw her struggling with the heavy door; she disappeared inside, leaving Gray on the step. The second bell was already ringing as I stepped through the door into the gloom of the hall. As I turned a corner Rose Dorn leaped out at me with a shrieking boo. I have never been amused by those who tell vulgar jokes, torture animals, or leap out of hiding places at unsuspecting people. Away she ran along the hall, her pigtails bumping on her back, her finger still trapped on the wooden paddle; and as I followed, distressed to hear a nearby class already reciting the Pledge Allegiance, a presentiment of Edwin's misery came over me like a winter rain.

"She said thank you," I reported to Edwin that afternoon. His recovery, already under way, now proceeded with great rapidity. Though by no means complete, it was, as I say, rapid: that evening he ate a tremendous meal, and the next day (Saturday) he rose from bed. That weekend we held interminable confabulations concerning the unspeakable virtues of intolerable Rose Dorn. I concealed my annoyance, thinking it far wiser to listen patiently, as I have always listened, and to pass stern judgments in secret. Edwin was still heartsore, soulsad, lovesick; who was I to prick his wound? Besides, he counted on me. He himself had never addressed Rose Dorn, while I had already established a relation. And yet as the weekend moved toward Monday, I was not easy in my mind, for all too vividly I remembered what had happened to poor Carol Stempel.

# 7

CAROL STEMPEL was in the top reading group. It was her only distinction. She was a tall bony dreamy droopy girl with stringy straw-colored hair hanging halfway down her back. She wore long faded dreamy droopy dresses from which emerged pale pipe-stem arms with red elbows; she wore blue-rimmed eyeglasses, and was forever taking them off to rub the lenses with a piece of faded yellow cloth which she extracted from a dark red eyeglass case. She liked to hand out paper, collect scissors, and water the plants. She was quiet, obedient, and barely noticeable except for her height. Her goal in life was to become as useful and unobtrusive as an eraser on a chalktray. At the age of seven she already resembled an old maid.

When the strange new girl with the blond pigtails appeared, Carol Stempel at first ignored her. Rose Dorn's noisy need for attention, her fakery, her tantrums, her nasty tricks of scribbling on other people's drawings and stealing pencils—these things were as embarrassing to Carol Stempel as they were offensive to me. But by the end of the second week, when Rose Dorn's peculiarities had isolated her from the rest of the class, Carol Stempel began to follow her movements with distinct interest. Perhaps she recognized a bond. Carol too had no friends, at least no close friends, though unlike Rose Dorn she was allowed to join in games of jumprope and could always be seen standing in a group of girls. But you could tell that she was not really one of them. Her height alone condemned her to uniqueness, for despite her desperate slouch she was easily a head taller than any other girl in the class.

It was not simply that she began to watch Rose Dorn—we all did that—it was rather that she watched with such intensity. Often you could see her far away at Table 6, staring across the room at little Rose Dorn in frozen fascination, her lips parted, her eyes wide, her pencil poised above her workbook. If at such a moment the boy beside her exercised his wit by moving a hand up and down in front of her stare, she would look frightened and confused, and blushing faintly she would lower her head and begin writing frantically in her workbook. Once on the playground I saw her jumping rope, holding her eyeglass case in one hand; as she jumped up and down, her long hair jumping behind her, she stared off to the right at Rose Dorn, who stood watching with her kitten some ten feet away. When Rose Dorn began to walk in a wide circle around the girls, Carol Stempel, still jumping up and down, turned her head farther and farther until she was looking over her shoulder. I believe she would have turned her head completely around until her neck looked like a corkscrew; but the girls' shouts shattered her trance, and like a cartoon character who walks off a cliff into the air, quite at ease until he looks down and sees that the ground has vanished, so Carol Stempel, who had been jumping perfectly until then, suddenly realized that her head was turned the wrong way, and clumsy with confusion she almost fell onto the tar as the rope came cutting into her leg.

But it was more even than the intensity of her watching that marked a change in Carol Stempel: it was the development of a deep mental sympathy with Rose Dorn. She became sensitive to Rose Dorn's moods. Her restlessness made her restless; her trances calmed her. She suffered her punishments, clenching her fists and frowning in anguish as Mrs. Cadwallader shook Rose Dorn angrily by the shoulder for some piece of viciousness or other. It was as if she were being drawn into the whirlpool that was Rose Dorn. It was as if, dare I utter it, Rose Dorn had cast a spell.

I recall a morning when Carol Stempel was watering the plants. She always watered the plants with great care, neatly tilting a small blue plastic watering can that she refilled at a sink in the back of the room. She was standing at the second window from the back, moving slowly from plant to plant along the windowsill. I was sitting at my table trying not to hear the babble of the middle reading group, gathered behind me in a small semicircle at the front of the room. From where I sat I could see three quarters of Carol Stempel's face at the far window; across from me, Rose Dorn sat frowning at her workbook. She had been turning pages restlessly as usual, and giving up at last she began to hunt about for something more interesting to look at. At the back of the room she saw Carol Stempel standing at the window. She began to stare intently with those eyes of hers. Carol Stempel was standing on her toes, holding the spout of her watering can over the rim of a red plastic flowerpot from which a dark green plant overflowed. Behind me a whining voice continued to mispronounce every other word; there was a sound of turning pages; I turned around to look up at the clock beside the flag. Suddenly there was a crash and cry. Mrs. Cadwallader jerked up her head. I whirled around. Carol Stempel, holding her cheeks in horror, stared at the watering can at her toes, from which a puddle of water was darkly pouring. Across from me, Rose Dorn was writing away in her workbook.

The climax came one stormy afternoon in early October. The sky had been clear all morning, but clouds began to appear in the early afternoon; by 1:30 a dark thunderhead had spread over half the sky like a seeping stain. Edwin loved days like that: inside, the high hanging lights were turned on, shedding over everyone a rich warm intimate yellow glow, while outside, like a piece of bromide paper in a pan of developer, the bright sky darkened into storm. Through the windows you could see paper bags and scraps of waxpaper tumbling across the deserted playground. The pale willow, drained of color, rippled like a curtain. The class was restless, waiting for the rain; heads at tables kept rising from workbooks to look out at the sky, and it was all Mrs. Cadwallader could do to keep the attention of the top reading group. I was relieved when the group broke up, for Edwin had received several warning glares. Back at his seat he barely pretended to work, but stared out the window with an eager and intense look. Someone gasped as a metal rattle sounded; we all stood up to look through the windows at a madly rolling garbage-can cover that came rattling past our windows, sweeping away from the building in a long wobbling curve and falling at last loudly on its back, where it shuddered to rest like a vast nickel. And still the rain did not fall. The restlessness swelled to excitement as a faint patter of thunder rippled across the gloom. Edwin especially could barely contain himself, for he loved to be frightened by thunder: seated in warm yellow light, on the bright side of darkness, on the warm side of coldness, on the still side of the wind, he loved to abandon himself to danger. Rose Dorn did not share the general enthusiasm. She was restless, certainly, but in a strained uncomfortable way. At the first patter of thunder she had looked up nervously; returning to her drawing, she grasped her crayon not in her fingers but in her fist, and proceeded to make fierce looping scrawls all over her paper.

Quite suddenly, with a sound of crumpled cellophane, it began to rain. The drops were immense; within minutes the playground was uniformly dark. The wind flung rain against our windows with a sound of fingernails against glass, and scraped the gleaming garbage-can cover in short sharp bursts across the tar. A zigzag flash of lightning sawed the sky in half, followed by words like CRASH! and BOOM! Edwin's nostrils flared; flushed and bright-eyed he searched the sky, as if anything so loud had to be visible. But Rose Dorn sat with her hands pressed over her ears. I remember noticing Carol Stempel: she sat working at her table in the back of the room, resting an elbow on a book and leaning her forehead on the palm of her hand; the fingers were spread over her head like a claw. Two-pronged lightning flashed; I counted to five; and the sound that followed made me think of a gleaming giant in technicolor with gold bracelets on his wrists, slowly swinging a hammer against a vast golden gong. Rain lashed the windows; the dark willow was barely visible on its dripping slope. Hardly had the last ripple of thunder died away when again the lightning came, a precise enormous many-veined flash that stood fixed for an instant, transforming the heavens into a vast nervous system: in the pale intense light, monstrous black telephone poles stuck up into the livid sky; far away white houses gleamed; and palely luminous through the sheeted rain, white crossbeams of distant frontyard fences gleamed. It was a magic moment, like a silver sparkle in roadside grass; but the longed-for dime is only the circle of silver paper on the cork lining of a bottlecap, and darkness, like a sadness, reclaimed the sky. I counted to five, but nothing happened. Donna Riccio rose from her seat and went up to Mrs. Cadwallader at her desk in the front of the room. Mrs. Cadwallader was explaining that the word was "rural," not "ruler," when the thunder began. It

started as a faint rumble, as of a distant train, and you had the feeling that you were lying on a track as the train came closer, growing
louder and louder as in vain you struggled to get free, growing
louder and louder but not yet appearing, growing so loud that
when at last it appeared you could not understand how so small a
spot could make so loud a noise, growing larger and larger and
louder and louder until it loomed above you like a falling mountain
and you shut your eyes and lay back and let it come hurtling over
you like the end of the world. For a moment I thought a window
had shattered. Only as the shock subsided did I realize that Rose
Dorn was screaming. She was holding her fists against her ears and
shrieking at the top of her lungs; her eyes were squeezed shut and
her face was twisted. Mrs. Cadwallader vastly rose. But suddenly,
as she made her way around the side of her desk, another shriek
began. Across the room, hands pressed against her ears and face
contorted, Carol Stempel howled in anguish while the boy beside
her, leaning away, stared in troubled fascination.

A week later, Carol Stempel was moved to another second-grade
class. I believe that saved her. I saw her sometimes on the playground, sticking up out of a new group of girls in her towering
slouch.

# 8

ON THE CORNER of a small shady side-street, across from the tall
wire fence that borders the playground above a kind of cliff or
steep drop, stands Rapolski's. To the right, as you enter through a
door set in the angle of two windows, stands the shining globe of
a bubblegum machine on its black base, resting on a recess before
a tall window with red backward letters. On the left, before a
window with green backward letters, lies a low glass case covered
with brown wood and containing pencil cases, erasers, colored
pads, yellow pencils, brass fasteners, and bottles of blue-black ink.
Beside it lies a taller glass counter with a sloping face, filled with
black licorice pipes, red licorice shoestrings, red-hots, packages of
bubblegum cards, black mustaches, packages of white pumpkin

seeds, packages of black Indian seeds, chocolate babies, root-beer barrels, Mary Janes. The tall sloping counter stretches past the window with green backward letters and continues in front of a wall that is hung to the ceiling with rubber daggers, plastic water pistols, whistles with white balls inside, strips of tattoos, false noses, one-way silver eyeglasses, handlebar mustaches, black masks, silver masks, rubber cameras, blue harmonicas. On top of the glass counter sit bright orange-and-green yo-yo's, small blue boxes of red caps for pistols, odorous stacks of bubblegum cards, turning stands hung with potato chips in waxpaper bags and small games wrapped in cellophane, and a transparent plastic container attached to a standing piece of cardboard, holding a layer of brown pennies mixed with nickels, for the March of Dimes. Old Rapolski stands behind the counter, smiling with broken teeth and watching with small dark suspicious eyes; across from him, before the dark windowless wall filled with shelves of cookies and cans, the older boys stand in noisy groups, flipping cards, combing their hair, drinking soda out of bottles, and playing crude games like Paper Scissors Stone.

The morning of Edwin's return was a bright gray morning. Even as we crossed the wide busy street in front of the school, past the wide busy policeman with his arms held out, Edwin began to look about anxiously to the right of the building, where a narrow flight of stone steps, bounded by the wire fence, led up to the high playground from the shady side-street. Slowly we climbed the wide flight of steps between the tree-covered slopes in front; more slowly we walked to the right along the high sidewalk that led to the top of the narrow stone steps; and as we turned to the left onto the side playground, through the space between the school and the wire fence, Edwin stopped in his tracks and searched the crowd nervously. His gaze swept along the wire fence on his right, turning where it turned to run along the shady side-street, and returning suspiciously to the massive oak that sprang out of the cement in the angle of the fence. An unknown girl stepped out from behind the tree. Turning away, Edwin walked slowly along the side of the school toward the back, gazing about and smiling at absolutely no one. At the corner of the building he stopped. Together we looked out at the crowded playground in back. It was only a matter of seconds before we saw the yellow pigtails: they were far away on the other side of the playground, near the willow on the narrow grass slope. Quickly Edwin withdrew to the safety of the side wall, peeping out from time to time to make certain that he was not taken by surprise.

In class he buried himself in his seatwork. Only once did I see his eyes rise from the page in the direction of my table, but he quickly lowered them as he met my stern gaze. She herself was having one of her good days, minding her own business and keeping quiet; twice she turned around in her seat, but luckily he was bent over his workbook. I had noticed immediately, with a mixture of relief and annoyance, that she was not wearing his ring. Of course he had noticed too. But after the lunch bell he did not hound me with anxious questions, as I had feared; instead, not looking me in the eye, he said that he had to go to Rapolski's. "You'll be late for lunch," I said, but I had the distinct impression that he did not know what I was saying. At Rapolski's he brooded intensely through the glass counter and even reached up to one of the wire stands on top, turning it slowly, like a fifth-grader.

Mrs. Mullhouse was disturbed by our late arrival. She was even more disturbed by our early departure, for Edwin insisted on leaving for school before the usual time. Back at Rapolski's he quickly made up his mind. His purchase surprised me: I had expected nothing less than a rubber spider. But perhaps he did not wish to overdo it; perhaps he wished to learn if she shared his taste; perhaps he had only five cents left (at this time he was receiving an allowance of fifteen cents a week). Even before he turned to me, looking directly at my nose, I knew that I was the one who had to deliver the goods.

The playground was practically deserted when we arrived. Edwin paced up and down before the tall wire fence, looking down at the little side-street along which Rose Dorn always came to school; a block past Rapolski's, the familiar street became suddenly strange, inhabited by tall frowning houses and dark twisted trees. Slowly the playground filled from three directions: from the wide busy street in front of the school, from the long sidewalk that bordered the far side, and from the flight of narrow stone steps that led up from the shady side-street, immediately across from Rapolski's. "Maybe she's sick," I ventured; he gave me a ravaged glance that made me feel ashamed. She appeared just behind a group of three girls who were walking arm in arm along the sidewalk, marching in step and giggling. She was dressed in her bright red coat with its hood in back, and as she walked she held her arms straight out at her sides, swinging them together for a clap and swinging them apart as far as they would go. Gray bounded along beside her, stopping now and then to pounce on a piece of cellophane. Edwin clung for a few moments to the wire fence, his fingers curled through the diamond-shaped openings; then he dashed over to me, uttered some nonsense or other, and immediately headed for a remote corner of the playground, beyond the willow, where the tar passed into dirt and weeds.

I took up my position against the oak in the angle of the wire fence, with Rapolski's behind me and the narrow stone steps on my left. I watched her head rising above the level of the playground as she climbed the steps on the other side of the fence; seen through the wire she resembled a jigsaw puzzle. As she turned in through the opening between the fence and the school, she saw me leaning against the tree but pretended not to. She walked along the inside of the fence, looking down at the steps and dragging a popsicle stick along the wire; she passed within two feet of me with her clicking stick. As she disappeared behind the tree the clicking stopped; I waited, but she failed to emerge along the fence on the other side. Sighing, I pushed myself erect, turned to the left, and proceeded to walk around the tree. To my surprise she was not standing in the angle of the fence. She was not standing anywhere; she had disappeared; and it was with an eerie feeling that I continued to walk around the tree until I had made a complete circle. Perhaps she had spread her arms and flapped away into the sky, perhaps she had fallen through the spaces in the fence onto the street below, perhaps she had simply melted away. I was pondering these possibilities when suddenly I felt a hideous sensation on my leg. I tore the vile thing off, suffering a nasty scratch, and hurried around the tree, just in time to see the end of a pigtail whisk out of sight. But I was not about to be made a fool of twice. I stopped, turned, and tiptoed in the other direction. She was standing with her back to me, bending forward and peering in the wrong direction; one pigtail lay on her back, the other hung down in front, invisible. Sharply I tapped her on the shoulder. She whirled around. A momentary look of wide-eyed terror gave way to narrow-eyed anger. She looked as if she wanted to punch me in the nose. I was determined to waste no time. "From Edwin," I said, holding out to her five long narrow strips of white paper covered with hard sugar spots in neat rows: two pink, two lavender, and one pale yellow. They were his favorite candy at this time: starting from the upper left-hand corner he loved to eat the bits of sugar from left to right, tearing each spot from the paper neatly with his teeth. She took them sullenly, as if she were doing me a favor. Suddenly she stuck the end of one strip in her mouth, letting it hang like a tongue, and looked up at me with a ridiculous false grin. I frowned in disgust. She frowned back, imitating me. Annoyed, I crossed my arms over my chest; she crossed her arms over her chest; I put my hands in my pockets; she put her hands in her pockets; finally I could stand it no longer and said: "Stop that." "Stop that," she mimicked, and the paper tongue fell; I frowned; she frowned; and I was wondering how to disentangle myself from this madness when all at once her face emptied and she began to stare past me into the distance. I feared a trick; if I turned, would she disappear? As she stared, again I felt a sense of something alien about Rose Dorn; for one brief moment I thought she was trying to cast a spell. I was relieved, this time, by the sound of the bell. She continued to stare, and I must confess that I had a start when, turning at last, I saw lone Edwin far away, standing on the grass slope beside the willow, slashing the grass with a willow switch.

# 9

I THINK Edwin would have been happy to pursue matters in-definitely in this distant manner, using me as a firescreen to protect him from that dangerous flame; unfortunately he had not reckoned with Rose Dorn. She was a bold little hussy, if the truth be told. Not that she liked him especially. In fact, I believe she actually disliked him from the start. But she liked to be liked; she loved to be loved; as I have said, she was always clamoring for attention. Edwin's fascination fascinated her. How could she fail to advertise it?

At my table the next morning I was in for a surprise. Rose Dorn sat over her workbook, drawing ears on the picture of a ball; but that was nothing. It was her left hand that startled me. Resting on the table, it was clenched in a fist; on the third finger loomed the pink compass-ring. Between her finger and the top of the ring was a space through which you might have inserted a straw.

By the end of the week everyone knew that Edwin loved Rose Dorn. Oh, she made sure of that. On the playground she showed people the compass-ring, saying: "Lookit what Edwin gamey." In class she spun around to catch him looking at her; blushing brightly, he tried to disappear. In the coatroom she would walk up to him and stare until he blushed; then pointing a finger she shouted: "He's blushing! He's blushing!" On Thursday a white-chalked heart appeared on the strip of concrete under the bricks in back, bearing the legend:

E.M.
L
R.D.

The sudden crude publicity of his private passion shocked shy Edwin; it was as if he were made to walk naked on the playground while everyone giggled and stared. And yet I cannot help wondering whether in some fashion he found it reassuring. For weeks he had burned in a private fever: might not the public side of things constitute a kind of proof of intimacy, a formal declaration that she was now bound to him, as their initials were bound in a heart of chalk? Even so, he was not prepared for the violence that first emerged that Friday afternoon. We had entered the side playground as usual and were making our way toward the back. Near the corner stood a group of girls, among whom were Trudy

Cassidy, Donna Riccio, and Diana Walsh. They had been watching
us, and as we passed they suddenly broke into a loud chant:

> *Edwin and Rosie*
> *In a tree*
> *Kay eye ess ess eye en gee!*

They sang it over and over, shrieking with savage glee, flinging the
words like sticks and stones; stunned and bleeding, Edwin stag-
gered away.

It was not until the following Monday that Edwin dared to approach her. Meanwhile he kept his distance, peeping and blushing,
while she stood in various poses in the spaces of his day, paddling
her ball, playing with her kitten, or simply staring. He received
his allowance on Sunday, and on Monday morning before the bell
he hurried over to Rapolski's, where after much brooding he purchased, for two cents, a hideous pair of red wax lips. To my surprise and relief he did not ask me to deliver them, but stuck them in
his pocket and hurried back to the playground. The bell had already rung and the line was moving forward. She was standing off
to one side—she never stood in line when she could help it—
paddling her ball while Gray leaped up at it with his claws. While
I kept my eye on Gray, Edwin stood with his hands in his pockets,
staring up at a little white cloud. As we passed Rose Dorn I saw
him withdraw a hand from his pocket. He turned; and staring suddenly at his toes he burst into a blush and passed on. As we passed
through the door she was still standing there, paddling away over
her leaping kitten.

He lingered in the coatroom, casting his fevered gaze along the
dark double row of coats toward the hall. She entered at last, seeing
us instantly and staring boldly at us as she moved along, holding
out an arm and brushing the coats she passed. Edwin reached into
the pocket of his hanging coat and threw me a look that was meant
to make me invisible. Quickly and judiciously I stepped into the
room.

At once poor Edwin came shooting out behind me. He looked
as if he had seen a ghost. Sliding into his seat as one might crawl

under a blanket, he assumed a rigid position and held his breath. In the corner of his right fist, a piece of red wax was visible.

She was there before us on the playground after lunch, standing beside the wide oak in the angle of the wire fence. As he stepped onto the playground through the space between the building and the fence, Edwin hesitated briefly; then firmly, as if he had come to some tremendous decision, striding sternly forward and looking neither left nor right, he hurried along the side of the school and turned the corner, shutting her out of view.

The long coatroom was shared by four classes, each of which had its section and its time. At the 3:10 bell our class filed in through the door in the back of the room, picked up its coats, and quickly returned to the room to wait for the second bell. On this particular day everyone except Edwin and Rose Dorn had returned to the room; I myself happened to be crouching on the other side of the rack, reaching for a lost glove. Under the row of coats four legs were visible. Below her right knee was a small white bandaid; on her left knee a double scratch stood out darkly against a bright red background of mercurochrome. "I've got this stupid thing," said Edwin, and they were the first words he had ever uttered to her. "Where is that stupid thing anyway. This is such a stupid coatroom. Oh where is that stupid thing. I don't know why I bought this stupid thing. You probably wouldn't want it anyway. Here. You can throw the dumb thing out if you don't want it. This is such a dumb school. I think I'll go to China."

Poor Edwin. He was not an eloquent lover.

# 10

AH, THOSE GIFTS! He gave her black licorice pipes with red sugar on the bowl, red licorice shoestrings, black licorice twist. He gave her chocolate babies, root-beer barrels, round red-hots, sugary orange slices, little red hearts that burned your tongue, triangular pieces of candy corn colored white and orange and yellow, squares of butterscotch wrapped in cellophane, strawberry candy that came in aluminum tins with little aluminum spoons, clusters of rock candy crystals growing on white string. He gave her five chocolate coins wrapped in gold foil, in a pouch of green netting tied with gold string. He gave her pieces of large pink bubblegum wrapped in blue paper and containing little colored comic strips. He gave her small wax bottles filled with sweet syrup: biting off the wax bottlecaps she sucked out the orange, raspberry, and lime.

He played the bubblegum machine passionately for her sake, giving her balls of white gum and black gum, red gum and yellow gum, green gum and orange gum, and all the prizes: miniature boxes of Quaker Oats, miniature red hot dogs in miniature brown buns, white teeth set in pink gums, little white baseballs with black trim, cream-colored lightbulbs that glowed blue in the dark, silver rings with green and red and yellow domes, little blue ships in little clear bottles, and colored charms with tiny loops on top: red dogs, green roosters, white Indians, green Indians, blue hearts, black pistols, green hands, green heads.

He gave her prizes from boxes of cereal: a small round magnifying glass with a clear transparent plastic handle, a blue plastic coin with an eagle on it, a star-shaped silver marshal's badge with a copper-colored pin in back, small tin cowboy buttons which you attached to a shirt pocket by folding back the prong on top, a red plastic caboose, a black plastic engine, a green rubber soldier wrapped in cellophane, tin railroad signs (Illinois Central, Southern Pacific Lines, Lackawanna Railroad), white plastic billboard-frames with colorful paper advertisements to insert, a five-hundred-dollar bill (THAT AIN'T HAY), a slim package of green clay, and the rings: a red watch-ring whose painted black hands pointed to three o'clock, a white ring through whose clear top you saw a clown alternately smile and cry, a blue ring with a blue telescope mounted on top, an olive-colored ring whose top opened up for secret messages, a yellow ring whose clear dome held a cowboy's face and two silver balls, an orange ring with an oval mirror set in the top, a black cowboy ring with a gold cattle-brand.

He gave her a black wax mustache and wax false teeth. When she wore the teeth to class, Mrs. Cadwallader took them away.

He gave her a magic trick consisting of a black ball, a blue plastic cup shaped like an egg and perched on a slim blue stand, and a circular blue disk that fitted exactly between the halves of the cup and held in its center, like the crown of a hat, the top half of a false black ball.

He gave her a blue-black plastic inkstain, a black rubber spider, a red rubber frankfurter, a white rubber fried egg with a yellow rubber bullseye, a yellow rubber pencil with a black rubber point. He gave her a brown rubber dog-dirt, but Mrs. Cadwallader took it away.

He gave her a dagger with a black rubber handle and a silver rubber blade. He gave her a gray plastic dagger with a retractable blade: she liked to stab herself in the heart and die, falling onto the playground with her pigtails streaming.

He gave her a dark green rubber frog attached by a rubber tube to a pink rubber ball: when you squeezed the ball the frog gave a hop. He gave her a yellow plastic chicken that stood on green plastic legs: when you pushed down on the chicken, a white egg came out.

He gave her fistfuls of glossy jumping beans, shaped like Mrs. Mullhouse's allergy pills. When she placed them on the table they rolled over and over, like tormented bugs.

He gave her a strip of blue tattoos. When she returned from the lavatory her right arm was covered up to the elbow by a blurred blue anchor, a blurred blue heart and arrow, a blurred blue eagle, a blurred blue angel, and a blurred blue sailor with a blurred blue hat smoking a blurred blue pipe.

He gave her a ten-cent balsawood airplane and a piece of stiff paper covered with shiny decals: under a thin stream of tapwater Edwin loosened, like a layer of colorless skin from a suntanned shoulder, a delicate and transparent sheath, containing a white star in a blue circle from which blue striped bands extended on the left and right; and holding the sticky shining emblem over a wing, carefully he pressed it into place. But she gave the airplane to Gray and attached to the pale side of her table two blue stars, the letters U.S.A., and the number 47, before Mrs. Cadwallader caught her.

He gave her one Japanese fan with blue mountains and yellow boats on it and another Japanese fan with a white Japanese lady on it. He gave her a special fan that opened in an unusual way: grasping the bamboo strips at the bottom you drew them apart as if you were pulling on a wishbone, bringing them around in a full circle until they lay side by side; and as they opened, soft paper dyed in bright colors stretched and opened like a flower.

One morning Edwin entered the playground, walked along the side of the building, passed the corner, and suddenly stopped. Ten feet away, Rose Dorn in her bright red coat was standing before two older boys with tall blond hair; one stood with his hands in his pockets while the other rested his hands on top of an upside-down bat. She was wearing a pair of one-way silver eyeglasses, which covered her eyes like a silver mirror and reflected a piece of one boy's face. In her yellow hair was a large red paper rose. Her fingers were full of colorful plastic rings and on each arm she wore a jingling bracelet of colorful charms. In her left hand she held an open Japanese fan. In her right hand she held a red-tipped candy cigarette that she raised to her lips and lowered, lifting her chin and blowing white breath-smoke into the bright chill air.

# 11

ALTHOUGH ROSE DORN liked Edwin's gifts, she showed no sign whatever of liking Edwin. It is true enough that she liked to torment him. Often, when Edwin arrived on the playground, she would start to run away, looking over her shoulder to make sure he was following; and handing me his books he would set off after her. On and on they ran, weaving through games of tag and ring-a-lievio, around lines of jumproping girls and groups of card-flipping boys, past faces staring up in the air at a pink rubber ball that someone had flung against a brick wall, between two boys who were shaking their fists at one another three times in preparation for shooting out their fingers, up the grass slope, around the willow, down the grass slope, past the basketball court onto the distant part of the playground where the tar turned into dirt and weeds, then back again, Rose Dorn well ahead of Edwin but losing all the time, running easily on short strong legs that moved back and forth very quickly, so that you were reminded of a fleeing cartoon character whose legs and feet are represented as a blurred spinning circle, while Edwin, slowly gaining, ran with long awkward curiously delicate strides, landing gently on his toes as if he were afraid of disturbing people, as one might run through a library, until at last, anticipating one of her many turns, suddenly he caught up to her, holding onto her shoulder and forcing her to stop; and still grasping her with one hand he would stand bent over slightly, smiling and flushed and breathless, unable to talk, holding the other hand against his thin heaving chest, while Rose Dorn screamed and squirmed and flailed her arms and even kicked at his shins until she broke loose; and running off she would again look over her shoulder at poor Edwin, who again set off after her in long, awkward, delicate, exhausted strides.

Another of her favorite games was to separate me from Edwin. She would come over to us on the playground and say that she had a secret for Edwin; and turning to me with a look full of shame and sorrow, he would watch me go off by myself while Rose Dorn, making him bend to her, uttered between the frame of her hands loud sounds of feigned whispering: pssh-pssh-pssh-pssh-pssh.

She liked to humiliate Edwin. Once she went up to Mario Antonio, kicked him in the leg, and ran to startled Edwin for protection. Mario, whose fourth-grade brother Tony was already well known in Juvenile Court, brushed Edwin aside, knocked her to the ground, and sat on her stomach and pinned her arms while she shrieked and kicked. Poor ineffectual Edwin could find nothing better to do than tug gently at Mario's sleeve, saying: "Hey, come on, stop it." Mario simply ignored him. Finally Edwin ran off to find help, or to disappear, or to die, but before he got very far Mario had already gone back to his friends. Rose Dorn never bothered Mario again, but that evening Edwin burst into tears. For the next week he beat up pillows and imaginary Marios, falling backward onto his bed, kicking Mario into the air, and leaping nimbly on him as he hit the floor. He spoke of buying a pair of boxing gloves, but he never did.

It was with no small concern that I saw Edwin beginning to go the way of Carol Stempel. Oh, not that he shrieked and dropped things; nothing so obvious as that. But he began to have the same curious sympathy with Rose Dorn that Carol Stempel had had. Her fits oppressed him; her restlessness infected him; her habits obsessed him. Unwittingly, as it seemed to me, he began to imitate her. He picked up her habit, for instance, of swinging her arms together in a clap and swinging them apart as far as they would go. He imitated her way of standing against a wall or tree with one foot resting heel-first on the surface behind her. She had a way of pushing her lower lip out and down like a kind of flap, so that she seemed to have no upper lip and a vast underlip; one day when I looked up from my table I saw him sitting with his lip folded down, gazing off in a Dornish trance, quite unaware that he resembled an idiot. When it was her turn during a spelling bee she sometimes frowned, puffed out her cheeks, and placed the tip of her forefinger on her lower lip. The first time I saw Edwin do that I told him that he looked like Rose Dorn; he blushed and never repeated it. But he picked up her habit of sitting in her seat with both elbows sticking through the space between the wide wooden slat on top and the narrow slat below. For a while he imitated her unspeakable habit of suddenly banishing a smile or laugh from her face and staring at you without expression; I believe she considered such insolence amusing. She was fond of sticking out her tongue, but thank God Edwin never sank to that.

She had a whole series of faces, three of which I saw Edwin perform for Karen: her Chinese face, made by pulling the corners of her eyes with her forefingers; her idiot face, made by crossing her eyes and pulling the corners of her mouth with her hooked pinkies; and her sick face, made by pulling down the skin under her eyes, letting her jaw hang slackly, and letting her tongue hang out.

To my horror he began to pick up her verbal expressions as well. She was fond of saying "Thank a-*you*," and Edwin began to say it constantly, angering everyone. "Thank a-*you*," he would say to

Mrs. Mullhouse as she served each item of his lunch. "Thanks, mom. Thank a-*you*." He assimilated several mispronunciations: "o-weez" (always), "prolly" (probably), "innit" (isn't it), "chock-lit" (chocolate), "Mondee" (Monday), "rayroad" (railroad), and "crane" (crayon). Other Dornisms that crept into his speech included: "It's Howdy Doody time" (in answer to the question, "What time is it?"), "goody goody gumdrops," "scaredy pants," "fa crine out loud," and "poopy" (a vulgar expression). She was fond of making vulgar sounds in class, and to my great disgust Edwin began to practice them on the way home from school, placing his tongue between his lips and sputtering with positive gusto.

And yet, despite these distressing instances of spiritual intimacy, in other ways he was barely closer to her than in the days of his distant fever. Of course there was the daily gift, followed by the daily tease. But even then he rarely spoke to her. For that matter he was rarely alone with her; indeed he rarely got near her at all. The only real opportunities for doing so were in the morning and afternoon before the bell, but as the weather grew colder Rose Dorn, like everyone else, began to arrive as late as possible. Even in very bad weather, when we were allowed to enter early, we had to sit quietly at our own tables until the bell. And during the day they were together only in the sense that they shared the same room. It may be necessary to remind the reader how, in those days, one's table was a personal island in an impersonal archipelago, bearing to the other islands a relation similar to that borne by one's own room to the other rooms in the house. Like it or lump it, as Mrs. Mullhouse might say, one's table was the center around which the schoolday turned. The only serious challenge to table-intimacy was the reading group that assembled at the front of the class, where table-democracy was replaced briefly by the hierarchy of intellect. Here Edwin and I met twice daily for twenty minutes at a time; but of course Rose Dorn was not in our group. And yet these meetings of the top reading group were points of high excitement in Edwin's day, for on his way to the front of the room he always passed Rose Dorn. Carrying his chair awkwardly against his leg, for we were forbidden to push our chairs along the floor, gripping it by the sides and leaning backward as he walked, struggling forward with clumsy steps, his face flushed, the tendons of his neck visible, Edwin tried to erase all signs of exertion from his face and to assume a look of casual ease, of utter boredom, as if the heavy chair he was carrying weighed no more than a pencil. Rose Dorn sat with her back to him, on the side of the table close to the wide uneven aisle formed by Tables 1, 3, and 6 on the left, and 2, 4, and 5 on the right (a numbering system that infuriated me), and as Edwin worked his way toward the front I could sense his growing excitement. Usually she sat perfectly still, so that gradually her right ear must have appeared, and part of her right cheek, and her eyelashes, and the line of her nose. Practically upon her, he would gaze down at the part in the middle of her hair, when suddenly she would look up, making him flinch and blush and stumble forward in a last burst of energy to the assembling semicircle in the front of the room, where he would drop his chair loudly to an invariable: "How many times have I told you *not* to throw your chair down"—as if he had flung it down like a baseball glove.

The possibilities of closeness were increased during play period, though closeness was rarely achieved. Twice daily during good weather we went outside for twenty minutes at a time, during which we held relay races and played such games as Dodgeball, Kickball, Drop the Handkerchief, Cat and Mouse, and Giant Step. Edwin looked forward eagerly to circular games because of the possibility that he might hold her hand; though when at last, during Drop the Handkerchief, he found himself actually doing so, he was thrown into a state of such utter confusion that when the handkerchief fell behind her he was unable to let go, but gripped her hand more tightly and stared in horror as Rose Dorn tugged and screamed. Once, during a relay race in which we had to stand in line with our legs apart and push a dodgeball through the tunnel to the end of the line, where the last person picked up the ball and ran to the front to begin again, Edwin stood directly behind Rose Dorn. At one point, bending over to push the ball through, he bumped his head against her behind, and straightened up in such panic that if she had not happened to roll the ball straight through his legs he would not have known what to do; while she, straightening up and placing both hands on her bumped behind, looked over her shoulder at him with a shameless grin.

As the weather worsened we played indoors (Red Fox, One Two Three Red Light, Dog and Bone, Simon Says, Hucka Bucka Beanstalk, Good Morning Judge, King and Queen). I shall report two occasions upon which Chance decreed that Edwin and Rose Dorn should play out their little drama in public. The first occurred during Good Morning Judge. Edwin was seated in the chair at the front of the room with his back to the class and his eyes closed. He had guessed five people in a row and seemed infallible. Mrs. Cadwallader looked around carefully and finally pointed to Rose Dorn. Sliding silently from her chair, she tiptoed quietly across the room to the windows and then, to fool him, stamped from the direction of Table 2. Standing behind him, in a high squeaky voice she said: "Good morning, Judge." Instantly Edwin's neck, as if it were a pale fruitjuice container into which cherry-flavored Kool-Aid had been poured, darkened perceptibly. "Ummmmm," he said, in a ridiculous imitation of uncertainty—"Donna?" "No!" squeaked the voice. "Ummmmm . . . uhhhhh . . . Billy?" "No!" squeaked the voice. "Ummmmm . . . uh . . . oh, I don't know . . . ummmmm . . . rrrrr—Rose?" "He cheated!" she cried, turning passionately to Mrs. Cadwallader as sly Edwin shyly turned, his neck now resembling a fruitjuice container into which cranberry juice had been poured.

But she made him suffer for a whole week because of a game of King and Queen. Rose Dorn's thick hair formed a flattish surface that was excellent for carrying erasers, and she would have been one of the best players in the class if it were not for her tendency to cheat in every possible way. Edwin's narrow and relatively sharp skull made it difficult for him to balance an eraser, but he was one of the fastest walkers in the class. It promised to be an exciting contest. They started against the wall across from the windows: Edwin stood by the front door and Rose Dorn stood by the back door with an eraser on her head. At the word "go," uttered by Mrs. Cadwallader as if she were commanding

them to leave the room at once and never come back, they both
began walking, Rose Dorn in little quick steps and Edwin in long
dipping strides that made his head seem to bob up and down above
the waves of his body. Halfway across the back of the room the
eraser fell and the girls shrieked; Rose Dorn hastily replaced it,
but with her first step it began to slide, and though she tipped her
head to balance it, by the third step it had fallen again; so that by
the time she rounded the back wall and began to walk along the
windows, Edwin was almost halfway across the back wall, dipping
and rising over his long legs. Halfway along the windows the
eraser again began to fall, but this time Rose Dorn, breaking the
rules, reached up and set it straight. The boys began to shout,
the girls were silent, and Edwin rounded the corner on his way after
her. Rose Dorn cut her corner, the little cheater, and began hurrying along the front of the room, but as she broke into a brief illegal
run the eraser fell again, bouncing on her shoulder, hitting the
floor with a puff of chalk, and tumbling away; as she leaped after
it she saw Edwin some ten paces away, striding along with glittering eyes in an expressionless face, as if he were insane; and she
cast at him a look of burning hatred. The class was yelling as
Edwin rounded the corner and came grimly gliding along the
front wall, some five steps away from Rose Dorn. Clearly losing
control as she neared the last corner, again she dropped the eraser,
this time catching it in her hands, and illegally placing it on her
head without stopping. As she scurried around the corner the
eraser began to slide but she held it in place with her hand while
angry shouts from the boys prompted a warning from Mrs. Cadwallader. But as Edwin rounded the corner he was only two steps
behind her, he was holding out his arm and straining forward
with his fingertips, gaining on her little by little; and just as she
passed the front door and approached the blackboard, some twenty
steps away from her starting point, he touched her lightly on the
shoulder. She slumped forward, grasped her shoulder in false pain,
and began to shriek "He pushed me! He pushed me!"—and as
the eraser hit the floor, sending up a cloud of chalk, she burst into
tears of rage, while cheers went up from the middle of the room,
and shocked Edwin, pale and open-mouthed, stared at her as if at

a china statuette that he had knocked from a mantelpiece onto the fireplace bricks.

If the schoolday itself afforded few chances for intimacy, the long hours after school afforded none at all. For Rose Dorn always went straight home. Edwin himself was under strict orders to return from school at once, though I think he would have lingered if she had given him half a chance; as it was, all he could hope for was a final stare. In two different lines they filed out through the front doors and down the steps to the high sidewalk. There she turned left with her line on her way to the stone steps that descended to the side-street, while Edwin and I continued straight ahead with our line, descending another flight of steps to the wide sidewalk at the edge of the dangerous road with its blue policeman. Sometimes he would have to wait a long time before the policeman allowed us to cross. Then turning to the left on his way home, and hurrying along to the first cross-street on our side, where a patrol-boy with a white stripe and a silver badge stood like a miniature policeman, he would look across to Rose Dorn's side, where sometimes he would see, beyond the tall cliff of the playground, in a perspective formed by a stone wall and a row of tall black trees, a patch of yellow over a bright red coat.

# 12

I SUPPOSE IT WAS INEVITABLE that he should follow her home. It happened after school one pale December day, when the sky resembled a vast frozen lake in which a cold yellow coin lay trapped. He had tried to get rid of me by requesting some preposterous favor that instantly put me on my guard. The three of us must have presented quite a sight to anyone spying from a distant rooftop: Rose Dorn skipping along beside her kitten and stopping now and then to write with a piece of chalk on the sidewalk; Edwin skulking along a block or so behind her, peeping out from behind trees and ducking behind garbage cans; and I skulking along behind Edwin. A block past Rapolski's we entered the strange land that we had glimpsed through the wire fence: dark twisted trees, like grim giants, rose up on all sides to guard the tall pale black-windowed houses, separated by black driveways and thin strips of lawn, while big brown hedges with white gates between them shut up the little front yards. I felt as if I were being drawn into some old storybook with towering illustrations; when I looked back, the real world had dwindled to a strip of light between the cliff of the playground and Rapolski's. At first the sidewalks on both sides were crowded with children going home from school, but as we proceeded the crowd thinned to a trickle; a last child turned; only Rose Dorn walked on. Her sidewalk chalkings turned out to be destructive scribbles over other people's initials, or unpleasant and meaningless scrawls: circles that did not join up, backward S's, uneven zigzags, fragments of stars. At last she turned to the right, looking back just as Edwin ducked into a driveway; I was stationed behind a tree. I waited for Edwin to turn the corner and then I hurried after them. When I reached the corner I saw a narrow street rising into the sky, flanked by peeling gray two-story houses with empty clotheslines stretched between them, as if they were being held up by ropes. They had tilted antennas on their roofs and staircases zigzagging down their sides; the sidewalks were full of garbage cans. I saw Rose Dorn at the top of the hill, silhouetted against the pale sky; she turned to the left behind a black drugstore as Edwin emerged from behind three garbage cans. Quickly I climbed toward the high black drugstore, which as I came closer revealed itself to be dark green; and stepping past the boarded window to a flight of cement steps at the corner of the store, cautiously I peeped out to the left. Rose Dorn and Edwin had disappeared. They had disappeared, I tell you, and all houses with them: under a pale sky the street dropped sharply between pale weedgrown fields, full of rusty objects and paper bags, that stretched on both sides into a distant mist. At the base of the sloping street, a thin black road stretched to the left and right; behind it, like a scribble of charcoal, a ragged black forest stood against the sky. The view of the forest was interrupted at the right by a high stony ridge that rose out of the hillocky field at the foot of the hill; at the top of the ridge, a little pointed tower on long metal legs perched like a vast spider. They had disappeared. It was like a turn in a dream, when you step out onto your back porch, hurry down the steps, turn the corner of your house, and find yourself on the brown sand of a deserted beach, with icy blue-black water stretching endlessly away. Overhead a white bird is crying, and when you turn back you discover that your house is a high white wall with pieces of colored glass on top. I wanted to turn back, but I feared that if I turned around I would see not the narrow street I had just finished climbing, but a strange new street, a nightmare street with dark pine trees on both sides and a broken white line down the middle. I wanted to wake up, I wanted to fall into a deep dreamless sleep, I wanted to be back in Edwin's room sitting on the bed under the map of the United States; and suddenly Edwin rose from behind a rusty car-top lying upside down in one of the vacant lots, and I barely ducked out of sight in time. At the bottom of the hill he turned to the right. Over the black tree-line the sky was almost white, and as I made my way down the hill toward the trees and sky I felt as if I were being drawn into a world bleached of all color and existing only in tones of black and gray, as if the landscape were its own photograph. When I reached the bottom I saw Rose Dorn turn left into the trees, while Edwin emerged from behind some thorny black roadside bushes. To my dismay he soon turned in after her. I followed anxiously, fearful of losing Edwin and fearful of plunging into the forest; I was relieved to discover that he had turned onto a narrow dirt road. A tilted wooden streetsign, nailed to a black trunk, contained wavy black blurs made by the rain. The road was so full of hollows that it seemed to ripple like a stream. It was a somber afternoon, but here it was already evening. Far ahead I saw a spot of yellow over a spot of red; Edwin's pale face peeped out from behind a tree; I followed. On and on I went, for minutes, for days; on the left, quite suddenly, the house appeared. It rose amidst the trees like some vaster and older tree: looming and gray and gabled, shuttered and shadowed, darkened by black windows: at once immense and lurking, like a

giant trying to hide. Only a sense of Edwin's imminent danger gave
me the courage to proceed. I stationed myself behind a mossy tree,
on spongy sod, and watched Rose Dorn walk along a weedgrown
flagstone path among the trees. From where I stood I could see,
through a tangle of trunks and branches, the front of the house
and one side. At the corner of the roof rose a small hexagonal
tower with a peaked black roof and two windows; along the front
of the house ran a long sagging porch with square gray posts, a
long gray railing, and long gray steps. The black trees seemed to
press up against the house, hiding many of the windows; the long
black branch of one fat tree crossed the porch rail at one end and
traveled crookedly over the porch itself, stopping in front of a
black window as if poised for a knock. Halfway to the front Rose
Dorn turned left onto another path that led to the side of the house,
where opening a gray door above three gray steps, and letting in
her kitten, she quickly disappeared. Edwin then emerged from
behind his tree and began walking toward the distant front porch.
I do not know what he had in mind. I do not think he had anything
in mind. As if spellbound he walked slowly and steadily along those
crooked flat stones, among those crooked black trees. A cry of
warning rose to my lips but I suppressed it, determined to remain
hidden should help be needed. I was wondering just what sort of
help might be needed when, with an abruptness that startled me,
Edwin stopped. I had been watching him so intently that I had
forgotten the house itself, and as I followed his gaze to the upper
row of windows I saw that one of them was open. Silent in her
black dress, her long black hair falling onto the sill, she sat in the
window and gazed down at Edwin. She said nothing at all; but as
if she had shrieked a witch's curse he turned and began to run down
the flagstone path, tripping suddenly and crawling wildly over the
hard red stones, too frightened to think of getting to his feet. I
glanced back at the house, fearful that she would come flying out
after him, but she continued to sit there, silently watching. And as
I watched, one of the windows in the high hexagonal tower
opened, and Rose Dorn leaned out. She was stark naked. Her pigtails were undone, and her yellow hair streamed below the level of
the windowsill. Grasping the ledge, and leaning on her belly, she

looked down at Edwin without a word; while he, stumbling at last to his feet and running out onto the dirt road, turned to the right and passed me as I swiftly ducked out of sight. For a while she remained there, watching. Then she disappeared.

I found him by the green drugstore at the top of the hill. Hopelessly lost, he sat sobbing on a cement step. His joy in seeing me was so great that he forgot to be angry at me for following him, and on the way home we elaborated a story to explain our lateness to frantic Mrs. Mullhouse. He never attempted to visit Rose Dorn again, though he was destined to see her house once more; nor did we ever speak of the visit in the evil months to come.

# 13

TWO DAYS LATER Edwin again fell ill. This time the familiar cold was accompanied by a severe sore throat, vomiting, and muscular pains. For more than a week I was not allowed to visit him, though downstairs in the kitchen I followed the progress of his fever as it climbed steadily up through 101, 101½, 102, 102½, 103, 103½, reaching a terrifying 104 before stopping and slowly subsiding. Mrs. Mullhouse spoke of the "grippe," a word that made me think of an eagle's claw. My own concern was less for his health than for his exile: shut up in his room with a burning throat, peering out from between burning lids with burning eyes at a burning world, his whole delicate and burning body grown so sensitive with sickness that a light turned on in darkness affected him like a fingertip thrust into his eye, must not Edwin have experienced his banishment with an equal intensity of awareness? My concern was mistaken. Bursting with health and imagination, I failed to perceive that intense physical suffering constricts the imagination by reducing the universe to a throb of pain. Only with returning health would he suffer the difficult, the intricate, the robust torments of imagination.

During the first morning of his absence I saw Rose Dorn looking at me from various parts of the playground, as if expecting to see Edwin pop out from behind me; as she entered the class through the coatroom she glanced at his empty chair. During the day she looked at me from time to time, perhaps expecting me to deliver a gift, but she did not address a single word to me, nor did I offer any information. After a few days she ceased to exhibit even a remote curiosity. I myself was delighted, thank you, to have nothing whatever to do with her. My only concern was what to tell Edwin when the inevitable questions should arise.

Again the day came when I was allowed to visit Edwin. Again I climbed the carpeted stairs, bearing for some reason another glass of orange juice. Again I found his door closed, but not all the way, and again pushing it open with my foot I entered to see Edwin seated crosslegged on his bed, dressed in his purple bathrobe and looking up guiltily from a piece of paper which lay on a dark blue book on his pillow. He quickly whisked it out of sight behind him. I said: "Your mother told me to"

"I don't want any stupid orange juice," said Edwin.

I walked across the room and placed the glass carefully on top of the second gray bookcase, fitting it precisely over the faint ring the first glass had left. Turning I said quietly: "Orange juice isn't stupid."

"I don't want any smart orange juice either," replied witty Edwin.

I sat down on the bed under the map of the United States and waited. He was evidently in one of his difficult moods. I knew that if I said anything at all he would lash out at me and try to destroy me, because I had seen him whisk that piece of paper out of sight. I began to count the slats of one of the blinds, starting from the bottom. My eyes became confused at 14 and I began again. This time the slats melted together at 9. I began again, and I had counted to 15 when Edwin said: "How was school?"

I continued to count silently, making it to 19 before an untimely blink scattered the slats. I said: "Okay."

"That's good," said Edwin. I maintained a rigid silence. Edwin said: "Was that stupid girl there?" "What stupid girl?" "Oh, I don't know. Trudy." "Yes, she was there." "Somebody ought to kill that stupid Trudy. The stupid jerk." I said nothing. Edwin said: "That stupid doctor is another stupid jerk. The big stupid jerk. I wonder where this stupid piece of paper came from. This is a stupid house." He crumpled it into a ball and pushed it into his bathrobe pocket. "Everybody is so stupid in this house. I think I'll go to China." "You don't know Chinese." "I do too. Cha koo ka. Kä chee chaw." "That's not Chinese." "It is too. Chee koo ka? Oo ka chee! Cha koo keeka. Was that other stupid girl there?" "What other stupid girl?" "You know, Ro, Ro, whatever her stupid name is. I can't remember." "Oh, Rose. Yes, she was there. Everybody was there. Donna said to tell you she" "Yes, uh-huh, all right. Did that stupid Rose girl say anything?" "Not about you." "Everybody is so stupid I think I'll just fly away. I hate all these stupid people. Would you promise to do me a favor?" "First tell me what it is." "Thanks a lot. Good night." And still dressed in his bathrobe he crawled into bed, pushed the book from his pillow, turned his back to me, and began to snore loudly. "All right," I said, "I promise." "It doesn't matter. Forget it." "I'll do it. I promise." Edwin turned over. "Well, I have to sort of send this letter. A secret letter." "Who's it for?" "I don't know." "You don't know?" "Oh, I don't know, maybe that stupid girl knows. Give it to her. She'll know." "What stupid girl?"

But already Edwin had sat up in bed, replaced the book on the pillow, and extracted the crumpled piece of paper from his pocket; and ignoring me completely he began to copy it over onto another piece of paper. When he was through he folded the letter in half over and over again until it was a tight little ball, and asked me to go downstairs for a piece of Scotch tape. When I returned he wrapped the letter-ball in a thick cocoon of tape, then folded another piece of paper in half once, placed the letter-ball on the crease, and taped up the sides and top. With a red crayon he printed on the center of one side:

*To*

**ROSE DORN**

In the upper left-hand corner he printed:

From Edwin.

While all of this was taking place I knew well enough that I should affect an absolute unconcern. When at last I took the clumsy envelope from him, it was with repeated assurances that I would not open it, or lose it, or damage it, or do anything with it at all except deliver it intact into the eager hands of his precious Rose Dorn. I was stung by his suspiciousness, and as I took my leave I turned in the doorway to say sharply: "Don't forget to drink your stupid orange juice." His shouted reply, as I hurried down the stairs, was unintelligible.

The human heart is a funny thing. The mind is full of dark secrets. Who can fathom the soul of man? Friendship is a mystery. Curiosity killed the cat. These and other reflections passed through my mind as, in my room that night, with patient fingers I slowly peeled the sticky tape from the paper it tried to tear. I do not, of course, mean to excuse myself when I remark that it was fortunate indeed that my scruples succumbed to my curiosity, since no copy other than my own is known to have survived. The little letter-ball contained a single poem. Untitled, it was printed in a crazy slant on one side of the unlined paper. I hereby give the poem in full:

> Rose Dorn, Rose Dorn,
> I am forlorn.
> My heart is torn
> By Rose, Rose Dorn.
>
> Night and morn,
> Rose Dorn, Rose Dorn,
> For you I mourn,
> My Rose, Rose Dorn.
>
> Why was I born,
> Rose Dorn, Rose Dorn.
> My mind is worn,
> O Rose, Rose Dorn.

*Rose Dorn, Rose Dorn,*
*I am forlorn.*
*My heart is torn*
*By Rose, Rose Dorn.*

It is not a masterpiece. Edwin never amounted to much as a poet, and if I include this poem in my biography it is as evidence not of his artistry but of his misery. As soon as I had read it I recognized, in memory, the dark blue book on his pillow: it was one of Dr. Mullhouse's dictionaries, the one which had on its front cover, in gold letters, the words ABRAHAM MULLHOUSE, and which contained in the back, between Common English Given Names and Orthography, a section called Vocabulary of Rhymes. We had played with the Vocabulary of Rhymes only a short while ago—Edwin had asked me how many rhymes I could think of for "at," and we had ended by looking up "cravat." Despite the poem's mechanical origins, the unprejudiced reader will recognize in those repeated "orn" 's a certain mournfulness, reminiscent of the dim blowings of distant foghorns on stormy nights. And surely, no matter what else one may think of it, the little poem represents a significant technical advance over his Abdul the Bulbul Amir days (see page 74).

I should add that Edwin continued to write poems to Rose Dorn during the next two miserable months, though he never showed her any but a few jingles scribbled on a Valentine card. His poetic activity at this time is interesting less for its own sake than as a harbinger of the great burst of creativity which he experienced that summer, when he produced no fewer than thirty-one fables and stories. Later he scorned the Rose Dorn poems, and I do not blame him; oddly enough, however, he expressed affection for the Valentine jingles. For Valentine's Day Edwin received thirty-four cards, which is to say, a card from everyone in the class except himself and Rose Dorn. She received only five cards: three from Edwin, one from myself—he made me send it—and one, unsigned, from an unknown admirer whose existence tormented Edwin to the end. On one of his three cards, Edwin wrote out a series or cycle of five little verses, based on the familiar jingle "Roses Are Red." The verses are here included for the sake of the curious:

1

*Roses are red,*
*Violets are blue.*
*I know a Rose,*
*And her name is You.*

2

*Violets are blue,*
*Roses are red.*
*I love you.*
*Sincerely, Ed.*

3

*If Roses are blue*
*And violets are red,*
*Then I must be you,*
*And you must be Ed.*

4

*Roses are rose,*
*Violets are violet.*
*I love your nose,*
*And I love your eyelid.*

5

*R oses are red,*
*O violets are blue!*
*S ugar is sweet,*
*E xcept near you.*

The sense of strain is evident in the last two verses, and explains why he did not go on to write the one thousand jingles called for, he once told me, in his original plan. But perhaps he was only joking.

"She said it was nice," I reported the next day when I returned to Edwin's room, noticing at once that someone had removed the glass of orange juice. "Is that all?" he said, utterly crestfallen. Fortunately he did not pursue the matter. She had torn open the resealed envelope in front of the wide oak, resting one foot against the tree behind her. Even when she removed the little letter-ball she continued to stare into the corner of the envelope, as if she had overlooked a prize. I paced back and forth in front of her, anxious to go away but knowing that Edwin would ask for her response. The little vocabulary-of-rhymes poem seemed to me suddenly quite moving; I was saddened by the mournful passion of its rhymes; in my mind, like trainwheels, the opening words echoed over and over: Rose Dorn, Rose Dorn, I am, forlorn, Rose Dorn, Rose Dorn, I am, forlorn. She, meanwhile, had managed to undo the knot of tape, placing the sticky mass onto Gray's neck, and was unfolding the page. She began reading and stopped almost immediately—probably at the word "forlorn," which I venture to suggest she did not know. Grasping the wrinkled page in one hand, and placing her hands on her hips, she stared at me with a blank face. Suddenly she screwed up her features, thrust her face forward, and stuck out her tongue. It was stained black from a piece of licorice she was sucking. I turned on my heel and walked away.

Later that morning I was interrupted at my table by a sound of giggling from Table 5. Donna Riccio and Marcia Robbins were bent over a piece of paper, and Jimmy Pluvcik, standing up, was leaning across the table for a closer look. For some reason the truth did not dawn upon me, or rather dusk upon me, until Mrs. Cadwallader had snatched the paper away. She stood reading it silently beside Donna Riccio, who had grown suddenly solemn. Rose Dorn, expressionless, watched sideways from her seat. Mrs. Cadwallader said to Donna: "And where did you get this thing?" "She gave it to me," said Donna, pointing to Rose Dorn. "I did not!" shrieked Rose Dorn. "You did too!" shrieked Donna. Finally I too was dragged into the vulgar fray when Rose Dorn revealed that I was the one who had given her the "thing." I refuse to go into the sickening details of this dispiriting episode. Fortunately

Edwin did not return to school for a few days, during which the incident was drowned in the whirlpool of Christmas preparations.

# 14

THE TURN CAME on a pale cold colorless afternoon in late February, at 12:06 P.M. to be precise. In the coatroom he had agreed to return early from lunch, in order to meet her on the playground at 12:15 (the last time they had made such an agreement, Edwin had rushed back to school after a hasty bite and waited with a stomach ache on the cold empty playground; she arrived five minutes before the bell, in a bad temper). We were seated in Edwin's kitchen— Edwin, Karen, and I—at the metal table with its white tablecloth bordered by red apples. Edwin sat bent over an old comic book to the right of his plate, engrossed in a Mickey Mouse adventure that was continued in the small heap of old comic books to the left of his plate; Karen was kneeling on her chair, licking her plate like a cat; and I kept my eye on the clock. At precisely 11:59 Mrs. Mullhouse, standing by the sink, proceeded to pour milk into the first of three tall glasses decorated with red and blue fish. As the swift red second-hand rounded the 7 on its way to the two upright black hands, Mrs. Mullhouse turned, bearing in one hand a glass of milk and in the other a large brown noisy package of M & M's. Edwin liked to drop ten M & M's into his milk and look at them through the bottom of the glass; as he drank he would watch for them with growing excitement, gazing delightedly at the swirls of brown and red and yellow suspended in the bright white milk like the ripples in fudge ripple ice cream, drinking with closed eyes the last sweet milk at the very bottom, and finally tapping the hard chilled M & M's carefully into his mouth. The eating habits of my talented friend were always a puzzle to me; in summer he liked to eat chilled grapes by arranging five on one side of his mouth and five on the other side and biting down on all ten at once with an expression of rapture, chewing with bulged cheeks as shiny grapejuice fell from the corners of his lips. As the second-hand joined the black hands I said: "It's twelve, Edwin." "Mmmm," said Edwin, not looking up. Karen spilled onto the table a bright bouncing stream of M & M's, and in imitation of Edwin proceeded to arrange them in long rows according to color, though she failed to keep the white M's upright (according to Edwin, the M stood for Mullhouse). Mrs. Mullhouse said: "Be careful you don't get those things all over the floor." I said: "It's after twelve, Edwin." Edwin said: "Why is everybody screaming at me?" It normally took fifteen minutes to get to school; twelve minutes, walking quickly and cutting across the lawn behind the church; ten minutes, running. Karen, grasping her glass with two hands, took a loud gulping drink and set down the glass with a muffled clank, grinning at me with her white mustache. "Shhh," said Edwin. Mrs. Mullhouse said: "We mustn't disturb His Royal Highness, honey." "Royal heinie," muttered Edwin, punning automatically and not even looking up. Karen said: "Roya heinie! Roya heinie!" Mrs. Mullhouse said: "Just like his father." I said: "It's four after, Edwin." He had not even dropped his M & M's into his milk. "What's the big rush?" said Mrs. Mullhouse. "You're always rushing, Edwin." "Edwin!" I whispered harshly, reaching over and tugging at the comic book, but he jerked it away and sat sideways his chair, holding the comic on his knees. At 12:06 I felt a ripple of excitement pass through me, as if I had just done something dangerous and irrevocable, like skipping a day of school. At 12:17 Edwin closed the last comic book and looked up horrifiedly at the clock. "Why didn't you say something!" he said angrily, pushing back his chair. "Finish your milk first," said Mrs. Mullhouse, but Edwin was already hurrying toward the front hall.

Why was Edwin late? He was late because I kept on reminding him of the time. He was late because it was cold outside and warm inside. He was late because, although on the one hand he wanted to run away with Rose Dorn and live with her forever on a green island and never grow old, on the other hand he wished she would disappear. He was late because she was always late. He was late because he had not yet had his milk and M & M's. He was late because he was happy, and seeing Rose Dorn always made him miserable. And perhaps, in an important sense, he was not late at all. For during those vital minutes, he had been living in a world where Rose Dorn simply did not exist; so that he could no more be said to be late for an appointment with her than she could be said to be late for an appointment with Mickey Mouse.

As we turned through the opening onto the crowded playground, some ten minutes before the bell, it was evident that she was not at the appointed place: the wide oak in the angle of the wire fence. Edwin insisted on looking behind the tree; of course she was not there. "Maybe she's sick," he murmured, but even as he spoke I saw, far away across the playground on the grass slope beside the willow, a patch of red, a glitter of yellow, a spot of black. I tugged at his arm and pointed. He began to run, and I ran after him, and she too began to run—not toward us, but along the far sidewalk toward the front of the school. She quickly disappeared behind the side of the building. When we turned the corner, just past the green entrance door over the single step, we saw only the thin empty strip of playground between the doorless brick wall on our left and the sidewalk on our right. Straight ahead, the tree-grown front lawn sloped to the busy street; through the bushes I saw dangerous cars rushing both ways. Suddenly I saw her red coat disappear beneath the hideous wheels of a honking car.

The back wheels passed over her, and she blew up into the air, revealing herself to be a red kerchief.

Edwin was running along the side of the building ahead of me; he turned to the left and disappeared around the front, into forbidden territory. I turned the corner, hot on his heels, and saw Rose Dorn at the top of the tall front steps, tugging open one of the big forbidden doors. As the door swung shut behind her, Edwin took the steps at the bottom two at a time; as he reached the top I reached the bottom; and suddenly I stopped. How can I convey to the unknowing reader the awesomeness of those high front doors? To climb the steps was unthinkable, impossible: it was like continuing along a strange sidewalk after seeing in the distance three unknown older boys, who already have noticed your approach and are all looking at you. One of them is leaning against a telephone pole with his hands in his pockets, one of them has just stopped throwing stones into a vacant lot, and one of them is combing his wavy blond hair. And so I hesitated, unable to follow Edwin, whom a slow door was already shutting out of view. Far away, across the busy street, a crowd of waiting children stared. Someone was pointing; the blue policeman turned, hand on hip, as if to draw his gun. Above, the door swung softly shut. Without informing my mind, my body reached a decision. Up the long steps I flew, not at all surprised to see Gray lying at the top with a big smile on his face and his front paws tucked under his chest. Inside I could at first see only brown darkness, which resolved itself into two brown doorless windowless walls leading to the main hall; in the stillness I heard a sound of running footsteps. Twice a day we passed out of school this way, but I had always stood in a screaming crowd; the silence and emptiness changed everything, as if a vital piece of furniture had been removed. I hurried down the short hall and turned right, in the direction of the footsteps. At the far end of the hall I saw Edwin disappearing down a staircase. Behind me stretched the half-familiar part of the school, where the first- and second-grade rooms were located; before me lay an identical brown hall that was utterly strange, filled with doors and dark spaces that to this day inhabit my dreams. As I flew along, it seemed to me that I was passing room after room, dozens of them, each thrusting at me through an open door a sudden and quickly vanishing vision of strange desks, a window, a yellow shade; in one room I saw a tall white-haired lady writing on the blackboard, who turned as I rushed past.

The steps were made of black metal. Overhead the white ceiling sloped like an attic. In a small dusty window I saw, in quick succession as I descended, the bottom of the wire fence, the top of the tree, the empty sky. The copper-colored rail, crawling above a row of green metal posts, turned suddenly at a landing, slithered down another row of posts, and terminated abruptly by curling under itself. I was staring down a long windowless hallway that narrowed like railroad tracks and ended in a tiny black metal stairway. The high walls, painted a pale shiny gray, and broken here and there by brown doors, stretched up to a white ceiling

hung with bright glass bowls at the ends of black chains. The un-
painted floor was like the floor of a cellar. The hall was deserted
except for a single aluminum snowshovel leaning against the left
wall partway down. I half-walked, half-ran along, stopping at
open doors to look inside; one dark room on the right was dimly
illuminated by a dusty stripe of light that fell from a single barred
oblong window at the top, through which I could see the shoes
and legs of children on the playground. As I advanced, listening
intently, and fearful of shouting in the bright silence, I heard noises
as of moving furniture in a nearby room on the left. I followed the
sounds to an open doorway, and as I stepped inside, suddenly behind me, over me, on all sides of me, the first bell began to bang.

The room was dark and windowless, but light from the hall
rolled along the floor through the open door, breaking into pieces
against a dark jagged pile of old desks. The room seemed to be full
of them; I could see that they were piled up on one another higher
than my head. There was a narrow passageway between the desks
and wall. I heard the sounds of moving furniture from the dark
back of the room and began to make my way along the narrow
dark corridor to my right. My eyes, adjusting quickly to the dark,
turned the blackness to shades of blackness, so that by the time I
turned left with the turning wall I could see the desk-shapes rising
over me with their metal bars sticking up and I could see, not far
from me, Edwin standing on his toes with his back pressed against
the wall, trying to peer over the pile. I did not understand what he
was doing. The desks shifted loudly, and nearby a heavy desk-
cover came softly sliding down. Only then did I realize what the
wooden noises were. Above us, invisible, Rose Dorn was somehow
making her way across the dark sharp rickety jumble. In my mind's
eye she crawled with bare knees over edges and screws. The heavy
desk-cover crashed at my toes; I leaped away. "Rose!" cried Edwin.
"I hate you!" she screamed, as from the doorway a deep voice
called: "Hey! Who's in there?" and shrilly, as if without mercy,
the second bell began to ring.

# 15

EDWIN'S RESPONSE to all this puzzled me at first: he blamed himself entirely. The vehemence of Rose Dorn's resentment, far from affecting him as a typical bit of nastiness, convinced him beyond all possibility of dissuasion that he had wounded her deeply and unforgivably. Endlessly he envisioned the pitiable scene that I assembled from his sighs: Rose Dorn standing with her kitten by the tree, eagerly searching for Edwin through the wire across the rush of traffic. The fact that she had never once been on time for an appointment did not weaken this vision; on the contrary, it increased his guilt by making him seem to abuse her very first fidelity. Perhaps she had had something special to tell him, something grave and unimaginable that would change his life forever. Perhaps she had wanted to share with him some sorrow or trouble; perhaps she needed help. Perhaps she had brought something to show him, something she had found, like a book of matches, or something she had made, like the potholders some girls made on metal frames. Perhaps she had had a wonderful surprise for him, a gift—a licorice pipe, or a whistle, or a flower. Perhaps she had wanted to invite him to a party, or make a plan to meet him on the weekend somewhere. Perhaps she had wanted to ask him if she could come home with him, and have dinner with him, and spend the night in the extra bed in his room, telling him things in the dark. On and on he went, spinning out one piece of wretched nonsense after another; and always he would end with the vivid picture of Rose Dorn's face growing sadder and sadder behind her cage of wire, until her large pale eyes became bright with held-back tears. Slowly they trickled down her cheeks in two wavering trails, running into the corners of her quivering mouth. This last picture was so vivid in Edwin's mind that it was as if he had been present at the scene of the crime, looking up at her as she stood

staring hopelessly through the wire fence, her fingers curled
through the diamond-shaped spaces. When I tried to modify his
picture by pointing to past instances, he did not argue, but looked
at me with gentle sadness, as if he forgave my failure to understand. The picture became for him the very proof of his iniquity;
having treated her like that, how could he expect forgiveness? No,
he was completely, irrevocably unforgiven; there was no hope for
reconcilement at all. And dragging himself forlornly up the stairs,
in silent sadness he would lie upon his bed, wise beyond his years.

At school he maintained a humble, humiliated remoteness. On
the playground before the bell he leaned alone against some un-
occupied portion of wall, resting one raised foot heel-first on the
bricks behind him, while far away a flash of yellow braided itself
in and out among a dark crowd. He was careful not to stand near
her in line, and he avoided her in the long brown bootfilled coatroom. At his seat he sat bent over the adventures of Bobby and
Betsy, never once raising his eyes. When, despite his precautions,
some accident of a game or spelling bee thrust them together, he
behaved with an intricate unawareness of her presence, as if she
had dissolved into light. Rose Dorn's method of annihilating him
was more violent: she jerked her head away from imagined
glances, ran in the opposite direction when he arrived on the playground, and pressed her face into the pages of her workbook when
with his chair he came struggling past her to join the top reading
group. But Edwin passed with lowered eyes, in serene humiliation.

And at last I began to understand. I began to understand that a
secret force was at work in Edwin, a powerful and devious force
that wanted to free him from Rose Dorn. Unable to forget her,
unable to endure her, weary to death of the vain struggle, Edwin's
battered spirit had at last discovered its freedom: it conspired
against her by taking her side. His powerful imagination was en-
listed in her cause; entering her ravaged soul, it condemned poor
Edwin to eternal damnation. Ah, he was so detestable that she
could never look at him again. Ah, he was so abominable that she
could never think of him again. Prince of mud, king of the dust,
he was beneath contempt. He was lower than low, he was out of
the question, he was nothing at all. Like a mad scientist in a foam-

ing laboratory, Edwin had found the secret chemical. Slowly, cunningly, triumphantly, he began to disappear.

# 16

ON A DRIZZLY SIZZLY steamheated afternoon, three days after Edwin's momentous lateness, a small and barely noticeable incident occurred, of which I was an accidental witness. I was sitting in my seat at Table 1, across from Rose Dorn. My eyes hurt from the strain of a tedious workbook exercise, and in order to rest them I gazed off at quiet Edwin in his seat at the back of the room. He was poring over his workbook with both arms resting on the table and his head bowed as if in shame. As I idly watched I noticed, in the blurred forepart of my vision, Rose Dorn turn quickly to look at him and quickly back. She saw me see her; and to my utter confusion, to my horror, she began to blush. And suddenly, for the first and only time, I was overwhelmed by a feeling of pity for Rose Dorn, who had lost Edwin forever. The feeling vanished instantly when she began to scribble vulgar mustaches and beards all over her workbook girls and boys. In the distance Edwin continued to sit with his head bowed, for all the world like some stone statue in a book.

That night I dreamed that I was seated in Edwin's kitchen at the metal table with the white tablecloth bordered by red apples. Mrs. Mullhouse was seated across from me, wiping a wet glass with a piece of tissue paper that kept on breaking apart and sticking to the glass. Rose Dorn was seated between us, reading a book. The back door opened and Edwin entered, holding in his right hand a pair of sharp cuticle-scissors, curved at the end. He walked up to Rose Dorn and began to stab her in the neck, making large stripes of blood pour down, while Mrs. Mullhouse, now wearing a pair of blue rubber gloves, stuffed a yellow sponge into the bottom of the glass. Rose Dorn fell forward onto her right cheek, her face ugly with pain, and tried to protect the left side of her face with her hands. "Stop that!" I said, and rapped the table. Edwin slashed nimbly around her hands and between her fingers, tearing her left cheek with loud ripping sounds, cutting off pieces of her soft upper lip, and plunging the sharp point repeatedly into her closed eyelid. I leaned forward and tried to cover Rose Dorn with my hands, but her head was just beyond my fingertips. I began to cry, and Edwin, turning to me as if he had just noticed me, raised the bloody scissors over my head. At that moment I awoke, feeling as if the darkness were a huge stone crushing me.

# 17

THE EVENTS OF THE NEXT TWO WEEKS come rushing at me as I write, and I find I must make a special effort to place things in their proper order. My general sense is of Rose Dorn running across the playground with a wild look in her eyes, brandishing a stick from which a rusty nail protrudes—but of course my memory has borrowed that stick from Arnold Hasselstrom. Yet the false fusions of memory may reveal truths beyond chronology, and the fearless biographer, in his tireless pursuit of the past, must be willing to heed the kind of evidence contradicted by clocks. Which is not to say, with my witty friend, that memory is merely one form of imagination. The true course of events must always be carefully distinguished from memory's false fusions, lest biography degenerate into fiction; and so, having presented Rose Dorn with the stick of Arnold Hasselstrom, I immediately return it to its rightful owner, with due apologies. Besides, she had weapons of her own.

She had no intention whatever of allowing Edwin to vanish in peace. On the very next morning after the incident recorded in the last chapter, she tried to trip him as he passed her table, carrying his chair to the top reading group. Mrs. Cadwallader noticed nothing. After the reading group he carried his chair all the way around the front desk and returned to his table by way of the windows. That afternoon as we entered the snow-patched playground I saw her standing by the side of the building with one foot resting heel-first against the bricks. In one hand she held a pink rubber ball. Edwin, who had suddenly begun speaking about the outlook for snow, proceeded to walk in a long curve toward the back playground. As he spoke he stared intently at me, as if anxious to gauge my true response by the involuntary movements of my facial muscles. I was arguing against the likelihood of snow, since the sky was cloudless and blue, when suddenly something fell out of the sky and landed at our toes, at once bouncing into the air. It bounced toward the wire fence in a diminishing series of hops, followed by bouncing Gray. Edwin said: "No, you're wrong, look at the little cloud there, I hope it doesn't snow, don't you see the little cloud there?"

The afternoon passed without incident. As the top reading group began to assemble, Rose Dorn asked for permission to go to the lavatory, and as she left the room Edwin, who had begun to carry his chair from his corner of the table to the aisle by the windows, returned and made his way down the central aisle as usual. When, twenty minutes later, the top reading group was dismissed, he returned by way of the windows. Rose Dorn ignored him, and as the day passed she made no more than the usual nuisance of herself, drumming her fingers on the table, uttering vulgar sounds, shifting about in her seat, and flipping the pages of her workbook loudly. At the 3:10 bell we filed into the coatroom, where I was so intent on lifting my heavy wintercoat carefully from its hook, so as not to damage the little silver chain that mama had recently sewn in to replace the original elastic band, that at first I did not notice Edwin frowning at the empty hook a few coats away. "It's gone," he said. I said: "Are you sure you" but without listening he began to walk along the aisle, anxiously checking the coats on the left and right, making his way through everybody coming at him, and at last breaking free into the region that belonged to another class. I followed, double-checking. At the end of the central coatrack, where an open doorway framed the hall, Edwin turned to the left and began walking back along the aisle on the other side, checking the coats of yet another class. I was approaching the last coats on my side when I happened to stumble over a projecting boot. I kicked it in the shin. As I turned to check the coats on my right I automatically glanced underneath at the boots. There, like a corpse, lay Edwin's coat. The dark blue cloth was filthy with dust, and one arm retained the blurred, dusty, but quite unmistakable impression of a foot.

It was only the beginning. On the playground she taunted him, calling him vile names. In games of dodgeball she aimed at his head. One day, running away with her kitten after having kicked Edwin, she fell down and cut her knee; shrieking and sobbing she limped inside and told a strange teacher that Edwin had pushed her down. Edwin was called into the principal's office, where I soon joined him as a witness; three other members of the class had seen Rose Dorn fall, and her case collapsed. One morning when Edwin opened his workbook he found that several pages had been scribbled on with black crayon. She told Trudy Cassidy that Edwin loved her; she told Mario Antonio that Edwin said he was a Jew; she told people that Edwin made pee in his pants. Passing his desk on the way to the coatroom, she knocked his books or crayons to the floor. She tortured her kitten in Edwin's pained presence, holding Gray upside down by the tail while he yowled and spat and clawed the air, or swinging him under her legs with both hands and flinging him up into the air, where he writhed and twisted.

And then, as if inflamed by Edwin's calm fortitude, or as if Edwin himself were too small to suffer her rage, she began to include others in her attacks. And it was here that her instinct for revenge began to display a certain shrewdness, since it recognized that her real enemy was not Edwin, whom she had never cared for anyway, but something quite different. Trudy Cassidy was her first victim: she came up behind her on the playground and pulled hard on her hair. Later in the day she tripped Marcia Robbins, who fell and began to cry; Rose Dorn was sent to the principal's office. But nothing could stop her now: she kicked Diana Walsh in the leg, with lowered head she butted Anna Litwinski in the stomach, and standing in front of plump Marcia Robbins she chanted "Fattypants Fattypants Fattypants Fattypants" until Marcia burst into tears. One day she stabbed Barbara DeAngelo in the forearm with a pair of scissors. It is true that the points were blunt, and everyone knew that Barbara DeAngelo was a big crybaby, but no one had ever been attacked with a pair of scissors before. But it was on Donna Riccio that she practiced the first of an outrageous series of attacks that quickly attracted the attention of half the playground.

I recall the incident very well. Donna was standing in the middle of the jumprope line, chanting away lustily with balled fists, and I was watching the game with Edwin at a distance of some ten feet, wondering how on earth they managed to jump into those two rapid ropes. As I tested my notion that the jumping-in took place immediately after either rope smacked the tar, I became aware of Rose Dorn standing almost beside me. She ignored me completely and seemed intent on the game. Donna sprang into the ropes, performed grimly an elaborate series of nimble little jumps, leaped out, and strode to the end of the line, where she balled her fists and began chanting again. At that moment Rose Dorn went up behind her. She paused, as if deciding; and with a sudden motion she reached down, gripped Donna's coat and dress, and yanked them as high as they would go, revealing for all to see a pair of pale blue underpants. Donna screamed, but some nearby boys were laughing, and Rose Dorn ran away. She did the same thing to Marcia Robbins, whose underpants were yellow, and Susan Thompson, whose underpants were white; Marcia Robbins burst into tears, and all three girls reported to Mrs. Cadwallader. Of course Rose Dorn was sent to the principal's office. But the attacks continued, and soon she was followed by a band of older boys who watched from a near distance, whistling and cheering.

One day she came to school with a box of wooden matches. Holding an unlit match in one hand and the box in the other, she came up to Jimmy Pluvcik, struck the match, and flung the flaming stick at him, laughing falsely as he ran away.

In the room she became increasingly unmanageable; her attack on Barbara DeAngelo was only the most memorable of a number of physical assaults, for each of which she was sent to the principal's office. Several girls were distinctly frightened of her by now; Marcia Robbins looked anxiously about whenever Rose

Dorn came within ten feet of her, though at a safe distance she whispered spitefully. I myself, for some reason, was less troubled by her violence than by her drawings. For as her behavior degenerated, so did her crayon drawings: the simple figures with red and blue arrows sticking through them were soon going up in flames of black and red and purple. She began to scribble over everything she drew, turning all pictures into holocausts. I recall one picture especially. With a black crayon she drew a round face, a stick coming down as if from a lollipop, a triangle at the bottom of the stick, and two stick legs with balls for feet. With a yellow crayon she drew three long lines coming down from both sides of the head, which remained bald on top. The face was blank. With a red crayon she began to color in the triangle in her usual way, following first the left slope and then the base and then the right slope, leaving a space in the center which she would finish any which way. But as she was following the right slope, suddenly the crayon shot away from the outline and began to swirl and crisscross all over the picture, as if the dress had become unraveled and, with a life of its own, were now winding the neck and face and legs in a loose red net. At this point she pushed the picture across to me; I looked at it, nodded, and pushed it back. But she was not yet finished, for now her red crayon began to rush furiously back and forth over the entire figure until it had formed a solid sheet of bright dark red. When she was through you saw a black outline behind a fiery shield of red, the whole thing surrounded by the white of the paper; and if you looked closely you saw, ever so faintly, the blurred remains of the hair, now no longer yellow but red-orange.

I never liked Rose Dorn; but I do not wish to temper the strict truthfulness of this biography by painting her one stroke blacker than she was. She did not always torment us. I don't know what else precisely she did do; I suppose she left us alone. We were thankful enough for that, after a while. And there were periods of deep musing, when rapt in revery and trafficking with who knows what monsters of the spirit, she seemed peaceful and even pretty; even sweet; even innocent. Her serenities had once been very important to Edwin: he saw in her then some essential angel that burned away all accidental devils (I myself had always believed that she was communing with pale-eyed fiends). But of course she would always spoil it in the end, just as she spoiled Edwin's passion in the end, because she had pale eyes and her mother was a witch and she was damned to hell no matter what she did.

It was not until a certain morning that Rose Dorn actually frightened me. It was a cold day, though no colder than usual; to my surprise she entered the playground with the red hood of her coat covering her hair. In the coatroom she dawdled. I watched Mrs. Cadwallader frowning at the empty seat, and at the clock, and at the coatroom door, and she had already risen in anger when a collective gasp sounded and Trudy Cassidy nudged my arm. Her face expressionless, Rose Dorn walked between the tables to her seat. That was all; but as we rose to our feet and began to pray I could barely remember the words. It was not until some time later that I could actually look at her. She was hideous, grotesque. She looked as if she had removed a wig. Her braids were gone, and her short pale hair, parted on the left and combed to the side, barely reached her ears. She looked like a boy. She was utterly changed, and I was reminded of Mrs. Mullhouse at the beach when she covered her hair with a white bathing cap and became a stranger, smiling with a mouth that had only a grotesque resemblance to the mouth of the real Mrs. Mullhouse. But whereas her face, in the white bathing cap, looked smaller and thinner, as if all the features had been pressed together, Rose Dorn's face looked larger and almost square; and her large pale eyes, staring out at you with no expression that I could recognize, gave you the feeling that they were dangerously exposed, as if her abundant hair had once protected them. Billy Duda said that her mother had cut off her hair. Donna Riccio said that Rose Dorn had cut it off herself.

She behaved so badly that she spent most of the day in the principal's office.

The next morning I was relieved to find Rose Dorn's seat empty after the second bell. It was a bright morning, with a touch of spring in the air, and her absence seemed in keeping with the blue mildness of the day. We all stood up, bowed our heads, and began to recite the Lord's Prayer, as if in thanks for the empty seat.

During the words "on earth as it is in heaven" I became aware of footsteps running along the hall; seven words later, at "bread," there was the sound of a loudly turning doorknob; and at "as we" my eyes tore open to see Rose Dorn standing in the room by the front door, panting loudly but frozen in an attitude of motion. Most of us had stopped and were looking at her with a kind of horror; a few girls grimly went on reciting the prayer with their eyes squeezed shut. Mrs. Cadwallader was saying the words louder and louder and at the same time glaring ferociously at Rose Dorn, as if the words were a curse or lash. Everyone knew that this interruption of the Lord's Prayer was sinful, hideous, and exciting, and that Mrs. Cadwallader would rise to the occasion; and indeed after the final words she stormed over to Rose Dorn and began to shout at her for not waiting outside until we were done, and then she shook her by the shoulder and dragged her by the upper arm out of the room into the hall, where she had to stay until we finished the Pledge Allegiance; but what had upset me more than all this was the look on Rose Dorn's face. For after her first look of confusion and uncertainty, her face had gradually filled with the knowledge of her trespass, and had taken on a look not of repentance but of sly pleasure. Her eyes had roamed over the class and had stopped at Edwin, who was looking at her with his mouth partly open; and as she awaited the onslaught of Mrs. Cadwallader her face seemed to be smiling, though her lips did not move. Later she returned to her seat. She was in one of her dreamy moods, gazing off with a strange light in her eyes.

The next morning she burst in upon our prayer from the rear door. Mrs. Cadwallader instantly stopped the prayer and marched toward Rose Dorn, who awaited her calmly, almost happily it seemed to me, at the back of the room.

I have always enjoyed riding my bicycle. Last Saturday, when for some reason all my sentences were stupid and ugly, and nothing made any sense at all, and mama was humming a lullaby although Edwin was dead, I took a long ride over white sidewalks under orange trees. Men in short jackets stood beside piles of burning leaves, resting their hands on rakes and watching the lines of dark smoke rise into the brilliant blue air. I crossed at the stoplight in front of the church and rode toward Franklin Pierce. At Rapolski's I turned right and rode along the side-street beside the high playground. Under the tall trees on both sides of the street lay long wavering lines of fading fallen leaves, and I was careful to ride through the snap and crackle. It was a quiet, peaceful street; a small child was throwing leaves up in the air and letting them fall all over him; in one driveway a man was squirting a hose at a shiny black Ford. After several blocks I turned to the right and began pedaling uphill between gray two-story houses. At the top of the hill stood a bright red drugstore. I turned left, raised my feet to the handlebars, and flew downhill between yellow and white ranch-houses. Between my toes I saw, across the street at the bottom of the hill, a line of small colorful houses that stretched to the left and right, blocked only by the cliff on which a silver water-tower sat. I applied my excellent brakes in time to stop at the street below, crossed carefully, and turning right, rode along the sidewalk that bordered the green lawns with their thin new maples. At Sunnyholm Drive I turned left, riding past rows of identical small houses where small children in red and blue jackets played on small back lawns. At last I came to the circular end of the street where, behind a high wire fence, black trees rose up. Then I turned around and rode back.

She died two days after the death of her hair. Probably it was the worst thing left for her to do. She was absent that morning, though Mrs. Cadwallader prayed with her eyes wide open; she seemed indeed to be enlisting the Lord in her struggle against Rose Dorn. It was shortly after play period that we heard the fire engines. At first invisible, they came wailing out of the morning like an agony of the sky, and suddenly appeared through our windows on the street by the sidewalk. Redly they rushed away, with black firemen stuck all over their backs like clinging cats. Mrs. Cadwallader let us stand at the windows; I counted three trucks and two red cars. Later another truck streaked by. At 11:15 a thin haze of smoke was visible on the horizon, far beyond the wire fence. At the 11:30 lunch bell Edwin and I hurried down the side-street, turning at the hill between the rows of gray two-story houses. People were running from all directions. At the green drugstore we looked down past the grassy lots at a long sheet of fire, shooting black smoke into the blue March sky. The policeman would not let us past the bottom of the hill. We climbed the ridge and stood in the shadow of the vast iron spider, watching the loud flames, which seemed at times to roll slowly and heavily, like honey. The ridge was crowded with spectators. Through the flaming trees we could see red fire engines on the nameless dirt road, and long pale curves of water from the hoses. "Look!" some idiot cried as the high hexagonal tower burst into sudden flame. Edwin watched without a word, sitting on the ground with his arms hugging his legs and his chin resting on his raised knees. He did not even flinch as the tower separated from the house and plunged, a fiery ball, down to the flames below. After a while Edwin stood up and we walked home without a word.

Mrs. Mullhouse, who had been following the story since eleven o'clock, was listening to the radio. Edwin had muttered something about watching a fire when we arrived, answering her flurry of questions with mumbles, and now he sat at the table picking at his napkin as the radio voice shouted quietly. They were pronounced dead on arrival. The fire was not yet under control. Mrs. Mullhouse stood with her back to us, making sandwiches and shaking her head. When she turned, with a plate in each hand, she made a curious sound, as if she were inhaling hard on a cigarette. Edwin sat with his hands pressed over his ears. His eyes were squeezed shut. His face was twisted.

# 18

RAIN WASHED ANOTHER WINTER AWAY, and warm winds came, like a blossoming of the air, carrying with them an odor of voyages. Again the maples put out their dark red flowers. In the Late Years, shut up in his room behind the closed venetian blinds, Edwin cursed the spring outright as the year's smiling devil, for it created in him a fever of restlessness that tempted him away from his cool,

cool sentences; but in the Middle Years he still left himself open to the full influence of the season, to its languor and its fever, to the violence of its mild afternoons. There was always a suddenness about the first real day of spring: Edwin once compared it to the movie version of the *Wizard of Oz*, which begins in brown and white and bursts suddenly into color. I prefer to compare it to a game we used to play at the end of Saturday matinees in summer. For hours we would sit in darkness, watching cartoons and pirates, and then the lights would go on, dimming the luminous red EXIT signs. The yellow overhead lights of the vast emptying theater filled us with a sense of lamplight and evening, and as we made our way slowly up the slope of the side aisle in an air-conditioned chill, we encouraged the illusion, thinking how cool it was, how tired we felt, how late it must be, imagining as vividly as possible the cool darkness outside, the headlights, the glowing blue BAR & GRILL sign across the street, the shadows of passing people growing longer and shorter in the light of streetlamps, and in a black satin sky, just over the horizon, a luminous orange moon—and suddenly we had passed through the door and were standing on a crimson rug in a flood of sunlight, beyond the glass doors the white sidewalk glittered under a blue sky, on all sides of us we felt the harsh hot gleam of glass and silver, and though we had known it would be exactly like that, still the delightful illusion of evening that we had created kept its force, so that for a moment we felt, in the heat and light of a radiant afternoon, a distinct sense of confusion, of loss, of bitter disappointment.

So spring surprised him: he had not expected quite that intensity of brightness. Spring that year was a great cracking and breaking, a green fever, an agony of trees; and for a moment Edwin was confused. For the death of Rose Dorn had plunged him into grief, and the season, like a bad stylist, failed to express his mood. At the same time, the season seemed to revive in him certain dangerous memories, best laid to rest. Perhaps the reason was this, that his obsession with Rose Dorn had been so much a part of fall and winter weather, of bare black trees and yellow leaves, of frosted windows and steamheated rooms, of white breath under freezing blue skies, that the bright loss of these things revived in him the loss of his first

love of her. Or perhaps it was simply that he had learned to deal
with her under the old conditions, which somehow explained her,
or explained at least his sorrow and failure, which were only like
the weather itself. But now new conditions had arisen, green warm
budding conditions that spoke at once of tranquillity and adventure, and tormented him with visions of voyages to remote green
islands where, in dark green shade pierced by rays of green sunlight, he and Rose Dorn would never walk.

Edwin barely spoke to me for a month. In class he leaned his chin
on his hand and stared; after school he dragged himself slowly,
slowly, slowly up to his room. "I don't feel like it," he would say,
and it was generally his sole contribution to the conversation. After
a month or so of this he came down with the chicken pox and was
shut up in his room for three weeks, during which I was not even
allowed to enter the house. He returned to school in early May,
looking paler and thinner than usual, and proudly displaying a
small round scar on his left wrist. He seemed somewhat more lively
but had to spend most of the next week making up schoolwork.
Thereafter his recovery was rapid. He began to throw himself into
games again, arguing hotly, making puns, inventing new rules. One
Saturday Dr. Mullhouse drove us all to a distant picnic ground,
where dark brown tables were scattered among tall evergreen trees
whose needles grew near the top. After lunch Dr. Mullhouse,
making obscure jokes about pine Cohens and evergreen Levis, and
wearing around his neck a light meter, a gadget-bag, and two
cameras whose straps were adorned with little leather cases for
filters, led us along a winding dirt trail that came out at a tall white
waterfall, dropping crookedly into a brown stream. Edwin was
delighted. There was also a stone bridge spanning the stream, and
there is a picture of Edwin leaning over the parapet, looking over
his right shoulder with a winking grin.

It was a warm blue morning in May. Edwin sat on the shady,
rippling root of a fat old tilted tree that leaned over the brook at
the end of Beech Street, casting a leafy shadow that rippled and
bubbled on the water as if it were about to break loose and stream
away. By his right foot lay a three-inch plywood boat shaped like
the pointed side of a house, to which a small cube of wood, serving

as a cabin or smokestack, had been carefully glued. I sat on a sunny root beside him, reflecting upon his difficult moods. There he sat, mournfully munching a peanut butter and jelly sandwich, sadly licking his sticky lips, pensively wiping his fingers on sticky wax-paper, and fixing his glum gaze on a quiet inlet in the uneven opposite bank, where from time to time the smooth surface of the water was gently shattered by the landing of some invisible insect. He had eagerly agreed to my plan of a little expedition to the end of Beech Street, going so far as to suggest that we make a whole day of it, complete with an elaborate lunch and various emergency supplies, such as pistachio nuts, cashews, licorice shoestrings, sugar wafers, and small red boxes of raisins. But once arrived, he mumbled something about having all day, chose the first shady spot in sight, sat himself glumly down, and fell into a condition of such gloomy meditation that I dared not disturb him, not even when he absently began to eat his lunch some two hours before the usual time. I was in foul spirits, for it seemed unlikely that we would ever get to sail our boat. But mostly I was distressed by what I considered an unhealthy backsliding into unruly grief.

Rippling and bubbling, the shadow extended more than halfway across the stream. A fringe of tall yellow grass was reflected as spots of yellow in the sunlit ripples of the opposite bank. But in the quiet inlet, the precise stalks were reflected as in a dark mirror. High overhead, in a glowing sky, a bright white three-dimensional cloud, molded with blue shadows, looked so plump and heavy that I don't know how it stayed up there. Spots of blue and white danced on the ripples. Here and there the leafy shadow was punctured by bright shifting patches of light—one of which, I suddenly noticed, played over an orange and black orange-juice can that lay, now dark, now gleaming, at the bottom of the water. Glancing at gloomy Edwin, who was still immersed in his lunch, I stood up, stepped to the water, scooped up a handful of small cold stones that gleamed in the sunlight, and proceeded to toss them at the winking can. I missed on the first three tries, but on the fourth I heard a highly satisfying clank.

"Shhh," said Edwin.

"But," I began to shout.

"Jeffrey," he said, and in that eager accent I recognized my old friend, "which is best: Edwin's Weekly? The Mullhouse News? The Mullhouse Post? or Edwin's Gazette?"

# 19

THE IDEA OF A FAMILY NEWSPAPER did not originate with Edwin but with page 46 of *A Boy's Treasury of Things-to-do*, which he had received for his seventh birthday (more than nine months before) and had not looked at until the day before the preceding chapter. No matter. The true artist is not an inventor but a finder and user—in this instance, of a boy's book of games. The paper first appeared on Sunday, June 3, 1951, and continued to appear regularly once a week through Sunday, July 1. After a lengthy pause occasioned by a visit from Grandma Mullhouse, during which Edwin displayed a consuming passion for Lotto, the paper reappeared on Friday, July 13. It continued thereafter on a regular daily basis, stopping abruptly—and forever—with the issue of July 31. (On August 1, Edwin's eighth birthday, he received among other treasures a Monopoly set, a Brownie camera with two yellow rolls of film, and a fascinating wooden box the size of a small desk-drawer, whose movable top, controlled by red wooden knobs on all four sides, was a raised maze full of numerous holes, past which you tried to steer a marble-sized steel ball.) Altogether there were twenty-four issues of what Edwin finally chose to call *The Family Newspaper*, the bland name suggested by his source.

The five weeklies and the first three dailies consist of three pages each, but the strain of daily production soon told upon Edwin, and the remaining sixteen issues are all two pages long. The format is simple, and is modeled closely on the newspaper pictured in the *Boy's Treasury*. The first page of each issue has a wide space on top, where the title appears in large capital letters; "THE" is generally but not invariably centered above "FAMILY NEWSPAPER." Beneath the title are two ruled parallel lines exactly one-half inch apart, in which the date is printed in small capital letters. The page is then divided into four columns, of various widths, by ruled vertical lines that extend from the dateline to the base of the page. Second and third pages are titleless but have a narrow space at the top where "page 2" or "page 3" is printed; the second page is visible above the first page and the third above the second, in the manner of a row of cards in a game of solitaire. The pages are joined at the top by means of three and sometimes four pieces of Scotch tape that begin below the dateline on the front page, proceed upward over succeeding pages, and end several inches down the back of the last page. The general appearance is far from neat. Not only are the strips of tape crooked and ugly, but the numerous short horizontal lines separating headline and article are drawn without the aid of a ruler; and to tell the truth, Edwin's printing is uniformly dreadful. All words are printed in small capital letters, and although the letters of the headlines are usually larger than the letters of the articles, this is not always the case, so that sometimes it is difficult to distinguish a headline from an article, especially since many articles are extremely short.

The bulk of each issue (not counting the last seven) is taken up by snippets of family news, generally no more than half a column in length and often much shorter; representative headlines are EDWIN PLAYS THE PIANO, FATHER SMOKES CIGAR, KAREN GOES TO NURSERY SCHOOL, NANNY BUYS A NEW COAT, EDWIN BROKE HIS WATCH BAND, MOTHER DROPS GLASS. In addition to the family news are items such as weather reports, lists of imaginary television programs, ridiculous baseball scores (CONNECTICUT 10, YANKS 7 AND ½), carefully numbered crossword puzzles without definitions, meaningless cartoon strips with stick figures and empty bubbles, pencil sketches representing photographs and signed PICTURES, INC., and a column called EDWIN'S BELIEVE IT OR NOT, in which he wrote down any old rubbish, such as IN CHINA PEOPLE HAVE 3 HEADS. A boy's magazine that Edwin had been getting since Christmas supplied him with riddles (WHY ARE WOLVES LIKE PLAYING CARDS? ANSWER ON PAGE 2), jokes (FIRST CANNIBAL: WHAT'S THAT BOOK YOU'RE READING? SECOND

CANNIBAL: IT'S CALLED HOW TO SERVE YOUR FELLOW MAN), and doodles (a bear climbing a tree, the neck of a giraffe going past a window, a fat man taking a bath, a trombone player in a telephone booth, two elephants' tails tied together, a fat lady diving, a tall man in a short elevator, a birdseye view of a boxing match, a checkerboard for midgets, a black cat at midnight). All of this trash, trivial and repulsive though it may be, is nevertheless of no small interest as evidence of the diverse influences upon Edwin's imagination, evidence which the biographer ignores at his own peril. For it is in this setting, like butterflies in a vacant lot, that Edwin's earliest stories appear.

Because they both belong to a pack.

The five weekly issues and the first twelve daily issues each contain a single story, from one to two columns in length. The last seven issues contain two stories apiece, which become longer and longer until the last two issues consist entirely of fiction. Altogether Edwin wrote thirty-one stories (fourteen in the last week), ranging in length from 89 words to 432 words. The transformation of a journal of fact into a journal of fiction is an event of major significance in the spiritual history of my artistic friend. The stories themselves are of little or no significance, except insofar as they reveal the form and content of Edwin's imagination, approximately one year before he was to begin his immortal novel. The shortness of even the longest stories forced upon Edwin a succinctness that at its worst is mere summary and at its best suggests dimly, very dimly, certain fairy tales. The style is uniformly unremarkable, imitated from various storybooks for children; occasionally Edwin introduces a large word for no purpose except display. A typical story begins:

> Once upon a time there
> was an ugly princess.
> Her name was Glug. Every
> body hated this ugly pri
> ncess. One day she was
> playing in the forest and
> she saw a beautiful frog.

His name was Thomas. He
had two brown eyes and a
beautiful green skin. S
uddenly, [etc.]

The difference between the hasty dashed-off simplicities of this
so-called style and the intricate simplicities of his final manner is
roughly comparable to the difference between a dull handful of
colored glass chips and their scintillating six-sided kaleidoscopic
transformation. Since, however, the subjects of the stories possess
a certain interest as imaginative information, I shall summarize
them briefly in the order of composition, allowing the reader to
arrange this mass of stuff in some more meaningful order if he can.
Here, then, are the thirty-one stories of Edwin's Middle Years—
and let us hope that no dull-witted disciple, in some future spasm
of misguided fervor, will ever hunt up the originals in order to
display their crudities to the public eye.

1–5. Uninspired tales centering upon Donald Duck
("Donald and the Witch," "Donald Goes to the
Moon," "Donald and the Flying Carpet," "Donald
Meets Edwin," "Donald and the Wizard of Oz"). In
"Donald Meets Edwin," the most interesting story
of this group, Edwin is presented as reading a comic
book from which Donald emerges one night. The
theme of creatures stepping out of books or off walls
or out of dreams is a favorite with Edwin and has
evident affinities with the last pages of *The Lonely
Island*.

6. The adventures of a dog called Grrr who is buried
alive. One day Grrr feels the ground give way under
him and begins to fall down a deep tunnel until he
hits a door. The door opens and he falls onto a vast
hand. The hand closes over him (there is an interesting description of the rising fingers) and he soon
finds himself in a dark pocket in the company of an
elephant and a dinosaur. Finally he ends up on a
sunny shelf beside another dog, and they all live

happily ever after (Edwin was partial to happy endings).

7.  A ridiculous fable about a hungry boy who sails to an island where the people are made of licorice. He bites off the king's finger and is pursued. He hides in a hill of raisins but eats so many that he is soon discovered; he dives into a lake of root beer but drinks it dry; he hides in a chocolate tree but eats all the M & M leaves. Finally he enters a chocolate-cake mountain, eats away the foundation, and is killed. Moral: DON'T EAT BETWEEN MEALS.

8.  "Pillow and Sam." The first of a series of dream-tales whose heroes are a boy called Sam and a pillow called Pillow. Sad and lonely by day, Pillow is happy only at night, when he and Sam go on adventures together. In this episode, Pillow and Sam follow a black cat into the woods. The cat leads them to a house. Pillow and Sam enter the house and are seized by a witch, who ties them up and places them in the fireplace. She lights a match; the flame gets brighter and brighter; the witch begins to resemble a window with venetian blinds; Pillow and Sam wake up.

9.  A not very funny story about a donkey called J.

10. An amusing story about a wave who runs away from the ocean and goes to live in a city. Unable to make friends because he makes everyone wet, he eventually wanders into a house, where a horrified lady, whose rug he ruins, calls the police. The police try to capture him but he slips through their fingers. Finally he leaps into a sink, disappears down the drain, and returns to the ocean, where he lives happily ever after.

11. A story inspired by my goldfish bowl, into which Edwin gazed for one hour. A boy standing on the seashore meets a green lady who takes him by the hand and leads him into the ocean. After a while they come to a stone house. The green lady turns to stone.

The boy looks at his hands and sees that they are changing to scales. He tries to escape but comes to a glass wall. The story ends with the words TO BE CONT'D but was never cont'd.

12.  "Donald and the Invisible Hand." A disappointing return to an early genre.

13–15.  Further adventures of Pillow and Sam. In each tale, a dangerous situation is resolved by waking.

16.  A story about the letter *l*, who is sad because he is the thinnest letter in the alphabet. One day he is chased home from school by *o*. His father, *L*, finding him in tears, explains to him that letters are not important by themselves but only as parts of words. He is part of "elephant," "eagle," and "whale," while *o* is part of "worm," "hog," and "toad."

17–18.  More Donald stories. The strain is beginning to tell.

19.  A sentimental tale about a little blind girl called Ann and her brother Dan. As they cross a bridge, Ann falls into the water and calls for help; smiling, Dan walks on. Ann drowns. In the last sentence we learn that little Dan is deaf, poor fellow.

20.  A continuation of *The Pied Piper of Hamelin*. Once inside the hill, the Pied Piper reveals to the children that he is going to eat them. The children begin to pray. As they pray, their shapes change slowly, wings appear on their long green bodies, and they fly out through a small opening in the hilltop. The children of Hamelin may still be seen today, for they are praying mantises.

21.  A story called "Alice's Sister," by Lewis E. Carroll. Influenced by Alice's account of her dream, Alice's sister follows a white rabbit down a rabbit hole. But this rabbit is a real rabbit, the rabbit hole is full of mud, and she cries until Alice rescues her. "It was only a dream," Alice reminds her sister, in the last line of this harshly realistic and highly uncharacteristic tale.

22.  A story, possibly influenced by *Through the Look-ing-Glass*, of a boy who steps through the lens of a camera. He becomes trapped in a piece of film. One day the film is developed and the negatives are hung up to dry; the boy calls for help but no one hears him. Finally the negatives are printed, and the boy steps forth. But from that day on, he is a black-and-white boy in a world of color. I once asked Edwin if the story was an allegory of the suffering artist in a society that does not understand him. "A what?" he replied. When I had explained "allegory" he frowned for a while and at last said no, he didn't think it was an alligator.

23.  The story of a giant called Jub, told by himself. In an amusing passage, he complains that giants have been misrepresented by men as violent and wicked. He, on the contrary, is a thin, sensitive giant who writes poetry and is shocked by the violence and wickedness of men.

24.  A story based on *Through the Looking-Glass*, about a boy who steps into a mirror. The mirror world is the same as the old world, but everything is reversed. Thus the boy walks backward, sleeps with his eyes open, eats dinner before breakfast, goes to bed when the sun comes up, wears shoes on his hands and gloves on his feet, cries when he is happy, laughs when he is sad, reads books from back to front, and is punished with ice cream and licorice.

25.  A story about a boy who dreams that he visits the fairy kingdom. There is a surprising—and refreshing—amount of specific description in this tale, pre-figuring *Cartoons*. The ending is a definite improve-ment on the Pillow and Sam series: the boy wakes up, but finds on his pillow a tiny green glass slipper.

26.  A story about an ugly princess who falls in love with the Frog King, whom she saves from a hunter.

Granted a wish, she asks to be his wife. Horrified, the Frog King nevertheless agrees to go through with the marriage, which takes place in a palace of gold, silver, and rubies. At the end, the ugly princess turns out to be a beautiful frog in disguise.

27. A similar but somehow less successful story about a writing desk that turns out to be a raven in disguise.

28. A shocking tale about a boy called Nedwi who shoots himself in the head. The ridiculous ending, in which you learn that the gun was only a cap pistol, does not diminish the horrible fascination of this ominous tale.

29. A story, appreciable only by initiates, about cartoons that come down off a wall and dance in a circle when their master goes to sleep. One day the master wakes up and sees them. They all dance together.

30. A story purporting to be the last chapter of *Alice in Wonderland,* in which the entire book, including Alice's waking from her dream, is shown to be a dream of the sleepy dormouse.

31. A story about the death of a crayon called Green, who gets smaller and smaller until he disappears. In the usual happy ending, we learn that Green lives on in the drawings of the boy who caused his death.

# 20

ALTHOUGH EDWIN NEVER KNEW his grandfathers, neither the German nor the Russian, each existed for him in an object. His father's father, the German, had left behind an intricate monkey carved from a peachpit, which Edwin's father kept wrapped in tissue paper in the upper left-hand corner of his top dresser drawer. Early in the

Middle Years, when Dr. Mullhouse first showed the monkey to
Edwin, he unwrapped it carefully and held it delicately in the large
palm of his hand; Edwin was then allowed to touch it and even to
take it in his own small hand. He felt that he had to be as careful
with it as with the delicate lenses and colored filters that his father
had begun allowing him to hold. The lenses and the peachpit
monkey were alike in their delicacy and in the tone of special
seriousness his father used in speaking about them, a tone that
invested them with a double sense of mystery and of mysteries
unveiled. But the peachpit monkey was different from the lenses.
For one thing, the expensive blue-tinted lenses with their collars
of silver were replaceable, however precious, but the monkey was
unique and irreplaceable, as unique and irreplaceable as a strip of
old negatives; and Edwin thought that if anything ever happened
to the peachpit monkey it would be far worse for his father than
losing a lens, worse even than losing his twin-lens reflex, it would
be, almost, like losing Edwin himself. Edwin knew it would be
like that because his father never spoke of the lenses with pride. It
was this pride, a different pride entirely from the joking pride
with which his father spoke of the glass-covered photographs hanging in the living room, that made the peachpit monkey precious
above all things, and first made Edwin experience what he later
called one of the deepest mysteries of his life: that his father had
had a father. And that same pride, like a bond between grandfather
and grandson, Edwin also heard in his father's voice when his father
talked about Edwin in front of grownups. One day during the
summer of *The Family Newspaper*, Dr. Mullhouse showed Edwin
a photograph of his father that he kept in a drawer. It was one of
those brown-and-white affairs, showing the upper half of a stiff
handsome gentleman with broad shoulders and a heavy pale mustache. The photograph meant as little to Edwin as the photograph
of a stranger, and he could never connect that unreal man, the very
image of his unknown grandfather, with the real, the intimate
peachpit monkey.

Above the old desk in the cellar, hanging from a nail in a wooden
beam, a pair of dusty scales rested in permanent imbalance. They

had belonged to Edwin's other grandfather, the Russian. Each of two yellow glass pans was attached to three gold-painted strings that came together in little hooks at the ends of a horizontal brass bar. From the center of the brass bar rose a brass arrow, which swung back and forth against a fixed upright as the scales moved up and down. Edwin liked to make the scales balance by placing in the trays special cylindrical steel weights with knobs on top; when the weights were lost he used marbles. But he was secretly disappointed with the scales, not because they failed to balance but because they hung in the cellar for anyone to touch. He thought they should have been wrapped in tissue paper and placed in a box in his mother's top bureau drawer. In the course of the Middle Years he forgave his mother. The scales had been part of her father's work: they had been used by him, not made by him, while the peachpit monkey had been made by his father's father and had always, in a sense, been wrapped in tissue paper. In the Late Years, when it became important to Edwin that artist's blood should flow in his veins, the peachpit monkey became a favorite symbol, while the uneven scales, hanging in dusty neglect, were improved by the knowledge that his mother's father, who had escaped to America from the Czar of Russia, liked to spend long hours reading books in Russian. Mrs. Mullhouse would say, smiling at Edwin's interest in her father: "Oh what a shame, you would have liked him so much," or smiling more sadly she would say: "He would have liked you so much." And Edwin would long to talk to a man whose blood flowed in his veins and who had escaped to America from the Czar of Russia.

# 21

THIRD GRADE SURPRISED ME: I had not anticipated desks. Darkly they stretched across the room in a grim repetition of emptiness. The strange room seemed at once smaller and larger than earlier rooms, a mystery that I failed to solve in the midst of the multitude of new sensations that pressed upon me. Over the blackboards the dark green alphabet cards contained mysterious white letters that bore only a loose, melting resemblance to the letters I knew, although the white numerals remained the same; on the teacher's desk a large colorful globe, the size of a beachball, rested on a shiny wooden stand. Unlike the tables, which were pale and clean and shiny-smooth, the desks were dark and old, and covered with little black grooves that seemed to be filled with ink or grime. When at last I opened my first desktop I was greeted by a damp, sour odor that instantly cast me back to the cellar of Edward Penn; again I walked down the wooden stairs and made my way along dim passageways toward that fabulous curtained den; while horribly visible in one corner of the desk, squatting there like a bloated bug, the black bottom of the glass inkwell hung over the pencil shavings, the black penpoint, the chewed lollipop stick, the scrap of sticky cellophane. That evening, in calm meditation, I solved the mystery of the room. It seemed smaller because it was filled and even crowded with desks, unlike the earlier rooms with their six tables and large empty spaces; larger, because the large number of empty desks seemed to express the sheer quantity of emptiness. Thirty-six empty desks, I reflected, are emptier than six empty tables. Edwin, who unfortunately did not possess a philosophical cast of mind, proved indifferent to these speculations but not to the fact that the room was, as he put it, "backward." For although Miss Coco's room was on the same side of the building as Mrs. Cadwallader's, with a view of the playground that excluded the far sidewalk and the willow but included part of the wire fence, her desk was at the opposite side of the room. This simple and not terribly interesting fact managed to fascinate and bewilder Edwin for two entire weeks; he could not get used to the idea that the front of the room was to the right of the windows and radiators, not to the left. He was also bewildered by Miss Coco herself. He had expected his teachers to become both larger and older as the grades advanced, for Miss Tipp had expanded into Mrs. Brockaway, who in turn had swelled into Mrs. Cadwallader; but Mrs. Cadwallader had collapsed into Miss Coco. Her short brown hair was turned up slightly at the sides, giving her head the shape of a bell. She had a little thin face in which large brown eyes kept watery watch above a long thin nose, reddish at the tip. In long thin fingers, reddish at the tips, she held in perpetual readiness a white handkerchief bordered with intricate lavender loops, which she continually lifted to her nose for little brisk rubs. She spoke in a little thin voice that barely changed during her various moods. Edwin was bitterly disappointed in Miss Coco, who could not inspire terror with a glance and whose very anger was thin and moist; perhaps this is why he began to whisper and faintly misbehave in class, a tendency encouraged by the accident of alphabetization, which placed him in the inconspicuous middle of the fourth row (I was seated in the third desk of the first row, by the door). But perhaps his restlessness may better be explained by the lack of any real challenge. In a ridiculously short time we had mastered our desks, learned to place new points on our black wooden penholders, learned to fill our inkwells from a large silver can in the closet, learned not to press down too hard when writing with ink, for then the point separated into two pieces; learned, even, the rudiments of script. But everything seemed merely a variation of what we already knew. Edwin did his work quickly and effortlessly, whispering to Anna Litwinski (who sat in front of him) and Susan Thompson (who sat beside him), making secret signals to Jimmy Pluvcik, and passing notes across the room to a new girl, Janet Kupek. For that matter there were several new girls in the class, none of whom inspired in restless Edwin more than a passing interest. There were also two new boys: Frank Picirillo, a troublemaker who quickly drifted into the society of Mario Antonio and Len Laska; and Kenneth Santurbano, a quiet boy in the top reading group, who was always being persecuted by Len Laska. The only classroom activity that truly interested Edwin was the twice-weekly spelling test on long thin strips of blue-lined white paper. Perfect papers received three marks: 100, A, and a shiny paper star that might be red or blue or gold. The starred papers were tacked in horizontal rows to the Spelling Board at the back of the room; and Edwin's row soon stretched well in advance of all other rows but one, which not immodesty but the spirit of precision compels me to reveal as my own.

It was shortly after Halloween that the new boy appeared. I say appeared because I don't remember when I first noticed him, though of course we all noticed him once he had appeared. There he sat at the back of the room, conspicuous and sullen in the last seat of the row beside the windows, with a bright blue lunchbox at his feet. Every other window was open, propped by a red dictionary, and you could see strands of his hair blowing in the chill November wind that came in over the steamblasts from the green radiator, whose black knob was turned all the way up with some notion on Miss Coco's part of a balance between Nature and Civilization. He was obviously miserable but he sat there stonily, staring at the pencil trough in his desk. The class tried to break him down with whispers, stares, and giggles, but he showed no sign of sensitivity other than an occasional quick look about the room, as if he were trying to take in the sheer physical size of the hostility. The most aggressive notice came from that clown Billy Duda, who sat at the end of my row and was always trying to impress Mario Antonio, Len Laska, and Frank Picirillo. All four were looking the new boy over mercilessly in the few minutes left before the bell, and indeed he presented no common sight. He wore what no one had ever worn before in Franklin Pierce, a tie, a real tie, a maroon tie over a dark green shortsleeved shirt; and on the floor by his feet, in loud defiance of a society of paper bags, stood that impossibly bright blue lunchbox with its silver clasp. He was small and solid and darkly tanned, with a head somewhat too large for his shoulders and aglow with pale unmoistened hair that seemed to have had the yellow burned out of it by the sun. His face was almost a triangle, rising from the sharp point of his chin to a large brown forehead; that, and his broad, conspicuous cheekbones, lent to his face the suggestion of a rude carving. His mouth was a small thin line, his long unboyish nose was not the kind that displayed its nostrils but the other kind with its slight overhang, and under his pale eyebrows a pair of gleams escaped from behind two slits. Later I was to learn that those slits could open suddenly over strikingly large green irises that seemed to have no depth at all but only a glitter, like the backs of spoons. And there he sat, glaring at his desk with one brown arm resting on the surface from elbow to clenched fist, and in general looking as if he were defiantly pretending not to have stolen something. Edwin had glanced at him from the middle of the room but had soon lost interest. Billy Duda was uttering loud witticisms about lunchboxes and Miss Coco was writing sentences on the blackboard when the bell rang. Miss Coco put down her chalk, gave her hands a few little slaps, and stepped around her desk to her praying position at the front of the room. But instead of folding her hands, she immediately fulfilled the wildest fantasies of the meanest members of the lowest reading group by saying: "We have a nice new classmate with us today and I'm sure all of us would like to meet him and find out all about him and where he's from. Arnold, will you please tell us a little about yourself, your name and where you come from? Stand up please, Arnold." At the first sound of the name a ripple of titters rocked the back rows; at the second, Billy Duda produced a repulsive sound by squeezing his palms together in some nasty way. Even Edwin smiled, but quickly frowned. Miss Coco said: "I don't see what's so funny. Would someone mind telling me what's so funny?" And raising her handkerchief to her nose she made little rubbing gestures as she gazed moistly from one face to the next. "William, would *you* like to tell me what's so funny? Mario, would *you* like to tell me what's so funny? No, of course not. Because there's nothing funny about a name, is there. Some of us are called William, some are called Mario, some are called Jeffrey, and some Arnold." She lowered her handkerchief. "It's hard enough to be a brand new boy in a brand new environment without us making it more difficult for him than it is already. You should always ask yourself how would *you* feel. So I think we all owe a great big apology to—to Arnie, from all of us. I wouldn't be a bit surprised if old Arnie there didn't want to share his experiences with us after the way we've acted today. And I wouldn't blame him one bit. But I'm sure you'll forgive us, won't you, Arnie. Now won't you stand up like a nice boy and tell us a little something about yourself?" All faces turned toward Arnie. He sat unmoving, staring at his desk. "Just a few words," said Miss Coco. From where I sat he seemed to turn a shade darker. Perhaps he was dreaming of green valleys in Norway, perhaps he was dreaming of bloody knives and shrieking schoolteachers, perhaps his mind was a void, but he sat unmoving, staring at his desk, and Miss Coco, radiant with compassion, said: "Do you want me to help you, Arnold?" The class was absolutely silent now; you could hear the minute hand jump on the big clock beside George Washington. With a sad little smile Miss Coco said: "Well now, you watch me and you'll see how easy it is, okay? Okay. And if I make any mistakes, you be sure and correct me, won't you now. Now let's see. My name is Arnold Hass, Hass, Hasselstrom and I have just come to Newfield all the way from Buffalo in the state of New York. Before that I came all the way across the Atlantic Ocean from Oslo, Norway. Norway is a very cold country far away across the Atlantic Ocean near Lapland. In Norway there are real reindeer and many lakes and mountains and Fords. There is always snow in Norway all year round and the girls and boys go skating, sledding, and skiing all year round. At Christmastime they fill their wooden shoes with straw and leave them outside the door for Saint Nicholas, who takes away the straw and leaves presents. But if you're a very bad boy or a very bad girl, then he leaves coal. It's so lovely in Norway with all the snow and the mountains and the lovely blue lakes and the ships and the. Arnold what are you"

A photograph would show Arnold Hasselstrom in profile, standing beside his desk with his back to the window and his eye wide open. Beside his feet lies an open lunchbox. Across the room Billy Duda is seated with a hand raised before his face and the fingers spread; on his face is an expression of terror. Behind him, on the blackboard, is a zigzag crack. Beside him, on the floor, lies a rock the size of a baseball.

# 22

His name was Arnold Hasselstrom and he never smiled. No one knew anything more about him except that he lived with his grandmother in the neighborhood beyond the white sidewalk on the other side of the school. Edwin and I never saw his neighborhood or his grandmother. According to the newspapers, her name was Josephine.

It was not until a month later that he and Edwin began their unlikely friendship. Meanwhile he accumulated an awesome record of violations, and might have been a hero if he hadn't been such a loner. He made it clear from the first day that he was not to be trifled with: that afternoon on the playground when two pals of Mario Antonio began to chant "Arrrrnie! Hey, Arrrrrnie!" he ran at them swinging a stick from which a rusty nail protruded. During the next few days on the playground before the bell he passed the initiation rites established by the tougher elements of Franklin Pierce. Watched by a semicircle of aspiring killers, among them Mario Antonio's fifth-grade brother Tony, Arnold Hasselstrom stood under one of the high windows at the back of the school and smashed his fist into the brick wall with all his might. He remained grimly expressionless then and afterward, when Tony Antonio clapped him on the back, but I noticed that he held his hand very carefully for the next three days, and once when he swung it carelessly against the back of his chair he winced with pain. The comb test was less painful though more colorful. Len Laska demonstrated. Making a tight fist he rapped his knuckles hard with a sharp-toothed pocket comb; then keeping his fist clenched he swung his arm in a circle fifty times, and when he held up his fist for inspection, the knuckles were lightly streaked with blood. He held out the comb to Arnold Hasselstrom. But Arnold Hasselstrom shook his head, and reaching into his back pocket removed a steel comb (cries of "Shee! Hey!"). Making a tight fist he whacked his knuckles five times sharply and began to swing; on about the fifteenth swing someone gave a shout and leaped back, wiping sprayed blood from his cheek. Arnold Hasselstrom kept on swinging, flinging blooddrops out of his fist as the circle of watchers moved away; when at last he stopped they came crowding around him, exclaiming loudly. When the circle broke up, Edwin and I caught a glimpse of a hand that looked as if it had been painted with red stripes.

No one except Miss Coco called him Arnold or Arnie or Arn: his name was Hass. No one smiled when Miss Coco called him

Arnold or Arnie or Arn. After the first morning he no longer brought his blue lunchbox to school, and he no longer wore a tie. He wore shirts of a single color, usually bright red or dark green, over tight black pants and heavy black shoes. In his pants pocket was a bulge that resembled a rock; in his shirt pocket he carried cigarette butts that he smoked in the bathroom. With a pearl-handled penknife he carved obscenities in all three toilet seats. One morning he appeared on the playground in a red-eyed stinking condition; inside he sat shaking in his seat, and suddenly vomited onto the floor. One day he raised his middle finger to Miss Coco, who sent him to the principal's office. Another day he took a swing at the principal, Miss Maidstone, who swung back (they got along quite well after that). He always said "I don't know" when called on in class. A special reading group was set up for him alone, one step below the lowest reading group, who were still on the first-grade level. His seat was soon changed to the front desk of the second row, two desks ahead of me and one desk to my left. He did no work at all so far as I could tell, aside from the inane sentences that he wrote fifty or a hundred or two hundred times in punishment for one of his endless offenses. Indeed he took to this work with a certain enthusiasm, which puzzled me until the day Miss Coco began scolding him over his shoulder. She had detected, in the middle of the page, certain sentences that I later saw when I happened to glance at the offending paper on her desk:

> Arnold Hasselstrom is a disobedient boy.
> Arnold Hasselstrom is a disobadient boy.
> Arnold Hasselstrom is a disodebient boy.
> Arnold Hasselstrom is a disobebient boy.
> Arnold Hasselstrom is a disodedient boy.

He was always making things difficult for himself that way, turning punishment into a reason for more punishment; but the acute reader will realize that I have sounded the first note of the subtle chord that was eventually to connect Arnold Hasselstrom, that disobedient boy, with angelic Edwin.

Although Arnold Hasselstrom spent his time with the likes of

Mario Antonio, Len Laska, and Frank Picirillo, flipping cards or pennies or jackknives in back of Rapolski's, or shooting flaming matches from matchguns made from spring-clothespins, he was never really one of them. He seemed to hold himself at a distance, as if he were passing his time among them on the way to something better. I think he despised them. They for their part admired him in a confused fearful way and never really liked him or felt at ease in his presence. No one could ever forget the rock he had hurled at Billy Duda; it set him apart as someone a little crazy, someone who might kill you if you made a mistake. And there was another difference: his deadly earnestness. Unlike Len Laska or Frank Picirillo, he never fought for fun. But when he did fight, he never held back. I had observed with interest that, with rare violent exceptions, other boys fought according to a never articulated but clearly understood set of rules, as if they were afraid of their own capacity to inflict injury or afraid of setting off some frenzy in their antagonist; but Arnold Hasselstrom fought to kill. Not to win, but to kill. He conducted every battle as if it were taking place on a cliff. Once he got into a vicious fight with a fourth-grader and was pressing his knee into the half-dead boy's throat before the older boys could pull him off. Another time he swung a baseball bat at someone's head, grazing an ear. But he was not invincible. Once when an enormously tall and fat sixth-grader, prodded by Arnold's enemies, was pushing him with the heel of his hand, Arnold aimed a vicious kick at the bully's crotch. The fat boy caught his foot, tipped him onto the tar, and proceeded to beat him up mercilessly, bloodying his face and getting him into a hammerlock that made him weep with rage and pain until, for the first time, he gave up. As the fat boy walked away, Arnold Hasselstrom picked up a rock and flung it at his head, narrowly missing; the sixth-grader returned and beat him up again, leaving him in a heap on the ground with blood and breathclouds pouring out of his mouth. Edwin and I saw that fight, held after school on a bright December day; the sixth-grader looked terrified, as if he were afraid he had killed a little boy, and he hurried away miserably among his cheerless friends. Arnold Hasselstrom did not come to school for a week. The sixth-grader looked worried during the whole time and never picked on him again. It was evident that you had to risk killing him if you were going to fight him at all.

And always at the end of a dark tunnel, shining like a prince in a fairytale, sat Edwin: Edwin, the brightest boy in the class (reputedly), laughing at his own jokes, exchanging notes with pretty Susan Thompson, working on special projects with Jimmy Pluvcik or Kenneth Santurbano or this biographer at the back of of the room while the rest of the class had to read in their social studies books; Edwin, who was saved from being the teacher's pet by his habit of gleefully pointing out her numerous mistakes in spelling and pronunciation; Edwin, master of the secret of success. Yes, I suspect that Arnold Hasselstrom was attracted less to Edwin than to a mode of existence that seemed the bright opposite of his own. In the Early Years there was a miniature toy that had enchanted Edwin: a little colored picture beneath a transparent plastic shield that seemed to be full of pinpricks. When you held it between thumb and forefinger and tipped it to one side you saw a slightly different version of the same picture, thus producing an effect of animation: a face with open eyes would become the same face with closed eyes, and by tipping quickly back and forth you produced a blink. Now let us say that the universe, for Arnold Hasselstrom, consisted of a ridiculous periwig, a frown, and a pointing finger. But tip it slightly to one side, in Edwin's direction —and see the frown change to a beaming smile, the pointing finger change to an open hand filled with shiny pennies. The ridiculous periwig, of course, remained.

One evening in the summer after Arnold Hasselstrom's death, as we strolled under streetlamps that had just burst into light although the sky was still gray, Edwin said, apropos of nothing: "But why didn't he beat me up?" I knew immediately whom he meant. "Oh," I answered lightly, "that old magic spell." This was a reference to a private joke between us that Edwin was under the protection of a fairy godmother who kept him from physical harm in return for a life of spiritual unease. Indeed it was an astonishing fact about him that never once in the course of his spiritually tumultuous existence was he hurt in a fight. A combination of cowardice and cunning, if we would believe Edwin; but I think it was something more than that, something at once physical and spiritual. The paleness and frailness that made him ideal prey for an occasional prowling bully rendered him immune from the onslaughts of the truly tough: it was no honor to whip Edwin. Of course they would have destroyed him if he had asked for it, but unlike Kenneth Santurbano he never asked for it. In class he never thrust himself forward except to expose Miss Coco's mistakes, his infectious humor gained him friends among the lower groups, and though he was outstanding in no playground sport he was good enough in all of them to be chosen fifth or sixth on a side (Kenneth Santurbano was always chosen last). But more than that, I cannot help thinking there was a kind of glow about him that warned off attackers, an emanation of spiritual particles that defined his difference; so that to strike him was not merely to risk breaking a very fragile and expensive vase but to violate a shrine. Not that he was totally immune, any more than Arnold Hasselstrom was invincible; indeed he was once saved by Arnold Hasselstrom from what could have been a very nasty fight. He fell into the faint beginnings of two or three other fights, all so trivial that I can barely remember them; each time he surrendered vigorously after letting just the right amount of time pass, so that his attacker had the illusion of having fought. But his general immunity was not won without effort. He exercised a continual vigilance, avoiding dangerous places and deliberately seeking out alliances among the strong. He cultivated a kind of distant friendship, for instance, with Mario Antonio, with whom he exchanged occasional jokes; and Mario's approval undoubtedly protected him from numerous unknown enemies of the thin and pale.

One afternoon after walking home from school with Edwin, I changed into my playclothes and discovered to my annoyance that I had to perform for mama a number of lengthy, disagreeable, and unnecessary tasks. At last I hurried across the back yard to Edwin's. I rapped; no one answered; and as usual I let myself in. As I passed through the kitchen I heard through the open basement door Mrs. Mullhouse telling Karen to pass the clothespins (in the winter Mrs. Mullhouse dried her wash on clotheslines strung across the cellar). I passed through the living room, climbed the carpeted stairs, and came to Edwin's closed door, on which I vigorously knocked. There followed a longish pause, broken by faint movements. Then "Come in," said Edwin, without enthusiasm, and I opened the door.

Edwin was seated on the near side of his bed with his back to me, looking at me over his left shoulder. On the bedspread before him lay the top of a familiar picture puzzle (Queen of the Seas. Over 375 Pieces) showing a three-master with puffed white sails plunging on dark blue water under a light blue sky. Beside him stood the green folding table, which held in its center an open Parcheesi board. On the board lay two red dice with white spots, one blue dice-box, two red pieces on the opening red space, one red piece on a nearby white space, one red piece on a white space on the other side of the board, one yellow piece on the opening yellow space, and three yellow pieces waiting to begin. To the right of the Parcheesi board lay the gray bottom of a puzzle box filled with a jumble of pieces on which could be seen an occasional bit of light blue sky, an occasional bit of dark blue sea. To the left of the Parcheesi board lay the black plastic Viewmaster and a scattering of slides in blue-and-white jackets. On the bed beneath the map of the United States were several rows of overlapping comic books; on the top rim of one of the two long pillows lay a black plastic dart with a pink rubber tip. On the far side of the bed sat a shoebox filled with marbles. On the far side of Edwin's bed sat Arnold Hasselstrom.

"Oh," said Edwin, lifting the top of the puzzle box from the bed and revealing, beside a brown leather sheath, a shiny hunting knife with a wavy black handle, "it's only Jeffrey."

# 23

So BEGAN THE ILL-STARRED FRIENDSHIP between Arnold Hasselstrom, that disobedient boy, and obedient Edwin. Opposites, they say, attract, and I would let it go at that if it were not for my suspicion that a more subtle combination of forces was here in operation. Unlike Arnold Hasselstrom, Edwin was incapable of saying "no" to a teacher, of openly and flagrantly disobeying authority— though perhaps "incapable" is a misleading word, since defiance would never have occurred to him. Obeying the sometimes unpleasant commands of grownups was a fact of life for Edwin, like being thin. And just as thinness had something to be said for it, although sometimes he longed for physical strength, so obedience was not without its advantages, although sometimes he may have longed for an impossible absolute freedom. But freedom was precisely the boon of obedience. Arnold Hasselstrom, who refused to obey commands that he disliked, was continually clashing with grownups; he had less freedom than anyone I have ever known, for he was always staying after school, going to the principal's office, losing privileges, and in general being watched and criticized and scolded and hounded by a whole army of suspicious adults. Edwin, who did whatever he was told, was left pretty much to his own devices. In this sense his obedience was perhaps not entirely virtuous, and resembled, in fact, nothing so much as disobedience. For the goal of disobedience is freedom; but the goal of Edwin's obedience was likewise freedom. And so although it is true that Edwin was an obedient boy, the very opposite of an Arnold Hasselstrom, still there was something cunning, something rebellious, something disobedient about his obedience.

They were soon fast friends. Or at any rate Arnold Hasselstrom became a frequent visitor at Edwin's, not only after school but on the weekends as well. My concern over possible bad influences made me anxious to be present at these meetings, despite the sense of strain I could not help noticing when all three of us were together. Let me say it at once: Arnold Hasselstrom did not like me. I, for my part, returned his feeling a hundredfold. Yes, I hated Arnold Hasselstrom: hated his dark humorless visage, his narrow almond eyes, his large brown hands that seemed awkward except when they were formed into fists; hated his habit of looking at me with an intense lack of expression that suggested to me the deliberate suppression of a sneer; hated above all his presence in Edwin's house. To my dismay, Mrs. Mullhouse took an immediate liking to him, referring to him first as "that quiet boy" and later as "that poor boy"—this last a reference to the fact that he lived with his grandmother, his mother being dead and his father (according to the newspapers, a sheet-metal worker and hunting enthusiast) having disappeared. He for his part seemed to take a fancy to Mrs. Mullhouse, and often when I entered the kitchen I would find him sitting at the table watching her load wet clothes from the washing machine into a wicker basket while Karen tried to unclench a playful fist that he had made especially for her. He was quite a hit with Karen, whom Edwin increasingly ignored; she was delighted by a certain trick he had of placing his palms together with the fingers spread, bending down the two middle fingers, pivoting his hands around those two fingers, and at last wiggling the two middle fingers back and forth on opposite sides of his interlocked hands. He performed this trick grimly, without a smile; but at these moments his intense lack of expression suggested the deliberate suppression of a smile. The pleasure he took in the company of Mrs. Mullhouse and Karen did not, however, extend to the company of Dr. Mullhouse, whose seriousness and whimsy both made him ill at ease. Seriousness for Arnold Hasselstrom was always a prelude to punishment; humor was a form of ridicule. Indeed he mistrusted all speech, which in his experience was a form of attack consisting of commands, criticisms, refusals, penalties, scoldings, challenges, insults, curses. Words, for Arnold Hasselstrom, were the sonic equivalents of blows.

And so he spoke very little to Edwin, in bursts of three or four words; his dark silence thundered in the room, drowning all talk. We played Parcheesi until I was bored to tears. Arnold Hasselstrom was fascinated by the game, and once when Edwin tried to teach him Monopoly, to Edwin's great embarrassment he proved unable or unwilling to learn. I noticed with distaste that Edwin quickly adopted Arnold Hasselstrom's method of shaking the dice. His own method was a long humorous excited shake of fist or dice-box accompanied by a hum or prayer, a shake from which the dice came spilling unexpectedly and usually from a great height, so that they bounced and danced and sometimes fell onto the floor; while

Arnold Hasselstrom's method was a short plain serious shake, which ended with the dice rolling down the broad slope of his extended fingers, whose tips touched the board. And I noticed how, in order not to seem boastful, Edwin imitated Arnold Hasselstrom's way of counting out each space as he moved a piece, instead of adding up the numbers in his head and moving instantly to the proper space.

Parcheesi was not their only pastime. It was Arnold Hasselstrom who inspired in Edwin a passion for bubblegum cards. One day he spread out on Edwin's bed five long rows of his favorite cards. They had titles like Trapped, Village Attack, Bombs on Target, Dry Landing, Tanks Are Coming, The Enemy Falls, Push to Pusan, Night Bombardment, Torpedo Away, Red Sniper. I have one before me now, called They Won't Stop. It shows a crowd of advancing soldiers carrying long rifles with bayonets; in the center a shirtless man leaps up in the air as three parallel white lines strike him in the chest. At the top of the picture is an explosion colored brown, red, and yellow. Three men on the left are bent over, and a man is lying on the ground with blood all over his arm. On the back of the card ("No. 28 in a Series of 152") are the words:

> Shortly after crossing the Kum River late in July the Reds made another full-scale attack on our new positions. Our tracer bullets mowed their ranks down like wheat . . . but they kept coming. Climbing over the dead bodies of their comrades the fanatical Red soldiers went for our lines!

Edwin also liked the more colorful series called Fighting Marines, in which the pictures were framed in a double line of red and blue. But he developed a veritable passion for Wings, not so much for the airplanes themselves as for their names: Sky Ray, Sea Hawk, Mustang, Thunderjet, Vampire, Invader. He also liked the colorful scenes behind or below the pictured planes: the purple water and the green land with wavy white lines below the PO-1W Lockheed, the pale orange sky and snowy mountaintops behind the Sea Hawk, and the dark orange and dark yellow sky over distant greenblack palm trees behind the P-4M Mercator. He enjoyed flipping, but Arnold Hasselstrom

introduced him to a more exacting sport: standing at one end
of the room and facing the bookcases, he grasped a card between his forefinger and middle finger, snapped his wrist, and
sent it flying smoothly across the room into the base of a bookcase.
Edwin practiced throwing cards for hours and soon was as expert
as Arnold Hasselstrom; I myself refused to join them. Astounded
by my aloofness, Edwin tried to lure me into enthusiasm by explaining the fine art of knocking down a leaner. "You gotta," he
said, in careful imitation of his latest friend, "hit'm ona bottom,"
for if you hit it on the top your card bounced back and the fallen
leaner might beat you anyway. An innocent pastime? Perhaps.
And yet the sight of the two of them standing there side by side,
grimly snapping their wrists, filled me with unease.

As if perpetually uncertain of his welcome, Arnold Hasselstrom
was forever giving things to Edwin. He began Edwin's card collection by giving him ten doubles, and he gave Edwin a small smooth
boomerang-shaped stone with which he said he had killed a squirrel.
But most of his gifts came from his grandmother's bedroom closet,
and these had to be hidden. The first such gift was a large brass
bullet, which Arnold Hasselstrom held out to Edwin in the palm
of his hand. He said it was for a rifle, and he warned Edwin not to
drop it. After a sleepless night Edwin placed the gleaming car-
tridge in a sock-ball and hid the sock-ball at the back of the high
shelf in his closet, behind a pile of old stuffed animals.

One day Edwin showed me a mysterious object that looked like
a dice-box or a roll of pennies. A red cardboard tube some two
inches long was attached to a brass base. It felt heavy, as if filled
with sand. On the red cardboard, in black letters, were the words:

REMINGTON

6

Edwin asked me if I wanted one too. I asked him what it was. He
said he didn't know. According to the newspapers, the police found
in Josephine Hasselstrom's bedroom closet a 20-gauge shotgun, a
.22 rifle, a .30-30 rifle, a dozen 20-gauge shotgun shells, six boxes
of .22-caliber cartridges, six boxes of .30-30 caliber cartridges, and
a "large" but unspecified number of .25- and .32-caliber cartridges.

Arnold Hasselstrom enjoyed not only giving things but also borrowing things: that too created a bond. Embarrassed by so many gifts, Edwin was only too happy to comply. Indeed he himself pressed Arnold to borrow three of his favorite comic books, hoping to share with his new friend the rare delights of his personal pleasure-garden, and forgetting that no garden was habitable by Arnold Hasselstrom that did not contain an abundant supply of guns, planes, tanks, and bombs. In the course of the next few weeks Arnold Hasselstrom borrowed occasional nickels from Edwin, which he forgot to pay back, a dark brown baseball bat that was too heavy for Edwin, a red-handled screwdriver from Dr. Mullhouse's green tin toolkit, a baseball dartboard whose three wooden darts had metal points and red plastic feathers, and a boxed basketball game with levers and a pingpong ball, which he said he wanted to show his grandmother.

Despite their friendship, on the playground they instinctively avoided one another. Arnold Hasselstrom disliked Edwin's friends, and his own acquaintances, some of them fifth- and sixth-graders, terrified Edwin. But Arnold Hasselstrom's careful failure to notice Edwin in public did not prevent him altogether from acknowledging a relation. I am thinking of one morning in particular. Edwin and I were strolling along the playground, discussing the possibility of a story without people or animals. I claimed, and I still claim, that such a story would quickly become boring. Edwin disagreed. As he was arguing that, on the contrary, such a story would be fascinating because people are boring, suddenly he stepped into a shoulder. The stranger tottered, regained his balance, and sprang furiously at Edwin, pushing him up against the bricks and holding his throat with one hand while he held a fist curled under Edwin's nose. A crowd began to gather. The attacker's looks did not inspire confidence. He wore a short purple jacket with the collar turned up, and his thick curly brown hair spilled down over his forehead in a V. I was wondering whether I should try to explain to the stupid bully that it was only an accident, or whether I should run to the front in search of the policeman, when suddenly Arnold Hasselstrom came hurtling out of nowhere, grasped the bully's neck from behind, jerked him away from Edwin, and without bothering to knock him down simply stood behind him and was in the process of strangling him to death when three older boys broke up the fight, holding Arnold Hasselstrom by both arms and one leg while he thrashed and writhed within a yard of his dazed antagonist, who stood bent over slightly, gasping for breath and holding his throat with one hand, as if he were trying to strangle himself. Edwin, unhurt, blinked in bewilderment.

One evening after dinner when I went over to Edwin's I found him pacing up and down in his room. He seemed glad to see me. Before shutting the door he stood for a few moments listening to the sound of voices downstairs; then holding a finger to his lips he motioned toward the bed beneath the map of the United States. Together we pushed the bed against the door. Edwin paused, listening; at last he set up a folding chair, carried it into his closet, climbed onto it, and removed from the top shelf a light brown shoebox with a dark brown cover. He carried the shoebox over to his bed. Holding a finger to his lips, he removed the top. Inside were five or six old cowboy pistols and a crumpled leather holster. He took them out one by one and revealed at the bottom a pistol I had never seen before. It was smaller than the cowboy pistols; the metal was not a bright shiny silver but the color of lead. There was no hammer, and the odd-looking trigger had space only in front and not on both sides. The black grip on the handle said COLT; it showed a black horse standing on two legs and holding a spear or arrow in its front legs, another in its mouth. Cut into the barrel in small capital letters were the words:

COLT AUTOMATIC
CALIBRE 25

Beside it lay a dark metal rectangle shaped like the handle of the pistol but smaller; it contained several holes, through which flashes of brass were visible. The bottom of the handle, I then noticed, was open and hollow. I made a reaching motion but Edwin knocked away my hand. Without a word he piled in, one by one, the shining cowboy pistols, placed the old holster on top, put on the cover, and returned the box to its hiding place on the top shelf. Only after he had folded the chair and closed the closet door did he say, in a whisper: "He asked me to keep it for him. In case he needs it."

# 24

THE DISINTEGRATION OF FRIENDSHIP is an instructive, and may be a delightful, subject for investigation. It was, therefore, with no small measure of interest that I watched the delicate structure tremble, crack, and fall. Edwin's first mistake was to ask his new friend to teach him how to fight. He did not realize that it was precisely his difference from Arnold Hasselstrom that fascinated Arnold Hasselstrom, who for that matter was not unwilling to show him a few elementary boxing tricks; nor did Edwin realize that by attempting to resemble Arnold Hasselstrom he could inspire only contempt. For of course he was ridiculous as a boxer. He was also a wretched nuisance, forever challenging me to bouts of gentle pugilism. No sooner would I enter his room than he would leap from his bed and fall into an Edwinian boxing stance. Bending over, curling in his shoulders, and making a curious circular motion with his hands, he would approach me in a series of tiny cautious steps, all the while bobbing up and down on bending and unbending knees and moving his head about behind his circling hands; long before he was near enough to touch me he would begin to stick out his left hand and draw it in; and as he came closer he would unconsciously begin to straighten up until, standing before me, he was bending over backward with his head pulled back and a look of determination and worry on his face, as if he feared that I was about to punch him in the eye. Naturally I refused to participate in an activity that I found at once preposterous and repulsive. Arnold Hasselstrom, I suspect, was not amused. Edwin would have done better, in his eyes, to express indifference or even contempt for fighting.

Edwin's second mistake was his persistent attempt to initiate Arnold Hasselstrom into the joys of reading. Arnold Hasselstrom had neither mentioned nor returned the three comic books that Edwin had lent to him in a fit of foolish generosity, and Edwin, too timid to ask for them back, was perhaps trying to stimulate his memory as well as his imagination. Slyly at first, by pretending to be in the midst of reading something when Arnold Hasselstrom arrived, and then more boldly, he sought to arouse in Arnold Hasselstrom an interest in his favorite books. But Arnold Hasselstrom showed no interest whatever in Edwin's books. His passion was Parcheesi. And this indifference, not merely to reading but to Edwin's favorite stories, inspired in Edwin quite helplessly his first faint feeling of contempt.

The first clear evidence of decay was a certain comic book that Edwin displayed angrily to me one afternoon in late February when we were alone in his room. For weeks he had worried about his precious comic books, and when, finally, he asked for them back, he learned to his horror that Arnold Hasselstrom was uncertain whether he still had them. Surprised by Edwin's alarm, he promised to search his house. He returned with one of the original three. It was this comic book that Edwin displayed to me that February day: swollen and wrinkled and discolored, it had evidently fallen into a puddle or perhaps lain in one for weeks; and the blurred, soiled cover was detached from the stapled pages. Arnold Hasselstrom had presented it without explanation or apology, and Edwin had been too embarrassed to ask for either. The other comic books were apparently gone forever.

And yet I feel certain that Edwin would have forgiven him if it had not been for his manner. I refer not to his pardonable impoliteness but to his inexcusable sincerity. For it was clear that Arnold Hasselstrom, who liked Edwin, was not being malicious or even thoughtless—he simply could not imagine anyone making a fuss over a couple of old comic books. He thus revealed to Edwin a remoteness from his world so absolute and appalling as to be comparable to the remoteness of the world of Edward Penn from that of General Eisenhower. Edwin's anger at the mutilated comic book was really, I mean to say, a form of spiritual revulsion.

Edwin's response to all this was as curious in its way as the memorable disappearing act inspired in him by Rose Dorn. For suddenly he was overwhelmed by a desire to repossess his property, all of which seemed to him in danger of being destroyed by Arnold Hasselstrom, and all of which, moreover, seemed to him absolutely necessary to his happiness and indeed to his continued existence— even the baseball bat, which was quite useless to him because of its weight. Arnold Hasselstrom had returned Dr. Mullhouse's screwdriver promptly, but he still had not returned the baseball bat, the dartboard, and the basketball game, not to mention some half dozen nickels (Edwin's allowance at this time was twenty cents a week). The bat, especially, obsessed Edwin. It infuriated him to think that Arnold Hasselstrom might think that the bat was useless to him because of its weight. He feared that Arnold Hasselstrom had lost the bat, or broken it, or left it in a puddle somewhere, or given it away. But for almost a week he could not bring himself to ask for the bat, partly because he feared to know the worst and partly because it was impossible to ask for a bat that he thought Arnold Hasselstrom might think was useless to him because of its weight, to say nothing of the fact that it happened to be the middle of winter. But hadn't Arnold Hasselstrom borrowed the bat in the middle of winter, for the purpose of practicing in his cellar? And Edwin wanted to know how he, Edwin, would ever learn to swing such a heavy bat unless he too practiced in the cellar. Meanwhile Arnold Hasselstrom continued to visit Edwin, quite unaware of the battle raging within his mild pale friend; and I could sense, as in a curtained room one senses the darkening of the sky, Edwin's growing anger at the sheer presence of Arnold Hasselstrom, who sat calmly shaking the dice over the Parcheesi board as if he had never so much as heard of Edwin's baseball bat.

Edwin asked for the bat, finally, staring at Arnold Hasselstrom's toes; to his astonishment Arnold Hasselstrom seemed annoyed. Instead of immediately offering to return the bat, instead of apologizing for having kept it so long, he asked Edwin why he wanted it back. "Why?" said Edwin. "Oh, well, why. I don't know. I guess I don't really need it." "You sure?" snapped Arnold Hasselstrom. "Sure," said Edwin. "Keep it. I don't really need it. Anyway, it's too heavy." And he felt ashamed of having asked for a bat that he really did not need and could barely pick up. But that evening in his room he paced up and down in front of me, throwing up his hands. Arnold Hasselstrom had no right to ask him why he wanted his stupid bat; he wanted his stupid bat because it was his stupid bat. And he needed it; he needed it right now. I listened patiently and, I confess, cheerfully as he continued in this strain, and finally I suggested that he simply ask for the bat again.

Two days passed. When at last he gained the courage to ask for his bat, Arnold Hasselstrom was ready for him. "You said you didn't need it," he said. Edwin was stunned. Immediately he saw the justice of Arnold Hasselstrom's position. At the same time he felt an irresistible craving for his bat, and with the vigor of desperation he replied: "I didn't need it then. But I need it now." And because he knew that this was an outrageous thing to say, he felt a surge of hatred for Arnold Hasselstrom.

The next afternoon I was in Edwin's room when we heard Arnold Hasselstrom's tread on the stairs. The very sound of his footsteps was now a source of annoyance to Edwin, who was also becoming heartily sick of Parcheesi. Instead of knocking at the closed door, Arnold Hasselstrom gave it a kick. Edwin flinched in disgust. "Come in!" he called angrily. Arnold Hasselstrom kicked again. Frowning, Edwin stood up and walked across the room. As he placed his hand on the doorknob I had a sudden vision of Arnold Hasselstrom standing on the other side with a gun in his hand. "Edwin!" I cried, as he opened the door.

There stood Arnold Hasselstrom, resting his right hand on the vertical baseball bat and holding under his left arm the boxed basketball game. "What," replied Edwin. "What?" said Arnold Hasselstrom. "Nothing," I replied. I noticed that the top of the basketball game was torn at two corners. But Edwin's ill will had vanished, and after a rousing game of Parcheesi he persuaded Arnold Hasselstrom to borrow a brand new red-and-black plastic roulette wheel, which when you pushed a lever spun beautifully round and round.

But that evening he wondered why Arnold Hasselstrom had not returned the dartboard. It was true that Edwin had not asked for the dartboard, but it was also true that he had not asked for the basketball game. But having just asked for the baseball bat he found it impossible to ask for the dartboard as well. Worse, he no longer had the new roulette wheel that he had just received for Christmas and that he had barely had time to play with at all. And he began to fear the visits of Arnold Hasselstrom, who always took something away.

Moreover, now that Edwin had his bat he began to brood over his two lost comic books. He longed to read them; he longed to see them; above all he longed to fill in the gaps in his collection, which without them was a poem lacking two rhymes. The comic books in question happened to be from two different years, so that the damage spread far beyond the two comics themselves. Two entire years, or twenty-four comic books, were affected by the loss. Not only that, but the stories in back were continuous, so that two serials, ranging over fourteen comic books, were permanently ruined. Sadly he spread out on his bed, in two neat rows, the twenty-two comic books that should have been twenty-four, leaving a space between the fifth and seventh of one row and the second and fourth of the other; and sadly he stared at the ugly swollen discolored thing with a stained and faded cover that formed the last comic book of the first row.

One of the missing comics was the very first he had owned, although by dint of judicious trading it was no longer the earliest of his collection. Vividly he saw the pair of yellow skis sticking out of a snowball under a red sky. Vividly he saw himself sitting on the stoop in his Indian headdress, vividly he saw himself lifting a box of marbles and lying on his bed as outside the rain pattered against his windows; and it was as if Arnold Hasselstrom had taken from him a piece of his past, making his life henceforward resemble a jigsaw puzzle from which a piece is missing, so that in the center of a billowing white sail you see a piece-shaped hole, through which the dark green table hideously shows.

And at last he asked Arnold Hasselstrom to look again for the missing comic books. He had found one; perhaps the others were lying in a corner somewhere, or under a sink, or in a pail. "Yeah," said Arnold Hasselstrom. As he was leaving he reached into his pocket, withdrew his hand, and stared at a palm that held a single dark penny. "You got a nickel?" he said, looking up at Edwin. Instantly Edwin looked away, saying: "A what? A knuckle? No I um maybe Jeffrey." Even as he spoke he realized that on the top of one of the gray bookcases, beside his little blue-and-gold tin cash-register dime-bank, lay six pennies. Arnold Hasselstrom jerked a thumb at the pennies. "Four cents?" he asked. "I need it." Edwin said: "Take it, take it," and sat on the bed while Arnold Hasselstrom, understanding nothing, held his left palm beside the bookcase and with his right index finger pulled four pennies across the wood into his palm.

The next day Arnold Hasselstrom failed to mention the comic books. As he was leaving, Edwin asked if he had looked. "Yeah," said Arnold Hasselstrom, giving him a look of guilty hatred. "But did you check every single place?" pursued Edwin, who had been taught never to say "yeah" for "yes." "Yeah," said Arnold Hasselstrom, a little too quickly, a little too sharply, so that Edwin felt compelled to say: "Well, maybe if you look again. Jeffrey, why is a raven like a writing desk?" "Because a writing desk is a raven in disguise," I replied with a smile. "No," said Edwin, "because they both have quills," and he began to giggle while Arnold Hasselstrom looked off with his lively deadpan.

The next day, as all three of us were playing Parcheesi, Edwin said as he shook the dice: "Did you find those comics?" Instantly Arnold Hasselstrom reached into the tight pocket of his pants, so that his shoulder was pushed up. I wondered whether he was going to shoot both of us or only Edwin. Withdrawing his hand, he tossed onto the Parcheesi board, one at a time, two bright dimes. One slid to a stop against a yellow piece, but the other rolled slowly, round and round, before it fell.

For a moment Edwin stared. Then he said: "It's not your turn," and rolled the dice. "Twelve. That puts me"

Arnold Hasselstrom's hand swept across the board. Most of the pieces and one dime struck the side of the bed, but two pieces and both dice hit the wall and rattled down behind the bed onto the floor. As Arnold Hasselstrom, wide-eyed, rose to his feet, I observed with interest that he did not once look at Edwin, who sat rigid with angry terror, staring at the table. Arnold Hasselstrom hit the table, which wobbled and almost fell. He picked up the

Parcheesi board, held it under his chin, and tore it in half along the fold. He flung the halves onto the floor and stamped on them with his right foot. Then he was gone.

"Well," said Edwin after a pause, "he didn't have to," and as he burst into silence I proceeded to pick up the twelve pieces, the two dimes, the two dice, and the ruined Parcheesi board, which even with the aid of masking tape would never, thank goodness, be the same.

# 25

THE DECLINE AND FALL of Arnold Hasselstrom would not occupy even a very small place in this biography, had it not occupied a very large place in the imagination of Edwin. Deterioration set in rapidly after the event recorded in the last chapter, an event which did not, incidentally, terminate their friendship: the decisive blow was Edwin's refusal to see Arnold Hasselstrom when, a week later, he rang the bell. Mrs. Mullhouse said he was sick, Arnold Hasselstrom went away, and that, as Mrs. Mullhouse put it, was that. Within two days Edwin was blaming himself for the whole misunderstanding, and was prepared to receive Arnold Hasselstrom amicably when he next stopped by. But Arnold Hasselstrom never stopped by. Edwin, who was willing to be reconciled, was apparently not willing to make the first move. It was not the first time I had witnessed in my friend a certain stubbornness that is perhaps part and parcel of the creative temperament. Arnold Hasselstrom never did return the dartboard or the roulette wheel, by the way.

Perhaps it was the death of his friendship with Edwin, perhaps it was simply the coming of spring, at any rate as the weather grew warmer a distinct change came over Arnold Hasselstrom. No longer did he sit in sullen silence, brooding darkly about ridiculous periwigs or whatever it was he brooded about: instead he was visibly restless and bored, and squirmed in his seat as if he were chafing against invisible bonds. One morning he fell into a vicious fight in the hall and nearly had his head cracked open against a radiator. Another morning he appeared in class with a dark bruise under one eye. One day he was absent. When he returned the next afternoon, handing Miss Coco a crumpled note that she read with a little frown, I was not surprised when she asked him to go with her to the principal's office. The forgery raised Arnold Hasselstrom in the eyes of the class, for no one had ever dared one before. A few days later he was absent again, and when he returned he did not even bother to bring a note, merely shrugging when Miss Coco questioned him. The next day he was absent again. This time he returned in a more colorful fashion. Kenneth Santurbano and I were working on a large map of Connecticut at the back of the room, and I had turned to consult the atlas concerning a small indentation in the southern coastline between Bridgeport and Stratford when I noticed a plump smiling man in the front of the room. According to the newspapers, his name was Mr. McKisco. He was wearing a long pale unbuttoned coat over dark clothes, his forehead was shiny, and his thin dark hair was combed straight back in little ripples. Beside him stood Arnold Hasselstrom. Mr. McKisco spoke a few words to Miss Coco, who nodded slowly; then he left, and Arnold Hasselstrom, with a distinct smirk on his face, walked to his seat.

During the next week Arnold Hasselstrom attended school regularly, behaving toward Miss Coco with a sullen obedience just short of insolence. He refused to talk to anyone else at all. On the playground, in the morning and afternoon before the bell, he stayed by himself. I watched him from afar as he sat defiantly alone on the sidewalk by the greening willow with his feet resting on the grass slope and his wrists resting on his knees, or as he stood alone in some empty corner of the playground with his hands in his pockets and his dark face turned against the wind.

One hot morning we entered the side playground, strolled to the back, and saw in the distance a large ring of shouting boys. Edwin and I glanced at one another and instantly looked away. As we hurried toward the noise my brain kept pace with my feet by repeating nonsensically the lines of an old poem: Rose Dorn, Rose Dorn, I am, forlorn, Rose Dorn, Rose Dorn, I am, forlorn. All over the playground groups of children went about their business, quite indifferent to the shouting circle in their midst. One group of girls was jumping rope a mere ten feet from the fight, and as we approached them a noisy chant briefly drowned the shouts:

> *All*
> *All*
> *All in together girls*
> *Never mind the weather girls*
> *Rain*
> *Snow*
> *Sunshine bright.*

But as we passed, already I heard among the shouts a voice crying: "Back! Back! Back! Back! Back!" The circle was three or four deep, and at first we could barely see past the older boys, who had the best places on the inside. Through arms and shoulders I had a confused impression of a white t-shirt, a light blue shirt, dark arms, a red shirt, a chin thrust back by a hand, a dark arm hooked around the grimacing face of Arnold Hasselstrom. We made our way around the circle, searching for a place; at a sudden opening Edwin squeezed in and was immediately shut out of view. I found my opening a few feet away, and managed to squeeze my way almost to the inner circle, where I was fortunate enough to find an excellent vantage point between two necks.

The fighters were barely moving. The tall boy stood with his arm hooked around Arnold Hasselstrom's head, just under the jaw, pressing it against his chest, while Arnold Hasselstrom, whose anguished grimace was directed at me, was pushing the invisible face over him with the heel of his outside hand. With his inside hand Arnold Hasselstrom was gripping the arm that hugged him, while with his free hand the other boy was gripping the hand that pushed against his chin and that was probably trying to get a stranglehold on his throat. The curious immobility of the fighters, which in one sense rendered their struggle unexciting and even uninteresting, in another sense conveyed an impression of intense seriousness that filled me with alarm. I recognized Arnold Hasselstrom's antagonist at once, an evil fifth-grader called Weasel who

was always cursing and spitting at people and who always had at
least three friends with him. He was more than a head taller than
Arnold Hasselstrom. His thin brown arms with their long thin
biceps were full of veins, and the close-shaved black hair on his
thin hard skull contained on one side a small triangular bare spot
that made you think of a notch in a tree. He wore black-and-white
sneakers with no socks, beltless pants the color of semi-sweet
chocolate, a white t-shirt, and a light blue unbuttoned shirt that
hung down below his pockets; one of the short sleeves was rolled
up above his shoulder but the other had fallen down. The match
looked unfair, and might have looked ridiculously unfair if it were
not for the general impression of solidity presented by Arnold
Hasselstrom, as if he were a stump battling a rugged vine. But he
seemed to be getting the worst of the still nearly motionless fight,
for his eyes were shut tight, drops of sweat beaded his eyebrows,
and his lips, stretched open over clenched teeth, seemed to be
forming a cry of pain. Suddenly Weasel leaned back and simultane-
ously whirled around in a half-circle, lifting Arnold Hasselstrom
briefly into the air and letting him down as he came to a stop. A
shout went up from the crowd, most of whom seemed to be
friends of Weasel's. Again he turned, lifting Arnold Hasselstrom;
when he stopped, Arnold Hasselstrom's hand slipped from the
jaw. Instantly Weasel smashed a fist into Arnold Hasselstrom's
face. Someone shouted "No fair!" Arnold Hasselstrom clutched
blindly at the invisible face above him, missing; again Weasel
smashed a fist into his face, hitting him directly in the eye. A shout
went up from the crowd. Twisting in pain, Arnold Hasselstrom
lowered his outside arm and tried to bury his face in it while
Weasel, with a look of malignant triumph, proceeded to form one
of those vicious fists with the third knuckle protruding, and began
alternately to rub his knuckles back and forth on Arnold Hasselstrom's head and to punch him in the neck and face. Someone
shouted "Break it up!" but no one took up the cry. Arnold Hasselstrom looked quite helpless now; there was nothing he could do but
shield his face by turning it inward, while Weasel punched and
rubbed. And as I watched Arnold Hasselstrom struggling, suddenly
I heard him shriek with pain. It was a high horrible sound that I had

never heard before, like the sound of some imagined animal in pain; and it was not until a few seconds later that I realized the shriek had come from Weasel. For suddenly Weasel had abandoned his hold and with both hands was tugging at Arnold Hasselstrom's hair, while Arnold Hasselstrom, with a sound like a growl, bit into his stomach. I half-expected to see him tear off a piece of bloody flesh, and no doubt he would have eaten Weasel alive if he had not had the better idea of hooking a leg around Weasel's leg and tripping him. He fell on top of Weasel, who somehow managed not to smash his head against the tar, and then Arnold Hasselstrom was holding Weasel's head by the cheeks and slamming it over and over against the ground. Suddenly there was a little pool of blood under his head. Arnold Hasselstrom stopped. He stood up. His left eye was swollen and bruised. On the bloody tar Weasel whimpered feebly. No one stopped Arnold Hasselstrom as he pushed through the opening circle and began to run.

When he reached the part of the playground where the tar turned into dirt and weeds, he picked up a stone and looked over his shoulder, but no one was following. He then ran up the narrow grass slope and onto the sidewalk, never once looking back. I watched him run along until he was shut out of view by a tall hedge, and when I turned I saw Edwin standing with his hands in his pockets, staring at the distant hedge.

According to the newspapers, Mr. McKisco was shot five times as he entered Arnold Hasselstrom's room. Three other bullets struck the wall to the right of the door. Arnold Hasselstrom then reloaded the .32 Colt automatic, picked up a cap pistol, and left the house. His grandmother was out shopping at the time of the shooting. He was found shortly before midnight in a wooden shack on a vacant lot in a remote neighborhood. Sergeant Flanagan said he hadn't wanted to shoot the boy. He said the boy had thrown out a gun, come out with his hands up, and suddenly started shooting again. I forget what happened to Sergeant Flanagan. A week later Weasel reappeared on the playground with a small white patch on the back of his head. "Jim always believed in boys," Mrs. McKisco was quoted as saying.

# 26

DURING THE MIDDLE YEARS Edwin and I saw well over two hundred cartoons. Intrigued by the titles, Edwin once began a list. I here give it in full:

Peeka Booboo, Lovey Dovey, Dandy Lions, Tamale and Tamale and Tamale, Scars and Stripes, Yankee Poodle, Hare-um Scare-um, No Chickee No Washee, Play for Cheeps, Finders Peepers, A Tail of Two Kitties, Much Achoo About Nothing, All's Wail that Ends Wail, Dutch Tweet, Kit for Kat, Kit-napped, Bumble Bzzzzz, Warp in the Woof Woof, Arf and Arf, Bow-wow Movements (or Loose Bow-wows), Oinkers Away, Tails You Lose, Sittin' Kitty, Go Fly a Kat, Warrin' Puss, The Brothers KaraMOUSEov, Winnie the Pooch, The Wind in Your Woolies, Little Red Robin Hood, The Fall of the Mouse of Usher, Pie a la Moo, Pooches and Cream, Quackers and Cheese, Cat Be Nimble Cat Be Quick, Kit Carson (Coonskin Kat), Kit and Kapoodle, Do-It-Yourself Kit, Kit and Kin, Wyatt Chirp, Mouse Breaking, Ro-meeow and Alleycat, The Quality of Mousey, Cat as Cat Can, Madame Pussycat (music by Poochini), Is There a Dachshund in the House?, Ali Baa Baa and the Forty Sheep, Fowl Play, The Howl and the Pussycat, Cocka-doodle Don't, Midsummer Mice Scream, Hare Today Gone To-morrow, Hare! Hare!, Hey Nonny Ninny, To Bzzz or Not to Bzzz, Pair o' Dice Lost, Hot Cross Bunny, Atomic Fishin', Kitty Cornered, Much Ado About Mutton (or All's Wool that Ends Wool).

A number of things about this list are of special interest to the student of Edwin's work. First of all, the influence of the animated cartoon is clearly verbal as well as visual: the titles are a feast of elementary wordplay. Second, a great many bits and pieces of adult culture first came to Edwin in this distorted fashion; indeed the cartoon titles encouraged in Edwin a tendency to think of adult culture solely as a source of puns and jokes. Often in the Middle

Years, on rainy afternoons, we would spend hours among his father's books in the three living-room bookcases, inventing cartoon versions of their titles. I recall simple ones like Moby Duck, Holy Bubble, and Alexander Poop, and more elaborate ones like Boogeyman's Conversations with Ghosty, Selected Bones of T. S. Alleycat, and The Whine and Call of the Woman Vampire. Edwin often missed the point of cartoon titles and had to ask his father to explain, for instance, Much Achoo About Nothing. Dr. Mullhouse was delighted by the whole business and was quite capable of tilting his head forward, raising his eyes solemnly to the top of his new bifocals, and telling Edwin in the full accents of professorial dignity that Much Achoo About Nothing was a play by William Sneeze. Edwin would frown for a few moments in desperate concentration before making the connection; his intense expression would melt to a blankness betrayed only by his suddenly knowing eyes, and at last his face would contort into a fit of the spluttering giggles, which he tried fiercely to stifle in order to command his father to be serious, but with each effort to overcome the spasm he set off another and greater one, so that he presented to the mildly smiling observer the interesting spectacle of a face grim and grinning in quick succession, as if it belonged to an idiot. Third, and most important, it seems to me, is a certain disturbing quality of the list, a quality that I shall define, after considerable meditation, as a repellent cuteness. I shall return to this quality in my discussion of Edwin's immortal masterpiece, in Part Three.

So much for the cartoon titles. The single most important influence of the animated cartoon upon Edwin's masterpiece—an influence that I shall discuss in a later chapter—is the cartoon image. Here I wish only to mention that the first direct use of images drawn from cartoons was made by Edwin in a poem written at the end of the Middle Years, some three months after the death of Arnold Hasselstrom (July 11–15, to be exact). This poem may be considered the last of Edwin's juvenilia or the first product of his literary maturity; at any rate it is the first motion in the long dance toward *Cartoons*. In it, for the first time, Edwin approaches a serious subject by means of comic and even ridiculous images, thereby producing a pale prefiguration of that elusive and absolutely original quality of his mature work that for the time being may be defined as a flickering combination of the grimace and grin. The poem is actually entitled "Cartoon" in one manuscript copy, although the single typed copy, which in Edwin's usual practice represents the final version, is entitled "To A.H." The version I reproduce below is that of the typed copy. Aside from its purely historical interest, and except (possibly) for the penultimate line, the poem is of absolutely no value. The scene is set not in cartoon-land, as the uninformed reader might suppose, but on Robin Hill Road, Newfield, where Edwin often walked of a summer afternoon on his way to the bakery for a loaf of sliced pumpernickel and a sugar cookie, and upon which he was fond of gazing at night from the dark window beside his pillow. The poem is a fitting if belated tribute to a dead friend, and a fitting but not, I hope, belated conclusion to Part Two of this darkening history.

## To A.H.

*Streetlamps, fellas, all in a row,*
*Like cartoon men with ideas in your heads,*
*Come walk in a loonytune night with me.*
*Changing, a stoplight blushes red*

*As the big-eyed moon looks winking down—*
*And blows out a star with a sudden sneeze.*
*A skeleton dressed in a tall silk hat*
*Chases a mailbox (rattling knees)*

*And mails a* DEAD LETTER. *Close-up, now:*
*My eyes show waves with sinking boats,*
*And terrified tears jump overboard*
*As the circle closes. That's all, folks.*

# Part Three

# THE LATE YEARS
## (*Aug. 2, 1952–Aug. 1, 1954*)

# 1

Toward the end of September a familiar change came over Edwin. Day after day from the middle of Row 1, I watched Edwin idling at the back of Row 4. Day after day I watched his gaze rise from the bright new pages of *Earth and Sky* or the faded pages of *Many Lands, Many People* to the clock or the flag or the piles of red dictionaries or the shiny blue map-cases hanging over the blackboard like rolled-up movie screens; and leaning his chin on his palm he would stare unseeing, minutes at a time. After school he walked home wearily, conversing in shrugs and sighs; and clutching the banister he dragged himself slowly, slowly, slowly up to his room.

It was painful for me to witness in Edwin this appalling repetition. Perhaps I had no business to interfere, perhaps in any case I could do nothing at all to help him, but I vowed, this time, to guard him against enchantment with all the means at my disposal. The source of the sorcery was not far to seek. There were four new girls in our class—Margaret Riley, Anna Maria DellaDonna, May Flowers, and Rose Black—and Edwin had maintained a suspicious silence about all of them. Margaret Riley was a thin nervous sickly girl whose big round eyes glittered in a little face the color of white paste. She looked as if she were dying of malnutrition. You could see the bone-bumps at the back of her neck, and you could see her shoulderblades sticking through the white sweater that she always wore over her pale dresses. From time to time she was racked by violent fits of coughing, during which her face became splotched with red. Anna Maria DellaDonna was a chubby bubbly girl with a bouncing black ponytail, black bangs, and eyes like black marbles. She was always collapsing into fits of the giggles, hunching up her shoulders and clapping a plump hand over a mouthful of shiny braces. As for May Flowers, she was the most artificial girl I have ever known. She resembled a wooden doll. A spot of red glowed at the center of each shiny cheek, her tiny rosebud mouth gleamed as if with varnish, and her shiny blue-black hair clung in tight little curls about her head. Her eyes, fringed with thick black lashes, were large, glassy, and piercing blue. One always imagined the lids closing with a soft click as the vast hand of her mother tipped her backward. Mrs. Flowers dressed her little daughter in a nice new outfit each day, slipping on the little white underpants and the little white undershirt, pulling down carefully over the shiny curls the red-and-white-checked cotton dress, fastening the shiny black belt with its silver buckle, slipping the little white socks over the polished feet, buckling the shiny black patent leather shoes, buttoning up the pretty navy blue coat with the gray fur collar, lifting her gently by the elbows past the little couch in the living room, past the little mantelpiece with the little candlesticks, past the little painting over the fireplace and up through the open ceiling into the sky; and swinging her through the blue, at last she set her down gently on the playground, leaning her carefully against the wire fence. And really she was an extra-ordinary doll, for she could not only close her eyes, cry, and wet her pants, she could also smile, talk, hum, cheat, and dream. She was smart enough in her shiny wooden way, and read aloud fluently in a bright sharp rapid aggressive voice. What a contrast to Rose Black, who was also in the top reading group but read in a fluent murmur. She was a homely, dusky, boyish girl with a large nose and a long serious mouth. She wore long drab dresses that must have belonged to an older sister, and scuffed brown shoes with worn-down heels. She kept to herself, though not defiantly; you sensed in her a relaxed self-dependence, as if she were used to being alone and rather enjoyed it. This in itself was cause for concern, for Edwin in the past had always been attracted to lone wolves and witches. But even more suspicious was her name: that eerie repetition caused her to possess quite helplessly an unpleasant fascination, as if she had donned the old red dress of dead Rose

Dorn. Sometimes, at certain angles, in certain shadows, I even fancied a distinct resemblance between them, as if Rose Black were an older, duller, duskier, dustier rose; a faded rose; a rose come back from the dead. And I recall with a shudder a certain morning when I saw her standing by herself near the brick wall in back: a shabby black cat was rubbing against her leg. I turned to Edwin, but he was watching a couple of black-jacketed blond hoodlums with white eagles on their backs.

Of course it was hopeless to try and learn from shy sly Edwin whether he had succumbed to the charms of Margaret Riley, or Anna Maria DellaDonna, or May Flowers, or Rose Black. And so I began to observe all four of them with an attention none of them deserved. I even went through the motions, on four successive occasions, of striking up an acquaintance I did not desire and later could not disown. I noticed at once that of the four only May Flowers actively pursued Edwin, poking at him with her bright sharp voice and fluttering her thick lashes whenever he came within ten feet of her. But I twice caught Margaret Riley staring furtively at Edwin from her seat beside him; and Anna Maria DellaDonna regularly collapsed into giggles, hunching up her shoulders and clapping a plump hand over her shiny braces, whenever Edwin uttered the faintest, most forlorn witticism. Only Rose Black displayed no interest in him whatsoever. Edwin himself, worsening daily, was careful to treat all four girls with the same gloomy, witty politeness; and everyone else, for that matter.

Within a week I was intimate with Margaret Riley, Anna Maria DellaDonna, and May Flowers. It was not without a certain ingenuity that I managed to conduct my investigations entirely unobserved by Edwin. If through the wire fence I saw Margaret Riley entering Rapolski's, I discovered in myself an overpowering urge for a piece of licorice. If over Edwin's shoulder I spotted May Flowers on the far sidewalk, I suddenly remembered that she had borrowed my green eraser. I snatched moments for private conversation during play period, and in the coatroom, and at the special groups that Mrs. Czernik liked to form for the purpose of making dioramas or building toothpick forts. By the bubblegum machine in Rapolski's I learned from Margaret Riley that Anna

Maria DellaDonna thought Edwin was handsome. On the grass slope by the willow I learned from May Flowers that Margaret Riley thought Edwin had nice eyes. While fitting a mirror-pool into the sand of a desert diorama I learned from Anna Maria Della-Donna that May Flowers liked Edwin first, Kenneth Santurbano second, and myself (with a giggle) third. During a game of kick-ball, when Edwin was on the other side, I learned nothing at all from solemn Rose Black, who apparently had no taste for idle chitchat.

Mrs. Mullhouse, alarmed by the familiar signs of illness but mis-interpreting their cause, began to supplement Edwin's absurdly healthy diet with huge brown vitamin capsules. Dr. Mullhouse mocked the whole enterprise and declared mistakenly that Edwin had never looked healthier in his life. But even he must have realized that something was wrong, for one evening when Edwin stumbled in the living room, his father looked up frowning over his bifocals and said: "Better get yourself oriented, boy. Before you have an occident." For that matter Edwin stayed on his feet rather longer than I had anticipated, though he continued to display all the symptoms of a consuming passion. I, meanwhile, found myself faced with a regrettable and entirely unforeseen turn of affairs. It was on the playground one morning in early October that Edwin and I were approached by Billy Duda, who had made great strides in loutishness over the years and was now trying to screw his oafish features into an expression of cunning. The reader will share my astonishment when, greeting me with a complicitous wink, jabbing me in the side with a conspiratorial elbow, and exhaling a stench that was probably the odor of his rotting intelligence, he said with a practiced leer: "Hey, Brain, how's Margaret?" "I don't know what you're talking about," I replied coldly, and indeed I didn't; but the impudent fellow only laughed, exposing his greenish teeth, and proceeded to lead Edwin and me to a portion of brick below one of Mrs. Cadwallader's windows. There, in white chalk, a lopsided heart was pierced by a crooked arrow; in the heart was the legend:

J.C.
L
M.R.

"It's a lie!" I cried, as Billy Duda ran off with a whoop of laughter; and Edwin lowered his eyes in gloomy embarrassment.

It was only the beginning. In my desk that morning I found an unsigned note reading JEFFREY AND MARGARET: I recognized the elaborate handwriting as that of May Flowers. Later, on the wide ledge of the coatroom window, I discovered the crude drawing of two kissing cartoon faces; over the first were the letters J.C., over the second were the letters M.F. And that afternoon, on the tar behind the oak in the angle of the wire fence, I discovered, chalked in hideous pink and green:

A.D.

L

J.C.

All of this was annoying in the extreme, and became positively sickening when, in class that afternoon, turning to observe Margaret Riley, I noticed that her glittering eyes were fastened upon me. Later I had the distinct impression that May Flowers, who sat one seat ahead of me in the adjacent row, was aiming a battery of fluttering glances in my direction. In the top reading group, which gathered in the first and second desks of each row, I happened to sit next to Anna Maria DellaDonna, who immediately turned into a jello of suppressed giggles; and May Flowers gave her a look of poison.

The morning came when Edwin failed to rise. As I rode to school with Dr. Mullhouse and Karen, now in Kindergarten, a sense of angry frustration gripped me. It seemed to me that I had been bungling about in an inexcusable manner; that I must discover at once which girl was the germ of Edwin's sickness, and effect an immediate and decisive cure. Far from allowing myself to become the reluctant fanner of another fire, I was determined to beat out the flames with my own bare hands. But how was I to learn which girl had bewitched him into illness? And how should I ever break the spell?

As I entered the playground, holding Karen by the hand, I saw Margaret Riley, Anna Maria DellaDonna, and May Flowers standing together in a little group not far from the tree in the angle of the wire fence. A flurry of excitement seemed to pass over them as I walked past; my polite nod was greeted by a medley of giggles. As I proceeded toward the back playground with Karen, I happened to glance over my shoulder at my little band of admirers, when behind the tree I saw, leaning alone against the wire fence with her hands in her pockets and the collar of her belted trench-coat turned up like a boy's, little Rose Black, watching me with a questioning gaze. Quite suddenly the answer to everything took shape in my brain.

In the coatroom I exchanged a significant look with Margaret Riley, who lowered her eyes and blushed. At my seat I leaned my chin on my hand and gazed dreamily at the ridiculous blueblack curls of May Flowers, who glanced over her shoulder three times and was finally thrown into the May Flowers version of blushing confusion. In the top reading group I released a wink in the direction of Anna Maria DellaDonna, who clapped a hand over her silver mouth and almost choked to death on an indigestible giggle. During snack period I composed, in my best penmanship, the following little verse:

> *Roses are red,*
> *Violets are blue.*
> *I love a rose.*
> *Do you know who?*

which later in the coatroom I delivered personally to Rose Black, lowering my eyes and reaching out shyly my trembling hand.

Edwin was sleeping when I arrived with Karen for lunch; Dr. Blumenthal was expected any minute. With cheerful candor I assured Mrs. Mullhouse that everything would soon be fine. "Oh I hope so, Jeff. I'm really worried about him this time. I hope it's not serious, do you think it's serious? Oh where is that stupid doctor, Edwin could have died of old age already."

That afternoon I discovered in my desk three folded notes. The first, showing a two-leaved stalk topped by a heart-shaped flower, and bordered by an intricate series of hearts and tendrils, was signed M.F. The second, written in a shy tiny hand, read:

<pre>
Jeffrey do you 1. hate me
              2. like
              3. love
</pre>

and was signed M.R. I crossed out 1 decisively and teasingly left untouched both 2 and 3. The third note read:

OPPI LOPPOVE YOPPOU

OPPANNOPPA MOPPAROPPIOPPA

I had no time to penetrate the logic of this ridiculous code, though it was easy enough to detect and then to eliminate the inserted *opp*'s. Things were going more splendidly than I had hoped; but Rose Black's silence puzzled me. I tried to attract her attention—she sat two seats in front of me—but even when she turned to pass some paper for a spelling test she resolutely avoided my gaze. I ignored her in the top reading group, during which I managed to return Margaret Riley's note. But during play period, when for a moment I found myself holding hands with Rose Black, silently, without looking at me, she slipped me a note.

Back at my seat I unfolded her message behind Chapter 2 of *Many Lands, Many People*. It read:

> *This rose is black*
> *And full of gloom.*
> *Yet I too love.*
> *Do you know whom?*

I cursed myself for my grammatical blunder; for a moment I wondered whether she was making fun of me. And yet, all things considered, I was pleased to have wrung from so elusive a soul so promising a response. At the 3:10 bell, when we all filed into the coatroom, I shattered Margaret Riley with a glance, reduced Anna DellaDonna to delirium with a smile, and shut up jabbering May Flowers with a wild flutter of my lashes. But each time I looked at little Rose Black, I saw only the serious brown back of her head. As I made my way down the front steps I watched that head in the line beside me; and as her line turned left toward the shady side-street, suddenly she flung at me a sharp, questioning gaze.

Dr. Blumenthal had prescribed small blue vitamin pills, and as I made my way upstairs bearing a pill and a glass of orange juice I reflected uneasily upon the next step of my campaign. Once I had persuaded Edwin that I was unalterably in love with all four girls, all of whom were unutterably in love with me, I felt certain that I should be able to extract from him a solemn vow. And it was this vow which would prevent him from pursuing her, whoever she was. Unfanned by the wind of public attention, unnourished by the fuel of gifts and glances, the flame that was consuming him would quickly die. It would not be pleasant to see the look in his eyes as I boasted to him of my quadruple conquest. Yet wasn't I right to risk a moment's pain for the sake of sparing him six months of anguish? At the top of the stairs I had a sudden vision of Rose Dorn, leaning from her tower with her long hair streaming; and as I pushed open the door of the dusky room I was not at all surprised to see Edwin seated crosslegged on his bed, dressed in his purple bathrobe and looking up guiltily from a piece of paper that he quickly whisked out of sight behind him. I said: "Your mother told me to bring up this stupid orange juice."

"Orange juice isn't stupid," said Edwin, eyeing me darkly. It was going to be a difficult visit. I handed him the glass and the small blue vitamin pill and sat down on the bed beneath the map of the United States. Edwin placed the pill in his pocket and drank down the juice with smacking and gulping sounds. After a while I began as follows:

"Something important happened to me today, Edwin. Something very important. In fact, today is the most important day of my whole life. Are you listening? Gee, I don't really know how to say this" (here my voice became hushed, hesitant, palpitant) "but, well, Margaret—you remember that day—and Anna Maria—and May—and Rose—you see I—I don't know how to—you see they —they love me, Edwin." I paused. Edwin lowered his eyes but said nothing. I continued eagerly. "And gosh, I was secretly in love with all four of them. But I never hoped, I never dreamed . . ." My voice trailed away in dreamy hope. "And you know, they even sent me love letters, Edwin. And you know, I have this strange, feverish feeling. But you know, one thing bothers me, Edwin. One thing bothers me. If I thought anybody else loved Margaret—or Anna Maria—or May—or Rose" (leaning forward I tried to discern his expression but he kept his face cunningly lowered) "or if I thought anybody was writing secret letters to Anna Maria—or Margaret—or Ray—or Mose" (not a motion, not a sound) "I don't know what I'd do, Edwin. I don't know what I'd do. I guess I'd—I guess I'd—I guess I'd just" (my voice fell to a whisper) "kill myself." I allowed the syllables to expand in the dusky silence until they filled the entire room. Edwin did not look up but sat with his eyes rigidly cast down; in the dim light of the drawn blinds he was the very picture, the very photograph, of grief. A faint tremor seemed to pass over him; I felt like a scoundrel. For a moment my resolve weakened, and I almost burst into apology. But recalling my purpose I hardened at once, and said with quiet firmness: "Well, I'm glad I told you my secret, Edwin. Please don't breathe a word of this to anyone. But I want you to promise me something, Edwin. Are you listening? I want you to promise me something very important. I want you to promise me in the holy name of friendship that you will never ever try to take away my Anna Maria —or my Margaret—or my May—or my Rose. Will you promise me that, Edwin? Will you? Edwin?" He sat with lowered eyes, trembling perceptibly in the cold breeze of my words. I rose and began to step toward his bed. Let him burst into tears, let him howl in agony: I wanted him to destroy that letter, I wanted him to swear that he would never look at those poisonous girls again. "Edwin," I urged, standing before him; but he sat with bowed head, unheeding. "Edwin!" I said harshly. Slowly he raised his dark, shiny eyes to my stomach, my chest, my chin; his lips were quivering. "Look at me!" I commanded, and as his eyes met mine his forehead wrinkled, his lips stretched open, and gripping the bedspread tightly with both hands he burst suddenly, helplessly, horribly into screams of laughter.

# 2

Thus, unwitting, was I witness to the feverish origins of Edwin's masterpiece. The whisked-off paper, I mean to say, was no love letter but the first page of the fiery work that had consumed his imagination for the past several weeks. Lest the reader chide me for exhibiting my mistake at such length, let him consider well my design in so doing. For was I really mistaken, after all? True, Edwin happened not to be in love with Margaret Riley, or Anna Maria DellaDonna, or May Flowers, or Rose Black. But if I had mistaken the object of his love, surely I had not mistaken that love itself. If outward signs mean anything at all, Edwin was as much in love with that book of his as ever he'd been with little Rose Dorn—indeed more so: for she had bewitched him for barely six months, while the book held him in its spell for a year and a half, teasing and tormenting him without mercy; though unlike Rose Dorn, this fleeing vision was captured in the end.

After Edwin's shattering laugh I found myself in a rather awkward position vis-à-vis my four girls. Fortunately it has been my policy in this work to huddle modestly in the background except when my presence is absolutely necessary for the illumination of some facet of Edwin's life. Suffice it to say that Margaret Riley, Anna Maria DellaDonna, and May Flowers proved conveniently fickle, though faithful Rose Black haunted me horribly with her sharp, questioning gaze. Finally I had to write her another note. As for Edwin, he recovered from his collapse though not from his consuming fever, so that Mrs. Mullhouse continued to feed him a steady dose of small blue vitamin pills supplemented by occasional big brown capsules—just, as she put it, to be on the safe side.

And now, reader, this radiant history is obliged to enter one of its less luminous eras. For although I saw Edwin daily during the difficult months of the making of *Cartoons*, and so in a sense fol-

lowed the slow creation from moment to moment, in another and
more important sense I did not see him at all. I don't mean simply
that he hurried home from school each day and shut himself up in
his room with no thought whatever of his abandoned friend; nor
do I mean to stress my misery when I add that those sad days
taught me many a grim lesson concerning the perhaps necessary
selfishness of the creative temperament. Rather, I mean that even
his presence was a form of absence. It was as if he had once inhabited himself completely, but now had moved to some small
part of himself where I could not find him. It is true enough that
Edwin's absence from himself allowed me a certain freedom of
observation, even if it was only an observation of abandoned
rooms. Thus I soon became expert at distinguishing among shades
of pallor and nuances of irritability. Thus too I quickly noticed
the new red cracks in his eyes, the new squint, the new habit, while
he read, of propping a weary eyelid by pushing up with a forefinger the skin beneath the eyebrow—and no wonder. For one
troubled night when I was unable to sleep, and emerging from bed
at 2:45 proceeded to creep into the chilly kitchen for a graham
cracker and a glass of milk, lo! through the kitchen window, over
the Mullhouse garage, I saw the bright yellow rectangle of Edwin's window, glowing like some unnatural sun.

The day provided me with little opportunity to enjoy even the
distant company of my lovesick friend. I arrived at Edwin's each
morning with my customary punctuality, to be greeted by Karen
and Dr. Mullhouse and Mrs. Mullhouse and ignored by bleary-
eyed and disgruntled Edwin. "The Prince of Wales will be with
you in a moment," Mrs. Mullhouse would say. "Hurry up, Edwin,
for heaven sakes. You're not the only one around here, you know.
Do you have all your books? Do you have your homework? Look
at your shirt, oh really. And look at your shoelaces. Really, I'm
surprised they let you in that place. Do you have everything? Does
he have everything? He'd forget his head if it wasn't screwed
onto his oh my God look at the time. Make sure you hold Karen's
hand, and don't you make faces at me young man. Make sure you
hold Edwin's hand, baby, tight tight tight. Now kiss mommy goodbye, mmm what a schatzkele. Keep an eye on Mr. Mopey Falopey,

Jeff, don't let him fall into any manholes or anything. And drive carefully, won't you, dear. And for heaven sakes make sure the doors are locked, remember what happened to Jimmy Pisarelli on Sullivan Avenue. Look at that. Just look at that. God love it, Edwin, people will think you're a refugee."

Dr. Mullhouse drove us to school in the morning on his way to work, letting us off a block before the blue policeman; Edwin sat crumpled up in a corner of the Studebaker, with his hands lying palm-up on his lap and his books lying in a fallen pile beside him. "All out," Dr. Mullhouse would say, leaning over and opening the door for Karen. Then looking over his shoulder he would wish me a hearty good morning, and dropping his voice to a dramatic whisper he would add: "Who in God's name is the ninety-two-year-old gentleman in the corner there?"

On the playground before the bell Edwin was melancholy and remote. He utttered isolated remarks that were not meant to be taken up, and remained aggressively indifferent to remarks of my own or Karen's. Indeed he seemed unpleased at having his little sister with him, and sometimes in a fit of impatience would tell her to go play with her little friends—a difficult problem for me, since I felt responsible to Mrs. Mullhouse for keeping an eye on Karen. Often he would simply leave us, and I would not see him until the bell; and after the bell, for all that he was in the same room with me, he might as well have been in Timbuktu.

The only real time I spent with Edwin was on our three walks together: home from school for lunch, back to school after lunch, and home from school in the afternoon. Karen, on a half-day schedule, accompanied us on the first walk, which seemed both to annoy Edwin and to provide him with a civilized excuse for absolute silence, since after all I could speak to his little sister if I had to speak at all. Not that he was always silent; for sometimes he erupted into complaint. "How come we always have to go to school," he would say, kicking an innocent leaf. "How come they never come to us." Or perhaps: "I feel awful. I think I'm dying." As a rule I chatted with Karen or Mr. Nobody and rested content with observing my temperamental friend. His health was distinctly on the decline, though one could by no means foresee the shocking developments that were to take place in a year's time. After all, his love affair was still in an early stage. In late October I noticed a twitch in his left eyelid; in early November I detected a tremor in his right hand. And of course he was reddish in the eyes, and blueish under the eyes, and a bit yellow about the gills—oh, he was a regular rainbow—but one somehow expected that; and besides, in other respects his appearance was distinctly improved: a slight tightening about the lips, and something in the eyes, gave his unstriking face its first suggestion of character; and indeed it was this very change that first caused me to doubt my skepticism concerning the evidences of physiognomy, and to feel that after all there may be a secret connection between what a person does and what he looks like.

Home from school, Edwin would at once disappear into his room; and except on the few occasions when I was invited by Mrs. Mullhouse for dinner, I did not see him again until the next morning. This was the cruelest blow of all, for over the years I had contracted a habit of spending the last hour or so before retirement with my then friendly friend. On the weekends, I may add, he was about as available as Edward Penn. Sometimes at night I would watch for Edwin from my kitchen window; but over the Mullhouse garage I saw only a glowing rectangle, as if he had been transformed into electricity.

And so that autumn I spent most of my time with 5½-year-old Karen. To my surprise I discovered that she was a solitary, serious, rather cynical little girl. The fact is, I had scarcely noticed her for the past three years. I taught her how to play checkers, dominoes, and gin rummy, and she in turn taught me how to play House, Doctor, and Paper Dolls. I became rather fond of paper dolls; between Halloween and Thanksgiving I cut out some three hundred costumes, each with its fringe of white tabs. We played in the living room or in her room while Edwin stayed stubbornly shut up by himself. A kind of friendship sprang up between us, though I fear my affection was less for her than for the notion that a friendship should have sprung up between us: us, two orphans of Edwin's affection: us, the abandoned ones. Indeed it had not escaped my attention, during the Middle Years, that Edwin had played less and less with Karen; and I now realized that she had quickly gone the way of his other toys. I wondered with some bitterness whether I too had served my turn. One rainy afternoon when Karen and I had run out of amusements, and had begun to turn through the family albums, it was something of a shock to come across that photograph from the Early Years in which Edwin and Karen are walking hand in hand along a bright, tree-lined road, stretching away in a shimmering perspective that grows brighter and brighter, as if they are being drawn toward some dazzling vision. That dazzle had proved a drizzle indeed. As I continued to turn pages I began to notice that the pictures of Karen from the Middle Years showed her with a variety of serious, sad, and sultry expressions on her face—the very record of Edwin's cruelty, written for all to see. I glanced guiltily at Karen, who was gazing at the pictures with innocent delight; and my heart wept for the sadness of all abandoned sisters, though even then I knew it was myself I grieved for.

# 3

ONE FRIDAY AFTERNOON in late November, on our chill way home from school, Edwin suddenly invited me to visit him the next morning at nine. I must have opened my mouth in surprise, for I had not entered his room for two months. How well I remember that longed-for visit. It was a bright blue morning, with a shine on things and a touch of ice in the air, and as I crossed Edwin's back lawn, walking the line where sun-green met shade-green, I glanced up at his double window, glossy, black, and opaque as licorice. When I rapped on the door, at nine precisely, Mrs. Mullhouse informed me that the Sleeping Beauty had not yet awakened. "He was so mopey all week I just didn't have the heart to get him up," she said as I stepped inside. "But if he thinks I'm letting him sleep past ten he's got another think coming." In the bright living room Dr. Mullhouse sat twisted in his chair, holding up a glass-covered slide to the window behind the lamp-table; I caught a glimpse of glowing red and green. "Hello," said Karen, who sat on the rug amidst a snowfall of paper dolls. "Oh, hello," said Dr. Mullhouse, turning around but still staring at the held-up slide, through which he suddenly looked at me, saying: "Well now, *that's* an improvement"—but whether he meant the slide or me I shall never know. Glancing at my watch, I joined Karen in her snowfall. At precisely 10:00 Mrs. Mullhouse said: "Jeffrey, you're sitting on a jumper." At 10:29 I heard the upstairs bathroom door slam shut; at 10:36 Edwin appeared at the head of the stairs, bleary-eyed and glum in his purple bathrobe. "Well well well," said Dr. Mullhouse from his chair, "you're looking chipper this evening. Did you sleep well? You're just in time for supper." Haughty, sulky, and rather rumpled-looking, Edwin proceeded into the sunny kitchen, where he ate his breakfast in pale silence, punctuated by occasional dark complaints. At 11:04 he rose from the table, looking at me as if he remembered me from somewhere. "You told me to come over," I said as I followed him upstairs, and at 11:06 he slowly opened his door.

Inside, it was already twilight. The blinds were closed, and long dark curtains covered the vertical edges of the windows. The ceiling light shone like an afternoon's pale moon. On the red rug beside his unmade bed lay a black checker, two of his father's blue examination booklets, a big thin glossy book called *Mowgli the Jungle Boy*, and a long yellow pencil. On the bed under the map of the United States lay a lone pingpong ball. I sat down beneath the state of Texas, and the pingpong ball came rolling against my thigh, while Edwin sat down crosslegged in the center of his rumpled bed, staring gloomily at his purple right knee. "Play some checkers?" I ventured cautiously. "Mmm," said Edwin. "Jump out the window?" I suggested cheerfully. "Mmm," said Edwin. Ten minutes later he got up suddenly and left the room. When I heard him close the bathroom door I rose, tiptoed over to his bed, and squatted down before the red rug. With trembling fingers I opened the first blue booklet. It was blank. The second blue booklet contained, on the first page, a meaningless list of words and phrases, among which I recall: deadpan, deadbeat, dead heat, deadlock, dead letter, deathmask, dead center, and Dead Sea. On the second page was the single mysterious phrase:

bats with bibs?

Puzzled and disappointed I returned to my bed, where again the wretched pingpong ball came rolling against my thigh. When at last the door opened, and gloomy Edwin entered, I could not resist saying with a smile: "Was that you flushing?" But Edwin, who never remembered anything and never, never understood other people's jokes, looked at me solemnly and answered: "Uh huh." He then resumed his position in the center of his bed, and began to tap a little marching tune with his fingers against his right thigh. I coughed into my fist. I examined my palm. I inspected the ceiling, where in the glowing lightshade I discovered the silhouettes of half a dozen dead bugs. At 11:45 I said: "Well, I have to go now. Lunchtime." And as if Edwin were intent on completing an analogy, suddenly his features became animated with true affection, and with absolute sincerity he told me how sorry he was to see me go.

# 4

In December I took up photography. I mastered film speeds, f-numbers, and focal lengths; I learned to use a range-finder, a light meter, a lens shade, a yellow filter. With the aid of a tripod I took pictures of star-trails at night, pointing my camera at the North Star; with the aid of a flash attachment I took pictures of myself in the mirror, carefully focusing at twice my distance from the glass. On weekends I went on photographic jaunts with Dr. Mullhouse and Karen, returning with shots of fire engines, tombstones, garbage cans, church steeples, and snowy vistas. I took pictures of Karen in her snowsuit, of Dr. Mullhouse photographing Karen in her snowsuit, of Mrs. Mullhouse pulling Karen on her sled; and there is an indoor shot of the Mullhouse family, taken with the aid of floodlights, that shows Dr. Mullhouse sitting on his chair staring vacantly at an upside-down book while Karen sits grimly on the chairarm glaring not quite at the camera and Mrs. Mullhouse leans in from the other side with a wild grin on her face.

Only once that winter did Edwin come briefly back to life. One morning in class he reached into his pocket and removed a slim black case that opened like a jewelbox; and removing a pair of round eyeglasses with colorless rims, quickly he slipped them on his face. I was hardly surprised, for Mrs. Mullhouse had told me about that trip to the eye doctor. Edwin was distinctly upset by his glasses: for the first few weeks he never looked people in the eye when he wore them, and he wore them as little as possible, taking them off twenty times a day and shutting them up in the case with a click. I myself had not yet acquired eyeglasses, and Edwin's fascinated me perhaps unduly: they seemed the sign of a special wound, like the white slings and casts of boys who were reckless of their bodies. But the eyeglasses had two other, and opposite, effects: they made Edwin look strange to me, as if they were the outward and visible sign of that inward and spiritual strangeness I had felt in him ever since he had fallen so desperately in love with his book; but at the same time they made him once again familiar to me, for by troubling and obsessing him, by making him self-conscious, they returned him briefly to the world, and made him creep from his hiding place to re-inhabit himself as of old. And so he complained bitterly to me about the way his glasses pressed into his nose, and hurt his ear, and wouldn't stay up, and wouldn't sit straight, and blinded him, and killed him, and gave him headaches and eyeaches and stomach aches and backaches and lord-knows-what-aches; and once he even blamed them for a swollen gland in his neck. He complained bitterly, I say; and his complaints were music to my ears. We exchanged gossip. We chatted about this and that. We even had a few games of checkers after school. When I asked him about his novel he laughed and said oh, that thing. Once he actually discussed in a serious but confused manner the problems involved in writing his book: "And you see, there are all these words, nothing but words, what are these words, and there they are, so that's what you're faced with, words, words . . ." "Do you mean," I suggested cautiously, "that the problem you face is the relation between your life on the one hand and your words on the other?" "That's it!" he cried, and a moment later: "Well, no, I don't know, what does my life have to do with it, what are you talking about, words, life, I don't know. How's April Showers, I mean May Flowers?"

But soon he was wearing his eyeglasses for the entire schoolday, taking them off only to and from school; and soon he was wearing them even then; and as the year turned, and the last snow melted in the shadows of trees and porches, again he retreated from the surface of his skin into his secret hiding place.

# 5

THAT SPRING, Edwin's penultimate, I took up philately and mineralogy. I sent away for whole bagfuls of used stamps and wrote to the Geology Departments of all 48 state capitals. In the course of a month I accumulated more than 2,000 American stamps, of which 1,853 were duplicates. I received labeled collections of specimens from Arizona, New Mexico, Colorado, and New Jersey, and a jar of sawed talc from Georgia. I also began to go on long bicycle expeditions around the neighborhood, accompanied at times by Karen, who sat in the basket like an enormous egg, because Mrs. Mullhouse feared she would fall off the fender-seat. I showed her scenes of interest from the life of her brother, as if he were dead. I showed her the stream that flowed past the bakery into the tunnel under Robin Hill Road, where Edwin picked up his boats and refused to continue, and the steep street beyond the school where gray two-story houses with zigzag staircases rose to a bright red drugstore, once dark green, and the bland house beyond the bakery where Edward Penn had lived. One day we had lunch together at the end of Beech Street.

It was a blue, too blue day, and as I sat on the root of the fat old tree, watching the shadow ripple and bubble on the water, years of memories rippled and bubbled in me, from the distant days of Edward Penn to the summer of *The Family Newspaper*. And suddenly I told Karen everything about Penn, the strange little boy who lived in a cellar; but I think she thought I was making it up, for afterward she said: "Tell me another, 'kay?" And so I told her all about Rose Dorn, the little girl who lived with a witch in the woods. At the end she wanted to know if Rose Dorn went to Heaven; I told her I didn't know; and she wanted to know if Gray went to Heaven; and again I told her I didn't know. "*I* know," she then said bitterly, scornful of my evasions. "They both went to Hell because they were bad." Somewhat taken aback by the strictness of her views, I attempted to give the conversation a lighter turn by saying with a twinkle: "And where will Edwin go?" But immediately she dropped her eyes, and hugging her knees and looking off across the yellow field she said evasively: "Oh you stupid. He's still alive."

# 6

I HAVE HAD SOME OCCASION, in my time, to reflect upon the admirable uses of adversity, but never more than during the bright, dark spring of 1953. Edwin's silence and absence were painful to me, and for that very reason I found myself yoked ever more tightly to our burdensome friendship. My many attempts to escape into sham hobbies were but further evidences of the true bonds they sought to sever. I do not recollect the precise day on which I clearly realized, what I had always dimly known, that I was going to write a biography of Edwin. Indeed it was not a sudden but a gradual knowledge, comparable to the growth of crystals of rock candy on a string suspended in a syrupy solution of sugar and water. Indeed I had, in a sense, been accumulating this knowledge over the long course of an observant lifetime. The reader will perhaps be surprised to learn that I did not instantly set to work, did not even begin to plan my book or take notes: I simply rejoiced in my new sense of purpose. Of course I continued to exercise my faculty of scrupulous recollection, satisfying thereby an inner need and at the same time readying myself for my great task. I knew that before beginning in earnest I should have to see Edwin's masterpiece; nor did I doubt for a moment that it was, in fact, a masterpiece. Already it seemed to me that I understood it perfectly, that book—for was it not the organizing principle of his life, the central magnet around which the innumerable filings of his experience were taking shape, just as my own book now began to attract to itself stray bits of memory that slowly discovered their appointed places in a previously unsuspected design? Even then I suppose I perceived dimly that the design was marred somewhat by Edwin's indefinitely continued existence, but at the time I was less concerned with the hazy future than with the luminous past. And so I dreamed, and waited, and assembled old puzzles with Karen, and above all savored the sweet sense of mission and meaning that my life had begun to assume. Mountainous meditations, you say, for so modest and molehillish a biographer. And why not? After all, there was nothing else to do.

# 7

IT WAS NOT UNTIL SHORTLY AFTER his tenth birthday that Edwin began to show signs of resembling himself again. Meanwhile he continued the feverish and spellbound pursuit of his merciless book, following it down the hill and over the nameless dirt road into the black forest and over the flagstone path into the very heart of the house itself. About the middle of May he began to sniffle a great deal, as if he had caught a slight perpetual cold; when it failed to develop into anything serious, Dr. Blumenthal suggested that he be checked by Dr. Piccolo, Mrs. Mullhouse's allergist. Tests showed him to be allergic to dust, feathers, pets, and pollen; Mrs. Mullhouse had to buy him a foam rubber pillow, which at first he refused to sleep on and later refused to do without, and once a week he had to be driven to Dr. Piccolo's for an injection. Edwin submitted to this routine with surprising meekness; later he explained to me that the allergy interfered with his work. All through this period I of course continued to accompany him to and from school, observing the familiar signs of weariness and irritability that later, in the fifth grade, were to take such an alarming turn. I never saw him after school, for he napped until dinner and then went straight up to his room. Often at night, unable to sleep, I would creep into my kitchen and watch Edwin's light until it went out: at 1:26, at 2:03, at 2:55. I even made a game of it, thrilling each time he broke a record. Once I watched from 3:27 (his previous record) to 5:06, when the sky was a deep melancholy blue and the birds had been shrieking for nearly an hour, before I had to crawl back to bed, exhausted, though his light still burned; but that morning Edwin looked surprisingly well-rested, and I realized that he had fallen asleep with his light on. But one gray dawn I saw the light burning again, and that morning Edwin's hands were trembling and his eyes red-slashed. And one night I saw the light go out at 11:16, and I longed to know what triumph or agony had sent him to sleep at such a ridiculous hour.

In July I took up chemistry. With the end of school (fourth grade for the budding novelist was a distant blur) Edwin no longer had to rise at 7:00, and so his light began to go off later and later. He refused to come out at all on the morning of the Fourth, though in the afternoon he made a sullen appearance, sitting on the back steps with a haggard expression and wincing each time Karen and Dr. Mullhouse set off a firecracker. One bright blue morning at 8:00 when I entered the kitchen to eat breakfast with mama, I saw his yellow window shining palely among the shadowed white shingles; as I was helping myself to a second bowl of Quaker Puffed Rice, the light went out. Naturally his hour of rising retreated steadily as his hour of retirement advanced. Sometimes Mrs. Mullhouse would invite me for lunch at noon, and as I was finishing my milk I would hear the sound of the bathroom door closing upstairs. "King Farouk is up," Mrs. Mullhouse would say, jerking her chin at the ceiling. At first she had refused to let him sleep past 9:00, but Edwin had apparently dragged his weary way through breakfast with an air of such melancholy outrage, such pained betrayal, that at last she had washed her hands of the whole affair. "If he wants to live like an owl," she would say, "that's fine with me. Let him. I certainly won't stop him. He can do what he likes. Of course he's ruining his health, you see that, don't you. Ten million little boys in New York are all dying to have a nice back yard like Edwin's, but he doesn't give a damn, excuse me, Jeffrey. We might as well live in a cave, for all the good it does him. We might as well live on East Tenth Street."

"Well, dear," said Dr. Mullhouse, "I entirely agree with you. Starting tomorrow that son of yours gets up at nine like a sensible boy."

"Oh, but Abe, you know he needs his sleep. And besides, he's working on that thing of his. You know, dear, it's really all your fault. If you hadn't given him all those damn books. Oh, how long does it take to write a little old novel, anyway? More milk, Jeffrey?"

Edwin's tenth birthday (the last party of his life) was a memorably melancholy affair. Grandma Mullhouse was present, which meant that Karen was sleeping in Edwin's room and that poor Edwin was leading abnormal hours, that is to say, normal hours. Edwin sat at the kitchen table with a green party hat on his head and dark shadows under his red-cracked glittering eyes. Piles of presents in colorful wrapping paper, tied with red and blue bows, towered before him. As he unwrapped each gift he worked his weary features into a feeble imitation of surprise and delight. He received a splendid hockey game with knobs and a steel ball (smile), a small but excellent globe on a red stand (smile), a model ship with elaborate instructions (smile), a bazooka that fired pingpong balls (smile), and a tall illustrated book called *Rockets and Missiles* (smile). I gave him a handsome edition of *Oliver Twist* (smile) inscribed "Ice again!" (frown), a reference evidently lost upon

Edwin, whose only comment was: "Mom, give Jeffrey some ice cream." Afterward he rested his elbows in a pile of crackling wrapping paper, staring gloomily as Grandma Mullhouse carried over a cake blazing with eleven candles (one to grow on). "Make a wish!" we all urged, and I have no doubt he did, but fortunately he managed to blow out only five candles.

And then, three days later, as I sat in the Mullhouse living room playing the hockey game with Karen, Edwin appeared at the head of the stairs. Slowly he descended, raising a handkerchief twice to his nostrils; and strolling over to us he sat down and said: "Hi, can I play?" It was the first time he had smiled at me in eleven months. "Be my guest," I said, and added casually: "Finish the novel?" "Nozzle? What nozzle? Oh, novel. Well, no, not exactly. I reached a point." A point, dear reader! But this smoke-screen of indifference only served to reveal to me the smoldering excitement beneath. It was then that I first urged Edwin to ride with me to White Beach, for old times' sake; and the very next day he accompanied me on that nostalgic and memorable journey, as recorded in Part One Chapter 3 of this history. A distinct relaxation now became noticeable in Edwin. For although he continued to work steadily on his book, he proved accessible to companionship and even exhibited a mild prankishness on occasion; and several times he actually suffered Karen and me to be present while he "revised." It was on one of these occasions, incidentally, that Dr. Mullhouse burst in upon us with his new twin-lens reflex and captured the second of the two delightful photographs described at the beginning of this work. Once or twice I slept over, as I often had in the past; and at the end of August Edwin accompanied me to Soundview Beach, as recorded in Part Two Chapter 4. I questioned him incessantly about that point of his, but received such vague and elaborate answers that I soon began to wonder whether he knew precisely what he meant. Indeed I have often marveled at the discrepancy between Edwin's incoherent and vaporous explanations of his work and the coherent and luminous work itself. Perhaps it is simply that the creative imagination by nature does not understand itself; or perhaps there is something about the mysterious act of creation that resembles a dream, which fades so quickly from the waking brain. Even such a mind as mine, tenacious of detail, feeling itself waking to the dusty items of the morning, will try to plunge back into the dissolving colors of some lucid and luminous land, only to find that the very energy of the trying hastens the dissolution; and all the azure and ivory of an abundant kingdom resolves itself into a corner of pillow and a piece of wallpaper. And all the king's horses and all the king's men cannot put that dream back together again. August ended, and with it the luxurious summer dream of endless azure time; and suddenly school was upon us, and again Edwin began to fade away; but that was all right; for now my own book began to stir in my brain like a bird, like a bird I tell you, like a bird.

# 8

So BEGAN THE FIFTH GRADE, Edwin's last. And suddenly, as if resentful of Edwin's recent affection for his old friend, his jealous book began to punish him cruelly, teasing him and tormenting him and mocking him and making him suffer such black despair, such crimson agony, as Rose Dorn had never inspired. Oh, she was a fiend out of hell, that book, a wicked fairy, an evil stepmother with a basket of poisoned apples; and he was so deeply in love, so deathly in love, that I feared for his health as I never had before.

His mysterious internal pains began in late September: he would walk to school stooped over slightly, holding one hand pressed against his stomach. Fits of violent vomiting soon developed which kept him out of school for ten days. His mother's usual intense concern developed this time into something more serious: she began to suffer from sudden headaches, during which she would sit with a fist pressed against her wrinkled forehead. Dr. Blumenthal put Edwin on a special diet that seemed to work, for the vomiting stopped and the pains did not return; but for weeks Edwin's tongue was coated with white, and he began to be persistently troubled by his bowels. All this I learned in great detail from Mrs. Mullhouse, who did not realize that she was imitating Mrs. Penn. Attacks of diarrhea alternated with attacks of constipation that sometimes lasted five days; severe attacks of indigestion left him prostrate and feverish. In addition to his other troubles, a urinalysis revealed an excess of sugar in his blood, as if his very corpuscles were degenerating. He was forbidden all sweets and forced to make do with Saccharine, which upset his stomach; and once a month he was required to perform the strange ritual of chewing on a special cube of wax, spitting repeatedly into a small vial, and presenting this sample of his saliva to Dr. Mullhouse, who mailed it away for analysis. Violent headaches woke him at night, and one day in class I saw him rise with everyone else at the recess bell and suddenly grip the edges of his desk, squeezing his eyes shut and bowing his head—the first of his dizzy spells.

But these violent and occasional afflictions caused him less suffering, I think, than the mild and unvarying underlying condition of intense nervous irritability. Bright light affected his eyes like flung sand; all noise tormented him. He said he was dying from lack of sleep because the attic made creaking sounds and the toilet gurgled all night long. Sudden sounds shattered him: we were standing on line one day, waiting to be let inside, when Edwin suddenly whirled around, his face filled with terror, because some clumsy fool had dropped a pile of books. Even his sense of touch underwent a change: he could not bear to handle grimy pennies or to run his fingertips along a dusty surface, for grime and dust affected his sense of touch the way the prongs of a fork scraped along a plate affected his sense of hearing. His very vision seemed to become infected by the general germ, for more than once as we passed some familiar and perfectly innocent mailbox or fire hydrant, Edwin expressed a sudden, violent revulsion, as if we had come upon the mountainous droppings of some enormous beast. Sometimes, leaning over a book in class, he would sit up suddenly with a startled expression on his face, having mistaken some spot in his eye for a crawling bug.

But even his nervous irritability was as nothing compared to the despair of spirit that emanated from him like an odor. In the Middle

Years, Edwin once expressed a fondness for the cartoon fellow who walks alone under his personal raincloud, which rains only on him in a beaming world—an image that might serve as Edwin's emblem during these black, bleak months. For the truth of the matter was simply that he could no longer progress with his book. This I gathered not merely from the stray moans and railings that had begun quietly in September and had swelled to a harsh sforzando by the end of October but also from the now distressing fact of his increased availability. No longer did he hurry upstairs when he arrived home from school, but lingered pitiably in the living room to talk with his mother or me. Meekly he asked Karen if she wanted to do a puzzle. He begged Mrs. Mullhouse to let him help with dinner and he asked me if he could see my photographs. He was feverishy impatient for the daily return of his father, for whom he fetched the black moccasins and chose a pipe ·from the metal rack. And now his earlier selfishness began to seem to me a strength he had lost; it was as if he were so weak that he could only be solicitous. Indeed the whole question of strength and weakness, in regard to Edwin, caused me no end of speculation. For if strength was the opposite of his present need for distraction, was it not also the opposite of his former grim obsession, which had about it some touch of desperation and fear? Was not strength rather calmness and relaxation, such as Edwin had experienced briefly after reaching that deceptive "point"? Or had his calmness been only a pleasant vacation in the midst of the long turmoil of his task? And was that "point" perhaps a deliberate illusion, imposed by some force within him that knew he must rest in order to gather his energies for yet sterner efforts? And was it possible that effort and struggle were themselves mere forms of weakness? And is it possible that a work of art is born not of strength but of weakness, of weakness trying to become strength, of weakness brought to such a pitch of frenzy that it becomes strength? But I fear this sudden gust of question marks has blown the reader's patience away; and I hasten to return to the milder air of periods and semicolons.

Unfortunately for the more romantic members of my readership, Edwin's heartbreaking physical condition was accompanied by a rather less endearing mental condition. A spirit of harsh contradiction began to prevail in him. He made cutting remarks about everyone and everything: he mocked little children, he railed at dogs, he lashed out against the wind. If as we drove to school some bright October morning I happened to make an innocent remark to Karen such as "Pretty nice day," Edwin would say snappishly: "I hate nice days," or "My Aunt Fanny," or "Stupid sun. Makes me sick." He seemed moderately unmiserable only on drizzly miserable mornings, when the gray light soothed his eyes and the general bleakness seemed a fitting expression of his mood; though even then, if I said anything at all, he would reply in a spirit of mockery and contempt. On the playground he liked to stand alone with one foot raised heel-first against the bricks, his hands in his pockets and his books in a pile beside him, while he surveyed the crowded playground with an exaggerated sneer. There were times, I swear, when he looked almost tough. Once as we were walking toward the back, a little bespectacled third-grader bumped into him accidentally, and Edwin, like a pale thin Arnold Hasselstrom, whirled around with clenched fists, saying: "Watch it, kid." The little fellow, himself an Edwin, could barely hold back his tears.

It was about this time that curse-words began to make an appearance in my friend's shocked vocabulary. "Hell" and "damn" were constantly on his lips, and on at least two occasions he actually used words so foul that I cannot, I will not allow them to besmirch this biography. In class he continued to receive 100's and A's, for by now good schoolwork was an unbreakable habit, but he was by no means a model student, and on his first report card Mrs. Kaplan gave him the first bad mark in behavior of his career. At times I thought of him as a frail hoodlum. At times, indeed, I was almost afraid of him.

It is now my unpleasant duty to report an instance of deliberate cruelty on the part of gentle Edwin, which the spirit of honesty forbids me to suppress. It was a bright, chill morning in early November. Edwin had been unusually snappish as we rode to school, muttering at the weather and sneering at happy little groups of first-graders. As we entered the playground, Billy Duda, passing with a group of younger friends, looked over at us and made a vulgar noise. Edwin glared at him with hatred but said nothing. As we stood on line, waiting for the doors to open, I overheard Mario Antonio say something unpleasant to Len Laska about Billy Duda. "Yeah," said Edwin immediately, in his toughest voice, "he's always askin' furt. Somebody oughta give it a him." Len Laska never cared for Edwin, but Mario Antonio and Edwin had retained for one another a kind of distant respect. Mario said: "What'd that —— do now?" "Aw," said Edwin, "he's always botherin' me. We oughta kill 'um." At that moment Billy Duda, standing out of earshot at the front of the line, made a series of grotesque girlish noises, and laughed his loud unpleasant laugh. Mario stood still, listening without expression; then turning his head to one side, he spat onto the tar. "The saft," he said, which for the edification of the genteel I translate: "This afternoon."

That afternoon Edwin, accompanied by Mario Antonio, Len Laska, David Bopko, and Chuck Tucey, found Billy Duda standing with some of his little fourth-grade friends on the far part of the playground where the tar turned into dirt and weeds. "There he is!" cried Edwin; and suddenly Billy Duda was running away toward the slope and sidewalk, followed by Mario Antonio, Len Laska, David Bopko, and Chuck Tucey, with Edwin somehow straggling after them, and me after Edwin. Mario Antonio tackled him on the grass slope, but it was Len Laska who pushed his face into some wet brown stinking stuff. Later, in the principal's office, a sobbing Billy Duda reported that it was Edwin who had shouted "There he is!", and when grim Miss Maidstone turned to Edwin and asked if it was true, Edwin lowered his bloodshot eyes and nodded. Chuck Tucey then boldly confessed that it was all Edwin's idea. Miss Maidstone looked at each of us in turn, and at last settled on Edwin. "That was a cruel, cowardly thing to do," she said. "Why did you do it? Answer me. Why did you do it? Look at me." But Edwin clenched his teeth and stared ferociously at his toes, for how could he tell her that he wanted to see Billy Duda murdered because there are all these words, nothing but words, what are these words, and there they are, so that's what you're faced with, words, words . . .

# 9

EDWIN'S IRRITABILITY began to affect, and infect, the Mullhouse family itself. Things were all right so long as he stayed in his room, but by November he was no longer shutting himself away, and ranged uncaged about the house, snarling and growling. It was Karen who came in for the worst of it; he teased and mocked her mercilessly, lashing her to tears. He was quite reckless about it, tormenting her even in the presence of Dr. Mullhouse, who could not endure ill will between his children. On one such occasion, as we waited in the living room for dinner, Dr. Mullhouse rose quivering from his chair, stalked over to terrified Edwin, and roaring "Get up!" held out his hand palm-up. Edwin rose shakily to his feet, placed his delicate small hand palm-down in his father's hand, and looked away as Dr. Mullhouse raised his right hand over his head and swung it down on the back of Edwin's hand with a sound curiously reminiscent of applause. "Oh Abe," murmured Mrs. Mullhouse, as Edwin ran weeping upstairs. "That boy," said Dr. Mullhouse, "has got to learn once and for all by God that in this house there is a thing called manners, and by God if he doesn't learn it quickly he's going to be in trouble. And by God I'll teach it to him if it's the last thing I do. I forbid him to have dinner with us tonight. I forbid it, is that clear? I don't even know if I want any dinner myself. Christ in heaven what incivility. Christ almighty it makes me sick to my stomach to see my own child act like that. Christ damn it all I don't ever want to see it happen in my house again. Didn't I tell you I don't want any dinner God damn it all to hell. I'm going out. I need some tobacco. Don't wait for me."

Mrs. Mullhouse too was a victim of Edwin's temper, though he inflicted on her an additional and more ingenious form of suffering: he began to display his misery before her in all its splendor. He was especially good at this during lunch on schooldays, when his father was at work. Sitting at the table he would carefully work into his rather inexpressive features a look of intense anguish: he would tighten his lips, wrinkle his brow, tense and untense the muscles in his cheek, and breathe with a little catch in his throat, as if his weary breath had climbed up out of a deep pit and barely had the strength to crawl out past his lips to die. At other times he would be more dramatic, leaning his elbows on the table and pressing his eyes into both palms with a little groan. He complained of intimate unpleasant pains in his blood, his bowels, his brain. And if Mrs. Mullhouse timidly went up to him and laid a gentle hand on his forehead, he would jerk away angrily, saying: "Oh, leave me alone. You're always touching me." "Oh Edwin," she would say sadly, "I'm not always touching you," and Edwin would say: "Yes you are. You are too. You're always touching me." And he would utter the word "touching" with an abrupt violence of loathing, as if he were spitting.

It was during one of these interesting lunches that an incident of violence erupted. In a sense I suppose Mrs. Mullhouse was at fault, for she should have known better than to mention his book. Edwin had been complaining of eye-aches and headaches, and Mrs. Mullhouse finally could not forbear saying: "God, if only you'd finish that awful book." Edwin looked up sharply, almost eagerly. "It's not an awful book," he said. Mrs. Mullhouse said: "I can't understand why it's taking so long. I once knew a boy who wrote a book. Of course he was much older than you. He wrote it in two months." "He must have been stupid," said Edwin. Mrs. Mullhouse said: "He wasn't stupid, he was very intelligent. That's why he could write a book in two months." "He makes me sick," said Edwin. Mrs. Mullhouse said: "Oh, everything makes you sick." Edwin, who by this time was panting, said: "Yes, but he really makes me sick. He makes me so sick I can't stand it. He makes me so sick I want to die." "Oh, stop it, Edwin. Please." "Stop what?" said Edwin. "Just stop it," said Mrs. Mullhouse. "But he makes me so sick," said Edwin. "Stop it I said!" cried Mrs. Mullhouse—at which point Edwin pushed out his chair, stood up, picked up his empty milk-glass, and flung it against the wall; and as the glass shattered, Edwin shattered into tears of rage.

# 10

READER! What is a book? A book is an intolerable pressure on the inside of the skull, demanding release. Woe to the writer, most wretched of the damned, who cannot finish his book; for then that pressure will seek some other, and darker, release. If Edwin had not been able to finish his book, there is no doubt in my mind that he would have turned into a hoodlum, or worse. Indeed I have sometimes wondered whether all the murderers and criminals in this evil world are nothing but tormented authors, writing their unwritable books in blood. I, for one, can testify that even a modest biographer may be driven to strange devices for the sake of his throbbing book. But let us not speak about that. Let us speak about Edwin. For quite suddenly he was back at work again, lord knows why, lord knows how; and really it was a good thing for everyone concerned. Of course I missed even his mocking and contemptuous company, but I knew now that it was only a matter of waiting. He still complained bitterly on his way to and from school, but somehow it was now a healthy irritability, the inevitable overflow of a vital and fruitful energy, and not a stopped-up energy turned poisonously against itself. Of his secret raptures, who can speak? But sometimes, unable to sleep, I would brood over Edwin's love affair as from my window I watched his yellow window; and I knew that even now he must sometimes hate that book, which for so long had been breaking his spirit, breaking his body, and breaking his stubborn heart.

# 11

THE LAST SUNDAY IN FEBRUARY (we are now in 1954) was a cold gray rainy day; a few sad patches of snow were all that remained of the luminous white kingdom I had watched from my window the night before. Karen and I were sitting on the rug before the fire, playing dominoes. From time to time stray raindrops hissed against the logs, as if to remind us that a chimney is nothing but a big hole in a house. Through the watery strips of window behind the open blinds, dark green and dark gray blurs were visible. The table-lamp was on, though it was only three in the afternoon; a cloud of odorous smoke clung about the glowing shade. Dr. Mullhouse, frowning into a book, sat in his chair with one leg hooked over the arm and a black slipper dangling. Mrs. Mullhouse sat on the couch, frowning into a book of her own; from the kitchen came an odor of roast lamb that mingled with the smell of sweet tobacco and harsh firesmoke. As I blocked the row with a double five I noticed that Karen was gazing up over the couch at the top of the stairs. There, peeping out from behind the balusters, was Edwin's bespectacled face. Raising a finger to his lips, and pointing to his mother, he began to crawl down the stairs head-first on his stomach. He looked like a long pale impish worm. "What are you two looking at?" said Mrs. Mullhouse. "Nothing," I said. "Your turn, Karen." Mrs. Mullhouse returned to her book as Edwin's outstretched hands disappeared behind the couch, followed by his head, his neck, his belt, his cuffs, and his shoes. Now nothing remained but the ascending brown balusters, caging an empty wall. "Your turn," said Karen. I realized that he had entered the most difficult part of his maneuvers, for the slightest noise would attract the attention of Dr. Mullhouse, who had only to glance to his right in order to see his son crawling along the floor near the foot of the stairs. I began to whistle. "What's that you're whistling, Jeff?" said Mrs. Mullhouse—a most embarrassing question, as it turned out, for I had summoned to Edwin's assistance the very first tune I could think of, which happened to be a popular schoolyard ditty beginning:

> *Oh they don't wear pants*
> *On the other side of France.*

An incident which I here record as evidence of what I have so often noticed in my lifetime, namely, that even the most careful and scrupulous biographer cannot be too careful and scrupulous. I extricated myself with a casual "Oh, I don't know," and Mrs. Mullhouse returned to her book, and that would have been the end of it had not Dr. Mullhouse looked up and said: "We used to call it 'They don't wear pants on the other side of France.' Salacious little thing, in my day."

"Yes, well let's not go into that, for heaven sakes. I'm sure Jeffrey has no interest in your salacious little days, dear."

"So much the worse for him," said Dr. Mullhouse, and returned to his book.

Mrs. Mullhouse was seated on the corner of the couch near the wall bookcase, with her tucked-up feet resting against the couch-arm, under a white sweater. As she read, her face was turned in the direction of her feet. Behind her, on the safe side of her head, the top of Edwin's head slowly rose into view. Karen began to bubble with silent mirth as his forehead appeared, followed by his eye-glasses, his nose, his chin, his neck, and the white triangle of his t-shirt in its dark frame of shirt. As Edwin brought one elbow onto the top of the couch and slowly placed his chin in his hand, facing the head that was turned away from his gaze, Karen erupted into muffled laughter. Mrs. Mullhouse looked up with a smile and a frown, her eyes darting over her dress and legs. "Come on, you two, what's the big" "Finished," said Edwin softly, and Mrs. Mullhouse burst into a scream as a maddened bird flew round and round its cage, while Dr. Mullhouse, looking up over his bifocals, said sharply: "What's all the racket? Where'd he come from? Finished what?"

# 12

FROM THE OPENING WORDS of Edwin's immortal masterpiece we enter a precise and impossible world:

A white crescent moon, wearing a red nightcap that comes down to a long-lashed eye, snores in a blueblack-ink-colored sky above a twinkling town where the purple houses breathe in and out, in and out. One by one the yellow lights go out, each to a musical note. Down in the drowsy town the blear-eyed streetlamps yawn and nod, a corner mailbox snores through its mailslot, and shoulder to shoulder on the swaying telephone wires, the purple sparrows huddle in feathery sleep. Two black hiccupping cats come staggering along the road with their arms around one another's shoulders, singing "Down by the Old Mill Stream," while up above, the grumpy moon stirs in his sleep, and in the lamplit roadside grass a cricket wearing a tuxedo falls asleep under the eaves of a dark blue mushroom. Two glowing fireflies trace the words GOOD NIGHT against the dark. Now one by one the stars go out, each to a musical note. The world sleeps.

These familiar images, drawn from animated memories of technicolor cartoons, make up a world that I have called precise and impossible, and are the very heartblood of Edwin's book. But the reader is mistaken who believes that Edwin shared with Edward Penn a desire for a free-floating cartoon universe bearing no relation whatsoever to anything in this world. For what shall such a reader think when on page 2 he finds himself before a tall moonlit door with cone-shaped bushes on both sides and the number 295 at the top? or when, entering the black front wall, and passing through the rattling inner door, he steps into a moonstriped living room and proceeds to climb the creaking stairs to a dark door, and entering comes to a slumbering form beneath a double window? That elaborate description of the snoring hero, whose every inhalation draws toward his crimson mouth a yellow-eyed black spider at the end of a violet thread, is most amusing. A sliver of moonbeam, shining diagonally through the edge of a window, "cuts the hero's throat in half"—a bright foreboding. Slowly the moonbeam travels toward the hero's eyes; and as it crosses the lids, they open suddenly, revealing, in anticipation of that final fourth-of-july burst of eye-images, two startled pink ostriches who stick their heads in the sand.

For despite Edwin's repeated claim that his book bore no relation to his life, *Cartoons* is nothing less than a scrupulously distorted version of that life. It is a feature-length cartoon in technicolor, taking place during one timeless and enchanted night, bathed in cool midnight tones of silver, blue-violet, green-blue, and blue-green, with occasional splashes of lemon and crimson. Each episode is a dazzling cartoon painting, a scintillating series of unforgettable images that forms a precise and impossible picture. But this is not to say that the effect is static, for the images are always leading us somewhere, as if we were following a slow pan on the screen; and of course the three central adventures are bound by the familiar cartoon plot of elaborate pursuit. I shall now briefly summarize *Cartoons*, both for the sake of those unhappy readers who may not have read it (I assume, of course, that it will have been published by the time of this reading) and in order to provide fuel, so to speak, for the fiery remarks that follow.

The hero, waking in the moonbeam, and after a comic series of stumblings in his room and on the stairs, issues from his house, turns to the left, and walks along a glowing green-blue version of what is unmistakably Beech Street. He is followed by a mysterious black-cloaked figure in a broad-brimmed black hat, the lower part of whose face is concealed by the cape that he holds high with one arm "as if warding off a blow"; his bright yellow eyes are alone visible. Purple bats flutter in the vacant lots, a green-eyed black owl hoots from the rippling branch of a fat black tree, the purple shutters of a dark green house are blown suddenly shut by the wind; and when the hero climbs a little moonlit hill at the end of the street, while the black-cloaked figure watches crouching from a field, we are not surprised to see, standing before a purple-black stream on which green-blue shadows ripple, a tremulous and transparent ghost. The hero and the ghost step onto a raft and make their way downstream—followed by a distant raft—to the ghost's home in a burrow or cave in the side of the steep bank (here Edwin seems to have combined Penn's cellar with Rat's home in *The Wind in the Willows*). The delightful description of the ghost's gloomy dwelling, in raw umber and blue-violet, is in my opinion one of the high points of the book. Who can forget the undulating fog-furniture, the clanking skeleton cat and the mouse of mist, the gloomy meal of moonbeam soup and cobweb stew served in hollow skulls by white-bibbed bat waiters, the skeleton-hand spoons and the lightning-flash knives, the row of black-framed family photographs each of which is blank, the coffin standing against the wall and containing on its shelves a dead letter, two deadlines, a dead heat, a deadlock, a deadpan, a death rattle, and a dead end, the fireplace where petrified wood is burned to produce the shadows of flames, the light-switch that causes an overhead cloud to drizzle, the bat-wing umbrellas, and the wonderful revelation that the melancholy ghost is an imaginative painter whose wildest fantasies resemble precisely the news photographs in the Sunday *New York Times*. After a curious game of chess, in which the pieces keep evaporating, the hero bids goodbye to the ghost and proceeds downstream on his raft, pursued by the mysterious figure in black, who emerges from behind some red-violet reeds. Rather abruptly the hero comes to a black forest on a hillside. He sees at the top, silhouetted against a big round yellow moon (Edwin forgets, or perhaps does not care, that his original moon was crescent and white), a crooked haunted house. The long climb to the house, in black and purple, in a traditional setting of green and yellow eyes, with the dark figure in slow pursuit, is a fitting prelude to the triumphant description of the stylized house itself: the bats fluttering from the windows, the tilted shutters, the owl on the gutter, the cobwebbed porch on which an empty rocking chair eerily rocks, the eyeless Raggedy Ann doll smiling in a corner, the sudden movement in a pile of old clothes as a green mouse scampers out, the front door hanging crookedly on a rusty hinge, the glowing green eyes behind the black windowpane, the creaking threshold, and then that evil front room: the piles of broken purple furniture striped by yellow moonbeams, the headless doll on the couch, the black furry spider on the coucharm, the green-eyed bat, the bearded grandfather clock who strikes thirteen, waking up a one-eyed black cat who has pieces of yellow straw and red wool in his jaws, the crumbling staircase with its tilted purple stairs and its lion-headed handrail that snaps at the hero's hand as slowly he begins to climb, pushing away cobwebs and sticky moonbeams, climbing higher and higher until he comes to a tall purple door; and peeping through the keyhole he sees a weeping yellow-haired princess in a crimson dress seated on an emerald chair beside an ebony spinning wheel. The door swings open, revealing a black-eyed witch with thick black eyebrows and long black hair and a long black dress and long thin pointed black shoes. There follows a long nightmarish chase through all the rooms of the house (my favorite is the Cobweb Room with its sticky cobweb furniture, its sagging cobweb stairway, and its clinging cobweb cats), as smoke flows from under the door of the princess's chamber and rolls down the tilted stairway in thick purple balls, until the house bursts into magnificent crimson and yellow flames that turn the midnight sky crimson and yellow, while frowning storm-clouds prepare for battle armed with bright yellow flashes of symmetrical zigzag lightning forged by a host of heavenly blacksmiths, and a gleaming giant smashes a vast gong. Angel-firemen dipping silver buckets into celestial streams pour down parallel slanting lines of violet rain. There is a beautiful description of calm after a storm, culminating in a midnight rainbow that casts rainbow shadows on the world below. The hero takes a last look at the charred ruin against the round and now scarlet moon and makes his way sadly through the dark trees, pursued by the figure in black, until he issues from the forest and finds himself standing at a far edge of town that he has never seen before. Slowly he wanders along the dark and crooked streets, silently pursued, until at last he sees a dim light in a cellar window, through which in vain he tries to peer. Nearby is a sloping and curiously realistic cellar door (such as Edwin had seen at the back of many a house on Benjamin Street). Lifting it, the hero descends a flight of dark stone steps and enters a large dim room filled with old suits of armor, rusty swords, Colt automatics, festoons of chains, piles of glossy black cannonballs, unnamed instruments composed of purple spikes and green toothed wheels, nooses of thick twisted rope dangling from dark ceiling beams, piles of pale crates labeled REMINGTON, steel traps that look like jaws—one of which snaps at the hero's heels as he makes his way toward the distant light, which comes not from a bulb but from a flickering candle; and as the hero crawls past a final obstruction and creeps under a table, he sees before him a vast black wolf chained to the wall, straining at the end of its chain and dripping saliva that gathers in dark gleaming pools. And as the hero watches, he notices a white-haired lady in shiny black boots on a blue piano stool in the corner, who slowly rises and approaches the wolf, and raising a lash swings it onto the wolf's back with a whistling snapping sound, drawing a great gash of crimson blood. Again and again she swings the lash, until the bloody wolf creeps to the wall; then the lady returns to her stool, where she falls asleep. There follows the hero's unsuccessful attempt to free the wolf, the pursuit by the lady, the chase through the cellar, and the hero's escape up the stone stairs and into the street, where for the first time he becomes aware of the figure in black. And now the book enters its final movement as the pursued hero hastens through a maze of misty streets—misty for no reason except that Edwin wanted mist—until he comes to the tall white door with cone-shaped bushes on both sides and the number 295 at the top. The concluding section of the book is a long chase through all the rooms of the hero's cluttered house, in which we are briefly introduced to slumbering cartoon parents and a slumbering cartoon sister, and in which all the formulas of the cartoon chase are used in a kind of crescendo of clichés as the clumsy pursuer is continually outwitted by the clever pursued (the double-barreled shotgun is twisted into a pretzel, the sledge hammer strikes the pursuer's toe and sends a gong into his eyes, the pitchfork-pierced belly turns into a sprinkler when water is swallowed), and just as we have become accustomed to these rather brutal conventions, and the smiling hero crawls complacently into bed beneath the same old spider, suddenly there is an unexpected reversal, the cloaked figure reappears and plunges a dagger into the hero's white throat, thick crimson cartoon blood pours out and forms symmetrical patterns on the white sheet, and as the circle closes, the hero's last moments are depicted in a series of images that appear in rapid succession in his eyes: two steamships slowly sink, the spinning wheels of a slot machine stop at two skulls, a cash register rings up NO in one eye and SALE in the other, two whistling bombs explode into two mushroom clouds, two black pussycats swallow two orange fish and remove from two black throats two clean white skeletons, two smiling divers plunge into two drained pools, two gray tombstones rise from two green mounds, and two winged heroes sit on two white clouds strumming two golden harps as two little circles close and That's All, Folks! writes itself across each eye. And with that bitter, mocking, trite, and flippant slogan, the novel abruptly ends.

Let others breathe on the clear cold glass of Edwin's immortal masterpiece the mist of analysis. Let others beat against the rich red brick of Edwin's art their heads. There are many things that I might say about his work, but I shall limit myself to a small number of major insights. It will not have escaped the attention of the most imbecile reader that a significant feature of *Cartoons* is a quality that I shall call *scrupulous distortion*. No object in Edwin's novel, with the amusing exception of the ghost's wild drawings, matches a real object in the real world. But the reader, and Edwin too, must under no circumstances forget one simple fact: *distortion implies that which is distorted*. Edwin's book, far from portraying a world that has no connection whatsoever with the real world, is bound to the real world more tightly than a photograph. Oh it is, Edwin, it is. For by the method of scrupulous distortion, Edwin draws attention to things that have been rendered invisible to us by overmuch familiarity. The familiar image that gazes sleepily at us from our bathroom mirror, or glides companionably beside us in the plate-glass window on the shady side of the street, has long since ceased to surprise; not so his prankish cousin in a funhouse mirror. We are shocked by distortion into the sudden perception of the forgotten strangeness of things. If, then, our first reaction upon plunging into *Cartoons* is that we have entered an unreal world, blissful or boring (as the case may be), gradually we come to feel that we are experiencing nothing less than the real world itself, a world that has been lost to us through habit and inattention, and that we are hereby being taught to repossess. So much is clear, and elementary. And most of us will go no further, happy in the recovery of a world we had not known we had lost. But some few intrepid wanderers will venture beyond this brightness to a dark misty realm wherein things cease to have definite and distinct shapes, and the very notion of a real world seems a scrupulous distortion, a specious clarity and hardness imposed on mists and shadows—as if sunlight itself were a form of stylization. And in this dark realm, but only here, Edwin's distortions are not distortions at all, but precise impressions scrupulously conveyed. For in this dark realm, Penn is in truth a ghost, and Rose Dorn a weeping princess, and Arnold Hasselstrom a chained and bleeding wolf. And as for that mysterious figure in black: "But don't you know?" said Edwin, and I suggest we leave it at that.

If distortion is the essence of Edwin's fiction, the means to distortion is of course the animated cartoon, whose influence on Edwin's art I have promised to discuss. It was the animated cartoon that taught Edwin to combine the precise and the impossible. It was the animated cartoon that provided him with a whole bagful of comic tricks. It was the animated cartoon, far more than the solemn and sentimental adventure film, that acknowledged frankly a violence in things, and provided Edwin with a method of reflecting the violence he had witnessed in the course of his own quiet life. It was the animated cartoon that provided him with the central theme of pursuit, which in his hands seems to be transformed into a vision of Destiny. But even more important, it was the animated cartoon that influenced the very soul or spirit of his book. In the last chapter of Part Two I mentioned a certain disturbing quality in Edwin's list of cartoon titles, a quality that I described as a repellent cuteness. Now I do not mean that Edwin was blind to this quality of cartoons, on the contrary he was especially sensitive to it and

sought it out deliberately for his book. For it is Edwin's achieve-
ment to have discovered Beauty not in the merely commonplace,
not in the merely ugly, not in the merely malodorous and disgust-
ing, but in the lowest of the low, in the vilest of the vile: in the
trivial, in the trite, in the repellently cute. And if, with Edwin's
permission, I may briefly leave the narrow bounds of the personal
for the free fields of the socially significant, I think it is permissible
to say that in his immortal masterpiece the false images that feed
our American dreams—the technicolor and stardust through which
America, poor savage inarticulate giant, expresses her soul—are
in a manner purified, are used seriously in a serious work of art but
without losing their gimcrack quality, so that every syllable (written in blood, gentlemen, in blood) seems to plead to be taken as a
joke only. It is as if Edwin wanted you to discover, as the hidden
intention of his book, the cute grin of a cartoon cherub—whereas
that grin is itself the mask, beneath which lies a grimace of earnestness. For it was Edwin's peculiar vanity to wish to seem not quite
serious.

# 13

WHEN, ON THAT RAINY SUNDAY AFTERNOON, Edwin announced that
he had finished, he meant that he had finished transferring into the
last of seventy-four blue examination booklets a more or less legible
version of the screaming scrawls that defaced eighty-one blue
examination booklets, themselves drawn from two sets of even
messier blue booklets and a scattering of single pages covered with
unsightly additions, corrections, suggestions, deletions, and so on.
It was in this more or less legible set of seventy-four blue booklets
that I first read Edwin's masterpiece—though not, I fear, until the
following Friday, despite my pained impatience, since Dr. and Mrs.
Mullhouse naturally took precedence over me. It was I who insisted
upon typing up the entire novel in duplicate, with two patient forefingers, on the big old machine on Dr. Mullhouse's big old desk

in the big old cellar, on a rickety folding chair, under a low-hanging bare bulb, while Edwin peered into the big hooped barrels under the stairs or walked back and forth paddling a vile pingpong ball up and down, up and down, up and down. It was not simply that I wished to possess a copy of my own but that I wished to read a copy free from the distracting personality of a particular handwriting. Each of the handwritten words seemed to be intimately mixed with Edwin, to quiver with his personality, to be uniquely his by virtue of their uniquely Edwinian curves and angles; but this was a false uniqueness, for it was a matter of surface only, and kept me from penetrating to the true personality that lay beneath those surfaces, in the shapes and shadows of the well-turned sentences themselves. I have never understood the adult fascination with author's manuscripts, and have refused to encumber my biography with inserted instances of Edwin's horrendous scrawls.

It took me more than one hundred hours to type that copy, at the rate of thirty-three minutes per page; the final typescript was 204 pages long, which rather disappointed Edwin, who was inclined to prefer the bulkier version in seventy-four blue examination booklets. Rather mechanically, as it seemed to me, he thanked me for my trouble. I reread the entire typescript backwards, checking for typographical errors and retyping each imperfect page, and I then read the entire thing forwards, in a single dizzy evening, with a pounding heart, and with a piercing pleasure ten times sharpened by the lucid impersonality of type.

Meanwhile three weeks had passed, and I had not yet revealed to Edwin my important secret. The truth of the matter is that I had once or twice been on the verge of so doing, when an unaccountable shyness rose up in me and choked me before I could speak. I must confess that I took myself completely by surprise. It was as if I had such tenderness for my project, call it what you will, that I feared the possible shock of an unfavorable reaction. For even biographers are subject to those little distresses of the nervous system that so engage our sympathy when the nervous system happens to belong to an immortal genius. And perhaps it was only this, that in the face of Edwin's recently completed work, in seventy-four blue examination booklets and 204 impeccably typed pages, I was bowed down by my own lack of accomplishment. And Edwin these days was filled with such confidence, such zest, such cruel good humor! His very friendliness seemed only a cry of strength, the cruel triumphant strength of one who has accomplished his task after staring for all eternity at the bloodshot eye of Failure. At times his joy seemed to me a wild victory dance about my prostrate body.

It was a windy Friday afternoon in March. I had not slept well the night before. As I walked home from school with Edwin, I knew in my bones that the time had come. And yet each time I glanced at him, that ridiculous shyness I spoke of came welling up in me like an attack of dizziness. Perhaps my condition was partly to blame, for my lack of sleep had resulted not in exhaustion but in that intense nervous agitation that is like a wider waking. And so, as we walked, I spoke not about my book but about his—rather rapidly and excitedly, I imagine, since once or twice he glanced at me with a startled expression. I continued to speak as we ascended his stairs and entered his room, continued to speak while modest Edwin stepped into his closet to change into his playclothes, continued to speak as he emerged carrying a pair of tall black sneakers with long white laces; and as he sat on the edge of his bed and bent over to tie his left sneaker, suddenly I blurted out: "Edwin, I'm going to write your biography."

Edwin continued to tie his left sneaker. When he had finished he lifted his face, slightly flushed, and said: "I'd like to get in some batting practice." Frowning he added: "If I can find my bat," and bent over again.

Now perhaps in my nervousness I had spoken too softly, perhaps I had emitted only a faint whisper, or a hum. Perhaps I had run my words together in a meaningless jabber. Or perhaps Edwin had been concentrating so intensely on those bright white shoelaces of his that the rest of the world had simply turned to dust. Whatever the reason, the effect on me was devastating, it was as if I did not exist, and in my sleepless and overwrought condition it was all I could do to keep from bursting into tears. But the very force of my effort at self-control provided me with the energy to speak again, and in anguish and anger I repeated: "Edwin, I'm going to write your biography."

Edwin sat up like a shot. And perhaps in my anguish and anger I had spoken more loudly than I knew, for he said: "You don't have to shout, you know." He added scornfully: "Anyway, how can you write my biography. I'm not dead."

"You don't have to be dead," I sneered, though as it turned out I was mistaken.

# 14

IT WAS ONLY A MATTER OF TIME before Edwin's indifference turned to passionate regard. I do not flatter myself that his change of heart arose from any mere desire to be of assistance to me. To put it bluntly: Edwin was bored. The reader must remember that for a year and five months he had filled his days to overflowing with the lively pursuit of his lovely book; completion was bound to leave a gap. If, in the first flush of victory, he seemed to experience only a sense of release, and returned with delight to the little games and passions of the past, swinging his bat in the chilly back yard, banging away at his Czerny five-finger exercises, playing the hockey game with passionate eagerness, and reading voraciously the trash he favored (glossy baseball magazines full of ugly statistics, vile baseball novels borrowed from the teenage section of the library), nevertheless his shiny new enthusiasm soon began to show a frayed edge of despair. He became afflicted with sudden passions that quickly died. One day he discovered a biography called *Thomas Alva Edison: The Wizard of Menlo Park*, and spent an entire afternoon turning a corner of the cellar into an inventor's laboratory; but his enthusiasm exhausted itself in the feverish collection of such treasures as the mortar and pestle from my chemistry set and an old brown mercurochrome bottle from whose dark cap hung a slim glass rod—and besides, he could think of nothing to invent. One day he dashed off a little play for three people based on the classic comic version of *Ivanhoe*. Karen was Rebecca, Edwin was Ivanhoe, and I was Brian de Bois-Guilbert; and he charged admission to his parents, each of whom had to drop a nickel into a delicately balanced section of vacuum-cleaner pipe that rose from a glass jar. On a vast sheet of brown wrapping paper he invented a simple game consisting of an elaborate winding trail called Paradise Street that led to a distant green Paradise and was divided into hundreds of sections that said GO AHEAD 3 or LOSE ONE TURN or bade you pick a card from one of three different piles; and he even made an enormous die out of red construction paper. He read a book on magic and gave a show, pouring into prepared glasses water that mysteriously turned blue or red (I had lent him my chemistry set) and performing miraculous feats of mind-reading with the aid of his medium, Karen, who transferred to Edwin the whispered numbers of Mrs. Mullhouse by means of an eyeblink code. One Saturday afternoon when Dr. and Mrs. Mullhouse were away, he transformed the entire house into a vast amusement park called EDWIN'S ISLAND, each room a ride: the bathroom was the ticket booth, in which toilet-paper tickets were dispensed; Edwin's room was the funhouse, in which you could jump over the River of Crocodiles from one moved-out bed to the other or crawl through a tunnel of folding chairs draped in dark blankets; the stairway was a roller coaster, down which you rode on a thick piece of cardboard; the cellar was a spookhouse, in which Edwin was the spook; but Dr. and Mrs. Mullhouse, returning to a living room filled with dusty dishes that had been brought down from the attic for penny-toss (I won the piano), quickly closed down the park. He plunged into schoolwork, making maps of the world whose dotted lines showed the voyages of Vasco de Gama, Ferdinand Magellan, Henry Hudson, Edwin Mullhouse, Bartholomeu Diaz. He became obsessed by word-games, forcing me into long vindictive bouts of Ghost, Geography, Hang Man. But all this energy was nothing but the rock and pitch of an inner dissatisfaction, and by the first week of April, as a sudden fierce snowstorm startled a balmy week of spring, Edwin was already darkening into gloom.

And so I was not excessively surprised when, one snowy afternoon in Edwin's room, as he paced up and down with his hands in his pockets among piles of old comic books and boxes of old toys, he turned to me suddenly and said: "*I* know. Let's play Biography."

"I don't know what you," I began, but he was standing before me, waving his hands about and talking rapidly: ". . . and I'll answer them, anything at all, and you can write it all down, we'll have pictures, maps, everything, wait, I'll be right back." And flying out of the room he rushed downstairs, where I heard various slams and clanks, and rushing upstairs he entered with a large pad of ugly yellow paper and one of Dr. Mullhouse's curving pipes; and thrusting a pencil and the ugly pad at me, and placing the pipe in his mouth, he leaped onto his bed, crossed his legs, folded his arms, and said between clenched teeth: "Mmmready!"

# 15

RAIN WASHED THE FINAL WINTER AWAY, and warm winds came, like a blossoming of the air, carrying with them an odor of voyages. On the strip of lawn between the pricker hedge and Benjamin Street, the maples put out their dark red final flowers. And as the year changed from black and white to technicolor, Edwin withdrew from the color and the clamor to the dimness and stillness of his beloved room. The bright light hurt his eyes, he said, but I think the reason was rather this, that during the long darkness of the making of *Cartoons* he had lost the habit of brightness, had created in himself an instinct for darkness. He now did his homework immediately upon coming home from school, and would go out only after dinner, when the sun had set behind the backyard vista of distant trees and pointed rooftops. And I, in order to see him, was forced to do my homework in my own dark corner of the bright blue day. But quickly I grew to look forward to those long evening rambles in the dusk and dark, to those deepening skies that made the pale streetlamps grow brighter and brighter, to those times half-night half-day when the vast advancing east is dark blue shading into black and the small retreating west is pale blue shading into white, and to the warm spring darkness itself. Edwin and I took longer and longer walks, in the nights that grew warmer and warmer; and as we strolled along familiar and less familiar streets in April moonlight, past yellow windows through which we saw lamps and elbows, past dark flickering windows through which we saw blue-gray television screens, over lamplit sidewalks strewn with mown grass, under dark boughs of budding maple and blossoming dogwood, now and again we would happen to step out of the familiar universe into a sudden sharp shock of sweetly scented air, sudden as spilled perfume, piercing as crystal, dark and sweet as the sound of oboes.

These were the balmy days of our early conversations, before they took that strange, fateful turn that wound its intricate and evil way to a certain shoebox at the top of Edwin's closet, where under a heap of silver cowboy pistols and an old leather holster lay Arnold Hasselstrom's gun. I followed no rigid and confining method but simply asked questions and let Edwin talk. And talk, talk he did. For if at first he was inclined to treat the whole thing lightly, as if it were all merely a game, in no time at all he was speaking in great bursts and rushes, as if he were relieved to have someone to talk to at last. And really it was not so surprising, for he had spoken to no one in a year and a half. What did we speak about? Nothing, I suppose, and everything: the moonlight, the meaning of *Cartoons*, the curse of allergy, Arnold Hasselstrom. When I asked him why he had ever accepted that gun in the first place, he shrugged and said: "Oh, I don't know," and turning he added with absurd solemnity: "Don't ever tell anyone about that— stuff, Jeffrey." "Oh, of course not," I answered, hurt by the implication that I might ever betray one of his secrets, and asked: "Next question: is the one-eyed cat supposed to be Gray?" "What one-eyed cat?" asked Edwin, in a surprise that was possibly genuine; for he was sincerely forgetful as well as cunningly evasive. And indeed after a time I was forced to realize that there was something distinctly unsatisfactory about these conversations, however delightful, for I was able to learn nothing I did not already know. My memory was ten times more acute than Edwin's; his understanding of his own book was questionable, to say the least; and there was a maddening evasiveness in him that kept me from ever penetrating to the heart of things. Perhaps the evasiveness was as often unconscious as cunning, the mere reflex of a shyness; but there it was, and I could do nothing about it. There were some things he simply would not talk about. He would not talk about Rose Dorn. He would not talk about Karen. He would not talk about his mother and father. He would, however, talk endlessly about Arnold Hasselstrom, whose dark wordless history seemed to obsess him like the riddle of existence. Of course he was bound to brood over his relation to that disobedient boy. "Remember the last time he came?" said Edwin one evening as we strolled under the streetlamps along Robin Hill Road. "And why didn't I answer the door? But no, I couldn't, and besides, he was such a—such a— he was always taking things, and he never gave you anything back, I mean even when he gave you something he wasn't really giving it to you, he thought he had to, and besides, oh, I don't know." It was always a puzzle to me why someone who wrote as well as Edwin should speak so badly. We came to the low concrete walls over the stream beside the bakery, and as Edwin leaned his arms on the top of a wall and looked out across the dark field and the dark stream, shiny in the moonlight, I asked: "Do you then blame yourself for the death of Arnold Hasselstrom?" Edwin flinched perceptibly but did not answer at once. After a time he said quietly: "I didn't kill him." After another silence he said: "I didn't help him, either." And after still another silence he said: "Phew! A biographer is a devil." "Oh, we're not so bad, once you get to know us," I said with a smile, and Edwin said: "And the way he just sat there, saying nothing, just sitting there, like a, like a . . ." "Bump on a log?" I suggested, and Edwin turned sharply as if he were going to reply, but apparently he changed his mind.

Our discussions of *Cartoons* were a grave disappointment. At first I had questioned Edwin incessantly about his book: its nature, its meaning, and its relation to his life. But very quickly I came to realize that Edwin was not able to offer any insights whatsoever into the nature and meaning of his book, and its relation to his life. For either he did not understand the nature and meaning of his book, and its relation to his life, or else his mind grappled with these matters in so curious and personal a manner as to be unable to communicate its findings to intellects organized in a more commonplace way. If, for instance, I asked him a simple technical question, such as "Why is the moon first a white crescent moon and then a round yellow moon?" he would answer: "Why? What do you mean, why? You mean: why?" "Yes: why." "Oh, why. Well, why. Well, the reason why, it's obvious, why is the moon first a white— I really don't understand your question, Jeffrey, are you sure you mean: why?" And although at first I suspected him of eluding a challenge, gradually it became clear to me that he really did not understand my question, or that he understood it in some partial or eccentric way that rendered it puzzling or insane. So much for the technical aspects of *Cartoons*. If, shifting my ground, I asked him some simple question of interpretation, such as "Who is the mysterious figure in black?" he might reply: "I don't know," or in a playful mood might answer, with an infuriating smile: "But don't you know?" And when on occasion I would venture to explain to him my own understanding of the nature and meaning of his book, and its relation to his life, he would burst into rude laughter, or he would listen with a kind of wide-eyed innocent interest, saying: "Why yes, I see what you mean."

I tried to discuss books with him but quickly lost patience. His literary taste was really unspeakable. At a time when I was discovering *Huckleberry Finn*, *Kidnapped*, *David Copperfield*, Edwin was still immersed in *Walt Disney's Comics & Stories*. He continued to devour teenage baseball novels, and to read with delight the same old blue biographies in the Childhood of Famous Americans Series that he had started reading in the summer between the first and second grades. He sought out the complete versions of children's books he had read in unsuspected abridgments (*Bambi*, *Pinocchio*, *The Wizard of Oz*), and he was an avid reader of Karen's library books and first-grade texts. The only piece of adult literature he seemed able to endure was *The Settlement Cookbook*, whose cookie recipes exercised over his imagination a strange power.

And by the end of April, despite his initial enthusiasm, he was already losing interest. A note of levity began to creep back into his talk. He began to prepare his statements beforehand, and to deliver them in a distressing tone of mock solemnity. "Life is useful," he would say, twirling an imaginary mustache, "for the purposes of fiction. Jot that down, Jeffrey." One day I received in the mail a long letter addressed to Dr. Jeffrey Cartwright, containing a reminiscence so highly wrought as to draw deliberate attention to itself as artifice (I have quoted from this letter, the only one I ever received from Edwin, in Part One Chapter 1). At the same time a moody restlessness was taking possession of him, so that at times he seemed impatient of all talk and barely tolerant of my companionship. It was during this period, therefore, that I began to apply myself to the systematic accumulation of objective data, copying the titles of Edwin's earliest books, tracing the hand and foot in MY STORY: A BABY RECORD, and so on. One night as we sat on the top of the steps at the back of Franklin Pierce, looking out at the deserted starlit playground, I asked Edwin something or other about *Cartoons*, and when after a silence I turned to him, I saw him shaking in silent mirth, with that same pipe curving from his clenched lips. Yes, he was bored, there was no holding him; and really there was nothing more to speak about. It occurred to me that Edwin had become distinctly less interesting since the completion of his book. That very night, when I returned to my room, I withdrew from my desk a brand new three-ring notebook in blue cloth that I had purchased some months before, and grasping a brand new perfectly sharpened No. 2 yellow hexagonal pencil I wrote without hesitation at the top of the first page EDWIN MULLHOUSE: THE LIFE OF AN AMERICAN WRITER. I stopped, knitting my brows; and after three hours of staring at the blue lines, and the red slash, and the three holes, and the bright white empty spaces, I closed the notebook and turned out the light, and crawled into bed and pulled the covers over my head, and you would be amazed if I told you how bright that blackness was, how lively that silence.

# 16

IT WAS A WARM BLUE NIGHT IN MAY. Edwin sat on the black, rippling root of the fat old tilted tree at the end of Beech Street, watching white spots of the shattered moon on the rippling black water. By his right foot lay a piece of waxpaper on which sat four slices of moonlit cucumber, three moonlit radishes, and half a pepper, moon red and moon green. I sat on a moonlit root beside him, brooding moodily over the unsatisfactory course of our conversations. Ever since that night on the steps of Franklin Pierce, his restlessness had increased until there was no knowing what he wanted. His mirth and mild levity, insulting to begin with, had taken an unpleasant turn toward crude clownishness and vicious mockery. At the same time he was capable of sudden seriousnesses, disarming solemnities, that were downright embarrassing to me. On one such evening, after hours of unparalleled poisonous nastiness, Edwin suddenly began speaking in a rush of sincerity; and instead of parting at his front door I followed him into the house, where we continued our discussion first in the cellar and later, when his parents went up to bed, upstairs in the living room. It was on this occasion, as reported long ago in the last lines of Part One, that Edwin told me I had "saved" his "soul" by making him think of his life as a biography—that is, a design with a beginning, middle, and end. But the next night he was at it again, saying how "stupid" and "boring" biography was—as if he were talking about Go Fish or Monopoly—and responding to my quiet remarks with snorts and silences. And this very evening, on our way to Beech Street, he had been, oh, unspeakably vicious, he had called me things I cannot repeat, he had treated me with such merciless malice, such eager loathing, that it was as if my very existence were hateful to him; and now he sat on his rippling root, crunching his vile vegetables as if he were devouring the bones of an enemy, and watching the shattered moon with a look of grim satisfaction, as if he were taking pleasure in the dissolution of the universe.

In the dark blue sky, a few yards away, the luminous half-moon looked suspiciously precise, as if it had been carefully separated from its missing half along a perforation. A nearby star, twinkling for all it was worth, resembled a flickering dot in a faulty neon sign. I reflected, not for the first time, upon the exaggerated reputation of the trite night sky, so empty of mysteries, so smug and small, in comparison with the terrible blue infinities of a blazing summer noon. On the pale field across the stream the moonlight lay like a sprinkling of sugar on a vast sugar cookie. The color reminded me of Arnold Hasselstrom's hair, and again I saw those pale strands blowing in the chill November wind that came in over the steamblasts from the green radiator in Miss Coco's room, ten thousand years ago. I was reflecting upon what it was that had attracted Edwin to that disobedient boy, when suddenly a shot rang out.

It was only Edwin, chomping on a plump radish. The sight of that moonlit medley of raw vegetables filled me with rage. I had reached the word "those" in the statement "If you have to eat those filthy things, at least close your mouth," when Edwin, turning to me suddenly, said with rude eagerness: "Jeffrey, suppose a person knew the day he would die." I distinctly remember that his mouth was full of radish.

# 17

EDWIN'S NOTION OF SUICIDE was strictly esthetic. So at least it seemed to me from the confused effusions of the next several nights. It was not so much the act that interested him as the design imposed by that act upon his entire life. "You know how you see the end, when you're writing," he said, cogitating under the moon. "Well, suppose life was like that. Then every day would be—special." Yes, it was the idea of design that led him on; it was as if he wished to imprison, in the glass globe of Art, the dancing and unpredictable waters of Life. None of which, incidentally, kept him from doing his homework faithfully each afternoon right through the end of June.

Was Edwin serious? Oh, as serious as ever he was, when he was playing; dead serious, I almost said. Certainly a new energy took hold of him that swept him through the next ten weeks and smack into the arms of the predestined day: he threw himself into the idea of doom with infectious zest. That very first night, at the end of Beech Street, he decided on the date: August 1, his eleventh birthday. It was clearly an artist's choice. After school the next day we learned from MY STORY: A BABY RECORD that he had been born at 1:06 A.M. The night was passed in a discussion of such matters as the means of suicide (I favored the gentle sleeping pill, Edwin the bloody gun) and the suicide note (I favored the voluminous justification, Edwin the brief farewell). It was I who jokingly suggested, at this time, a splendid line that brought a smile to his lips: "I aspire to the condition of fiction." After that night, the event itself seemed to drop out of Edwin's mind as he began to steep himself in the excitement of his new sense of existence. His most trivial acts, he seemed to think, glowed in the backward-reflected lurid light of his foreseen death; they "fit in," you see, to the main design. He continually urged me to record some silly remark of his in my biography. "Jot that down, Jeffrey," he would say, sitting crosslegged on his bed and leaning back against the wall with his hands clasped behind his neck. He was only half joking.

As for me, I was a most uncomfortable participant in this latest game of his. There was something unwholesome about it, something that crept into my brain and made me dream of bright green bugs on black moss; though once or twice when I expressed my reservations, Edwin turned to me angrily and called me a "spoilsport"—his mother's word. Which raises, I suppose, the whole question of Edwin and play. For you see, it was at this time that the simple games of the Early Years were first revealed to me in a sinister light. I thought of little Edwin gazing in the ground glass of his father's Graflex, and removing photographs from the long blotter roll, and staring at his three-dimensional Viewmaster reels, and brooding over his colorful comic books; and it now struck me that this early habit of viewing the unshaped world in a shaping frame had produced in him a desire to view his entire life in the same way. His novel, I began to realize, was one such frame; and now he wished to carve from Time itself a final frame. But surely, you say, it was only a game. Surely he had no intention—oh, no doubt, no doubt. Innocent games, guilty games—how can a mere biographer unravel it all? So much is certain, that despite my forebodings, I could not escape being drawn into the current of his excitement. Frail Edwin generated a powerful force of personality when he was playing; you either kept out of his way then, or were swept into his stream. And so despite myself a kind of mild excitement began to take possession of me, as long ago when I had set a secret fire.

Winter after winter I had watched the flames in the Mullhouse fireplace, but not until the summer after my fifth birthday did I dare to summon the forbidden demon. I had discovered the matches some months before, in a white metal drawer in the kitchen, but mama's stern injunction checked me as I reached. Checked me, but fevered me too, so that what was forbidden in deed was performed in imagination many times. A mild excitement took possession of me and began to grow until my fingertips tingled with the forefelt tension of a scraped wooden match. One bright day mama was out. In a kind of numbness, but with perfect lucidity, I opened the white metal drawer and removed the matches. I carried them downstairs into the hot dim cellar; through a high window I saw blades of green grass against a bright blue sky. As if I were repeating mechanically an action performed many times in the past, I found a piece of old newspaper and a dusty jar. I crumpled up the newspaper and stuffed it into the jar, whirling suddenly at an imagined noise. I moved against the wall under the high window so that no one happening to look in could see me crouching there. Easily, and without surprise, I struck a match. At first the hard ball of paper resisted the flame, and I nearly burned my fingers as I tipped the blackening stick deeper into the opening of the jar. I dropped the match and struck another. An edge took fire. The ball of paper seemed to writhe in pain, and as the flames began to shoot up over the lip with a madness I had not foreseen, my hurt mind writhed, and I watched in terror, for it was as if my sin had taken upon itself a shape of flame that would consume me in an orange blast. But in the very center of my terror was a relief so deep that it was like the end of terror.

# 18

CURIOUSLY ENOUGH, I find there is little that is worth recording in the rapidly lapsing life of my self-doomed friend. I say curiously, for deluded Edwin seemed to think that I was eager to record practically everything. In so thinking he was guilty of two grave errors: for not only did he once again reveal his misunderstanding of the biographer's art, which of necessity is more highly selective than the self-centered novelist's, since the biographer has an entire rather than a partial lifespan to choose from, but also he failed to perceive that the remaining days of his diminishment held no more interest in themselves than, in the Early Years, the days before Christmas had held in themselves. We strolled, we chatted, we recollected; but really it was all a matter of marking time. Edwin's various sensations, under the June moon, interested me not in the least. The three-part division of his life had already established itself in my mind, and it was emphatically clear to me that we had passed the middle of Part Three and were mere chapters, mere pages, from the tragic end. He had written his book: now he must bow and depart: all else was in a manner superfluous. At times, I confess, I found myself thinking of Edwin as recently deceased. Perhaps for this reason my memory of that June is less of Edwin than of the attendant moon, which seems to me now to have passed through its phases in rapid motion, as in a science film. But with the end of school (the reader will be happy to learn that on his last report card Edwin received A's in all his subjects and S's in all departments of behavior) a new note is struck, as if creative Edwin

recognized the propriety of a gentle coda. And so I feel that some
mention at least must be made of July, the final month of Edwin's
pre-posthumous life.

Always the days grew longer, pushing back the dark, and the
summer moon in the thirsty summer nights began to glow with a
cool, fresh brightness, like a lemon-ice.

One hot night I woke from a dream of twisted white animals and
sat up in bed. Through the drawn blind over my open window the
heavy odor of mown grass mingled with a faint trace of lawnmower gasoline. A beam of moonlight, creeping past an edge of the
blind, lay in broken pieces in my room, striping the dark sill,
dropping to the floor, rising up the right side of my bed, crossing
over my ankles in a wrinkled stripe, disappearing, reappearing
suddenly on the seat of a wooden chair to the left of my bed,
scattering among the folds of a flung shirt, and lying at last in
bright fragments on three different shelves. A branch scraped
against the screen, and as it did so a white dog frozen in the snow
of my suddenly remembered dream slowly lifted its head and
melted away. The branch scraped again, and as I rubbed my tired
temples I happened to recall that no branches grew beneath my
window. The tallest sunflower beneath my window barely reached
the sill. My blurred confusion had just focused into fear, and with
a thumping heart and held breath I was straining my ears toward
the window, when through my screen I heard the harsh whisper:
"Jeffrey. Jeffrey. Jeffrey."

I flung off my sheet, leaped out of bed, and pulled aside the
blind. Edwin's half-luminous face, falling into shadow on one side
of his nose, stared up at me not two feet away. He was standing
with his heels on the grass and his toes in the dirt of the moonlit
flowerbed; he wore his dark summer jacket, zippered up to his
chin. In one hand he held a bright white handkerchief; in the other
hand he held a dark paper lunchbag. In the lenses of his eyeglasses
I saw my window in its setting of moonlit white shingles. "What,
why," I began, glancing at my clock, which said 2:24, but "Shhh!"
said Edwin, motioning for me to come out; and stepping away
from the flowerbed he raised his luminous handkerchief to his
moonlit nose, holding it there as he glanced about in an excited,

secretive, conspiratorial manner. Within minutes I had dressed, crept through the kitchen, closed the back door, and tiptoed down the steps into the side yard, where for a moment I did not see Edwin sitting on a wheel of the lawnmower under the moonlit willow tree toward the front of the house.

As I brushed aside a curtain of willow leaves, Edwin held toward me a partially chewed carrot that had been scraped and salted. I refused it with an impatient gesture. "Is anything," I began again, and Edwin interrupted with: "I couldn't sleep. Let's do something. Let's go somewhere. Shhh! What's that?" It was a piece of crumpled waxpaper, uncrumpling slightly with faint creaking sounds. "I don't really," I began. Ten minutes later Edwin was bumping up and down behind me and his lunchbag was bumping up and down before me as all three of us rode along moonlit and lamplit Benjamin Street, past dark slumbering houses that had gone to sleep hours ago.

So began the first of those late nocturnal excursions by bicycle that lend to Edwin's final July its special shade of moon and night— as if, perhaps, he wished to immerse himself more deeply in darkness before taking the final plunge. The first few nights we simply rode along nearby streets, taking fearful delight in our ghostly privilege as the only waking souls in a sleeping world. We would float along past silent moon-enchanted houses guarded by hissing sprinklers and topped by television antennas showing black and sharp against the dark blue luminous sky; past half-built houses with skeleton roofs, high stepless doors, and holes for windows through which pieces of starlit sky were visible; past hillocky vacant lots from which came a steady sound of crickets on six different notes. The entire town seemed a vast department store that we had broken into, its toys and treasures lying in neat accessible rows under the frosted moon-bulb. The sudden distant headlights of occasional cars were the suspicious flashlights of unseen guards; a few dogs howled from kitchens or back porches as we crunched past. We were never caught. After the second night Edwin did not even try to sleep, but simply waited for his parents to fall asleep before sneaking from his house to my waiting window. Soon we were making long excursions to specific places:

and it is this, really, that lends to July its unique quality, the quality of a gentle leavetaking.

Our first excursion was to Soundview Beach. I parked at the long deserted bicycle rack, far from the solitary streetlamp I had never noticed in the bright light of the obscuring sun. Removing our shoes and sneakers we walked across the cool black road to the crest of cool sand that rose in moon-illumined folds and creases to a dark azure sky. At the top of the crest we saw the foam of long low waves shooting down the shore in a luminous white line; the water fell back slowly from a strip of dark moon-polished sand. Three solemn lifeguard seats sat watching the show. The nearest one, a few feet to our left, towered over us as a highchair towers over a baby; the farthest one, beyond the black refreshment stand, was the size of a dollhouse chair. At the feet of the nearby towering chair, an overturned lifeboat lay like a vast white seashell. Edwin and I walked down to the water's edge, where we mingled our feet with the shine and foam. For a long while we stood in silence, staring out at the distant lighthouse whose little yellow light seemed to illuminate the entire horizon, revealing the division between black water and blueblack sky. "I wonder if Penn lives in that lighthouse," I at length remarked, turning to Edwin. He had disappeared. A row of four precise footprints in hard wet sand walked from the water and vanished in the dry sand above. High up on the beach behind me I saw lone Edwin seated in the lifeguard's chair, staring out to sea with moonbright eyeglasses and an indistinguishable face; and as I gazed, the odd thought struck me that I had never seen him so distant from his lonely shadow, which lay in sad banishment far up on the moonlit sand, huddled at the end of the long sharp shadow-lines of the lifeguard's luminous chair.

In no particular order, yet as if we were completing a series, Edwin and I visited a new place every night. We sat under the watertower on the moonlit cliff, overlooking the remains of Rose Dorn's forest; in the blackness of the new moon we crept into Penn's old yard and peeked through a cellar window at a black wall. One bright night we peered through the black windows of the old stone library at shelves of moon-striped books. In vain we tried all the exit doors in the deserted parking lot of the local movie theater. We were more successful in entering the railroad station, where one night we recklessly appeared under cover of the last train, and discovered to our dismay that the old movie machines had all been replaced by new white-and-silver ice-cream machines, and that the old hand-cranked machine with the faded advertisement at the top had been replaced by a red machine that printed your name on a piece of metal. But our boldest and most memorable adventure was our farewell visit to Franklin Pierce.

Although I by no means approved of Edwin's dangerous and irresponsible plan, under the gentle fury of his insistence I found myself giving way, as if unable to refuse a dying man a drink of water. On the far part of the playground where the tar turned to dirt and weeds, softly I laid my bike. Silently we crossed the moon-washed expanse of the deserted playground toward the dark back of the school, followed by two long shadows. Both back doors were locked; the classroom windows were ten feet over our heads; the cellar windows were barred with iron. "Let's go," I whispered, looking nervously about, while Edwin continued to stare up at the high windows. I whirled at the sound of an approaching car, not yet visible on the street by the dark sidewalk; in brief bursts its headlights illuminated a fire hydrant, the base of a telephone pole, the skirts of the willow. Edwin and I pressed against the wall as a small truck emerged from the side of the school, throwing patches of light fitfully before it and soon rattling out of sight. "Let's go," again I whispered. But mad Edwin began to stride toward the very side of the school that had just frightened us. He had already disappeared around the corner before it occurred to me to go after him. Even at this hour there was occasional traffic on the wide street in front of the school, and as I turned the corner, just as Edwin turned the corner in front, I saw through black trees and bushes the moonlit ruby hat of a passing police car. Not daring to shout I hurried after him. When I turned the second corner I saw him halfway up the bright front steps, unspeakably visible in the brilliant light of the moon. And as I rushed after him, suddenly I found myself smiling broadly in the brilliant light of the moon. When I reached the steps he was tugging noisily at the big locked doors above; and half giddy in the intense moonlight, moon-mad and moon-bold, I threw all caution to the moony winds and rushed up moonily the moon-flooded steps, dreamily expecting to be shot from behind. Two steps from the top a fresh brown excrement gleamed in the moonglow as if it were made of plastic. "How do you do?" I could not help saying; smiling, I bowed. "Make a ladder," whispered Edwin, looking fearfully about, and as I linked my fingers he stepped with one foot onto my palms, holding onto my shoulder with one hand. In each of the side walls that framed the deeply set front doors, a dark window sat in a frame of brick. As Edwin pushed at the bottom rail of the window in the left wall, there came into my mind the words: "All of this is called the frame, boys. This piece here is called the sash: it holds the glass." But what was the name of the side piece? "The other one," whispered Edwin. We moved to the other window. As Edwin groped at the stubborn glass, I groped for the proper word. I saw the bottom rail rise slightly from the black sill, thinking: top rail, bottom rail, something, something. Already the window was wide open. Edwin's pants and sneakers stuck out above my head and were slowly disappearing into the dark. Top rail, bottom rail, sash, sash? With Edwin's help I pulled myself onto the sill, and before I knew precisely what was happening I found myself inside.

We were standing at the back of a brightly moonlit classroom, striped with parallel desk-shadows. Distorted windows of mad moonlight lay on the long blackboard at the side of the room. Edwin began moving toward the teacher's desk in front, and as he passed before the row of windows I had the presence of mind to whisper: "Get down!" Crouching beneath the sills, between a row of desks and a row of cold radiators, slowly he made his way to the front of the class, where straightening up he tiptoed to the teacher's desk and sat down in a flood of moonlight. "Edwin!" I whispered. As I started after him, creeping along under the windows, Edwin giggled, rose, and went to the blackboard. With a stub of chalk he began writing in rapid shrieks. "Stop it, Edwin!" I whispered, and as I hurried after him he put down the chalk and dashed to the front door, where turning the handle he vanished into the dark hall. In a sloppy hand he had printed: JEFFREY WAS HERE. I searched in vain for an eraser and finally had to use my palm, leaving a little pale cloud on the dark night of the board. Then stepping into the hall, and closing the door softly behind me, I saw his black shape tugging at the locked door of a nearby room to the right. "Stop it!" I half-shouted, and suddenly he was running down the hall toward the distant steps down which he had chased Rose Dorn long ago. Elongated versions of the little square windows at the top of the shut doors lay against the wall to my left, and as I hurried after Edwin I saw my shadow passing against the moon-windowed wall.

The metal steps were invisible. In a small black window I saw a black treetop in a blueblack sky. The smooth black rail above its invisible, remembered posts guided me on my slow way down, and at the bottom I stared at utter blackness, shaped by memory into ceiling, walls, and floor. At first I heard no sound, but soon I heard quite clearly a gentle patting in the distance: Edwin's sneakers. "Edwin!" I whispered, but my playful friend did not answer. Slowly I made my way through blackness, clinging to a sandpapery wall that suddenly turned into the smooth wood of occasional doors. I was startled by the nearby jiggle of a doorknob, followed by a cinematic creak. Tensely I groped my way to the open door, and as I stepped inside, suddenly I heard in memory a tune I had forgotten I was looking for: top rail, bottom rail, stile, stile.

The room was even blacker than the black hall. Almost at once my straining fingers touched a piece of cool wood. Gazing not forward into opaque blackness, but backward through transparent memory, I filled the room with a jagged pile of old desks. A narrow passageway appeared between the desks and wall. Deep in the blackness I heard the sound of moving furniture and began to make my way along the invisible corridor to my right. I could see nothing at all. I did not know what Edwin was doing. The desks shifted loudly, and in my brain a heavy desk-cover came softly sliding down. For a moment Rose Dorn crawled with bare knees over edges and screws. The desks shifted again, and quite suddenly things were out of control. A far desk crashed, and another, and another: it was an invisible landslide of desks, slipping and crashing down. "Edwin!" I cried. "Over here!" he shouted, startling me—for he called from the direction of the door behind me. In a roar of crashing desks I groped my way back to the door, and side by side with silent Edwin I hurried along the darkness and up the metal stairs. Side by side we pushed on the metal bar of the back door and stepped into the clear moonlight. Side by side we ran along the playground toward the distant bicycle, gleaming like a vast coin.

Only when the school was out of sight did we begin to speak. In excited whispers Edwin explained that he had tried to climb onto the desks, just for fun, but at the first sign of collapse he had circled along the corridor to the doorway behind me. He hoped nothing was broken. I too hoped nothing was broken. Now that we were safe we both felt a surge of pride in our moon-madness, and as we turned onto Benjamin Street we burst into loud, dangerous laughter.

Our final visit, on the penultimate night of Edwin's life, was to White Beach. As we rattled over the wooden bridge, closed to midnight traffic by means of a moonlit chain hung between two posts, the smell of saltwater mingled with the sound of water slapping against piles. The narrow footpaths on both sides of the bridge were deserted, and on the solitary black pile that stood alone in the bright black water, no moonlit seagull posed. "Look!" I whispered, "no seagull." "What seagull?" whispered Edwin. In the parking lot, deserted except for a single dark station wagon, I parked my bike sideways between two parallel white lines. Quickly we walked toward the miniature forest, and as we stepped out of the trees I sensed immediately that something had changed.

In the distance I saw a faint sparkle of black water. The merry-go-round building shone with a strange ghost-whiteness. The arcade looked somewhat larger than before, and I admired a handsome effect of shadow-stripes: cast by the posts at a sharp angle inward along the ground, they stood straight up against the bright façade. And yet the change I sensed had nothing to do with the artistic effects of moonlight and moonshade. "Do you notice anything?" I whispered, turning to elusive Edwin, who had already reached the merry-go-round and was standing on tiptoe at a little black window, peering intently through the blinders of his hands. "Look," he whispered as I came up to him. Through the window

I saw the frozen horses, their hooves still raised, their faces straining in patches of moon. "Actually," I said, turning to Edwin, who again had left me and was halfway to the arcade. I hurried to catch up with him, and together we walked along the striped arcade toward a polygon of night. "Look!" said Edwin, skipping excitedly ahead; but not until I had stepped through the polygon and looked about in bewilderment did I suddenly realize what from the beginning I had perceived. The concrete basin of the motorboat pool, shaped like the state of Nevada, had disappeared. For a moment I wondered whether I had dreamed our ghostly visit there last summer. But as I strolled about on the moonlit ground, I came across a little patch of concrete, lightly covered with dirt; and as if my eye had suddenly been granted the power of penetrating the earth's crust, I saw or felt the concrete outline of the motorboat pool, stretching away under its layer of moon-pale earth. In the dirt-filled basin I now detected a slight rise, as over a grave. Near the center someone had inserted a short tilted stick, which cast a shadow twenty times its length. "Let's go," I softly pleaded. But Edwin was having a grand old time, and we did not leave for at least another hour.

# 19

THE SUN HAD SET and the last light was draining from the sky as, with a splitting headache and a faint sore throat, swiftly I made my way across the darkening grass. I had not slept well the night before. In one hand I carried a small overnight bag containing a pair of red pajamas, a pair of maroon slippers, a black bathrobe, a green toothbrush, and an illustrated copy of *Huckleberry Finn*, wrapped in pink paper decorated with blue birthday cakes. This last was really for Mrs. Mullhouse, whose suspicions I thought might otherwise be aroused. Everything was going splendidly, splendidly. It had been easy enough for Edwin to arrange that I should sleep over that night, for tomorrow was a special occasion, and as a

matter of fact everything was going splendidly, splendidly, except
for the pressure of black dread crushing my heart, and that splitting
headache. All the hot morning, all the hot afternoon, I had walked
in a bright blaze of pain. More than once I had lain down in a vain
effort to sleep, when shortly before dinner, falling into a fitful and
exhausting nap, pursued by Edwin I raced through fields of strangling grass, over sliding hills of shells, through dark passageways lit
by flickering torches, until coming at last to a red metal stairway
with a yellow rail, swiftly I began to climb. At the top I pushed
open a heavy trapdoor and stepped onto a sunny roof. Women in
bright bathing suits and one-way silver eyeglasses sat about in gay
lawn-chairs. Beside a white table I found a yellow rubber float.
But when I sat down the sky darkened and a child began to cry,
and far below I heard the sound of crashing waves. My float began
to slide, faster and faster I rushed along, tumbling over the edge I
gripped the sides as down and down I plunged, faster and faster the
black waves rose to meet me, and I would have drowned for sure
if I had not wakened with a splitting headache. The pale west,
drained of blue, glowed with an unhealthy brightness, and as I
climbed the back steps I saw through the screen-door the soothing
lamplight from Edwin's living room, on the dark side of the house.
It was 8:32 by my watch when the door opened and Mrs. Mullhouse said "These damn flies hello Jeffrey," and as I stepped inside
I realized that Edwin had less than five hours to live.

In the kitchen I lifted a finger to my lips, unzipped my bag, and
handed the pink and blue package to Mrs. Mullhouse. She immediately pressed it against her stomach and began to look about in
terror, gripping the side of her face and breathing rapidly, as if
I had handed her a stolen radio. Finally she dashed over to a high
white cabinet and placed it between a large yellow bowl and a pile
of white dishes. Then drawing the back of a hand across her forehead, shaking off imaginary drops, and rolling her eyes at the
ceiling, she said in a loud voice: "I wonder where that bug-bomb
went to." She cupped her ear, as if waiting for an answer; gave a
comic wink; and together we strolled into the living room.

He was lying on his stomach across from Karen, delicately tipping up an orange pick-up-stick from the colorful pile between

them. Karen was leaning over, watching ferociously for the slightest motion in the pile. They had often played together since the completion of Edwin's book, but now the sight of the two of them playing there, while Dr. Mullhouse sat in his chair with one leg flung over an arm and his old black moccasin dangling, filled me with sudden tenderness, and in the overwrought state of my nerves I might have shouted out who knows what dark secrets if Karen had not shrieked: "It moved!" "It did not!" cried Edwin, and Dr. Mullhouse, looking up abruptly, said: "Enough of that. Do you want to ruin my illusion of domestic bliss? Good evening, Jeffrey." "It did not," whispered Edwin. "It did too," whispered Karen. Loudly I said: "Can I play?" and joined them on the rug, a smiling bringer of peace with a splitting headache.

Not even the shadow of a secret glance passed between Edwin and me. Indeed I was struck by his apparent absorption in the game. Relieved that he had chosen to hide behind that plausible mask, I awaited impatiently the moment when we should adjourn to his room. But as we played round after round, in lamplight that brightened as the sky grew black, I realized that he was actually and utterly absorbed in that unspeakable game; and his absorption seemed to me monstrous and grotesque, for it was all I could do to keep from leaping up and pacing about with my hands behind my back. Still more grotesque was the cheerful ease with which he handled the inevitable references to the next day's festivities. When from the couch Mrs. Mullhouse suddenly said to Karen: "How does it feel to have a big brother eleven years old?" Edwin said with a laugh: "But I'm not eleven yet." A few moments later a discussion began concerning when Edwin should open his presents. "Oh I think you should wait," said Mrs. Mullhouse, "don't you? Grandma's coming on the 1:57 and you know how much she likes to watch. You wouldn't want to spoil her fun, would you?" "But whose birthday is it," objected logical Edwin, "mine or hers?" "He's got a point there," offered Dr. Mullhouse. It was finally decided that Edwin should open his presents neither in the morning nor at dinner, but the moment Grandma arrived. During the entire discussion, mirthful Mrs. Mullhouse tried to catch my eye.

At 9:14 Mrs. Mullhouse said: "Well, Karen, time to go beddy-bye." "Just one more game!" pleaded Edwin, who was keeping score and who was leading by over 300 points. At 9:27 Dr. Mullhouse said: "It's nine-thirty." "Okay, okay," breathed Edwin, as he stared at the trembling stick that I was slowly pulling out from between two reds, while Karen stifled a yawn and rubbed her eyes. At 9:34 he cried: "I won!" whereupon Karen stood up and began to kiss everybody good night. At 9:36 she began to clump her way upstairs, bearing with her a dirty white bear with red ears. I glanced longingly at Edwin, who said: "Now that she's gone we can really play. A thousand wins. I'll keep score." Frowning suddenly, and raising a fist as if to strike me, he added: "Odds or evens?"

Ten minutes later Mrs. Mullhouse went upstairs to tuck Karen in. From time to time I heard a murmur of lines from *A Child's Garden of Verses*. When she returned she sat down on the couch beside her book, and resting her right elbow on her knee, and leaning forward, she placed her chin on her hand and began to stare at Edwin. "What's wrong?" said Edwin, who was leading 95 to 17. "Oh, nothing," sighed Mrs. Mullhouse. "I was just thinking about my handsome birthday boy." Edwin, lowering his eyes, flushed with pleasure. "You know," she continued, "I can remember when you were such a fat little baby." "Fat!" said Edwin. "Was I really fat?" "Like a lambchop, Edwin. And noisy? If you didn't wake up ten times a night, crying and screaming. Day and night you always wanted your mommy-mommy. Oh, it's true. Daddy wasn't allowed to give you the formula, oh no, it had to be mommy, such a kvetch. That was when they were still having those air-raids, remember? and we were all so scared. But he just slept like a log, that one. And I thought: God in heaven, is this a world to bring a son into. I can still remember walking in Times Square. Everyone was looking up at the Times Building, it said the Japanese had bombed Pearl Harbor. That was before you were born. I'm so sorry you never knew Father, he would have been so proud. He and Daddy used to have long talks together, you remember how he used to: Abe? oh, he's not even listening. And stubborn! Really, Edwin, sometimes I wondered what I had given birth to. You were always having these attachments for things, you just wouldn't let go of the percomorph-oil spoon. Then you ate my white button. I almost died I was so scared. Stupid me, I called the fire department by mistake. And you always made Daddy tell you two stories at night, one wasn't enough. Then Karen was born and when you came in to look at her you didn't say anything at all. I didn't know what to think. But you were such a good brother, always reading stories to your little sister and tucking her in. Eleven years old. Look at him, Abe. Such a handsome birthday boy."

"Mmm?" said Dr. Mullhouse, looking up from his book. "Are you talking to me?"

At 10:21 he again looked up from his book and said: "Isn't it about time you boys started thinking about bed?"

"Just let me get to a thousand," said Edwin, who had 804. Holding the pick-up-sticks in a loose careful sheaf, he tore away his hand and watched them fall into a nearly perfect spoke-design.

He won at 10:43. The final score was 1,012 to 96. As Edwin stood up, Mrs. Mullhouse said: "Now remember, be quiet going upstairs. And I don't want you staying up till all hours."

"Yes," said Dr. Mullhouse. "Lights out immediately, is that clear? You've stayed up far past your bedtime as it is."

"Your towel is on the lower right, no, left, no, right," said Mrs. Mullhouse.

As she hugged Edwin good night she said to Dr. Mullhouse: "Hey, old man. What do you think of my handsome birthday boy?"

"I think he'd be a damn sight handsomer if he weren't half dead from lack of sleep. Frankly, mama, I wouldn't marry him myself." He paused, looking critically at Edwin. "But he'll do. Now go to bed, for the love of Christ."

"And remember, you two," called Mrs. Mullhouse as we were halfway up the stairs. "No clowning around."

It was 10:48 when we entered Edwin's room. I closed the door behind me and turned to Edwin with a sigh of relief. But ignoring me completely he disappeared into his closet, emerging moments later with his skyblue pajamas and his purple bathrobe draped over his left forearm, and holding in his right hand a pair of soft beige moccasins with dark blue Indian chiefs on the toes. "I'll change in the bathroom," he remarked, and as he opened and closed the door I heard from downstairs a brief murmur of conversation.

As soon as I was alone I hurried to the closet, set up a rickety folding chair, climbed onto the padded seat, and proceeded to search on the dark deep cluttered shelf for an old shoebox filled with cowboy pistols. The closet lacked a light of its own, and my efforts were only partially illuminated by the light of the room. There were piles of old comics, old stuffed animals, a plug-in electrical baseball game with pitching and batting diagrams, a frame for weaving potholders, a shoebox containing a pair of old sneakers, a Viewmaster box containing little green houses and little red hotels and a little silver dog, an empty white shirt-box, an eyeless zebra, volume one of *A Child's History of the World*, a small rubber football, a broken shooting gallery, a smashed Indian headdress, a valentine from Donna Riccio, a shoebox containing dusty rolls of old negatives, a coloring set consisting of twelve unsharpened colored pencils and six eerie white landscapes filled with blue numbers, a cowboy boot with a picture of Roy Rogers on it, an old sock-ball containing a rifle bullet, a piece of folded typewriter paper on which was scribbled a rejected Rose Dorn valentine poem ("Blue are violets/ Red are roses/ Sweet my Rose/ From head to toes is"), a green glass ashtray from White Beach, a shoebox containing a complete set of Parcheesi pieces and a small stack of Freedom's War cards bound by a red rubber band, a shirt-box filled with crayon drawings done in Miss Tipp's class, the missing vial of tannic acid from my chemistry set, a shoebox containing puzzle pieces from at least two puzzles and a hunting knife with a wavy handle, a piece of old tracing paper on which was a picture of Donald Duck's head, a pile of Golden Books, a pair of earmuffs, a whiffle ball, a mousetrap, a water pistol, a shoebox containing ("What are you doing?" whispered Edwin) a pile of gold-starred spelling tests. Whirling, and peering down at his pale frowning face, I whispered: "Looking for—looking for—" "Get down!" he harshly whispered, and the rickety chair almost collapsed under me as I quickly obeyed. "But where," I said. "Shhh," hissed Edwin, adding in an indignant whisper: "You're not even changed."

I carried my bag into the bathroom and changed rapidly into my red pajamas, my maroon slippers, and my black bathrobe. I did not remove my watch.

When I returned I found frowning Edwin seated on the edge of his bed, leaning back on his purple elbows. As soon as I closed the door he stood up and said in a low brisk voice: "Okay, listen. You guard the door. If you hear anything, clear your throat twice, like this." He cleared his throat twice, like that. I nodded solemnly and took up my position at the door. As I stood with my ear pressed against the wood, listening to sounds of movement in the living room below, Edwin walked briskly to the closet and climbed onto the squeaking chair. Almost immediately he climbed down. He tiptoed toward the bed in his soft moccasins, bearing in his arms a light brown shoebox with a dark brown cover, and as I straightened up he whisper-cried: "Stay there!" Placing the shoebox on the bed he quickly lifted out five silver pistols, a leather holster, and a .25-caliber Colt automatic. Quickly he began to replace the pistols. "The clip!" I whispered. "The what?" he whispered. Aloud I said: "The other thing," slapping a guilty hand over my mouth. Edwin glared at me and then took out the clip, staring at it for a moment with a puzzled expression. Rising, and giving me another dirty look, he carried the clip and pistol to his chest of drawers, where he suddenly squatted and began slowly pulling out the crowded bottom drawer, looking up nervously each time it squeaked. He placed the gun and clip beneath a large green rubber frog-foot, which he covered with a pair of cowboy pajamas and a folding chessboard. Then he closed the drawer, reloaded the shoebox, replaced it on the closet shelf, folded the chair, and closed the closet door; and turning to me at last he said quietly: "Okay." The time was 11:09.

A rather awkward silence followed. I sat under the Gulf of Mexico, scratching my legs, cracking my knuckles, and picking at the spread, while Edwin sat motionless in the center of his bed, his pale face colorless above his purple bathrobe, as if the blood of his cheeks had flowed into his robe. From time to time he sniffled flamboyantly. At 11:14 he suggested that we play another round of pick-up-sticks; I emphatically refused. At 11:16 he offered to give me a lead of 800; I rudely ignored him. Time passed, during which I wondered why no one suggested that we turn out the light and lie down. I was on the verge of suggesting that remedy, and indeed my lips were parted, when Edwin, annihilating a yawn, suddenly whispered: "The letter!" Springing from the bed, he began searching wildly among his shelves, muttering in his mother's tone: "Oh where is that stupid pencil." I had no idea what he was up to, and for a moment I had the odd sensation that he was mocking me in some elusive Edwinian way.

He found the stupid pencil on top of the chest of drawers. He found a piece of stupid paper under his stupid bed. Sitting cross-legged in the center of his bed, and placing the piece of paper on a large flat book, he began to write furiously. A few moments later he said: "How's this?" and read softly: "To whom it may concern. I, Edwin Mullhouse, heretowith commit suicide. Yours truly, Edwin." He looked up expectantly. I said: "Heretowith?" "Actually," said Edwin, "I don't like this stupid note." He crossed it out violently and began writing again, while I cracked the knuckles of all ten fingers twice. "Listen," he said, "how's this. To whom it may concern. I, the undersigned, heretowith condemn myself to death by suicide at 1:06 A.M. on August 1, 1954. Goodbye, cruel world. Yours sincerely, Edwin A. Mullhouse, author of *Cartoons*."

"You mean herewith, Edwin. Or hereby."

"Wait a minute. I've got it. I've got it. To whom it may concern. I, the undersigned, heretowith blah blah blah author of *Cartoons*. Now listen to this, listen to this. P.S. Goodbye, life. I aspire to the condition of fiction."

It was, I confess, the needed touch. I did my level best to persuade him that "heretowith" should be changed, and I am sorry to say that my advice was contemptuously ignored. Edwin, as I have had occasion to remark, had an unpleasant trace of vanity in him that was, no doubt, the natural green stain on the bright copper of his creative genius. As a result his final message to the world is marred by the embarrassing presence of a nonexistent word. It is really a shame. Edwin quickly copied the note onto a clean sheet of paper, and we were discussing where to put it—I was for placing it modestly on the rug beside his bed (where it finally fell), he was for fastening it to his body in some ill-defined fashion—when the sound of footsteps was audible on the stairs, and leaping up, and wildly motioning for me to crawl into my bed, Edwin dashed to the door, turned out the light, and dashed back to bed, where he lay breathing heavily in blackness.

The footsteps stopped before the line of light under the door. In a low voice Dr. Mullhouse said: "Shhh, they're sleeping," and his footsteps creaked away down the hall. Immediately Edwin began to snore loudly, inhaling with vulgar snorting sounds and exhaling with a whistle. At the second exhalation he exploded into giggles. In my tense agitated impressionable condition, I too exploded into giggles. The door opened, and Mrs. Mullhouse whispered angrily: "Hey you two, what did I" and suddenly she too exploded into giggles. And stepping into the room, and closing the door behind her, she began to tiptoe toward giggling Edwin, who trying in vain to suppress his mirth, burst into irregular wild ripples of giggles as slowly, slowly she stalked through darkness, until suddenly she whispered "Gotcha!" and Edwin burst into screams of wild laughter as the door opened and Dr. Mullhouse hissed: "Shhh!"

The departure of Mrs. Mullhouse was followed by some fifteen minutes of creaking footsteps, opening and closing doors, and hissing tapwater. At 11:47 by my greenly luminous watch the line of light under the door went out and a last door closed.

The room was dark but not pitch black. Beyond the closed black blinds of the double window I could see the dark hump of Edwin's raised knees; and the dark head over the pale pillow was faintly visible beneath the vertical strips of polished black night at the edges of glass between the blinds. "Edwin," I whispered. "Shhh," he whispered, "they're not asleep." Minute after green minute I lay in black silence, listening to Edwin's regular breathing; by 11:54 I wondered whether he had fallen asleep. Another minute, like a little life, completed its circle. And all at once, just like that, he began to chat quietly about one thing and another, saying "Remember the time?" and "Remember the day?" I, too, sweetly reminisced. It was as if we were five years old again, dear comrades rejoicing in our youthful adventures, fettered in friendship by the binding dark. Indeed I have often reflected upon the intimate quality of darkness, so different from the estranging day; and perhaps the reason is this, that with the fading of objects we lose our faith in the solidity of objects, so that a great dripping and melting takes place, stone flows into stone as mind into mind, our bodies themselves melt and drip away, and in the all-dissolving and annihilating dark, the daylit multiverse becomes a cozy universe at last. Some such sensation, short of thought, flowed in me as we softly spoke; oceans of green time flowed; and it was with a rude jolt that I heard Edwin suddenly ask: "What time is it?" It was 12:29 by my glowing dial, and Edwin whispered: "They're asleep now."

With a dark swish he flung the covers back. Rising darkly, he made his soft way across the room to the black chest of drawers, where he kneeled darkly five feet from my straining eyes. Slowly and creakily he pulled out the heavy bottom drawer. For a while he groped inside. Then slowly removing two black objects, and carefully pushing in the drawer, he returned to his bed and sat down softly. "Jeffrey," he whispered. "Jeffrey." With a dark swish I flung the covers back.

I sat down close to him in the middle of the bed. Sitting in Indian fashion, we faced one another nearly knee to knee. In the imperfect darkness I was able to distinguish his features faintly. "Hey," he whispered, "how do you work this thing?" and handed me the gun and clip. "Careful," he whispered. And although I had never held a real gun in my hands before, it seemed a mere matter of instinct to slip the loaded clip into the hollow handle. A dim memory from an old movie stirred; with some difficulty I removed the clip and examined the gun with my fingertips. I found the safety and quickly discovered its relation to the trigger. Setting it, and explaining the mechanism to Edwin, I was about to push the clip back into the handle when Edwin thrust his handkerchief at me, whispering: "Fingerprints." For a moment I did not understand. Then with a wild, forlorn feeling, with a feeling of doom, of farce, of unspeakable melancholy, I realized that he wished to prevent a grotesque contingency. Carefully I wiped the clip and gun and then reloaded without touching metal. For indeed I had no desire that his suicide should be mistaken for murder. I then wrapped the gun in the handkerchief, preparatory to handing it back to Edwin; and only then, dear reader, did I suddenly feel the weight of the loaded gun pressing into my palm, and in a burst of lucidity I knew, I saw, I felt, that it was all horribly real, and that if I did not stop him, if I did not say something . . . "Edwin!" I whispered. "Hey," he whispered, "don't point that thing." And angrily he seized the gun.

In the darkness he began to examine his dangerous toy, bringing it close to his eyes, turning it over, holding it against his ear like a clock. "What time is it?" he whispered. "Quarter of," I whispered. "Tell me when," he whispered. "Okay," I whispered. Several days passed. "What time is it?" he whispered. "Twelve to," I whispered. "That's all?" he whispered. "That's all," I whispered. Then raising the gun to his right temple he whispered: "Like this?" And moving the barrel awkwardly to his forehead he whispered: "Or like this?" And slowly turning the gun toward me he whispered: "Or like this?" "Stop it!" I whispered, pushing away his hand, and Edwin began to giggle.

That giggle seemed to release something in Edwin. It marked the beginning of a madcap mood that swelled to a mindless frenzy of frantic mirth, as if he were a bubble of mad merriment about to burst. And perhaps it was only a sign of my overwrought condition that in some dim way I felt he was making fun of me. Leaping lightly from his bed, he scurried across the darkness to my bed, entering feet-first and disappearing entirely under the heaving covers. Beneath the black map of the United States I perceived a dark, wriggling mass as Edwin proceeded to turn himself around under the sheets and clumsily make his way to the foot of the bed near one of the black bookcases. A final groping from the inside of the low-hanging spread at the foot of the bed reminded me of Edward Penn behind his curtain. At last, with a gasp, Edwin's dark featureless head appeared, followed by the confused rest of him as huffing and puffing he crawled forward on his hands, one of which, as I knew by an occasional soft clank, contained the gun. His head reached the bookcase, knocking softly against a box, and he had to twist to one side as he continued to crawl from his soft cage, pausing to reach back with one hand in what was apparently a modest effort to hold up his invisible pajama bottoms. Free at last, he crouched in the black space between the bookcase and the bed, and suddenly began to pull out boxes and books, piling them up in front of him to form a wall. I sat rigidly on his bed, listening fearfully for sounds from the hall; and as I stared in dazed disbelief toward the quiet commotion at the foot of my bed, suddenly something came hurtling out of the dark and hit me softly in the shoulder. I gasped, and mad Edwin giggled, and the next missile hit my knee. They were his slippers. I clutched them in fearful silence, wondering whether the next thing to come spinning out of the dark would be a loaded gun. "Bang bang!" he whispered, his dark head bobbing up and down from behind his barricade. Suddenly he leaped onto the bed and began bouncing or dancing in wild silence across it, holding up his arms; a rectangle of light from a passing car rippled over his face like an illuminating mask. Then stepping onto the floor he began to spin round and round: holding out his arms he whirled faster and faster, he seemed a dark dancer whirling in darkness, I saw for a moment the glint of the gun, and suddenly he flung himself onto the bed before me, landing half on and half off but freezing as he fell, gripping the spread and squeezing his eyes shut as in his brain the black room turned and turned, and as if infected by his dizziness, I too felt the dark walls turning and turning. And as he lay there before me, clutching his gun, it seemed to me that he was already dead.

The magic potion wore off, and Edwin, breathing rapidly, climbed onto the bed and took up his position crosslegged before me. "Time?" he whispered. There were three minutes left. And now I noticed that Edwin was grinning, rather fiendishly it seemed to me, and in a mirthful whisper he said: "Make sure you put that in your book," and softly laughed. Oh, he was mocking me, he was mocking me, and again I felt a sense of dim foreboding, as if I feared for my life, and with a curious feeling of self-pity I whispered: "You're making fun of me, Edwin." "Who, me?" whispered Edwin, blinking in dark astonishment. "Why should I make fun of you? Time?" There were two minutes left. And again pointing

the gun at me he whispered: "You're so serious, Jeffrey." "Oh
what are you doing, what are you doing," I moaned, pushing away
his hand, and still grinning he whispered: "What'd you get me for
my birthday?" "Huc" "Don't say!" he whispered, "I want to be
surprised. Time?" There were ninety seconds left. And now
Edwin became serious, bowing his dark head in thought. After a
time he looked up and whispered: "Well, it's been nice knowing
you, Jeffrey." And despite my sense that things were somehow
rushing out of control, I was moved almost to tears by the sound
of those words. Placing his hand gently on my shoulder he whispered: "Goodbye, O friend." He began to giggle but stifled his
mirth. "Time?" "Twenty seconds," I whispered. Placing his hand
over his heart, and looking up at the ceiling, he whispered: "Goodbye, O life." Looking at me he added: "Jot that down, Jeffrey."
He released the safety and whispered: "Start counting." "Thirteen," I whispered, staring at my glowing wrist, "twelve, eleven,
ten, nine, eight, seven, six, five, four, three, two, one"—I raised my
eyes—"zero." And calmly raising the gun to his right temple,
Edwin whispered: "Bang, I'm dead," and fell backward on the bed
with his eyes shut, clutching the silent gun. A moment later his
eyes opened and he said: "Now what?" In a split second I was
leaning over him, gripping his gun-gripping hand; and I remember
thinking, quite lucidly in the midst of a dreamy numbness, that
the entry under "I Am Born" in MY STORY: A BABY RECORD allowed
a certain leeway in the matter of seconds.

# 20

ON A RADIANT BLUE APRIL AFTERNOON, in an odor of dust and sunshine, I strolled past Edwin's house on my way to Beech Street.
Through the blossoming trellis I caught a glimpse of mama and
Mrs. Hooper standing by the flowerbed. As I passed the house I
glanced at the backyard hedge, over which the skeleton of a new
house loomed: a man in blue overalls and a red shirt was seated on

a plank in the air, banging away cheerfully with his hammer. I
crossed Robin Hill Road and made my way along noisy Beech
Street. There were children everywhere. Two little girls came
clattering along on silver roller skates, another little girl jumped
up and down solemnly over her red-handled white rope, three little
boys were having a vigorous game of three-way catch, and farther
along a game of hit-the-bat was in progress. Halfway down, the
old sidewalks ended and the new, darker sidewalks began. The
trees in front of the new houses were thin and bare, and some of
the lawns were flat dark tracts of earth stippled lightly with pale
grass. In a vacant lot between a new white house and an even newer
house without roof and windows, a large sign shouted: SOLD. Slabs
of wood, bags of nails, cement blocks, buckets, and rolls of tar-
paulin lay about in front of the skeleton houses, and in the vast
rectangular earthen hole of one small lot, a sad yellow tractor
looked as if it were awaiting burial. At the end of the street I
passed the two brown posts with their red reflectors. I climbed the
rise and descended to the stream, where for a while I stood looking
across at the unchanged yellow field. Then strolling some little
distance to the right, I sat down on the rippling root of the fat
old tilted tree, and leaning back into the shade, and extending my
legs into the sunlight, I brooded over my final chapter.

Edwin's funeral was strictly a private affair. I, unfortunately, was
too sick to attend. My presence was, however, required at the
routine inquest, where Edwin's note and *Huckleberry Finn* also
made an appearance, and where Edwin's suicide was rendered
official. I dimly remember telling a white-haired gentleman that
Edwin had received the gun from Arnold Hasselstrom, and I distinctly recall three yellow shades that stood at three different
heights. But it is all rather hazy, for already I was hard at work
upon Edwin's biography.

I began it some three hours after his death, at 4:28 A.M. to be
precise, despite my exhaustion from the domestic mayhem that
frothed and bubbled in the wake of my shouts. During those hours
my headache slowly spread downward through my entire body and
erupted in my eyes in the form of red slashes. I left finally in the
company of mama, who had appeared with a kerchief over her

curlers shortly after the departure of the ambulance, and who had plunged into hysterical conversation with a sympathetic police-man. Once in my room I opened a drawer in my desk and removed my three-ring notebook and a sharp No. 2 yellow hexagonal pencil. At the top of the page were the words: EDWIN MULLHOUSE: THE LIFE OF AN AMERICAN WRITER. Introducing a careful caret be-tween LIFE and OF, I added the words AND DEATH above. Without hesitation I set to work, writing furiously the first draft of what are now the first, second, and fourth chapters, and finally fainting into sleep. The next day my sore throat had spread and I felt rather feverish, but I wrote on and on, all day and all night, and when I fell asleep I dreamed of a page of words that kept changing their shapes: blue fall, bloe fell, bell fel, beff lef. When I woke I instantly set to work, and indeed by the end of the first week it was clear to me that I had to keep writing on and on, for if I should stop, if I should brood . . . I did not see much of the Mull-houses that August, for they were often in New York; besides, a reluctance, a shyness, kept me from intruding on their grief. Once or twice I did allow myself to be dragged over by mama, but there was a terrible strain in the air, Edwin seemed always about to enter with his dripping wound, and I was relieved to escape into my happy pages. And by September they were gone. Three days after Edwin's death a FOR SALE sign appeared on the front lawn; the moving van arrived at the end of August. According to mama, they were going to New York and then abroad; their plans were vague. I waved goodbye to all three of them as they drove off forever in the black Studebaker. Mrs. Mullhouse promised to write, but not until two months had passed did we receive a perfunctory postcard from San Marino. Thereafter we heard nothing. Many and many a time did I send up a silent prayer to the guardian spirit of Biography for having impelled me to make a copy of *Cartoons;* for of course they took everything. When I finish my book I shall type another copy of Edwin's book and submit it along with my biography to one of the professors at Newfield College, who should be able to help Edwin and me find a publisher. The Hoopers moved in just before school began. Janey was entering the first grade and Paul was entering the fourth. Janey was a stupid little thing, always watching television, but Paul was a pale solitary fellow with a slight limp who spent his time devouring big books about dinosaurs and other Mesozoic monsters.

School interrupted my heavy labors, but by September I was glad of some relief, for the strain of writing all day long was well-nigh intolerable. I found it positively pleasurable to lose myself in the elaborate study of subjects that bore no relation whatsoever to my life, lovely subjects such as current events, social studies, science, and mathematics. I mastered the major imports and exports of every Central and South American country; I brooded endlessly over the labeled parts of a carefully dissected flashlight battery. I began to read newspapers regularly, pondering the national deficit, nuclear disarmament, and the prospects for world peace. Nevertheless my biography proceeded by leaps and bounds, so that by the end of October I had already reached the death of Rose Dorn. A kind of alarm came over me; I forced myself to go more slowly, to reflect more deeply, to write more carefully, to revise elaborately all my earlier pages. It took me two whole months to tell the story of Arnold Hasselstrom; it took me three whole months to tell the story of the creation of *Cartoons*, a labor I completed on the last day of March. But then despite myself I became caught up in the conclusion, and in one feverish week, as spring was bursting and cracking all around me, I wrote the series of chapters that culminated in Edwin's untimely death.

Over the yellow field, the sky was so blue that blue is not the word. Obeying an obscure impulse, I moved into the sun and lay down on my back. The sky seemed to be composed of an endless series of translucent blue panes, or rather of a single endless transparent blue substance that was at once solid and impalpable, for although it pressed down onto the very grass, crushing the blades under its heavy blue weight, crushing my supine form, at the same time it invited my mind to travel upward and ever upward in dizzying spirals of brighter and brighter blue, of formless and sinister blue—for who has not felt that there is a terror in blue noon skies such as no midnight blackness, frank in its emptiness, soothing as failure, can ever harbor. And as I gazed in helpless fascination at that terrible blue sky, which crushed my body and sucked out my soul, which soaked my soul as cotton is soaked in blue dye, oh! I seemed to read an image of my fate in that vast oppressive vacancy of blue, blue, blue. And when I thought of Edwin's fate—of old Edwin cozily tucked up between the loving covers of my soon to be completed book—I felt a sudden envy of him, a sudden anger, as if he had fooled me after all, as if in some manner he were still mocking me, as if, almost, he were smiling at me from my own pages. No, I would not mourn for Edwin. All things considered, his fate was not so bad; he was being well looked after. And he had come through with flying colors, all innocent and sainted; I was the foul devil lashed to a relentless hell. Pinned under my blue boulder, I could not help feeling that he had managed things with his usual cunning.

A sudden sound shattered my thoughts, shattered the sky, flung me to my feet. Ten feet away stood little Paul Hooper, peering at me through his thick glasses. "Your mother said come home," he stated in his precise fashion. I dusted myself off, sent up a silent curse to the big blue spook in the sky, and proceeded to walk home with limping Paul. On the way he told me his theory that just as the dinosaur proved unfit to survive because of the overdevelopment of its body, so man has proved unfit to survive because of the overdevelopment of his brain. He invited me to see his oil paintings of the creation of the universe, the cooling of the lava, the formation of the seas. For him, I gathered, the real world had ended with the extinction of the ceratopsians, approximately seventy-five million years ago. He is really an interesting little fellow and I expect to be seeing more of him in the near future.